The Healer

by Jan Hogan

—

Published by Vegas Vibe Books

The Healer
by Jan Hogan
© 2016 Jan Hogan

ISBN-print: 978-0-9968833-0-6   ISBN-Kindle: 978-0-9968833-1-3

This book is dedicated to John LY

Special thanks go to: Sami for her vibrant energy; Review-Journal editor Lisa Valentine, for understanding my vacant stare after pulling another all-nighter; to F. Andrew Taylor for his photography and PhotoShop expertise; to Karen Leslie and David Brichetto for their eagle eye editing. Couldn't have done it without you.

3

This book is purely a work of fiction and for entertainment purposes only. The information it contains is in no way intended to take the place of modern medicine or suggest that it is to be ignored. Any so-called remedies in this work are not intended to provide medical advice or take the place of medical advice and treatment from your personal physician(s). Readers are advised to consult their own doctor(s) or other qualified health professional(s) regarding the treatment of medical conditions. The author shall not be held liable or responsible to any degree for any misunderstanding or misuse of the information contained in this book or for any loss, damage, or injury caused, or alleged to be caused, directly or indirectly by any treatment, action, method or application of any plant, mineral, food source, product, item or other type of remedy contained in this book. The information is not intended to diagnose, treat, cure, or prevent any disease.

The U.S. Food and Drug Administration has not evaluated the statements in this book.

The Healer

by Jan Hogan

CHAPTER ONE

1875 – Sacramento, California

Here it came, another one. She gritted her teeth. *Oh, shit. Oh, shit. Oh, shit.*

"Push. Push," her housekeeper chanted from the corner.

Felicia Fontinello grabbed the upper arm of the midwife who was standing beside her and squeezed. She hoped it hurt because these contractions were going to kill her. She sent a hard look up at her. "Get this damn thing out of me," she seethed.

"Yes, ma'am." The woman winced and pulled her arm free. She moved to the end of the bed, between her legs. "Just a little bit longer. I can see the head."

You said that earlier, you bitch. Every nerve was on fire. *Get this damn kid out of me.*

"You're not pushing," the midwife said.

Like hell I'm not. Just let her grab that skinny little neck and squeeze and let's see how she felt. But, no, the midwife, whatever her name was, wasn't going to let herself get grabbed again.

"Give it one big push," the midwife urged.

"You can do it," said the housekeeper, standing by with the towels.

Felicia let out a yowl. The contraction passed.

Her husband was never, ever going to touch her again, not if she had anything to say about it. She slumped back against the bedding. "I can't handle another contraction."

"Of course you can. Women have been giving birth all through history," the midwife said.

"Let me die."

"Silly, you're not going to die. Now, gather your strength. The next one should be here in about a minute."

Another one? In a minute? No, she couldn't take any more of this. How come her mother had never told her it would hurt this damn much? Not that she'd told her much about anything, just to "do whatever Phillip says." Yeah, well, she'd done what Phillip wanted and look at where it had gotten her – big as a horse and wearing a tent for a dress. What had ever possessed her to allow Phillip into her bed?

Of course, she'd known it was her duty to give him a child when they'd gotten married. The Fontinello blood line had to be preserved of course. That had been clear. He needed an heir, a son, to take over the business and see it grow even bigger. The man was past forty. His former wife had been barren. So, it was up to her.

"Give me a son, Felicia," he'd whispered as he'd pumped away inside her nine months ago. "Give me a son."

OK, fine, he needed a son. But no one ever explained exactly what it entailed when it came to delivering on that agreement. This pain was unbearable.

Here it came, another one. Oh, shit. Oh, shit. Oh, shit.

"You've got to push," the midwife said. "Push."

Shut up, you bitch. She gasped. *This pain, this pain, oh my God. Make it stop!*

"Keep pushing." The midwife shot her a look above the drape and pouted. "You're not trying."

Like hell she wasn't. *I'll show you who's not trying. Just let me get my hands around that neck of yours...* Felicia sat up, arms outstretched.

"There! That's better. You're pushing now. A little more, a little more."

Wait. That's what it took? Sitting up? She leaned forward and sat up as far as she could.

Get this damn baby out of me right n-

There was a pop in her abdomen.

A squalling erupted from somewhere between her legs. She couldn't see through the darn drape. "He's here? He's here?"

The midwife's facial expression turned gentle. "There you go, little one. Welcome to the world."

Felicia collapsed back on the bed, bathed in sweat. He was out. Her son was born, little Phillip Junior was born. Finally.

"Aren't you a sparkler?" the midwife cooed.

Fine, fine, cut the cord, clean him off and give him to her.

The midwife cut the cord, set the knife aside, - "OK, the afterbirth is out" - then took him to the corner and fussed with him.

Do what you have to do and leave me with my newborn. This was taking too long. "Let me see him."

"What?" the midwife asked, stiffening.

"My son, let me see him."

The midwife hesitated.

What was wrong with this woman? She'd been irritating, bossing her around. Well, it was time that she had a taste of her own medicine. "Bring him here," she commanded, drawing out each word.

The midwife approached, holding little Phillip wrapped tightly in a blanket.

He was all cleaned up so she didn't have to deal with that blood and smelly goo. Nasty stuff, that. She reached out and took her child. "Now, leave, both of you. I want to be alone with my son." It felt so good to say that, my son.

The midwife and the housekeeper exchanged a look, took their leave and shut the bedroom door behind them.

Ah, this was better. *Look at you, little one.* She held him up.

He blinked back at her, eyes unfocussed.

"You're perfect," she told him. "Your life is going to be fabulous. You have money. You have status. You have power. And all because you're the son of 'the' Phillip Fontinello." She cradled him to her and he began moving his mouth, rooting around. Probably hungry. She exposed her left breast and he clamped on. *Ouch, easy, easy.*

He suckled away.

Now that Little Phillip was settled, she could check him out. She tugged the blanket away. Look at those little feet and those tiny toes. They looked like pearls. Perfect, just perfect.

She took his hands. Tiny fingers, perfectly formed. So sweet. One, two, three, four, five of them on the right one. She took up his other hand. One, two three, four –

What! No, this couldn't be. Six fingers? What the heck?

She yanked the baby away from her breast and stared as it began squalling in protest as the blanket fell away. Wait. Where was his penis? There was only a slit.

No, no, no.

It was a girl.

Not only that, it was deformed. Six fingers on one hand? This was an abomination.

Her heart beat faster.

All those months – the morning sickness, the weight gain, the constant peeing, the mottled skin, the inability to find a comfortable sleeping position – she'd endured it all to give Phillip a boy. And she'd never complained, not once. No, not her. She'd bit her lip and endured it all.

Now, she had this, this, this deformed *curse* to give him.

It wasn't fair. She'd worked so hard. She'd done all the work, day and night. Now, she had to present him with this utterly deficient *thing*?

No, no, she couldn't. She just couldn't.

There was a glint on the bed.

The knife. Yes, that was the solution, the only solution.

She could fix this, part of it, at least.

She grabbed the thing's left hand and held it flat against the night stand.

She could do this. She separated the thing's five normal fingers from the one that stuck out like a flag pole, telling the whole world the Fontinellos had created an abomination. If anyone saw it, Phillip would be the laughing stock of Sacramento.

There was only one thing to do.

She grabbed the knife tighter, hefted it high above her head and – *now!* – brought it down with all her might.

Felicia Fontinello sat before her vanity. She eyed her reflection. She really was beautiful, if she had to say so herself. Even though she was 26, she didn't look a day over twenty. Well, maybe twenty-one. Staying out of the sun - that was the secret to keeping a youthful appearance.

She opened a jar, scooped out some night cream and smoothed it on her face.

She stopped, staring at the reflection.

There is was, on the edge of her left hand, the reminder of the obscenity that had dictated her childhood. The scar still showed on the outside, a thin silvery line where the surgeon's scalpel had sliced. Oh sure, you had to look closely to see it, but it was there if you looked hard enough.

Ruby's was more prominent, so she made the child wear gloves.

The Purssington Curse, her mother had called it. Or the Extra Finger from Hell, when she thought her daughter was out of hearing range.

Sometimes it skipped a generation. Most times it didn't.

Lucky her.

It had caused more embarrassing moments in her life than she cared to recall.

When she was a child, the preacher had warned her parents that she was "this close" to being taken over by the dark side. He'd ordered them to take the switch to her if she rebelled in any way.

Every time she'd gone to church, he'd stared at her in that intense way of his, making her wish she could shrink into the pew and just disappear.

Then that little turd Jimmy Stoddard had called her the 'Child of the Devil.' He'd chided her with it every time he saw her. Even Bethany Tanner, her best friend, yeah right, had labeled her a witch, in front of the whole classroom, no less.

After that, the entire school had shunned her, chanting, "Finger bitch, sign of a witch" over and over until she'd run home in tears.

She'd told her mother that she was through with being called a freak, an abomination. She'd given an ultimatum. Have it surgically removed and then send her to live with her aunt where she could start her life anew.

The doctor had come well recommended. The surgery had been done in secret when she was twelve. When she woke up, she was in a carriage, on her way to her aunt's home a hundred miles away.

No one had ever known. None of her relatives, none of her friends, none of her beaus.

And certainly not Phillip when she'd met him ten years later. Him, the catch of the century. Tall, handsome, he'd swept her off her feet. He'd wooed her for months. And she'd fallen for his trap.

Then she'd discovered what the wedding night was *really* all about.

Felicia shuddered involuntarily at the memory.

She'd done her duty, endured his base desires and produced a child. An abomination, yes, but a child nonetheless. Thank goodness she'd taken care of the Purssington Curse on Day One or he would have thrown them both out into the street.

Now, Phillip entered and strode across the room. He slid his hands down her shoulders. "You look lovely." He bent down and kissed her neck. "I seldom get to see you in your night clothes. I've missed you."

He was pathetic with his whispered endearments. She knew what he wanted. "I gave you a child. Don't expect another."

He straightened up. "I wanted a boy."

"And you fathered a girl. Too bad. You had your chance." She flicked him away like he was a pesky fly. "Now, get out of my bedroom."

Felicia patted her mouth with the napkin and got up from the table. It was nice visiting friends and catching up with all the news. "Well, Penelope, it's really been lovely hearing about your honeymoon, but we have to go."

"No, don't leave. I didn't get to tell you about our last week. We spent all of it in Rome."

Rome. She loved Rome. If only Phillip would take her on a grand tour of Europe. All he ever did was work, work, work. Yes, he read bedtime stories to Ruby and indulged her with her constant talk of plants, but fathers were supposed to be involved in their children's lives. "Some other time. We really must be off." Ruby was three. She could be her excuse. "Little Ruby needs her nap."

Penelope gestured to dark-haired child, playing with blocks on the floor nearby. "She's been a delight. You must love having a daughter."

If only she'd stop coming up with these odd pronouncements, like at dinner last night. Ruby had stated that blades of grass followed the sun as it crossed the sky. Sure they did. Where *did the child come up with such things?* "Come on, Ruby, Put the blocks away. It's time to go home."

Ruby complied.

Good, she still had her gloves on. Sometimes she tore them off and then everyone could see that scar. It was horrid looking.

"Let's go home now." Felicia headed to the door. "Say 'bye bye' Ruby."

Ruby trotted over and threw her arms around Penelope in a hug. "Bye bye. See you soon." She looked up at Penelope. "Bye bye to you, too."

"Aren't you sweet? I get two goodbyes?"

"Yup. One for you and one the baby that you made last night."

Felicia froze. Surely she hadn't said that. What three year old even knew about such things?

Penelope was red-faced. "What are you talking about?"

"It's growing in your belly." She giggled and poked at their hostess' skirt. "Right there."

Oh, God, this was embarrassing. She grabbed Ruby's hand. "I'm so sorry. Children, they say the oddest things sometimes. Let's go, Ruby." She yanked her away and hurried the child out the door and down the steps. How *dare* this little brat embarrass her like that? They got out to the street. "I'm never taking you anywhere again."

"Enough play time," Mary Dubrowsky called out and ushered the kindergarten children inside the school. Little Ruby Fontinello was lingering again. She sighed. What an odd child. And what was with the gloves? Did the child wear them twenty-four seven? "Come on, Ruby. It's story time."

"What plant is this?"

Another question. This child was full of them. "I really don't know."

"Can you find out?"

Can you just obey me? For once? All week long it had been this way, ever since the start of school. "Yes, but not now."

"I really need to know."

"Of course you do, Ruby. Now, come inside."

"Bobbie has an obstruction."

Her ears were playing tricks on her. "Excuse me?"

"It's in his intestine."

"You know the word 'intestine?'"

"Upper intestine. Of course, it would fix itself if he ate the right foods. But he won't. So," the little girl shrugged, "you know what that means."

She was afraid to ask. "What does it mean?"

"He's going to die," she said matter-of-factly.

Mary's hand flew to her chest. The child was serious.

"I already told him."

"That he was going to *die*?"

Ruby pointed. "That's why he's crying over there in the corner."

This was the last straw. Ruby Fontinello was not welcome in her kindergarten class any longer.

Ruby Fontinello tugged the hand of her nanny. "Hurry up, I want to show Daddy what I found." This was so exciting. She'd led the nanny out to the woods, so few of her nannies wanted to go, and there she'd found the flowers, their faces raised toward the sun. It had been like she'd meant to find them. But then, she'd dreamed of the flowers just the night before.

Some people didn't understand that the earth offered so many wonderful things. There were things in nature that could help so many people. If their tummy hurt, a plants could help. If they had a headache, a plant could make it go away. If they cut themselves, a plant could keep the germs away.

Helping people was good. It was fun. Besides, it was the right thing to do.

They reached the back porch of the sprawling Victorian. Ruby let go of the girl's hand. She was too slow and this was too important. She ran inside. "Daddy, Daddy, look what I found." She raced into his office and jumped on his lap.

"Flowers?"

"Blue flowers," she corrected him. They were so pretty. But there was more to them than being pretty. She knew it deep inside her. She should know what exactly they could do, but it was just outside the grasp of her mind. "What are they?"

Phillip Fontinello smiled. "Let's find out."

She knew what that meant. He could look it up for her. He was such a great daddy, always helping her.

Ruby jumped off his lap and found the book on the shelf. It told all about the flowers. It sure was big, heavy too. She pulled it out and hurried back to him as fast as she could, hefting it up to him. "Here, Daddy." She climbed back onto his lap. "Hurry up before my tutor comes."

He flipped the pages and adjusted his spectacles. He found a picture of blue flowers. "These?"

"No."

He flipped more pages. "These?"

"No, Let me." She scanned the pages, one after another, searching. Not those. Not those. "Here they are."

"Let's see, ah, they're called campanula. It says here that its roots can be boiled tender like parsnips are and eaten warm, best covered with sauce. Sweetish tasting, with a pungency to it, young roots can be eaten raw with vinegar and pepper."

Food? That was all it was good for? But she'd been sure there was more. "Is that it? Nothing about making people feel better?"

Daddy scowled as he read. He flipped to the next page. "Found it. 'A decoction of the roots is good for all types of inflammation of the mouth and throat,'" He closed the book. "So, they're not just pretty flowers."

"I knew they were good for something."

"Did you now?" He looked amused. "And how did you know that?"

"The flowers told me, in my dream." Or, they'd told her something. What exactly, she couldn't put her finger on. If only she could remember her dreams better.

Daddy patted her head. "Dreams don't tell us about flowers, Ruby."

"Mine do." She slipped off his lap. Sometimes adults could be so funny. How had she known? She just did, that was all.

Mommy was at the back door, waiting for them and waving them in. She was dressed in one of her traveling suits.

Ruby raced ahead of her nanny, holding her prize against her chest. This has been the best-est day ever. She'd gone into the woods and out had come a baby looking for a home. It had walked right up to her, like it knew they belonged together. "Mommy, Mommy, look what I found."

Mommy frowned. "What is that?"

Ruby held it up. "It's a kitten. Isn't it cute? Can I keep her?"

Mommy ignored her. Her mouth was tight as she waited for the nanny to catch up. "What is all this?"

The nanny stopped, hesitated. "She found it near the edge of the meadow. Seemed abandoned."

"So you let her take it?"

"Well, there didn't seem to be any harm in –"

"I repeat: You let her take it?"

"Yes, Ma'am."

"I don't like cats."

Mommy sure was talking funny. Like, one word at a time. Ruby knew she had to make her understand. It was alone. Without its mama, without its sister s or brothers. It had nowhere else to go. "It's not a 'cat,' Mommy, it's a kitten."

"I told you, you're to call me 'mother'. As for that thing you're holding, it'll be a cat soon enough. They're filthy."

The door opened.

"What's filthy?"

It was Daddy.

Ruby held up the yellow kitten to him. He would realize just how special this was. "Look what I found."

Daddy took the kitten from her outstretched hand and held it up. "Well, well, what have we here?"

"It's my kitten. I'm going to name her Diamond Twinkle-sky Crystal Magic Jewel. Isn't she cute?"

Daddy handed the fuzzy kitten back to her. "Looks to be about four months old. Maybe it's hungry. Let's go find a saucer of milk for it."

What a good idea. Daddy understood the importance of today and how it was the best-est day ever. But then, he knew a lot of things.

Felicia leaned closer to the bathroom mirror. Her gums were red. They hurt. She twirled at the sound of footsteps.

Oh dear, Phillip was home. He made it clear that he ruled the family and whatever he said, was gospel truth. The Fontinello name was not to be scourged with short-comings, inadequacies or, God forbid, scandals. A sixth finger would have marked Ruby with all three.

The child was a conundrum. Even without the extra finger to mark her as strange, she drew attention to herself in other ways. She'd embarrassed the Fontinello name more than once with her innocent proclamations. One never knew what she'd come up with next.

Felicia's entire life was spent ensuring Ruby didn't do something to make Phillip think twice about keeping them around. At least she'd been able to bear him a child, unlike his first two wives.

She hurried out of the en-suite into the bedroom, put on a serene face and greeted him at the bedroom door, ignoring the pain in her gums. "You're home early."

He pecked her on the cheek. "I'm going to San Francisco on the five o'clock train." He walked past her, pulled his travel satchel from the wardrobe and began packing. He glanced over. "You can go with me, you know."

And be bored to tears? "It's about work. What would I do?"

"Go shopping."

Hmm, that sounded good. She needed a new outfit. And a hat. There were perks to being Phillip's wife and if you wanted a hat, there was no better place than San Francisco to find one. "Maybe."

"When my meetings are over," he said, "we can have dinner and take in a play."

He was being nice. Well then, she could be nice, too. "Well, if you really want me there, I suppose I could join you." She pulled out her own satchel and began filling it.

There was a shriek from downstairs.

Phillip looked up. "Ruby!" He raced for the door and ran downstairs.

Felicia hurried to keep up with him. "What's the matter?"

"Daddy! Mother! It's Whiskers. She's having her babies. Come see."

That's what this was about? A cat giving birth? It had better not be on her new sofa.

After Ruby had pronounced her cat was pregnant, she'd questioned Mildred, Maude and all the servants, asking if her daughter witnessed the female cat being in heat with a tomcat. None of them had seen a thing. In fact, all of them were of the thought that such a young cat could not possibly be developed enough to carry a litter. After all, the filthy thing was only a few months old herself. But now, here they were, being born.

She rounded the corner.

Ruby was sitting on the floor next to a box lined with a towel.

Whiskers, a much easier name than Rainbow Starlight Diamond Glitter Whatever Else, was licking a scrawny little white kitten with a pink face. It looked more like a rat than a kitten.

Felicia peered down at it. There was so much blood, it made her skin crawl. "How many of them are there, anyway?"

"This is the first one, Mother. I knew she was about to have it by the way she was behaving."

She shuddered involuntarily. "And you *watched* Whiskers give birth?" The girl was beyond comprehension. Who would intentionally do such a thing?

"It's the best-est day ever," Ruby said.

"There is no such word," she said.

Phillip peeked into the box. "What a cute little kitten. Our household is growing. We'll have to order more cream be delivered. Keep an eye on Whiskers for us while we're out of town, Ruby, OK?" He patted Ruby's head and returned upstairs.

Some help he was. One cat was plenty as far as she was concerned. Ruby had been right. A cat could give birth when it was only a few months old. But … how had she known that? Maybe her path had been crossed by a witch while she was carried in her belly. She shook the thought away and went to leave. "If any of that blood gets on my floor, you'll be the one cleaning it up," she warned.

"Don't worry, Mother. I'll take care of things. Whiskers is going to be fine." She hesitated. "It hurts, doesn't it?"

"What hurts?"

"Your mouth, around your teeth."

What? How did she know that?

"It's nothing major, Mother." She pulled something out of her pocket and handed it over. "It's blue spruce sap. Make a tea of it to rinse in your mouth for ten minutes three or four times a day. That'll make it go away in a couple of days." She turned back to Whiskers who was panting. "It's all right. There, there, it's all right."

Felicia stared at the sap, shook her head and left the room.

Maude, the Fontinello's housekeeper, eyed the young woman standing in the front hallway. This house went through nannies as though it had a revolving door. "Let me see your papers."

"Yes, Ma'am." She handed them over.

"I'm not a Ma'am. Call me 'Miss'. I'm not ancient, after all." Though she might well be, the way she was feeling these days. She'd caught a chill or something and it was dragging her down.

"Yes, Ma'am. Miss, I mean." The young woman looked around with wide eyes.

Felicia Fontinello had insisted on using one of the fancy pantsy servant finder services in Chicago when she could have merely hired a local person for the child's nanny. Her own cousin fit the bill. But, no, Felicia only wanted the best. This girl, Matilda Moore, was eighteen, had a clean background, did not have rickets or consumption, and her pastor said she was clean of dress and manner. She'd been through the service's "rigorous and thorough" classes for dealing with children from kindergarten through age twelve.

The girl's papers seemed to be in order. She handed them back. "Your quarters are just off the child's room. Follow me." This one would probably last a month, just like all the others.

The young woman hesitated and leaned close. "The service said you needed someone able to handle a compulsive child who was head strong," she whispered. "Is she that bad?"

"Ruby?" Maude made a wishy-washy gesture as she headed up the grand stairs. "She's ... different." Better warn her now before this Matilda opened her mouth and blurted something in front of Felicia. "Listen up, because I'm only going to tell you this once and then you're never to speak of it again."

Matilda hurried to take the stairs beside her. "Yes?"

"Ruby had an accident on the day she was born." Sure, blame it on the child. "She, uh, crawled over to the burning fireplace –"

"She could crawl on the day she was born? That's unbelievable."

Wait until she heard the rest of Felicia's story. "She crawled over to the burning fireplace and stuck her hand out."

Matilda looked aghast. "What? Into the fire?"

"You'll see a scar, a burn mark, on the outside of her left hand. But do not, and I repeat, do *not* say a word about it."

"Why not?"

Because that's not what happened. The newborn's screams had brought her and the midwife running back into the room to see a torrent of blood streaming off the child's hand while Felicia just watched, still holding the knife. She could still see it plain as day, even after all these years.

"What have you done?" the midwife had screamed as she'd swooped in and snatched the newborn away from Felicia. "She'll bleed to death. Quick, Maude, grab that poker."

It had been lying on the grate, its end in the fire, glowing red. She'd grabbed it. "Now what?"

"Press it to her wound. We've got to cauterize it or she'll bleed out."

She could still smell the flesh being burned, still hear the newborn shrieking in pain. Poor Ruby. They hadn't been sure she would survive, but she had, thank goodness.

But she couldn't tell this young nanny that. She couldn't tell anyone, not if she wanted to keep her job. And who would want to hire someone as old as her? No, best to keep quiet and play along with Felicia's irrational story. At least she didn't make Ruby wear those ridiculous gloves 24/7 anymore.

Maude reached the top step. "From now on, you'll use the backstairs like the rest of the servants. There are eight bedrooms up here. Ruby's is down this way at the end."

"I've never seen hallways so wide."

And she wouldn't ever again. Felicia had argued over the plans with the architect day and night and, as always, had gotten her way. Too bad she hadn't added one of those new contraptions, an elevator. It sure would be kinder on the knees.

They reached Ruby's room. Matilda's was attached and they shared a bathroom, situated in between like a pass-through. That, thank goodness, was one of the things Felicia has insisted on for this new house. It made her and the other servants the envy of their peers.

Matilda peeked into Ruby's bedroom. "Not pink?"

Hardly. Ruby could be as strong minded as her mother. "The child insisted on moss green and a cedar plank wall."

"So I see. Do you know why she wanted cedar?"

"For the fragrance. She likes to go out into the forest." Likes? Insists. It was only fifty yards off their back porch and this new nanny would learn soon enough how the youngster was drawn to it. Let her find out on her own and see how well the service's classes had prepared her for a child like this. "And, as you can see, a canvas cover instead of a ruffled canopy over her mattress." Canvas? Call it what it was – a tarp, like some hunter might use.

"My goodness."

The girl was getting the idea now. "Your room is through here." She led her through the bathroom.

The new nanny's face brightened. "Very nice."

"Ruby gets a bath every night."

"Not just Saturdays?"

"The lady's orders." There were lots of orders.

They entered her room. "You have your own entrance to the hall, too, of course." She pointed at the door. "And the back stairs are just a few feet away."

Matilda set her suitcase down and looked around. "I hadn't expected anything quite so, well, plush."

The velvet covered settee, the artisan-quality chifforobe and headboard set, she meant. Yes, the Felicia had her standards and they were high, even for the household's servants. The expensive furniture pieces were the madam's castoffs. "Dinner will be at six. You're expected to sit next to Ruby and correct her on any manners."

"Of course."

"Then, you'll whisk her away so the madam and the master of the house can have their peace and quiet. You're not to be seen after dinner, either."

"I'll keep her occupied. I brought some fabulous young people's books." She looked around. "Where is Ruby? I'd like to meet her."

"Yes, I guess it's time." Maude sighed and gestured her back to the moss-colored room. "Ruby likes to be outside so she's often on her balcony."

"Oh, that sounds delightful."

Just wait. She crossed to the balcony door and opened it. "Ruby? There's someone here to meet you."

Matilda stepped out onto the balcony with her. She turned her head side to side. "No one's out here. She must be downstairs."

"No, she's here." Maude cupped a hand to her mouth. "Ruby," she yelled, "come here, please."

There was a scrambling sound above them, then the youngster appeared – oh, goodness, she'd changed to men's dungarees again. "Here I am." She scrambled down the trellis like some kind of monkey and dropped down the last couple of feet to land with a thump.

Matilda looked from Ruby to the roof and back to the child. She cleared her throat. "My, what an entrance."

"Are you my new nanny?"

"Yes." The girl recovered and crouched down. "I'm Matilda. Nice to meet you."

Ruby shook her hand like a sailor, pumping it heartily.

Matilda winced and stood up again.

Ruby gestured to the trellis. "You sure you don't want to climb up on the roof? It's a great view."

Poor Matilda. She looked like she was drowning and had no idea how to save herself. It was time to step in. "Now, now, Matilda is tired from her journey."

"But –"

"No buts. I'll let you two get to know one another." She turned to leave.

"Want to see my kitty cats, Matilda?"

Those cats. The girl let them into her bedroom in the middle of the night so they could sleep on her bed. Good thing the missus didn't know. "Remember, dinner's at six and Ruby will need to wash up and put on a dress for it." They couldn't have the child convincing the new nanny she could show up at the table in dungarees and with smudges of dirt on her face or Felicia Fontinello would throw a fit.

Ruby looked behind her as she climbed the hill. "Hurry up, Matilda, you're falling behind." Maybe her nanny would finally get dungarees. She was being slowed down by the long dresses she wore. But then, all her nannies had been slowed down by long skirts. Silly girls.

What's this? A Jack-in-the-pulpit was right in front of her. They were really hard to find. Should she pluck it and show Daddy? Hold on, if they were hard to find, maybe it was because other people had done that and now there weren't many left. No, she'd leave it alone, let it be.

"Thank you, forest, for letting me see one," she murmured and, giving it one last look, moved off.

There was a lot to see and do out here in the woods. She'd spotted a rabbit, watched a hawk soar high above the tree tops and found a weasel's hole in the ground.

This trail, she'd never seen it before. It sure was faint. It *was* a trail, had to be. Someone had used it. There was a broken branch, a depression in the soft dirt, yes, it had to be a trail, just not used much.

She turned off and followed it, ignoring the twigs that caught at her hair, the branches that brushed her face. Where, oh where, did this thing lead? She'd never explored this way before.

She followed it up the hill, around a bend and –

There was a small opening, a clearing. And there were pinion pines here. Excellent. She hurried over, reached up and plucked off two pinion nuts. They were hard to crack open, but they would be worth it.

She used her thumbnail to break apart the seam, then peeled back the one flap. The other two sides were easy after that and, voila, there was her prize, a small, but oh so yummy nut.

She sat down and popped it in her mouth. Delicious. She worked the other one open and ate it, too. The forest had all kinds of things to eat.

Like, what were these dark berries? She'd never seen them before. They looked kind of like the ones she'd tried that one time, the ones that had made her feel sleepy.

These were smaller and easy to overlook, clinging to the underside of prickly leaves on a low bush. If the leaves were prickled, then it was trying to keep small animals from eating its berries. And they were dark, so they were packed with good things.

She reached in. Ouch, these prickles were stinging her. She felt the berries, grasped them and yanked.

Got them, a small cluster of them, at least. She inspected the berries closer. No, she'd never seen any like these. Bet they tasted good. There was only one way to find out. Ruby leaned back on one elbow, tipped her head back and opened her mouth in anticipation.

A shadow fell across her face.

It was a small woman with yellowish skin and small slits for eyes.

She sat up. "Who are you? Where did you come from?"

The woman's hand slapped the berries away.

Ruby gasped as they tumbled onto the ground. No, her berries! Her eyebrows knitted. "Hey. Why'd you do that?"

The woman shook a finger at her. "Good for the man, not good for the woman. No eat." She turned and walked off.

Ruby stared after her. "Good for the man, not good for the woman. No eat," she muttered. Who *was* this woman?

CHAPTER TWO

Ruby pulled the covers up to her chin as she settled into bed. She was going to have one of those dreams, she could feel it. It would come in the middle of the night, so the sooner she fell asleep, the better her dream would be.

She closed her eyes and drifted off.

Someone was with her. They were tall, dressed in white, but she never really saw them, couldn't even say if they were men or women. They just *were*. But the sense of them being there with her was undeniable.

"I'm listening," she said.

Miss Maude had a problem, the being on her left told her without speaking. They showed her Miss Maude's thumb. Ruby could see it in her mind.

There was a wart. It didn't hurt, but it bothered the housekeeper to no end.

Funny, but from the way it was presented, the beings let her know it wasn't anything life-threatening, nothing even to cause a visit to the doctor. But, they showed Miss Maude was fretting over it, wringing her hands with worry when no one was looking.

She was shown was a tree. The bark looked familiar. That smell it – it was cedar like her wall, but not exactly like her wall.

The beings cut into the tree to reach the part near the center.

She pressed her fingers against the pulp. It was soft, moist. The fibers came away easily.

Daddy had given her a jackknife. She could gouge it out with that.

"How much of it will I need?" she'd asked. She didn't want to kill the tree, just get its medicinal portion.

The picture in her mind changed. There was a pile of it in her hand, no more than the littlest measuring cup the cook used in their kitchen. She could feel the heft of it.

"I understand," she said. "Where do I find this tree?"

She was flying over her house and shot north, far across the forest. One hill, two, three, past a waterfall. She settled on the ground. So specific, this must be a special tree.

"I think I can find it."

The beings left.

Ruby adjusted the blankets and buried her head into her pillow. Miss Maude needed her. She would help. She fell back asleep.

Matilda scrambled up the hill after her charge. This was so much easier in dungarees. "Ruby, where are we going?"

"I think I found the trees."

She had no idea what the child was talking about. "What trees?"

"Red cedar. They were in that book Daddy bought me. Come on."

Hadn't they walked half the Earth today, already? "How much farther?"

Ruby pulled out her scope and peered through it. "I think I see some. Follow me." She started off.

Matilda sighed. The father bought his daughter things, like the scope, to make up for the time he was away on business. He bought her digging tools, a rucksack, bought the herbs that Ruby said she needed. Didn't he understand that the youngster needed his time?

Then there was Felicia Fontinello. The mother barely wanted anything to do with the child. So, she and Ruby's tutor were left to pick up the pieces. The two of them had compared notes soon after she'd been hired and both had come to the same realization, that Ruby had intelligence, but not in the normal sense. Instead, Ruby had her own way of seeing things, of *knowing* things.

It was uncanny, eerie even.

She caught up to Ruby and ran a hand across her brow. She was sweating. No proper woman would be caught dead out here and certainly not sweating. "Why on earth did we have to find these trees, anyway?"

"Maude has a wart on her hand."

"So?"

"So, if Mother sees it, she'll send her away."

Maybe she hadn't heard her correctly. "Dismiss her, you mean?"

Ruby paused. "Don't you think so?"

"Did your mother tell you that she'd fire anyone working in the house with a mark like that?"

"She doesn't have to come out and say it. Can't you feel it?"

Now that she'd brought it up, there was that sense to Mrs. Fontinello that if something wasn't up to snuff, out it went. It had all the household workers walking on egg shells, trying to never stand out for fear of her wrath. "Maude can't leave. She keeps the household running like a clock." They'd fall apart without her.

"So, that's why I need the cedar."

"But, for what?"

"To make a salve. If I crush it into a pulp, boil it down and add it to a cream, I can bandage her wart and it'll go away."

Really? Cedar could do that? "Hold on. You have cedar on your wall. Why did we have to hike all this way?"

"I need the inner bark. And it has to be fresh. I'll add bloodroot to it too, but it's pretty caustic and I'll have to be careful handling it."

So many specifics. Surely, that hadn't come from a book. Ruby wasn't known for her reading skills. "How do you know this?"

Ruby smiled. "I dreamed it."

Felicia stood before her mirror and patted her hair. This new hair-do was certainly very flattering.

The doorbell rang. That meant Mrs. Teedamann was here. She hurried downstairs. "Mrs. Teedamann, how nice to see you again."

Ruby burst in the door behind her. Oh, dear, she was in dungarees and that dirty old man's shirt again. How embarrassing.

"Who's this?" Mrs. Teedamann said.

"I'm Ruby, how do you do?"

At least the child had the presence to curtsy. But that horrible outfit, it was no way for a proper young lady to dress.

Mrs. Teedamann reached out and grabbed the fabric with a jerk. "What in Heaven's name is this?"

Ruby lost her balance and fell into her. "Denim." Her hand pressed into Mrs. Teedamann to regain her balance. She looked up into their guest's face. "You have an upset stomach."

Mrs. Teedamann nodded. "It's nothing. I just need to take some bicarbonate of soda."

"No, don't do that." Ruby held her hand around the woman's stomach area, her eyes focused on ...nothing.

"Ruby, what in heaven's name, what are you doing?" Her daughter was turning a perfectly lovely visit for tea into a circus act. How dare she? Felicia hurried forward. "Stop that. She's our guest, for goodness sake."

Ruby ignored her to look up at Mrs. Teedamann again. "Bicarbonate of soda is too strong for you. It'll swing things in the other direction. You need something more soothing. Chamomile. Yes, that's what you need."

Enough of this. Felicia grabbed Ruby's arm. "Upstairs, young lady. I don't know what you're trying to do, but we're not amused. Now, go. Your tutor's been looking for you and it's time for your studies."

"Sorry." Ruby hightailed it up the stairs.

"You'll have to excuse her. She's rather, um, headstrong." *And an idiot.* Something had to be done about her or the entire town would be talking about this odd person who was surely some kind of changeling.

Felicia adjusted her bonnet. It wouldn't do to let the sun ruin her porcelain complexion. She'd been forced into this, so she'd better make the best of it. A community garden to help feed the poor. OK, so it was a good cause, but did she *have* to get her nails dirty? Couldn't she just write a check? Giving money was so much ...cleaner.

At least Ruby was here. She could be the one to dig in the dirt, get on her knees and press seeds into the ground. Maybe everyone would assume she was a boy in that old hat.

It was a big turnout. Women were smiling, laughing, lining up to get hoes and shovels and bags of seeds, like this was a picnic. Really, who'd thought up this dirty deed, anyway?

"Ruby, you like to dig in the dirt, right?" Her clothes certainly looked like that's what she did when she'd come home from the woods. "You can do it for both of us."

"OK, Mother. I'll go and get a shovel."

"No, wait." *Until the crowd thins out so no one gets a close look at you.* "Let the others choose their shovels first."

An old woman, a foreigner with slit-like eyes, was coming toward them.

Ruby tugged on her sleeve. "I've seen her before. In the woods. She slapped berries out of my hand."

What was a Chinese woman doing here? Oh, that's right, a Chinese group had moved north of town to help build Phillip's latest venture, a railroad branch to Carson City, Nevada. Why anyone would want to go to Nevada, she couldn't fathom. But he'd pulled in big backers. They must have seen an economic advantage to having such a branch running from Sacramento.

The kicker to the deal was finding cheap labor. No one was cheaper than the Chinese. Let them break their backs doing the hard labor.

Now, one of their kind was walking toward them. She shuddered. What did she want? A handout? A Fontinello didn't carry money. Every merchant in town knew to send a bill for whatever she picked out at their store.

Why, the woman was walking right up to them and stopping inches away. Intentionally, no less. How rude. She needed to be put in her place. She straightened her back. "What do you want, old woman?"

The Chinese woman ignored her to stare into Ruby's face. She reached out with a craggy arm and grabbed Ruby's chin with her boney fingers, turning the child's face this way and that.

How dare she, and in front of other people, no less. "Just one moment, whoever you are –"

The old woman let go. "She's been touched."

Touched? What? "I beg your pardon?"

The Chinese woman tapped the side of her own head. "Touched," she repeated, shook her head and made a wishy-washy gesture.

"What are you say –?"

The old woman turned around and moved on.

What in the world was that all about? She'd declared her daughter as being "touched" – touched in the head, she meant.

Wait. Suddenly things made sense.

The sixth finger had been a sign. She should have paid more attention to it. Ruby had not only been born deformed. Her brain was deformed, too. It had taken a witch of a Chinese woman to point it out.

Ruby pressed her ear to the bedroom door. Mother and Daddy were talking. It was about her, no question about it.

"I tell you, Phillip. She grabbed Ruby's face and leered at her. It was so strange, I was ready to yell for a policeman, not that they're ever around when a lady needs one."

"She grabbed Ruby's face?"

"And stared into her eyes. Then she was talking about how Ruby wasn't quite all there. It was crazy."

"All there? What do you mean?"

"That she was not right in her head. I mean, right in front of everybody, she practically declared your daughter to be mentally delinquent."

Hold on. She'd said "touched", that's all.

Mother winced. "I didn't know what to do. If no one had known about Ruby's strangeness before that, then they certainly knew now. I was so *embarrassed*. Everybody was there, Phillip. Everybody was watching."

"Everybody? Oh, come on, now. You're making a big case out of nothing."

"That witch knows things. She could be dangerous."

"She's a harmless old Chinese woman."

"One who singled out *your* daughter."

There was silence.

What was going on in there? Were they whispering?

"She's your daughter, too, Felicia."

Estelle Krofton held the hand of her toddler, Charity, as they went down the street. They been out to the meadow for a picnic and now were going for a treat – ice cream. She was such a sweet little child.

Charity tugged on her skirt. "Mommy, I don't feel so good."

It was the heat, most likely. The child was looking a little flushed. The ice cream would help cool her off.

"Not much longer." Estelle twirled her umbrella. She wanted some ice cream, too. Vanilla, no, chocolate.

Oh dear, there was Felicia Fontinello and that strange girl of hers, the one who, years ago, had declared her to be on her period before she even knew it herself. It was like the girl had intruded into her most private space. It was wasn't, well, *natural* to know things like that.

A lucky guess. Yes, that's what it had been, a lucky guess, nothing more than that.

Now, she had to be polite even though Ruby Fontinello always seemed to be looking at the air around a person, not at the people themselves. So strange. She held Charity's hand tighter.

Felicia nodded. "Hello, Estelle. A lovely day, no?"

"A gorgeous day."

"You must see this new necklace Phillip bought me." She placed her hand below her neck. "See?"

Another piece of jewelry? Like the woman didn't have enough already. But she would nod and comment on it, just to be polite.

"Mommy," Charity whined.

"Just a moment, honey." She peered at the necklace. The size of the stone was impressive. "Diamond?"

"With sapphire accents."

"Lovely. I've never seen a cut quite like that." She pulled back. Oh dear, that weird child, Ruby had worked her way next to Charity.

"Mommy," Charity whined again. "My tummy."

"What about your –?" she gasped. "Oh, my god, her mouth, she's bleeding!" Frothing was more like it. She grabbed Charity. She had to help her, had to find a doctor.

"Stop," Ruby shouted. "Help *is* here."

Did Ruby see a doctor in the crowd over there? "Where?"

Ruby jumped behind the two-year-old, got on her knees and wrapped her arms around Charity's waist. She squeezed.

Charity burped.

What the hell was she doing? "Get your hands off my child!"

Ruby squeezed Charity again, hard.

Charity vomited.

Enough of this. Felicia's strange daughter was killing her little girl. "Get away from her, get away, now!"

Ruby stood up. "She ate choke cherries." She pointed at the ground. "See?"

Choke cherries? Oh, dear, Charity must have found some while they were in the meadow and eaten them. But

...how had Ruby known? "We were on our way for ice cream," she muttered. "But I'll just get her home to rest."

Ruby shook her head. "No, she needs the ice cream. It'll help her feel better."

It would? Well, OK. That made sense. "But how did you know what to –?"

Felicia and Ruby moved off.

Estelle watched them leave, blinking in confusion. What had just happened? She knelt down and checked Charity, wiping her mouth with a kerchief. "How do you feel now, sweetie?"

Charity nodded. "All better, Mommy. Ice cream now?"

She stood up and stared at Ruby's retreating figure. "Yes, yes, ice cream. That's what she said to give you."

Ruby came downstairs for breakfast. Daddy had brought home a crate of pears the day before. She couldn't wait to have one.

Mother was at the table. There was a bowl in front of her and a pitcher of milk.

"What's that, Mother?"

"Cereal. It's a new food. You just add milk and, voila, you have breakfast." She scooped up a spoonful and popped it in her mouth. "Delicious."

She made it sound like there was nothing else like it. Ruby peered at it. It looked weird, like thin wood chips. "What's it made of?"

Mother stopped. "I have no idea. Corn, maybe. No, wheat, yes, that's it, wheat."

"It doesn't look like wheat."

"Well, they added things to it in the factory."

It came from a factory? She'd seen a shoe factory once. It hadn't been very clean. "Like, what things do they add?"

Mother picked up the box and turned it this way and that. "It doesn't say." She took another spoonful, chewed, swallowed and said, "It doesn't taste like wheat. It doesn't taste like anything I've had before."

So, it was processed at a factory, came from a box and it tasted like, well, nothing from nature. "Shouldn't food come from the earth, Mother?"

"This comes from the earth, only, by way of a factory, is all," she said. "It's just, dressed-up to make it taste good. Try it."

"Real food doesn't need to be dressed-up." Ruby grabbed a pear and polished it against her shirt. "I'll have this, thanks." She went to leave.

"Wait. Where are you going?"

"To the community garden. Matilda is coming with me. I'll be home in time for my tutor, don't worry." Other kids in town went to school. But mother insisted she be taught at home for some reason. Probably so she didn't make a fool of herself at school.

Learning reading, writing and arithmetic just didn't appeal to her. Not unless they were books on trees and herbs. Thank goodness Daddy understood her and filled her room with books on plant ecology.

The community garden was busy. A group of young ladies were off to one side, near the forest, giggling and laughing as they approached the garden. They weren't much older than her. She'd never seen them before. "Who are they, Matilda?"

Her nanny's face grew red. She looked down. "I don't know them."

But she knew something about them, obviously. She just wasn't saying. Ruby sighed. "It doesn't matter." She grabbed two rakes off the equipment rack and handed one to Matilda.

She walked over to the center of the garden and began working the soil.

Matilda took up a position on the row opposite her. It was nice out, but then, California weather usually was. That's why there were so many different types of plants being grown here. She entered the rows of corn, pulled out her canteen of water and took a drink.

Where had Matilda gone? Oh, she must be over by the spinach and potatoes, beyond her direct line of sight.

There was still chatter and giggles coming from the edge of the forest.

Ruby wandered over.

There were six girls. Two of them were leaving. All of them were pretty, in silky clothes. Instead of tight sleeves, their dresses had long, draping edges off the elbows, exposing their forearms. Their skirts were layered with a frilled top layer that was more netting than fabric. The effect was whimsical, fun, alluring even.

Mother and their neighbors didn't have exotic clothes like these.

Ruby ventured closer to the remaining four girls. "Hi, I'm Ruby."

They all turned, breaking apart.

Now she could see that they'd been talking to the old Chinese woman, the one who'd come up to her and peered into her face when she and Mother had first come here. There she was, sitting crossed-legged on the ground with baskets around her. The baskets had little pouches in them. "What's this all about?"

The girls giggled like it was a secret. "Just our monthly needs."

Needs? What did that mean?

The pretty blonde waved the girls off. "Ignore them. I send all my girls, the girls from my house I mean, here to get their medicines. Lord knows we need them."

They bade goodbye to the Chinese lady and skittered away, their sleeves flowing behind them like flags.

"You." It was the Chinese lady. "Help me up."

Ruby offered her a hand. The Chinese woman's hand was gnarled but soft.

"Bring my concoctions."

Concoctions? What concoctions?

Oh, the fabric pouches, she meant. Ruby quickly picked them up, put them in the baskets and scrambled to catch up to the Chinese woman who was now well into the woods. "Hey, wait up. Where are you going?"

The woman kept going, ignoring her. She was putting more distance between them.

Ruby stopped and glanced back to where Matilda was intent on wielding a rake. Maybe she should stay at the community garden.

She looked back to the woman in the forest. But she wanted to learn more about this strange person. After all, she'd proclaimed that she'd been "touched," whatever that meant.

Stay or go? Which decision was right?

These pouches of hers, maybe they held the answer.

She sniffed. Odd, she knew that smell. It was marigold. This other one – she sniffed again – was anise. The Chinese woman must have been handing them out.

"She knows about using these things," Ruby murmured. "Things from the earth."

She turned her back on the garden and ran after the Chinese woman. "Wait, wait, I'm coming."

CHAPTER THREE

Ruby caught up to her. "Who are you?"

"Stop talking and listen to the forest," she said.

She could hear the forest, too? She kept following the strange woman. This was a part of the woods she'd never been to before.

There was a stream. They followed it uphill. They came to a meadow.

All around it were tents with Chinese people moving about. There were at least a hundred tarp dwellings. She had no idea this was here. These must be the workers who Daddy had brought in for his railroad branch venture. She'd heard Mother talking about it a few months ago.

The old woman went up to a log cabin and stopped at the front door. "My home. Take off your shoes." She opened the door and entered, her slippers left outside on the porch.

The door closed behind her.

Ruby dropped the baskets, plopped on her butt and yanked off her boots. She scrambled back to her feet, picked up the baskets of pouches and hurried inside.

It was dark but her eyes began adjusting.

The old woman was stirring a pot at the hearth across the room.

What was she making? Soup, maybe? Ruby moved closer. "Um, where do you want these?"

The old woman fluttered her hand in the direction of the corner.

Ruby went over and set down the basket. "Who are you? What were you doing at the community garden? Do you grow food there, too?"

She gave a snort. "You ask too many questions."

It was a rebuke. Mother did that a lot. OK, maybe if she just asked one thing at a time. "Who *are* you?"

The woman stopped stirring and eyed her up and down. "Who are *you*?"

Her face heated up. This woman was mean. She stood straighter. "I'm Ruby Fontinello."

"I know."

She knew? How? Certainly Mother had never played hostess to a woman like this at their home. No, Mother would tip up her nose at such a person. "How do you know?"

The woman resumed stirring.

All right, so she wasn't talking. Two could play this game.

Maybe there were clues around the cabin – a photo, a train ticket, a letter of introduction. She turned.

Whoa.

There was a wall of makeshift book shelves. It towered above her. There were books up the ceiling. Look at those titles. There was a farmer's almanac, a book on animal husbandry, weather patterns and, what was this section?

She scanned the titles.

Herbs for the Modern Woman, The Role of Plants in Today's Busy World, Back to Basics, Medicines of the Earth, Healing From Nature. She pulled the last one off the shelf and opened it to a random page.

"The inner core of the cedar tree contains natural anti-bacterial properties..."

It was exactly the information that her dream had told her. And here it was in a book.

She dropped to the floor and read more, flipping page after page. There were so many things in here, it would take twenty years of dreaming to learn all this. But here it was, in a book. It was everything she could possibly want to know.

A shadow fell over her.

Ruby looked up at the Chinese woman who stood over her. "Tell me, where did you buy this? I want one, too."

"You're not ready." The woman took the book from her hands. She set it back on the shelf.

But, but, I wasn't done with it. "I sniffed your pouches. I know marigold is good for soothing a sunburn."

"And sprains and rashes and tonsillitis."

Those, too? "And the anise – it's for sleep, right?"

"And to aid digestion, expel abdominal gas and clear the breath."

So many uses. "Why do you have so many books?"

"So I can know many things." The woman gestured at the wall full of tomes. "Some women travel with a wardrobe full of clothes."

Like Mother.

"I travel with a wardrobe full of knowledge."

Who *was* this woman? She wore simple Chinese clothes, a long dark tunic with pants that fell to her ankles. Her hair, streaked with gray, was cut at her shoulders with bangs. Her skin was wrinkled with age but soft to the touch. And now she was a reader of books. Wait. The books were in English. And she was speaking in perfect English, not the hesitant gibberish she'd spoken at the garden. "What's your name?"

"Meifeng." She sat down across from Ruby. "Yes, I'm educated."

"But ...in China, right?"

Meifeng drew herself up straight. "I speak five languages."

That many?

"How many do you speak?"

Her face felt hot. "Only one."

"I was a doctor in my home country but I came here to look after my people."

"You're a doctor? Wait a minute. Doctors don't hand out herbs."

"Maybe they should. I also use acupuncture."

Act you ...what? "I don't know what that is."

"You can learn." She reached out and held Ruby's face in both her hands. "Don't talk. Look up."

Ruby obeyed.

"No, don't move your face, just your eyes. Look up."

She looked up without lifting her chin.

"Follow my finger." Meifeng held up her index finger, moved it left to right, then back again.

"What's all this about?"

"Shh. Stick your tongue out as far as you can."

Well, all right, but it seemed kind of rude.

"Hold your hand straight out to the side, close your eyes and touch your fingertip to your nose."

Ruby followed her direction and jabbed the side of her cheek. Oops. "Let me try again."

"No need." Meifeng cocked her head. "Were you dropped on your head as an infant?"

"No."

"Fell down a flight of stairs as a toddler?"

"No."

"Hmmm. Why do I see you out in the woods?"

This was one she could answer at length. "It's like I'm drawn to it. There's so much to see and do. Mother thinks it's silly but I like to find herbs and plants, taste them, smell them and learn what they can do."

"I see. How does just tasting them tell you anything?"

She thought back. "Well, if they make my tongue numb, I know they're probably not good. If they taste bitter, then I figure there's a reason, like maybe they don't want animals to eat them."

Meifeng nodded. "That's one reason, I suppose. You like learning about plants?"

"Oh, yes." She couldn't help the grin the spread across her face. "There's nothing better."

"Why?"

"So I can help people. That's why I have dreams."

"Ah, what dreams?"

Ruby told her how things were shown to her in her sleep.

"Who is telling you these things?"

"I don't know who they are, exactly. They guide me. Like, they told me that raspberry tea is good for a woman's cramps."

"They told you that?"

"I never really see them because they stand beside me. But they show me things, things that heal."

She told of Maude's finger from years ago. The wart had disappeared within a week.

She brought up Mother's swollen gums. They'd returned to normal and hadn't bothered her since.

"And Mrs. Teedamann cured her upset stomach after following my advice."

"Goodie for her."

"I want to learn more."

"Is that so?" Meifeng got up and dusted off her pants. "Time you headed back. Bring your mother to the garden tomorrow before the sun gets too high. I'll be there. I need to speak with her."

Ruby hurried down the trail.

There was a caraway plant. She barely registered it. There was a big borage plant. She ignored it. There was false indigo. There was wormwood. There was no time to collect them now.

She rounded a corner, running hard.

She had to tell mother, had to – *oomph!*

She sprawled on the ground.

She'd run straight into someone – it was a boy, no, a young man. "I'm sorry," she blurted.

"Are you all right?" he asked, helping her up.

"Y – Yes, I'm fine."

He was a little taller than she was, probably sixteen, two years older than her. And he was – she caught her breath – so good looking. Wow.

Her face burned. She should be in a dress, should have her hair pulled back with a ribbon. She blinked at him, unable to look away.

He smiled, a great smile. "You shouldn't run through the woods if you don't know your way."

"Yes. I'll remember that."

He turned to leave.

No, don't go. "I'm Ruby." She kept staring at him and stuck out her hand.

"Tadashi. Pleased to meet you."

Tadashi? "Oh, you're Chinese." That sounded stupid. "But, no, you don't look Chinese." That sounded even stupider.

But it was true. He didn't look Chinese. Not like Meifeng, anyway. The old woman's eyes were smaller, her face rounder than this young man's. Tadashi was Asian with that pale skin, obviously, but his face was longer, his chin pointed. And his eyes, he had noticeable eye lids. Thin, yes, but still noticeable.

"You're all right?" he said. He cocked his head. "You sure?"

"Yes." Gosh, he sure was cute.

"Well, then." He nodded goodbye and turned.

No, don't go. I just want to get to know you. But there was nothing she could do to make him stay. She watched him until he was swallowed up by the forest.

"Ruby? Ruby?"

Someone was calling her. It was Matilda.

Her nanny came up the trail. "Ruby, who was that? Where have you been?"

"Oh, Matilda, the most amazing thing happened," she blurted. "I met Meifeng. She took me to her home. It's deep in the woods, farther up this path. There's a whole camp full of Chinese workers."

Matilda gasped. "And you were there? By yourself?" She fanned her face. "Lordie, your mother will dismiss me for sure."

That was silly. Besides, she wouldn't let Mother do that. "Did you know the old Chinese woman is a doctor? The one who sits at the edge of the community garden? She's a full-fledged doctor." She thought back to their talk, how the woman had a cabin full of medical books. "She knows all these things about plants and herbs and we had the most amazing discussion." She was babbling, but she couldn't help it. It was so exciting to finally meet someone who shared her interest in how to use things found in nature.

And then there was Tadashi.

A thrill passed through her.

Tadashi.

It had been exciting to meet him, too. Very exciting.

The killer entered his house. He'd been a bad boy. He'd been to the whorehouse.

His inner voice spoke up.

Shame on you, bedding that filthy whore. You're no better than a dog, going after a bitch in heat.

He stared at his feet.

But how could he resist? She was so pretty, so soft and she knew special things, things that made his body feel alive.

You're weak. You're pitiful. Giving in to the enticement of that whore.

He'd done her twice, paid extra. It had been worth every cent.

Was it worth your soul? She was laughing at you the whole time, laughing at your weakness. Women like her are the devil. They only want to snare men, weak men, gullible men. Men like you.

He clutched his groin, remembered her touch, her soft skin. He'd let her do those things to him, things that were special.

You fell for it, an easy target. Targets need to put aside their urges. They need to stand up to the devil.

His little voice was right. He'd been bad. Next time, he'd stand up to the devil.

Ruby pulled the covers up to her chin. She thought of the young man she'd run into and her heart fluttered.

Tadashi. Who was he? Where had he come from? Why hadn't she ever seen him before? Did he live in the Chinese encampment?

Running into him the way she had – was it fate?

He was handsome, but in his own way.

Those eyes. Those lips.

She wanted to kiss him. There, she'd admitted it. She wanted to kiss him.

Her face flushed at the thought.

She groaned. She'd probably looked a mess. There had been mud on her boots, on her pants. And she couldn't say how long it had been since her favorite shirt had seen a hot iron. Heck, there had probably been sticks in her hair from when it had caught on the branches.

Of all the times to meet someone who appealed to her, and she'd looked like something that lived in a cave.

Had he seen beyond that, seen that she was all-right looking?

She threw back the covers, jumped out of bed and hurried over to her mirror, turning her face this way and that.

Ordinary.

She was ordinary-looking.

Brown hair to her shoulders. Other girls had long, luxurious hair.

She stepped back. Her body was small, thank goodness. If she had to wear a pinched-waist outfit, she could pull it off. But ...did she really want to?

Nope.

Maybe Tadashi didn't demand a perfect twenty-two inch waist. Maybe he would accept her for who she was. He'd better. If he didn't, then it was his loss.

She returned to bed. When would she see him again? She couldn't wait.

Ruby jumped up from the breakfast table and wrung her hands. "Mother, you *have* to go. She's waiting for you."

Mother continued sipping her coffee. "I am *not* going to meet with that woman. I'm not at her beck and call."

"She didn't order you to go, she just wants to talk with you."

Mother gave a huff. "Talk? She probably doesn't even speak proper English. And she makes herself out to be better than trained doctors."

"You're making excuses. Why won't you go?"

"She talks to those, you know, *girls.*" She shuddered.

Girls? Maybe she meant the young women with the fluttering sleeves. There was something going on about those girls, but there wasn't time to delve into it now. "Meifeng only wants to talk to you."

"Oh, really? About what? The weather?"

"About me, Mother. She gave me some kind of examination." At least it seemed like an examination.

"Examination? Oh, really? Without my permission?" Mother set her arms akimbo. "Let her send a bill for this so-called examination and then she can wait for payment. Wait forever." She buttered her toast. "I want you to stay home today. Your tutor says you're behind in your studies and we can't have that, now can we?"

"I, uh, left something at the community garden."

"Well, go retrieve it then, but after that, you're to be hitting the books, young lady. Do I make myself clear?"

"Yes, Mother."

Ruby trudged to the community garden.

There was nothing to retrieve. She'd lied.

She had to break the news to Meifeng. Not only was Mother not coming, she would never come to speak with her. Great, just great. It was up to her to relay the bad news.

Meifend was at her usual spot, discreetly out of the way, but visible should anyone be looking for her. There was a man there talking with her, a tall man.

Better wait off to the side, out of sight. If he was there to see the doctor, she wasn't about to intrude on his troubles.

The Chinese doctor spoke in a hesitant way, chopping her words.

He was given a pouch and instructions. Money changed hands.

He nodded and stepped back.

Finally, Meifeng was free.

The man turned to go and spotted a young woman approaching.

There was fluttering material around her arms. It was one of the girls from the other day, the one with blonde hair. "Hi, Wendell," she sang out. "Haven't seen you around lately."

His face turned bright red at her teasing manner.

"You know we all miss you, sugar. Don't be a stranger."

He nodded and hastened away, head down.

That was weird. Why didn't he want to talk to the pretty girl? They obviously knew one another. Who was she, anyway?

The girl spotted her and brightened. "Oh, were you here first?" She gestured and the fabric followed her movement. "Go ahead. I can wait."

"Thank you. I won't be but a moment." Ruby stepped up to Meifeng. This was so awkward, apologizing for someone else. "Um, I'm sorry but Mother isn't coming."

"I'm not surprised." She patted the grass beside her. "Have a seat." She handed her some pouches. "See if you can identify these." Meifeng turned to the pretty girl. "Anastasia, come closer. We're all women here."

Her name was Anastasia? Like, from the Bible?

Meifeng frowned. "Didn't I give you enough herbs yesterday? Or is there something else?" Her English was suddenly perfect.

Now she understood. Meifeng spoke in Chinese Pidgin English, acting as though she wasn't educated, with some people but showed her true self to those she'd dealt with before. Would she have used Pidgin English if Mother had come today?

Anastasia stepped up.

"Meet Ruby. Ruby likes herbs and being in the forest."

"Well, hi there, sugar," Anastasia said.

There it was again – Sugar. Maybe she called everyone that. Maybe she forgot names easily. There was probably an herb for that. "Nice to meet you." She held out her hand.

Anastasia's hand was soft, but not as soft as Meifeng's were.

A monkey suddenly leaped up on Anastasia's shoulder and began playing with her blonde hair. Where had he come from?

"Now, Buster, stop that."

She'd never seen a real live monkey before. "He's your pet?"

"From a customer who asked me to look after the little guy then never came back for him." Anastasia made a rolling-eyes face. "I should have known better."

It was a white faced capuchin. Grace had had her study monkeys and do a man-monkey comparison. "He's cute."

"How can I help you, Anastasia?" the Chinese doctor asked.

"One of the girls is having cold sores. Occupational hazard, but not good for business, if you know what I mean."

"Lips or ...?"

"Or." Anastasia gestured in a resigned manner. "Anything you can do?"

Ruby bent over the sacks she'd been given and inhaled as she lifted each one to her nose. It was like being in the forest. The burlap odor was heavy and got in the way, yeah, but she knew these herbs. Easy stuff.

Meifeng turned to her. "Ruby, any ideas?"

Me? She'd only been half listening. "I don't understand. A cold, you said? With sneezing and coughing and sores, too?"

"Never mind." Meifeng rooted through her basket and pulled out a bag. "Here, Anastasia. Have her drink a tea of this four times a day. Make it as strong as possible. I'm afraid she'll be unable to work for at least a month."

Anastasia nodded and paid for the herbs. "Thank you. Nice to have met you, Ruby." She got up and left, fabric floating behind her.

So, she *did* remember people's names. "Who is she?"

"She and the others came to town with the railroad."

Which meant, what? That Daddy had hired her? She'd never heard of a woman building a railroad. But it wasn't like she'd ever been to the construction site. "Mother's not coming."

"I'm not surprised. Look at these herbs," Meifeng said. "Can you identify them?"

She peeked in the pouches. "St. John's Wort, hyssop, sage and safflower."

"And what do each of them do?"

"Our cook uses St. John's Wort to make our bread's texture better. But I would give it to someone for arthritis."

"It's one of the uses, yes."

There were others? It was the only one her guides had shown her.

"It has an effect on the nerves and on infections. It's one of the herbs I just gave Anastasia for her friend." She reached over and heft one of the bags. "This one?"

Ruby sniffed it. "That's the hyssop."

"You didn't look inside?"

She shook her head. "I could smell it."

"Did you smell anything else?"

Like the burlap? "No. I just assumed that was all that was in there."

"Never assume. It's a mixture, hyssop and lemon balm."

Wait. She knew of this one. "Hyssop helps someone with blocked lungs or a cold."

"Yes," Meifeng said. "It's an expectorant. It knocks out germs. Science has yet to catch up to this plant. It's another herb that was in the bag I gave Anastasia. So was lemon balm."

"You had these pre-made? You *knew* what she'd need?"

"An educated guess. Various ailments are found in any town. I made concoctions ahead of time, is all."

Be prepared, it was a smart move. "Mother's not coming."

"You already said that. I'm not surprised."

"I'll keep trying."

"Fine."

There was a lull. Here was her moment. "Who is Tadashi?" she blurted.

"Tadashi Moro?" Meifeng lifted one eyebrow. "He's my son."

Who looked nothing like her? Maybe he was her nephew, her brother's child? Or her sister's child? That didn't make sense, either. Meifeng was quite old. Her brother or sister would have to be at least thirty years younger to have a nephew that age.

"He doesn't look Chinese."

"He's not."

A group of women were entering the garden. There was Mrs. Wilson, Miss Porter and her Aunt Martha. They were coming closer. They wanted to speak to Meifeng, obviously, and probably one on one.

Darn, she wanted to ask more about Tadashi. "I'd better get going."

"Can you come tomorrow?" Meifeng asked. "That is, if you want to. I'd like you to help me decide which concoctions people need."

Really? Her? Ruby brightened. Nothing could keep her away.

Ruby hurried to the garden. Was Meifeng here?
There she was.

She raced up to her. "I'm sorry. I'm sorry. Mother forced me to study my books. She wouldn't let me leave the house. I wanted to be here last week, I really did."

"It's all right. I figured something like that was going on." She patted the ground beside where she sat. "I want you to join me, that is, if you can."

She could spare an hour. "I want to help."

"Good." Meifeng gestured. "Look there."

Ruby followed her pointed finger. Women and children were entering the garden. She recognized them. They were the ones who lined up for free food every week. They must need low-cost medical help too.

"Our patients are coming."

She'd said "*our* patients." Her heart beat a little faster.

The first woman came up to them, hoisting a crying baby of about three months on her hip. "She cries all night. I've tried everything."

Meifeng took the child, placed her across her lap and inspected her, pressing on the baby's stomach with her palm, feeling her spine down to her pelvic area. The Chinese doctor picked up the child and probed the baby's mouth. She leaned closer and whispered, "You see, Ruby?" She indicated a red area on the baby's gums.

It seemed like she should whisper, too. "It's infected."

"No, merely a tooth coming in." She straightened up, lesson over. Meifeng gave the baby back and reached into her basket of pouches. "I give tea. Need hankie."

Ruby shot a look at the old Chinese woman. I give tea? Her mentor's grammar was better than that. How could she relay vital medical information if she spoke Pidgin to people?

The mother dug in her pocket.

Meifeng opened a pouch and sprinkled a large handful into the mother's waiting handkerchief. "Take this much." She demonstrated. "Boil like tea, not drink. No, no."

"It's not meant to drink," the mother said. "I understand."

"Make strong. Take cloth. Soak. Let baby bite." She pantomimed dabbing cloth in her cupped hand, brought it to her mouth and made a gnawing motion.

"Yes, I see," the young mother said, pulling out some cash and handing it over. "Thank you." She left.

Another woman stepped forward. Her dress was out of style and threadbare in places. She had a child, a boy, of about four. "He wets the bed." She made an exasperated face. "Every night. My other three never did that."

Meifeng nodded. "I fix. Hankie?" She reached into her basket, opened pouch after pouch – yarrow root, sumac berries – and measured out the amount by eye into the woman's outstretched handkerchief.

Yes, those would help clear the kidneys, but there was another thing that the mother could try. It was on the tip of her tongue. If only she could think of it.

Meifeng began gathering the points of the hankie to close it up.

No, not yet. "Add White Pond Lily," she blurted.

Meifeng stopped. She shot a look at her, nodded slowly, pulled out another pouch and added a pinch of dried pond lily.

The transaction was completed and the mother left.

Meifeng glanced over. She kept her voice low. "No more yelling out herbs. Whisper to me if you have something to add."

"Yes, ma'am."

A skinny girl of about fifteen, her age, came up. They'd be in the same class if she attended school. The girl wore tattered clothes that hung off her frame. "My little brother has the measles."

Meifeng nodded that she understood. She reached behind her and retrieved a small vial. She pulled out the stopper and held it out to Ruby.

She wanted her to smell it, obviously. Ruby leaned in and inhaled. The odor was distinct. "Catnip oil."

Meifeng recapped the vial and, using pantomime, showed the girl how to apply it. She waggled a finger. "No drink."

The girl nodded. She shifted her weight from foot to foot. "All right. I, uh, don't have much money."

"You good people. Take. No charge."

Ruby whispered, "Why did you warn her not to drink it? It's not like it's toxic."

The Chinese woman waggled her hand. "I didn't want it wasted."

They saw person after person, so many she lost count. All these people had heard of Meifeng, who listened to their symptoms, handing them what they needed to get better. But, she was acting as an outsider, never letting on that she spoke perfect English. Whatever the reason was, she didn't want people to know she was well-educated.

The sun was near noon. So soon? But she'd only just begun to get the hang of all this. And there was still a line. "I have to get going or Mother will have my hide."

"School is important."

She kept her voice low. "Yeah, well, I'd rather have this as my schooling."

Meifeng hesitated. "Look at me."

"Why? What is it?"

"Do your eyes always do that?" she whispered.

"Do what?"

"Shimmy side to side like that."

"I don't notice anything."

"And you do a squinting kind of thing right afterward."

If she did, she really hadn't taken note of it. "I do? What does it mean?" Was something wrong with her?

Meifeng patted her hand. "I really need to speak with your mother and father."

"Father is gone a lot on business." Like, he was away more than he was home. It was Mother who ran the household, who made all the decisions for the family. And she'd refused, in no uncertain terms, to meet with the Chinese woman, someone who thought she was better than trained doctors.

Felicia looked up from her writing desk. What was that?

There was a commotion at the front door. The maid was raising her voice.

She'd better check this out right now. She gathered her skirts and hurried to the front of the house. "Amelda, what on earth is going on?"

There was a small woman trying to get around the maid.

How uncouth. Didn't this woman have any manners? You didn't just barge into someone's house. "Who are you? What do you want?" she demanded.

"I am Meifeng. I need to speak to you."

Oh, really? It was doubtful she had anything of value to say. She was not exactly the type of person to whom a person of high standing would normally pay any attention. "There is nothing you have to say that could possibly interest me. Go away." She turned and walked off. Honestly, some people had no idea of their place in the world.

"It's about Ruby. I know what's wrong with her."

What? Her heart rate surged. How could she know? How could she know that Ruby's finger had been whacked off? There was barely a scar. Everyone accepted that it was from a burn. Yet this small, strange woman certainly sounded sure of herself. Better find out just what, exactly she *did* know. She composed herself and turned back around. "There's nothing wrong with her."

"Oh, but there is."

"I see nothing wrong with her."

"You can't see it. It's up here," Meifeng gestured, "in her head."

Her head, meaning her brain? Well, yes, Ruby had always been sort of odd. She'd been checked out by the best physicians but the San Francisco doctors had found nothing wrong. But she, herself, had witnessed Ruby do things, small things, exasperating things, and been perplexed by what had caused them. Lord knows, the girl had certainly embarrassed the family a number of times. One never knew what was going to come out of her mouth.

Maybe this woman could help.

"All right." She let her in. "I'll give you five minutes."

CHAPTER FOUR

Felicia led Meifeng to the next room. She had no idea what this woman knew but it was to her advantage to find out, and the sooner, the better. She closed the doors and gestured to the parlor sofa. "Please be seated."

Meifeng perched on the edge of the cushion. Perhaps she'd never seen a settee before. Wouldn't surprise her. "Cut to the chase. What's wrong with my daughter?"

"I want to mentor her."

Preposterous. "You? You're no one. I hire the best tutors."

"From whom she learns nothing."

Wait a minute. This woman was speaking in proper English. Something strange was going on here. "What did you say?"

"She's been helping me hand out medicine."

"Those dried plants that you claim have magic powers? Ha! That's not medicine."

"It's not magic. It's medicine from the earth, used for thousands of years. They're all the body needs."

"Fine, fine. You pass out withered plants. People eat them and voila, they feel better. And now you've involved my daughter and she feels important, special. How nice."

"She knows of what she speaks."

There she went again, using English in its proper form. Who was this woman? "It's a passing interest, something she's never encountered before. What do you expect from a child?"

"She's not a child. She's growing into who she's meant to be."

"And what's that, pray tell?"

"A healer."

Ruby? She's a moron. "So, you're saying that she has a natural ability, an affinity for knowing what's wrong with people and how to help them get better?"

"She needs to explore that and I can help her."

And how much will this cost? Let her guess – a fortune. She lifted a single eyebrow. "As her, shall I say, 'questionable' mentor."

"I'm a doctor, Mrs. Fontinello, and a surgeon. I've amputated arms, set broken bones. I've removed gallbladders, appendices and delivered babies who were breech by Caesarean section."

She'd done all that? "You can teach Ruby those things?"

"Of course. She has a natural affinity for healing."

And for little else. "If she's a healer, then why does she have trouble with her studies? Why does she say the most absurd things?"

Meifeng sighed. "That's where the tricky part comes in. Have you noticed that Ruby has nystagmus, an irregular eye movement? It's indicative of a brain disruption."

"Brain 'disruption?' Are you making this up?"

"Her eye movement is likely due to something that caused one area of the brain to not develop fully. It's likely from an event that occurred when she was young, way in her past. Was she dropped on her head as a baby?"

"No."

"Had a severe illness as a toddler?"

She thought back. "No, nothing."

"Something happened, Mrs. Fontinello. Some kind of big event, especially traumatic on the body, especially debilitating for a small child."

A sniffle here and there, but no major illness, not even something that caused a fever. "There's nothing."

"Yes, there is. Think harder. Did Ruby fall into a cold stream and catch a chill? Did she get hit in the head by a ball? Suffer something like, like, –" she cast about for an example, "– like a cut that couldn't be staunched?"

She flinched. *Like all that blood she lost when I hacked off her extra finger?* That had to be it. That had to be this major event the Chinese woman insisted Ruby had suffered. It was just cutting off a finger. The damned thing didn't belong there. It was an aberration, marking the family as inept, cursed even. No, she'd be damned if she let someone, a stranger no less, tell her that she'd been in the wrong. She crossed her arms. "I don't know what you're talking about."

"It'll come to you. The thing is, that part of her brain has to be regrown."

What the heck was she talking about? "I've never heard of such a thing. What does that entail?"

"A combination of introducing herbal properties in a specific order and then challenging the brain with tests that will activate that portion of her brain."

"You know how to do that?"

"I have colleagues who have worked with brain-damaged people in the past. They've authored medical books on the topic. I can write to them and consult with them if I need advice."

"But ...you can help her?" *So people won't look at Ruby and comment on what a strange child she is? So the Fontinello name won't have that stigma to it any longer?*

"I'm not sure, Mrs. Fontinello. But I want to try." She leaned forward in her seat, eyes imploring her. "Ruby deserves someone to step in and help her. Don't you agree?"

Any mother would. "I always knew there was something 'off' about her."

"I warn you. It will take a while to fix what's been done. It's a slow process."

This brain deficiency, maybe it was what caused Ruby to act differently. Maybe it was what caused her to know things like how to address her hurting gums. Lord knew, she'd used the sap a number of times through the years and it had always worked.

"You need to understand. This is a day-to-day approach to healing her. She'll have to live with me."

"What? No, no, no. No child of mine is going to live in a tent. My husband told me where you people camp. It's primitive."

"My home is the logger's cabin that was already on the mountain. Rest assured, Ruby will have a roof over her head."

"And what about all those –" she shuddered "– Chinese workers who live there? They're men. Men have desires. What if they see a young thing like her and get, you know, ideas?"

"We are a civilized people with a high regard for tradition and honor. Besides, the workers put in long hours at the railroad. Then they have to trudge up to their camp. All they have on their minds is sleep, I assure you."

Well, all right, if that's how it truly was. Still, this proposition had come to her so quickly. What to make of it? Ruby? Brain deprivation? But yet, it could be reversed with treatment. "I'll have to think about it."

"Don't think too long. Ruby is already, what, fifteen? This is a slow process and a long one, years-long, Mrs. Fontinello. Think back and see if you can remember what it was that may have caused this." She stood up.

Felicia showed her to the door. "How do I contact you?"

"The community garden. I'm there three mornings a week. If Ruby lives with me, she'll come along when I tend people there, so it's not like you won't see her."

Just a few mornings a week? That was all the time she'd get with her daughter? "One more question. Why do I hear you speak Pidgin English to people at the garden, but here, today, you expressed yourself perfectly, as though English is your first language?" She narrowed her eyes. "Are you trying to deceive people?"

"Some people are more apt to be their true selves if they think you don't understand everything they say. I've learned it's more advantageous to let people think I'm a mere foreigner who is beneath them."

Felicia closed the door behind her. Ruby? Fixed by a Chinese doctor? If it could reverse what she'd done on her birthing day, how could she *not* agree to this idea?

Ruby turned in her sleep. Her guides were here. She couldn't wait to find out what they'd show her this time. They were outside a house – whitewashed with a red roof. She was beckoned inside by some unseen force.

The house was small, neat, with a parlor done in garnet colored sofas and heavy curtains. Not a lot of light could come in with those heavy drapes.

Look, there was Anastasia. She was clutching her stomach. Not good.

"If you'd touched her belly instead of just shaking her hand hello, you would have caught this," her guides told her.

Anastasia plopped down on the sofa and made a face like she was in pain.

"Tell me how to help her," she said.

Instead, her hand was lead to the young woman's stomach area.

Yes, she could feel it now. There was distress in the intestines. "This happens to her a lot," Ruby murmured. "She can't process food all the way and it causes her discomfort. Hold on." She felt farther down. "Oh, I get it. It's not what she eats, it's stress that's causing this." What the pretty girl would be so stressed about, she had no idea.

She drew her hand back. The words "magnolia bark" appeared in front of her. She could see the tree, its bark marked with Braille-like bumps. The pictures changed. Pieces of the bark were being crushed in a tiny bowl with a pestle, like their cook used with cloves of garlic.

She opened her eyes.

It was morning. She tossed the blankets aside and jumped out of bed.

She ran down the stairs. The grandfather clock read twenty after seven. If she hurried, she could make it to the station before the eight o'clock train for San Francisco took off.

She grabbed her coat, bolted outside and hightailed it down the street. The tracks were way on the other side of town. Great, just great. She'd have to hurry.

Ruby ran, settling into a good pace.

The town was just waking up. Children were going off to school. The milkman was delivering jars from his horse-drawn wagon.

She got farther across town. Now, instead of maids hanging up wet wash, mothers did that task, snapping the fabric tight to avoid as many wrinkles as possible.

She kept running, dodged a stray dog that trotted out of nowhere and jumped a water puddle.

Hopefully she'd put enough money in her envelope to get what she needed.

White steam was rising beyond those buildings. Good. If it was black smoke, then she would have been too late. Black smoke meant the iron horse was already moving.

She was almost there. She picked up the pace and leaped up onto the train platform. The train stretched before her, fifteen or twenty cars, with the engine down farther.

She trotted along on the planks, dodging luggage left on the platform and men milling about in duster jackets.

She approached the engine. "Max," she yelled. "Max."

A head popped out of the window. "Ruby? That you? Hey, that cough? It's all gone."

A tincture of white horehound, worked every time. "I need an herb from San Francisco."

"It's a turnaround trip, you know that."

"Send a boy to get it while you prep the train for the journey back."

"All right, all right."

She jumped up on the side of the huge engine and passed up her envelope. "The money's inside. Give some to the boy you send as a tip."

"You know I can't read. What is it you want?"

"Magnolia bark." She'd written it down but had no idea if the shop that supplied her used people who knew written English.

"Magnolia? Like that song?" He sang a few bars, a ditty that had been popular during the War Between the States.

Close enough. No one had ever raved about Max's singing. But if it helped him remember what she needed, she wasn't about to stop him. "Yes, like the song."

She hopped off the side of the engine. "See you tonight when you return."

Now, to check on her own herb patch at the community garden. She hoped no one had thought they were weeds and dug them up. It wouldn't be the first time. People just didn't understand.

She hurried back down the platform, jumped off and stopped.

Tadashi was here.

A thrill coursed through her.

What was he doing here? She couldn't let him see her. Not dressed like this, in dungarees. Had to hide.

He was talking with some Chinese workers, too far away to hear anything. But she could peek out and watch him, watch how he moved, how he gestured. It was obvious he was in charge, directing things, even though he was about her age and the others were much older than him.

Who was he, anyway? She couldn't wait to find out.

Felicia stopped the tutor. "Oh, thank goodness, you're here, Grace. Come to the parlor, I want to talk to you."

The young woman, a teacher from a good Boston family, removed her bonnet. "Is everything all right?"

"How is Ruby doing with her studies?"

"She's quite bright and –"

"Don't patronize me. You and I both know the girl does as little as possible, just to get by. What I want to know is if you've noticed any patterns, hesitations, little clues that she's, well, not entirely understanding what you're teaching her." Is she touched, like Meifeng had said?

Grace paused and wrung her hands. "Mrs. Fontinello, I've tried every way I could think of to try and get her to grasp my lessons. We have to go over and over things. No matter how I present the information, Ruby seems to barely catch on. Well, unless it's about plants and nature."

"I see."

She gestured helplessly. "Other girls her age are two or three semesters beyond her. I don't know what I'm doing wrong." She looked down at her feet. Her voice came out softer. "If you want to fire me, I understand."

The girl had tried, no doubt. But perhaps Ruby needed a different approach. "No, that's not what I was going to say. Keep trying." She dismissed Grace and paced across the parlor rug.

If only Phillip were here, they could discuss this Chinese woman's proposal. But no, he was gone, pulling together more railroad deals. All he cared about was this network of rail branches. Meanwhile, she was here to deal with things that truly mattered.

She had to look at this logically, had to do what was best of the family.

Ruby couldn't very well ignore her studies to run off with this Meifeng person to hand out plants. Her daughter deserved a proper education or she'd wind up like one of those girls across town in that red-roofed house.

She shuddered. Dreadful, the things those girls must be forced to do. How degrading.

Stop thinking about those women. They have nothing to do with Ruby and her fate.

"Damn it, Phillip, why do you leave all the hard decisions up to me?"

OK, if the girl was a natural at using plants to heal people and she liked it, no matter how people snickered about it behind their backs, then maybe this was a way for her daughter to feel useful, to have a purpose. And if Meifeng could restart her brain, then all the better.

She stared at her reflection in the mirror.

Who knew losing all that blood as a newborn would have caused such a thing?

"And you're to blame," she said to her image.

She left the room, mind made up.

Ruby watched the train approach the station. Finally, it was here. She waited for the engineer to shut down the boiler and finish up.

Max jumped off the train, lunch box in hand. "Sorry, Ruby, there was a near-washout at the gorge and we were delayed."

He stuck his hand in his pocket and rooted around. He pulled out a small bundle.

She checked it. Yes, it was magnolia bark. "Thanks, Max. If there's anything I can do to –"

"Sarah's having a tough time with this latest pregnancy."

They only had, what, six kids already? "I'll go home with you and see what's up."

They headed a few streets over. Max made good money as a train engineer, but each time another baby came, their expenses grew.

Sarah was finishing up some canning when they walked in. Her belly was bulging out. It looked like the baby would come within the month. "Ruby? Is that you? Can I offer you a bite to eat?"

"Max said you're having a tough time. What, exactly, is wrong?"

Sarah sighed. "My legs are swelling up so much my skin feels like it's about to burst, it's so tight."

"Sit down, let me see."

Her legs were swollen, all right. Her ankles were like tree stumps. This was bad. "It's water retention. Start some water boiling. Wait here."

She stepped outside. Stinging nettle could be used, but was better if dried first. Horsetail, rosemary, hawthorn –any of those would do, but they didn't grow just anywhere. Dandelions, now those were everywhere. She peered out the window.

There was a patch of them over there. She hurried outside and scooped up the plants, breaking the stems near the ground. When she had a full handful, she returned to Sarah.

"I already had a pot of water warming," the mother-to-be said.

"Let's make a tea of this," Ruby said, adding the plants. "Really get it boiling so it draws out the elements." It was not just a diuretic, it was a way to sooth the entire body. "You can add the flowers to your food, too."

"Like, to my cereal?"

That stuff Mother was so keen on eating? From a factory? Was she serious? "I was thinking more of eating them with your vegetables or with fruit."

"Well, I suppose I could do that, too," Sarah said. "But that cereal, have you tried it? My children can't get enough of it. They eat it night and day. It's so good to see them have healthy appetites."

And as a result, she'd likely be back one day to deal with their health issues, too. Sigh. Ruby gave Sarah instructions on how much of the tea to drink. Hopefully, she'd caught it in time. If not, there could be a bad end to this, so bad that the children would no longer have a mother. But how could she tell her that? "If you're not better in a couple days, let me know."

Max came over and put his hand on his wife's shoulder. "Thanks, Ruby. I should pay you for your advice."

"Don't be silly. I'm happy to help. Besides, you got me my tree bark, didn't you? So," she said, gesturing, "we're even." She bade them goodbye.

Now, to go see Anastasia. Her guides had shown her a house with a red roof. A shoemaker's shop was still open. She popped her head in. "Excuse me."

The man looked up from pounding nails into the sole of a boot. "Yeah? What do you need, boy?"

She froze. He thought she was a boy. Had Tadashi thought the same? "I'm trying to find a house with a red roof. I think it's around this area." At least, this was the direction Anastasia had headed in when she left the garden.

"The youngest madam this side of the Mississippi? Five blocks that way," he said, jabbing a thumb over his shoulder.

So, to the south. It was the direction of the train station. Odd that she hadn't seen it.

The light was fading. She'd better hurry.

One block, two, three. There it was, up ahead.

Just as she approached, the door opened. A young woman had a lantern, hung it on a nail and lit it.

"Hi there, is Anastasia here?"

The young woman looked over. "Sure, honey, she's inside." She hesitated. "You're a tad young for this, aren't you?"

Young for what? "I met Anastasia at the garden."

The young woman gasped. "You're not a boy. You're that girl who hangs out with Meifeng."

There it was again, being mistaken for a boy. But then, the sunlight was nearly gone.

"I'm Esther, come on in." The young woman waved her inside and shut the door behind her. She went to the bottom of the stairs and called out, "Anastasia, someone is here to see you."

There were footsteps overhead trotting their way, then Anastasia appeared on the stairs. "Oh, Ruby, it's you. I thought Esther meant a cust –, well, never mind. What can I do for you, sugar?"

"I brought you something." She held out the pouch of magnolia bark and told her how to prepare it. "It'll help you with your bowel issues."

"OK, I'll try it right now and -." Anastasia stopped. "Wait, I didn't tell Meifeng anything about gut issues."

Ruby spotted a clock. That late? She had to get going.

She bade the girls goodbye.

She hurried home. Mother would tan her hide for sure for staying out so late.

If only the train hadn't been delayed. If only Sarah's edema hadn't taken so much time, but what was she supposed to do? Ignore the mother-to-be's near-critical condition? No, she couldn't do that. She broke into a run.

Her home was up the hill.

She was in sooo much trouble, she just knew it.

She turned the corner.

There was the house. The lights were on in the front parlor. That was strange. Mother only used it to receive guests. Who could possibly be there? And at this hour?

She ran up the steps, tore across the grand porch and bum-rushed the front door. "Sorry, Mother," she called out, panting. "Time got away from me and I ran all the way here." She rushed over to the open parlor doors and stopped.

What was Meifeng doing here?

Felicia poured Meifeng more tea. She looked up just as Ruby burst through the door and clomped into the foyer. Couldn't the girl try to act more civil, a tad more subdued as befitting her gender? But no, Ruby had never fit the mold. "Do come in, dear, we're just discussing your future."

Ruby looked from one to the other, still rooted to her spot near the doorway.

She tried again. "You're winded. Take a moment to catch your breath and we'll talk."

Ruby recovered her senses and stepped into the room, leaving a trail of dirt behind her. She nodded hello to the Chinese doctor before plopping into a seat in her dusty pants. "What is this?"

Felicia winced. Her new silk cushions. "Tea?"

"No, thank you, Mother. What's going on?"

"Meifeng has made a proposition about which I've given considerable thought. She's been impressed with your fledgling knowledge of plants and how they can help those who can't afford modern medicine. She seems to think this is an innate talent of yours, that you're predisposed to learning more." *Lord knows the child shows no such propensity when it comes to traditional schooling.*

Ruby shot a look at the Chinese woman and scooted forward in her seat. "Yes?"

"She's suggested that she become your tutor, that you go with her to learn more and see if, perhaps, this is something you'd like to pursue. It would entail immersing yourself in her day-to-day life, working beside her and preparing medicinal remedies as per her instructions. You would also go with her to see patients who decline Western medicine's obvious advantages and choose to use Asian methods instead." She tried to keep her bias out of the conversation, but it was difficult. After all, she was subjecting Ruby to the influence of this woman who claimed Eastern medicine was far advanced and that Western medicine was only now catching up. Sure, it was.

Meifeng shifted in her chair. "Ruby, it would involve you coming to live with me at the cabin full-time."

Ruby's eyes lit up. "Seriously?"

Wait one moment, here. "Not entirely," Felicia interjected, stopping her.

The pair looked at her, waiting.

"I will only agree to this if you are here three afternoons a week to continue taking instruction from Grace. Your schooling is important and I won't have a daughter of mine walking this earth with only a rudimentary understanding of art, history and literature. The Fontinello name means something in this world, after all." She jutted her chin and huffed. "And when you're here, you'll wear a dress, for goodness sake."

Ruby launched herself off the chair, rushed over and threw her arms around her neck. "Thank you. Thank you. Thank you."

Goodness, child, don't choke me. She extracted herself. "I expect you to abide by the rules."

"Three afternoons a week, yes, Mother. Live with Meifeng learning medicine the rest of the time, yes, Mother." She danced back to her seat.

Did she really grasp what this meant? That they'd be apart much of the time? "I'm only agreeing to this because Meifeng has discovered a condition that you have."

Ruby lost her grin. "What condition?"

Oh dear, she'd frightened her. "Now, it can be improved, the good doctor feels, but only with constant supervision and intervention. You'll be under her care. This condition came about because of ...scarlet fever, which you had as a toddler." Sure it was. "I'd totally forgotten about it, but she said it likely affected your brain development. To get you functioning at your optimum level, you must be under her care night and day."

Ruby looked over at Meifeng. "Is this true?"

"There are neurological signs I've noticed," she said, nodding.

"Your father knows little of this." More like, the bare minimum. But how could she admit that her attack on their newborn had come to this? At least she'd sent him a telegram that Ruby would be seeing a doctor for a "hiccup" in her development. "He's busy still in Chicago, so the decision was left up to me. He's not one to dwell on matters such as this anyway." Last year, the man had suggested sending Ruby to school in Connecticut. Sure, like Ruby would fit in at a finishing school. Obviously Phillip had no clue how Ruby was received in polite society, how people whispered about the child whenever she made some faux pas and snickered at her behind her back. "So, I've had a bag packed for you." She pointed to a carpet bag in the corner. "You're going with Meifeng. Tonight."

CHAPTER FIVE

Ruby hurried after Meifeng as they hiked up the mountain. She sure was spry for an old woman. But then, she wasn't carrying a twenty-pound satchel of shoes and clothes and toiletries.

She hoped Amelda had remembered to pack her illustrated book of plant identifications and botanist Georg Forster's book on exotic flora. He'd accompanied James Cook to discover far off lands, reporting amazing species.

The satchel had looked so out of place in the front parlor. She hadn't even noticed it when she'd come home.

She went back to that moment when Mother had said she was to accompany Meifeng, felt the sting of Mother's words: "So, I've had a bag packed for you. You're going with Meifeng."

"Now?" she'd asked.

"What? This isn't what you want?"

"No, no, Mother, I do. I really do. It's just so ... sudden." And it had been. It had come out of the blue.

"Be that as it may," Mother had said, "this is your opportunity. Your *only* opportunity, you understand? It won't come again." Mother had drawn her shoulders back. "Make a decision."

Now, here she was, trekking up the mountain with just the full moon to guide her, hoping she didn't step on a piece of branch and sprain an ankle. That would be bad, out here in the middle of nowhere. But Meifeng seemed to have no such thoughts, stepping along without hesitation.

There was a heavy noise. It was from behind her.

Someone was coming up behind them.

Who would be out in the woods at this hour?

For what purpose?

What if it was a man?

Her heart pounded harder.

What if he was carrying a gun?

What if he wanted to do someone harm?

Maybe they should hide.

"Meifeng," she hissed. "Someone's coming."

The Chinese woman barely turned. "Men."

Men? More than one?

The sound came closer. She risked a look behind her.

Men. Many men.

They wore tunics and cropped pants like Meifeng wore. They must be men from the encampment. They sure hiked fast. They came up behind her. She stepped aside and let them pass, nodding at the men as they swooped past her.

The last one came upon her and stopped.

His hand shot out toward her.

He grabbed the satchel from her arms.

"What are you doing?" she gasped. "That's mine."

He smiled just as a cloud finished passing in front of the moon.

Oh, it was Tadashi.

"I'll carry it for you," he said and started off with her twenty-pound bag.

He was here. He was helping her. What a nice thing to do.

And she'd practically accused him of robbery. *Good going, Ruby. You sure know how to make an impression.*

But he hiked faster and soon outpaced her and Meifeng. Maybe she'd have a chance to talk with him tomorrow.

They gained the meadow and the Chinese encampment.

The men were already spreading out, starting campfires. The encampment was set up with six or eight tents clustered around a central campfire, so each one didn't have to make their own. Smart.

Beside the campfires, little orange glows began popping up across the meadow. Men were lighting lanterns and taking them inside the tents. It looked so pretty. Silhouettes moved inside the tents, their shadows playing along the lines of the canvas walls.

Her stomach grumbled. "What are we having for dinner?" she asked Meifeng as they approached her cabin.

Their cook had made a roast. She'd inhaled its aroma as soon as she'd arrived home. But she didn't smell a roast here. She didn't smell much of anything.

Tadashi had left her satchel by the door.

She yanked off her boots and picked her bag up, following the doctor inside. "Can I help set the table?"

Meifeng lit a candle.

Wait a minute. There was no table in here. She hadn't really paid attention to such things when she'd visited before.

"No time to eat," Meifeng said. "We'll be too busy."

"Doing what?"

"Our work's just begun, Ruby." She grabbed some pouches, a large pot and slung a bag with a wide strap over her shoulder. She pointed to one corner where a wicker basket of cloth sat. "Bring that along. Let's go." Meifeng blew out the candle and stepped outside. She started off.

Ruby grabbed the wicker basket. "Wait. Let me put my boots on."

"No need."

"Where are we going, anyway?" She hurried to keep up. Ouch, a rock. She hopped on one foot as she rubbed the pain away. "Hold up." She hurried after the doctor who was crossing the meadow.

Meifeng stopped at the farthest campfire where nearly a dozen men were seated around it on log benches. She greeted them in Chinese as she set down her gear and they answered her back.

Ruby hurried up. Now what? What were they doing here?

Meifeng set the pot beside the crackling fire and stepped back. Another pot was already at the fire, being heated. Maybe was stew or soup, something for dinner.

A man stepped up with a wooden bucket and poured water into Meifeng's pot. He did it slowly, watching the doctor.

"Ting," Meifeng told him.

He quit pouring at her command and set the bucket down.

Oh, so "ting" must mean stop.

The doctor reached in her shoulder bag, pulled out short, thin branches, then began snapping them into twigs. She dropped them into the water.

Ruby moved closer. She recognized this. It was witch hazel, a small shrub with twisting branches. When it bloomed, it had yellow flowers.

Ten minutes after it had been boiling, Meifeng signaled Ruby. "I need the cloths."

From the wicker basket, she meant. Ruby pulled out a couple of the cloths. Each one was two feet wide by three feet long. "Do you need more than this?"

"More like ten, a dozen even."

She counted out ten more cloths and passed them to her.

"Watch me." Meifeng said to her as she tossed the cloths in the bucket, took a stick and swished them around. She used the stick to pull out a cloth and let it drip. After it cooled a moment, she lay it across the bare back of one of the waiting men.

He must have removed his tunic when she wasn't looking.

"Hsit," he said, nodding and giving her a smile.

Sore back muscles. That's what was going on here.

Meifeng repeated the process with the next man.

"Here, let me help." Ruby found a stick. All she had to do was copy what the doctor had done. She approached the pot. The water level was low and the smell was more noticeable here. Meifeng had used a lot of plant material to get this concentration of witch hazel. She made sure to keep the side of her left hand away from the hot water.

Working as a team of two, they finished with the first campfire in no time.

They moved to the next one and repeated the process.

One man wanted the cloth only across his shoulders.

Two others wanted their calf muscles wrapped.

They moved on, doing the next cluster of tents.

The moon was now behind the far grove of trees.

Ruby stretched her own back muscles. This was tough work. They'd done six campfire clusters already. "Do we have to do the entire encampment?" It would take until midnight. Longer, even. She yawned.

Meifeng shook her head. "No. The rest of the camp has been doing this at the same time. It's just that these men don't own an extra pot."

Which meant that Tadashi's group of tents owned an extra pot. Too bad. She was hoping to see him, stretch a hot cloth across his back and talk with him. Besides Meifeng, he was the only one here who seemed to speak English. But she hadn't even caught a glimpse of him.

She trudged back to the cabin behind Meifeng.

"We get up early," Meifeng warned.

She was so tired now, she could drop to the ground and let the grass be her mattress.

Ruby sat on the cabin floor and accepted the bowl from Meifeng. It was warm and felt good on her cold hands. She scooped it up with the odd little spoon she'd been given. There was ginger in this, but nothing else stood out. And it had a weird green plant with flat blades in it. She held up a piece. "What are these pieces?"

"Sea weed. It'll ensure that you'll never get gout."

So, it must be high in iodine. "The witch hazel routine, do you do that every night?

Meifeng shook her head. "Only once a week. It's time consuming, yes?"

Well, if the water was already boiling when they arrived, it wouldn't have been so bad. "Yes."

"How did you sleep?"

Like a rock. "Thank you for the cot. I was expecting to sleep on the floor."

"It was left over from some woodsman." She glanced around and gestured. "At least he built a sturdy cabin."

Sturdy was an understatement, with these thick beams and the second story loft where Meifeng had retired last night. Whoever built it had had help. But she wasn't her to learn about architecture. "Are all the men railroad workers?"

"Yes. They go down the mountain and assemble at the train station each morning."

That had to be a sight. If Mother had come upon them, she would have clutched her hankie and shrunk back in horror. But Mother wasn't the type to get up with the sun. Ruby thought back. "I've never seen them assembled there."

"They're not at the platform with the regular citizenry. They board the boxcars that sit to one side of the rail yard."

Now she understood. And then they were transported along whatever line they were building until they reach the newest section to be laid. "Father told me that he needed to hire more. He showed me plans to have rail lines connect all over the West. He said every city should be connected and in all directions."

"Your father and his railroad partners have big plans. Maybe he should see how those plans affect the people who work for him."

Meaning what? "Like, he should come see how the men had sore muscles and needed the healing of your herbs?" She sipped her soup.

"The men who live here have strong backs to lay all those lines of track."

Here was her opening. "Tadashi has a strong back." She hid her smile by looking down into her soup. "He carried my bag for me."

"I'm glad to hear that my son has manners," Meifeng said. "But then, he has been exposed to Western culture more than the others."

"Come clean, he's not really your son."

"Not all sons are blood relatives. He's adopted. I took him in as a little boy. Sort of like I'm taking you in."

"How come he doesn't look like the other men?" He was way more handsome.

"He's not Chinese. Tadashi is half Japanese, half American."

"Is that why he speaks English so well? Because you took him in?"

"He has been educated. That's why your father's foremen uses him as in intermediary. He translates orders to the men, probably sees the plans and helps determine how much material will be needed. Now that he's seventeen, he's ready to make his own way in the world. He's old enough, experienced enough. He knows what he's doing." Meifeng made a rolling-eyes kind of face. "Sure he does."

So, he was eighteen? And she was going to turn sixteen soon. Perfect.

Meifeng kept talking. "Sometimes I have to rein him in, remind him that his lessons are not over, much as he would like them to be."

That meant Tadashi only worked part of the time. Maybe he came here to study. Maybe she would bump into him when he did. Unless she was in town, being tutored when he came to the cabin. "I wish Mother hadn't insisted that I keeping returning home to keep up my education."

"One day you'll appreciate that she did. My own studies took years, even took me to Paris. It was very expensive. Thank goodness my family has royal blood and could afford it."

Ruby choked on her soup. "You're *royalty*? Honest-to-goodness royalty?" Surely she was joking.

"Not so royal to warrant being at court and having to follow all the rules. Just enough to have respect and follow my heart. I'll never want for money."

"So, what are you doing here? Living in a cabin?"

"Because this is where I was called to be. I'm a doctor, Ruby. My people need me." She paused. "Do you think any of these men could show up in town and expect your doctor to tend to them?"

They'd be sent packing, laughed out of town. No, the Chinese were not regarded the same as white people. Was Tadashi regarded that way as well?

"You have money, too," Meifeng continued. "If your father is a smart business man, and I see no reason to suggest otherwise, you'll never have to work a day of your life if you don't want to."

She'd never considered that.

"The question is, what do you want to do with your life, Ruby Fontinello?"

Meifeng glanced at Ruby, sitting near her at the community garden. Did she grasp the little boy's problem?

She probably did. This was a simple one, a sore throat. But left untreated, it could develop into something more serious. Best not to jump in and hand the girl the diagnosis. Let her figure it out for herself.

She'd been working with the girl for a month now, feeding her the herbs that would clear out her system so that when the other herbs were introduced, her body could more freely use them. The big question was, could Ruby's body not just repair the damage that had been done, but begin growing the brain cells that should have formed when she was developing as a child? It was a big unknown.

Ruby leaned into her and whispered. "This could turn into strep throat if we're not careful. I'm thinking he needs to use lichen, but in a mouthwash form."

Amazingly, she'd nailed it. Lichen was perfect for this patient. "Be sure to tell the mother how to boil it down to get a high concentration."

The girl's hand hovered over the basket of pouches. She had a look of confusion.

Oh, the pouches were labeled in Chinese. Ruby must be afraid of handing out the wrong one and Lord knows she'd look like a fool if she opened every pouch to see what was inside. "It's this one," Meifeng said.

Ruby gave instructions to the mother of the little boy.

Good, good. Yes, good. She'd covered every point.

A boy from the mercantile hurried up. He had a large sack over one shoulder. It bulged here and there but didn't seem too heavy. "Your order came in," he told Ruby and set the sack down. It clattered.

"Finally." Ruby thanked him, tore it open and pulled out an item. It was a metal cooking pot. "For the men in camp who couldn't afford an extra one. I ordered ten." She returned it to the sack. "Now we don't have to spend two hours helping them. They can do it themselves."

Smart girl. And quite generous of her. But they still had patients waiting.

Anastasia was here. She should be done with the parsley treatments for that urinary tract infection. She must be here for some other issue. Meifeng gestured her to come forward.

Anastasia was such a sweet girl, better suited as a business woman than a prostitute. But everyone had to find their own way in life. She was one of the few people with whom she conversed in full English.

Ruby spotted her and brightened. "Come, sit down. Are you ready for more pregnancy prevention herbs?"

Not if she was taking the proper amount, she shouldn't be. But then, prostitutes tended to hesitate after they measured out the amounts, then add a dash more than was necessary. She called it the "just in case" syndrome. It was understandable. In their profession, they couldn't afford to get pregnant.

Anastasia nodded. "I think one of the other girls may have dipped into my canister. Either that, or I'm going soft in the head."

Meifeng thought back to the herbs she had with her. There were so many that could keep a woman from getting pregnant – thyme, golden thread, antelope sage, rosemary. The trick was knowing how much to take.

Anastasia looked a little down. "Sad day. We got word one of my friends, a girl I worked with in another town, was killed." She blinked away tears. "She didn't deserve to die."

"I'm sorry." Meifeng reached out and took her hand. It was a risk in that profession. Men got their pay, went out drinking and decided a girl was what they needed. They could get rough with the girl, demand more things than they'd paid for and expect immediate cooperation. She'd seen more than one girl with finger impressions around her neck. "I can give you a soothing tea if you like."

"Yes, thank you." The pretty blonde turned to Ruby. "My stomach issues, everything's better. I didn't realize how poorly I felt until you gave me that bark stuff."

"Magnolia tree," Ruby said.

This was news. When had Ruby given her such medication?

Anastasia looked confused. "But I didn't tell you that anything was wrong."

"You didn't have to," Ruby said. "My guides showed me what was going on while I slept."

Meifeng threw out a hand to catch herself from falling over. Had she heard correctly? Ruby learned of things through osmosis?

"Sometimes that happens," Ruby continued, "especially if I'm near a person or touch them."

"But we only shook hands," Anastasia reminded her.

Ruby gave a little shirk of her shoulders. "What can I say? They tell me what to do. They haven't been wrong yet."

Holy crap, Ruby was more than just interested in helping people get well. She had dreams, apparently. Enlightening dreams. And guides? Who had guides?

No, Ruby was way beyond any other student she'd taken under her wing in the past. She had more than just a passing interest.

Ruby finished her lesson with Grace and headed up the grand stairway. Thank goodness that was done. She couldn't wait to get out of this dress. Who decided that women had to wear these things anyway?

She reached her room and stripped off her dress. Her tunic with the Mandarin collar and her cut-off pants were set out on her bed. The maid must have washed and ironed them. Silly people, clothes were meant to move with the body. Who cared if they got wrinkled?

She put them on and caught sight of herself in the mirror. Was she more presentable now that she kept her hair clean and combed? Would Tadashi think she was pretty?

Ah, Tadashi. Those eyes. That smile.

She'd barely seen him since she'd gone to live with Meifeng. She'd finally learned which tent was his and she'd gotten a glimpse of him here and there. But that was it. It was so darn frustrating, knowing that he was near, but unable to find an excuse to go see him.

She headed downstairs.

Mother was there. She had a note. "For you."

It was from Max. Sarah and her unborn child were dead. He was burying her along the coast.

Her heart lurched. "Oh, no." She'd tried to intervene but the pregnant woman been too far along with the condition. Now, Max was left with the children to raise alone. She'd failed. She gave Mother the news.

"That's a shame."

She went to step past her.

"You can't leave, Ruby. You're to have dinner with us, remember?"

Was she serious? "We talked about this, Mother. I came here two hours earlier than usual today, just like you wanted, so I could have lunch with you and Mrs. Jenkins and the deacon. I put on a dress. I made polite conversation. I poured tea." Even though it was that awful factory-made stuff and not worth a penny. "I played the perfect daughter for you."

"You don't have to act so snippy about it."

"We had an agreement. You decided to change it, just for today. I get that. I'm glad you're flexible. We had a nice luncheon and that makes up for me not being here for dinner tonight. Now, it's time for me to continue my studies."

Mother brightened. "With Grace, you mean?"

"With Meifeng. She's waiting for me." She brushed past her and stepped out the door. The sun was getting lower in the sky.

She headed to the mountain trail. Maybe Meifeng would quiz her again, blindfold her and hold various roots and herbs and barks under her nose.

"What's this?"

"Ginkgo."

"Used for ...?"

Me. It's one of the herbs you have me drink. "Memory, blood flow, ringing in the ears, dementia, and to boost oxygen in the blood."

"What's this?"

"That's easy. Jasmine." It was Mother's favorite kind of perfume. "Good for depression. It's an antiseptic, can be used as an expectorant."

"One more thing."

What else? "It promotes sleep and lowers anxiety?"

"Yes, but it's known as a romantic plant, too. So if you find someone you'd ever like to entice," Meifeng teased, letting the sentence dangle.

They'd both burst out laughing. Learning with Meifeng was nothing like her required studies with Grace, the tutor at home.

The trail didn't seem so steep now that she took it almost every day.

She reached the clearing and saw a light on in the cabin. Meifeng must be reading.

She slipped off her boots and opened the cabin door. "I brought some more shiitake so we can make –"

Tadashi looked up. He was sitting on the floor, an open book on his lap.

Her heart fluttered. What was he doing here? Was he here to see her?

Meifeng stepped away from the hearth. "Oh, you're back. Here, I'll take the mushrooms."

Ruby handed them over. She dropped down beside Tadashi, sitting cross-legged like him. "Hi."

"Hi, yourself." His eyes sparkled.

It was like electricity striking her, that smile. *Don't just sit here smiling like an idiot say something.* "So, what book is that?"

He showed her the cover.

It was in Chinese. Those scratches and markings, she hadn't a clue what they said. But why let that stop her? "Oh, 'The Book of How to Make Your Own Ocean Freighter Out of Tooth Picks in Thirty Days or Less' – I read that one already."

He hid a smile. "And did you build your own freighter?"

"Yup, sailed around the world in her just last week."

"That so?"

"Only one problem. Every time I ate a meal, I had to pull off one of the toothpicks from the hull to clean my teeth." She sighed. "Made a hole in the hull."

"That's bad."

"Sank the freighter."

"That's even worse."

"Had to swim all the way home from Tahiti."

"Really?"

"Boy, are my arms tired."

Meifeng came over. "Very funny. Actually, the book is an intensive in body function. It would be wise for you to know such information."

It sounded fascinating. "Has it been translated into English? I can order it from the book store in San Francisco." Mother was always going to that city, saying how she longed for "real" culture. She could have the book in her hot little hands within the month.

Meifeng shook her head. "Sorry. Publishers in the United States don't see value in presenting medical information that comes out of China. The doctors there have only had, what, two thousand years of practice with such things."

Ruby heard the disdain in her voice. The doctor was being facetious. "Well, is the information available in another book? One that's written in English?"

"Not that's this specific, especially about connecting the information with the meridian lines."

Connecting it with the what?

Meifeng paused. "There *is* a way for you to gain the information." She gestured. "Ruby, meet your new tutor, my son."

What? What was she talking about? She shot a look at Tadashi.

He blinked in obvious shock.

"Think about it," the doctor said. "If you could read Chinese, you'd immediately know what the labels on the pouches said. And if you spoke Chinese, you and I could converse in front of patients and discuss what tack to take with their treatment. Yes, I think this would be highly beneficial. Tadashi, you stay for dinner. We need to discuss this, work out a schedule."

Ruby called up a goodnight to the doctor in the loft, fixed up her cot and got into bed. There was no way she could sleep, not after what had happened tonight.

Tadashi had had dinner with them, stayed all evening. He'd teased her about her toothpick freighter, complimented her on her off-the-cuff storytelling.

There had been magic in the air. It was like everything had fallen into place.

Tadashi was going to be her tutor.

That meant he was going to sitting beside her, close enough so that bumping up against him would be unavoidable.

Both of them would be going over the text together, trying to concentrate, but knowing there was that electricity between them

Even better, he'd felt that charge, too. She could see it in his eyes, the way they'd lit up at Meifeng's suggestion. So, he wanted to work with her, too.

She tossed and turned, too charged to sleep. Oh gosh, her hand was drifting to – yes, she had to do it this time –her private parts. It was the only way she could find relief. Her finger found the spot. The pleasure hit her like a rocket.

Damn, Tadashi, you don't known how badly I want to kiss you.

Phillip spotted Ruby coming down the street. Felicia must have insisted their daughter forego her Chinese garb to wear a dress to meet him, but, look at that smile, she seemed so happy. And that was what counted. He held out his arms. "Thanks for meeting me for lunch."

Ruby gave him a big hug. "I'm surprised you have time to see me, Daddy."

She had a point. Work was taking him away from home nearly every week. Lord knew, Felicia didn't care.

She looked around. "I don't get to this part of town much. It's growing."

It would grow even more once he secured these new routes for the rail lines. Railroads, they were the workhorses of America and the Fontinello family would be riding the wave as they steamed across the country. Well, that was the plan anyway. "Say, I've got a quick meeting before we can get lunch. Do you mind?"

"I've got time."

He escorted her to the three-story city hall building. If he could just get a signature, he could move on to the next step. They took the stairs to the second floor and he stopped before a set of double doors.

A secretary looked up from her post as they entered. "Yes, sir. May I help you?"

"Phillip Fontinello for Ross Wallace. We're expected."

She showed them to an office down the hall.

Ross Wallace had a large office with big windows overlooking the city. He got up from his seat and scurried around his desk. "Phillip, good to see you. Who is this?"

He made introductions. "My daughter's studying, er, international culture." That was the terminology they'd agreed to use, should anyone see her in her tunic. He used it now, even though she wore a dress.

"Please, both of you, have a seat." The city councilman returned to his post behind his desk, sitting back in his plush chair.

"We won't be but a moment. I was just wondering, did you get a chance to look over the proposal?"

"For making Sacramento the hub for a spider's web of rail lines? It's an industrious plan." He spread his hands and grinned. "What's not to love?"

"So, I can count on you. Good. Do you think the other council members will jump on board?" Or did he have to wine and dine them, too? "What's the chatter you've heard?"

"All of it good, I assure you, Phillip. Let's see, you needed a signature from me, right?"

"Right. But I was hoping to also have another councilmember sign on, also."

Wallace sat up suddenly. "You know what? Stewart just walked by, so he's in his office. Let me grab your paperwork and I'll chase him down." He ruffled through some papers in his desk drawer, found what he wanted, popped something in his mouth and hurried past them. "I'll just be a moment." He dashed out.

"This is a really big step," he told Ruby.

"I'm sure." She got up and slipped behind the desk, slid open a drawer, glanced in and closed it. She returned to her seat.

The councilman came back. He handed over the papers. "Two signatures." He clapped him on the back. "We'll get this project off the ground, I promise you."

"We" –as though the idea was his. "Thanks, Ross, appreciate this." Two signatures, what a relief. He ushered Ruby out and they took the stairs. "Why did you look in his desk?"

"Didn't you notice? He popped something in his mouth just before he left the office."

"His sweet suckers? Ross is known for importing them, not that he shares them with anyone." He wouldn't even tell people where he got them. Probably some perk from a shady deal.

"His sweet suckers are causing him a number of health problems," she said. "Not to mention his predilection for pork."

She was right. Every time he'd taken the man out to dinner, the guy had ordered pork chops. But Ruby had never witnessed that. "How do you know he likes to eat pork?"

"I could smell it on him. His body reeked of it."

It did? Ruby must have one super sensitive nose.

Ruby sat across from her father in the hotel's grand dining room.

The seat cushion on which she sat was even deeper than those at the house. A hand-cut crystal candle holder was on the table. The gold-plated dishes awaited a four-course meal.

It seemed strange to be in such an austere setting after leading so simple a life with Meifeng for the past three months.

The waiter came over with a silver pitcher and poured water in their glasses. "Do you need more time to study the menu? No?" He hovered near her. "For you, miss?"

"A salad, plenty of mushrooms, cucumber and cherry tomatoes." She handed him the leather-bond menu.

He took it and nodded. "And what else?"

"That's all."

"Nothing more, miss?"

"Please put the vinaigrette on the side."

He hesitated. "When you finish and want more to eat, just let me know your selection."

There was no reason to want more. The salad would be plenty.

He moved to the other side of the table.

Father closed the menu and handed it to the waiter. "I'll start with the turtle soup –" he leaned in "– bring plenty of those cheddar biscuits that your chef makes, please. Then coquilles Saint Jacques for a starter. The foi gras sounds good and the peach cobbler for dessert."

Did the man have any idea what he was doing to his digestive system?

"Very good sir."

The waiter left them. A four-piece string orchestra began playing in the corner.

"You only get that because of the railroad," Father said.

"The string quartet?"

"The extensive menu. Did you see all the different things it offered?"

And hardly any of them prepared in a healthy way.

"We can bring things in from the coast and have it on your dinner plate that night."

"That's so interesting, Daddy."

"You're too young to remember this but it used to take days to get goods to this part of California."

"How are things going with the new branches you're trying to start?"

"Well, Wallace's support is a step in the right direction. I'm hoping it will persuade land owners down the line. Some of them are stubborn, but I'll win out, I'm sure of it. Right now, our biggest hurdle is that we're having supply issues." He frowned. "If it weren't for that, we'd be farther ahead, miles farther, than we are."

The waiter swung by with two small plates, setting them down before each of them.

Father put out a hand, stopping the waiter. "What's this?"

"A sampling, compliments of the chef, Mr. Fontinello. Shrimp scampi."

"Very nice of him. Thank him for us." He picked up the seafood fork, stabbed the snail and popped it in his mouth. He closed his eyes and made a moaning sound. "Delicious. Try yours."

No, thanks. It was covered in butter. "You can have mine if you want, Daddy." She passed him her plate and spotted a flurry of movement behind him at the entrance.

It was Tadashi.

Her heart raced. What was he doing here?

The old maitre d' was blocking him from entering and had hold of one of his arms.

"How long has Tadashi worked for you, Father?"

"Huh? Oh, that young man who speaks excellent English? About a year now."

That long, and she'd only just become aware of him, or Meifeng, too. "Turn around. He's here."

Father twisted in his chair, caught the eye of the maitre d' and signaled him to let Tadashi approach.

Tadashi shook off the restraining arm of the old man, who scowled and turned away. He hurried forward. Tadashi nodded to her briefly before he turned to her father. "Begging your pardon, sir. A telegram came in marked 'urgent' and I thought you'd want to read it right away." Tadashi handed the telegram to him. He glanced at her and caught his breath. He seemed to suddenly realize that she was in a proper dress ...with a tight-fitting bodice. He blinked, obviously interested.

He liked this top, did he? Maybe he'd like this presentation of it even better. She pulled back her shoulders, pushing out her chest.

He stared and swallowed hard, his face turning pink.

Father sat up sharply.

She flinched. Oh, God, had he noticed her blatant, saucy pose? She ducked her head down, sure it was as red as Tadashi's right now.

Father yanked his linen napkin off his lap and wiped his mouth with it. "I've got to go see the governor. You'll have to excuse me." He pushed back his chair. "We'll have to reschedule this for another time. I'm sorry, Pumpkin."

It had been her pet name when she was small. Funny that he would use it now.

Father bent and kissed the top of her head. "Enjoy your lunch. I'll tell them to bill me." He hurried out.

So much for their special father-daughter lunch. But at least she'd gotten the chance to see Tadashi again. Now, if only there was a reason to make him stay. She had to think up some way to engage him in conversation. "I'm sure Father appreciates you bringing him the telegram." *Even though he never thanked you.*

"My pleasure." Tadashi hesitated and glanced down at her chest again. "Yes, well, I'd better go. It was nice to see –"

Someone pushed him sharply from behind.

He caught himself just before he fell into her table.

"Yes, you'd better go," the waiter hissed. "We can't have the likes of *you* lingering in here with our esteemed patrons."

How rude.

Tadashi straightened up and, with a quick nod to her, strode out.

Ruby watched him leave. Was that the way white people normally treated Tadashi? Didn't they know how smart he was? How kind and upstanding?

The waiter grinned. "Guess I got rid of that riff raff, huh?"

She stood up, staring him down. "Cancel my order. I'm suddenly not hungry."

Ruby slipped into the pew next to Mother. "Where's Daddy?"

She made a gesture of disinterest. "Work. Where else?"

On a Sunday?

Mrs. Krofton's usual spot was noticeably vacant.

Mrs. Tidewater spotted her, slipped out of her row and tiptoed over. "Ruby, dear, Can you come by the house after service?" she whispered. "Henry is sick in bed."

"Of course."

Eleanora Glanford leaned forward and tapped her on the shoulder. "My little Suzie's got a boil on her neck. Do you think you could see her this afternoon?"

"I'll be happy to." She should have anticipated this and ordered more herbs to have on hand.

She nodded hello to people as they filed in. Melvin Vincent's flesh looked less yellow than when she'd first treated him a week ago. Adeline Fisher's hair was growing back. Patrick McDurberry's burned hand was healing.

Daddy hurried in. "Sorry. Couldn't be helped." He gave her a perfunctory kiss on the top of her head. "Guess what? I located that missing shipment of rails. They should be arriving the day after tomorrow. They were in Ohio. Can you believe it?"

Two thousand miles away, that far? She would have thought they'd gotten side railed in a train yard in Berkley or Stockton. But, Ohio? "How did they wind up there?"

"Beats me. But I'm making up for lost time. I ordered the crew out to get out to the end of the line and start grading. They should be loading up right now."

But it was Sunday. The Chinese workers needed their weekends to rest after a long week of back breaking work. "Couldn't it wait? If the rails aren't yet here, then –"

"Work can never wait," he said.

Maybe if she appealed to his bottom line and played dumb. "Gee, Daddy, isn't it more expensive to have them work on a Sunday? Overtime, isn't that what it's called?"

He scoffed. "Chinamen don't get overtime, Ruby. That's only for Caucasians."

So, he was going to have them work on their day off without proper compensation. Someone needed to pay attention to today's sermon.

Ferguson LaVy looked up from milking his cow.

Someone was standing in the doorway of his barn, not twenty feet away. Whoever he was, he was just standing there.

Ferguson leaned back on his milking stool. "Can I help you, friend?"

"Are you the owner of this farm, Ferguson LaVy?"

"One and the same."

"Heard there was a railroad agent who came to call here, trying to get a lease to use your property."

Aye, that was true. "And I told him it's not for sale."

"He wasn't here to buy it. He was asking you to sign a lease."

"For a hundred years. May as well be for sale."

"Perhaps you need to be ...persuaded."

He didn't like the sound of that. Ferguson stood up and stepped away from the cow. "Perhaps you can turn around and tell the railroad I gave you the same answer as the railroad agent. It's not for sale, not for lease, not for anything."

"Mighty hard to work a farm with a busted up leg, Mr. LaVy."

So, this was a shakedown, was it? "You'd best move along, friend. I've got no quarrel with you."

The man gestured. "Mighty hard to work a farm with a broken arm, too."

Ferguson's heartrate increased. If only he had his rifle nearby, he'd make sure this guy went on his way but quick. "I don't take kindly to threats."

"Your choice, busted leg or busted arm."

"Get off my land."

The man produced a bat.

Ferguson figured he could take him. Maybe this guy didn't realize that the LaVy name had a long history of standing up for what was right. Grandpa was a prizefighter and had taught him how to take care of himself. He advanced to meet the threat and put his fists up. "Why don't you drop that and fight like a man?"

Two more men appeared. Both had bats.

Three against one? He was a dead man. Ferguson turned and ran.

Too late.

Strong hands grabbed him.

The blows hit him from every side, over and over again. He crumbled, tried to protect his head.

A bone cracked. His arm. Ahh, that hurt.

A blow landed on his chin. Then another. He saw stars.

More pounding. More pain.

"Sign or it continues."

"I'll sign, I'll sign."

Tadashi looked up. Ah, Ruby was finally here. He could start her lesson. "About time."

"Sorry, I'm still getting the hang of mixing herbal formulas," she said, taking a seat beside him.

He handed her the paper on which he'd written some of the major characters of the alphabet.

Her eyes got big. "I have to learn all this calligraphy? Are you joking? There are dozens of characters here."

Wait until she found out there were as many as 40,000 characters, though many were variations on a core symbol. She could probably get by with learning a few thousand characters. He'd better take this slow. Meifeng had said Ruby's brain was still lacking. "You'll do fine. After all, you have the best teacher in town – me."

Him? Was this a joke?

He pulled out five scraps of paper and handed her one. "This symbol is what you'd call your pronoun 'I', which also works when you want to use the word 'me'," he said. "And this one here, is 'you,'" He gave it to her. He wrote some more. "This is 'sky' and these are 'sun', 'wind', 'clouds', 'rain', for when you need to talk about the weather."

"What about actions?"

"You can learn verses another time."

She giggled. "Verbs."

"That's what I said, verses."

Ruby giggled again.

Surely she wasn't laughing at him. Look at that face, it said that she wasn't being mean. No, she was playful, happy, being a little silly. OK, maybe he *had* said it wrong. "Here are other words – 'home,' 'family,' 'town,' 'brother,' 'sister,' 'mother,' 'father.'"

He set them down in front of her. "See the difference?"

"Gee, they kind of look the same to me."

It was obvious if she just tried. He pointed. "See the tail over here on this one and the swish over here?"

Ruby frowned. "Just give me a moment to study them so I can cement them in my brain." She took the five pieces of paper and stared at each of them intently. She went back and filed through them again.

He studied her face. Did she know how long her lashes were? How they swept over her eyes just so? And those cheek bones. No one in China had anything close to cheekbones like hers. The rest of her was nice to look at, too, real nice. The way those pert breasts jutted out at him like they were beg-

She looked up.

He flinched. Damn, had she seen him staring at her chest? "Yes?" His voice had risen in pitch. Darn. "What is it?"

Ruby shook her head. "I'm not getting this, Tadashi."

It was sweet, the way she said his name.

"Can you help me?"

Of course he would. Maybe if she drew the symbols as well as studied at them. He handed her a quill pen. "There's not a lot of ink, so don't waste any." He reached behind her for the bottle. It was back here somewhere.

She turned her head and looked into his eyes.

He caught his breath.

Her face was inches away from his, a mere kiss away.

CHAPTER SIX

Tadashi stared at her mouth. Time stood still.

Ruby's lips were so close, so desirable. One kiss. That was all he wanted. Would she let him, if he made a move?

It was suddenly hard to breathe.

He stared at those eyes, eyes shaded by those long, dark lashes as she looked down.

One kiss.

Ruby turned her face away and the spell was broken.

Damn, he should have kissed her.

His hand found the ink bottle. He pulled it out from behind her and uncapped it. He cleared his throat. "Here. Try to draw them."

She dipped the quill pen in the glass ink well and began drawing.

"That's it, not bad."

She tried again.

A child could do better, not that he would tell her that. "A little shaky but you're getting the hang of it."

He hid the papers. "See if you can make the letter A from memory."

Ruby groaned. "Better to ask me to lasso the moon." She cast him a scared look, dipped the pen and made hesitant marks.

It looked nothing like the letter A. *She just saw this. It should be simple.* "Try again."

She crumpled the paper and threw it. "I'm sorry, I just can't seem to grasp this." She jumped up and put her hands to her temples.

Maybe Meifeng hadn't taught her to meditate yet. Maybe Ruby wasn't completely detoxed from her Western diet. She needed reassurance. "Calm down. It's your first lesson."

"It's just that I want Meifeng to be proud of me. I mean, she took me in."

"She took me in, too." He spread his hands. "I was living in the gutters, living like a wild dog. No one wanted me because I was a bastard. But Meifeng found me and raised me as her own child. She educated me, told me I could be anything I put my mind to."

Ruby let her hands drop and came close. "That's so sweet."

More than sweet. I would be nothing if not for her. "I owe her my life."

She nodded. "All right, let me try again. And I'll keep trying until I get this right."

That's the spirit. He reached in the box. Empty.

"There's no more paper." And hardly any ink. The encampment just didn't have a need for such things. "Looks like today's lesson is over."

The railway worker in Chicago eyed the three-car load in front of him and scratched his head. "Hey, didn't we already get all the rail ties for the Springfield delivery?"

His buddy came over. "Yeah, last week. Why?"

"We just got three more car loads." He didn't know where they'd come from. He didn't know who they belonged to. They'd just shown up and landed in his lap. "What should we do with them?"

"How the hell do I know?" his buddy shrugged and pointed. "Just park them off to the side and wait for somebody to claim them, I guess."

"You're right. It's not our problem."

Tadashi walked down the rail line and approached the supervisor's shack. He knocked.

"Yes?"

He peeked in. "Excuse me, Henry, but the men are almost out of rail ties. Where's the next load?" He looked down the track. It was clear except for the engine and the flat cars that took the workers to and from town. Other than that, there was not a railcar in sight.

The supervisor looked up from his paperwork and blinked in sudden realization. "What do you mean? There are no more cars with materials? Are you joking?" He dashed outside and checked for himself, looking this way and that. "What the hell?"

"Are more on their way?" Tadashi asked.

"No, and there weren't any at the train yard when we left this morning. How did this happen?" Henry ran a hand down his face. "Phillip Fontinello is going to put my ass in a sling for this debacle."

"What shall I tell the men?"

"That we're out of materials, I guess." He threw up his hands in surrender. "We'll have to send them home."

They needed the day off. First it had been twelve-hour days, then fourteen. Sometimes, the men were told to work sixteen hours. They were exhausted.

Tadashi returned to where the workers were finishing up. He got their attention. "Looks like you've got the rest of the day off, boys." And probably the next day as well. There was no way Phillip Fontinello could locate the three or four railcars of materials he'd diverted in twenty-four hours.

Ruby stretched her neck to see over the people in front of her.

It was a parade. There were horses and lasso demonstrations by their riders. They made sport of throwing their lassos at the bystanders.

A little boy, a toddler really, was caught. He went crying to his mother who laughed and pulled the rope gently over his head.

Another lasso caught a pretty girl.

It was Anastasia. She let go a peel of laughter as the cowboy pulled her closer to him. She slipped out of the rope, waggled a finger at him and gave him a saucy smile.

How did she make it look so easy? The girl knew how to talk to men, how to get their interest.

They needed to talk. Ruby skirted the crowd, hurrying over. "Anastasia," she called out as she got closer.

She caught the girl's arm and pulled her to the side. She got a whiff of Anastasia's perfume, rose water. "The medicine I gave you. How does your stomach feel now?"

"Didn't I tell you? Worked like a charm."

Yes, but that wasn't what she really wanted to talk about. "You know I've been living at the encampment."

"To learn more about healing, yes, I heard."

"I have to ask you something." She paused. This was suddenly so hard to say. "There's a boy," she blurted.

Anastasia grinned. "Ah, now I understand. Let's find a place to talk."

They found a spot under a tree to sit.

Anastasi's eyes were bright. "You met a boy, huh? You're, what, sixteen? That's the right age to start thinking about boys. I mean, some girls get hitched at sixteen. So, tell me about him."

"He's not Chinese. I mean, he's Asian, yes. Part. Well, half." She was making a mess of this whole conversation. "What I mean is -."

"You like him."

"He's got the most interesting features and he knows a lot of things." She told how Tadashi had taken up her satchel and carried it up the mountain as though it weighed no more than a feather. "The men use witch hazel compresses at the end of their work week. They take off their shirts." Her faced heated up. "I'd be so embarrassed if I had to administer it to him." Though at night, alone on her cot, it was all she thought about.

"Maybe you should offer."

How brazen. "No, no, I couldn't. I just couldn't."

Anastasia twirled a lock of her blonde hair. "Maybe he'd like it if you did," she said in a sing-song voice.

Would he like it? Or would he dismiss her?

"It's your duty as a healer, isn't it?" Anastasia let go of her hair. "Seems to me it would be a perfectly respectable offer."

That made sense, perfect sense. She'd be helping Tadashi with his health. It was sort of like him teaching her Chinese, but he was forced to do that, Meifeng's orders. No, this would be a true test of how he felt about her.

If he rejected her offer of a witch hazel treatment, she'd know for sure whether he liked her or not.

But if he accepted, that's when things could get interesting. She could see it now. She'd help him out of his tunic top, get to see him bare chested and feel his muscles as she draped the wet cloth over his taut, muscular shoulders. Something deep in her stirred. "I've got to head back." She jumped up and began trotting away. "You're brilliant, Anastasia."

"Let me know how it goes."

Meifeng looked up as the cabin door swung open. "You're late. Is everything all right?"

Ruby made a rolling-eyes face. "Mother finds 'things' for me to do while I'm still in a dress. Today it was taking hymnals from church to a meeting hall." She set down her pouch. "It's like she's showing me off, assuring everyone that I'm not in a Chinese tunic *all* the time. 'Doesn't she look lovely in this dress?' and 'I bought her this dress because I knew how much she'd love wearing it.' It made me want to scream."

Meifeng hid a smile. Knowing Felicia Fontinello, Ruby's depiction sounded like a spot-on assessment. "I see."

"At least she's going out of town next week."

"Help me cull these blueberries of their stems." She'd found them in a little canyon across the ridge while looking for plants.

Ruby hurried over. "You're making a poultice. The stems can't be used? Why? Do they make the poultice less effective? Render it useless?"

Silly girl, not everything they did was focused on medicinal healing. "No, they're for tonight's meal. You don't want to eat stems, do you?"

Ruby stood beside her and began picking through the berries. Her fingernails were short, one was broken. No doubt Felicia Fontinello would have a heart attack if she saw that. You could insist someone wear fashionable clothes, but you couldn't dictate the path that they took in life.

That scar beside Ruby's little finger. Now that the sun was shining on it, it stood out more. She'd said it was from a fireplace poker. Hold on a second, what kind of burn went so deep that it gouged into the muscle? Something wasn't right here. "When you meditate, what do you ask to see?" *Anything from your past?*

"That I be shown how to heal someone, like Mr. Lewis and his foot, or little Tommy Bennett and his breathing." Ruby kept working. "My guides usually come through."

Maybe you should ask them what really happened to your hand. But she couldn't say that. Guides never showed a person their own fate. Still, something far more traumatic had happened to Ruby than touching a fireplace poker. The only person who likely knew was Ruby's mother. And she wasn't talking.

Ruby slipped off her cot and slid her feet into her boots. Sometimes she went barefoot, but this was the middle of the night. She didn't want to risk stubbing a toe or stepping on a sharp rock.

She pulled a sweater around her cotton night shift and stole out the door. Stupid of her not to visit the latrine before going to bed.

The moon was hidden behind some clouds but there was just enough light to see where she was going. She started out for the row of outhouses. They were about a hundred yards from the edge of the encampment and downhill.

An owl hooted. A twig snapped deep in the woods. A deer? A raccoon?

She pulled her sweater closer. Maybe she should carry a stick if she was going to venture out this late alone.

She reached the latrine area, ducked inside one and did her business.

Ruby stepped out and hiked back up to the encampment.

Everything was so peaceful, so silent. The camp was totally silent.

Tadashi's tent was right over here, at the very edge. She'd watched him leave after one of her language lessons and followed him. Thank goodness he hadn't seen her. Nowadays, she made any excuse she could think of to happen over that way. He might be strolling back to it, one never knew, and they could bump into one another.

She detoured over to where his tent stood. Here it was, his tent. He was inside, sleeping, a mere ten feet away.

Did he sleep on his side? Stretched out on his back? Or curled up in a ball? Did he mumble when he dreamed? Maybe he was the kind who tossed and turned to get comfortable, then slept all night through.

She reached out. If she could just touch the canvas, be that much closer to him.

There was movement from inside the tent.

She froze.

He was awake.

A match was struck. A lantern door creaked open. It was being lit.

Crap, what if he discovered her standing just outside his tent flap, peeking in where the two flaps failed to meet?

Maybe he had to use the latrine, too. Wait, no. He wouldn't light a lantern for that. He must need it for some other purpose. She didn't dare move a muscle.

Tadashi set the lantern on a table. He stood up.

He was naked.

Ruby caught her breath.

Oh, dear Lord, look at that. Look at that body. He was even better than she'd imagined. How fit. How lean. She watched his silhouette.

He stretched, then pulled out a book, sat down and began reading.

She couldn't stop looking at his figure. He was just so damn perfect.

Part of her wanted to stay. Part of her said to go.

She winced silently and eased away. She'd surely spend the rest of the night tossing and turning after this.

Anastasia crossed the parlor to answer the knock at her door. "Coming." Another client? At 8 a.m.? Guys sure were horny lately. She opened the door.

It was Ruby.

"What are you doing here, sugar?"

"I need your advice."

The poor thing looked desperate. What could a sweet thing like Ruby want from someone like her? "Come on in. Let's go to the kitchen. I need a wake-me-up. You want coffee, too?"

Ruby shook her head.

Maybe herbal healers didn't drink coffee. She didn't know what she was missing. "Suit yourself, honey."

Over in the corner, Buster screeched in his cage. *Be quiet.* She pulled a shade over his cage. That would shut him up. "So, Ruby, what's this about advice?"

"How can I make a guy like me?" Ruby blurted.

So, *that's* what this was about. She poured herself a cup. They sat at the table. "Tell me about this guy, the Asian."

Ruby's eyes were lit up. "He's a couple years older than me, but he's so smart and nice."

"And good looking?" He was probably some hunk. Too bad her clients usually didn't fall into that category.

"How can I get him to notice me?"

"That's easy. Smile."

"I do smile."

"At him, I mean. And lock eyes with him, for longer than most people would consider, well, normal for regular company."

"So, I should stare at him."

"God, no, honey. He'll think you're demented. Smile at him in that cute, 'I'd like to get to know you' kind of way." She winked. "Works every time."

"I wish I was pretty like you."

"Sugar, you already are pretty. Did you offer to give him the witch hazel treatment?"

Another girl came in the room. Her hair was mussed and she wore a silk kimono kind of gown. "Good morning, Anastasia." She spotted Ruby. "Oh, hi. You a new girl?"

Shut up, Lillian. "This is Ruby. You remember, from the community garden? She's with Meifeng."

"Sorry, too early." She made a lopsided smile. "And too little sleep. Occupational hazard." Lillian crossed to the coffee pot.

"Ruby's met a boy and thinks she isn't pretty enough for him."

Lillian scoffed. "Any girl is pretty enough if the guy is drunk."

"Be serious. She isn't the type to wear makeup. She just wants some pointers." Her girls were always having makeup sessions. But any changes had to be subtle for a girl who was from high society.

"Let me see." Lillian came closer, cupped Ruby's face in one hand and studied her. "Eyebrows," she decided. She sipped her coffee.

Yes, perfect. She should have seen it herself. "Let me get my tweezers."

Two minutes later, she stood back and studied her work. She now had Ruby's brows perfectly shaped. "It really brings out your eyes, sugar." She nudged Lillian. "What do you think? Poof the hair as well?"

"To lengthen her face a little? Yeah."

It would have to be a low bump, though. She steered Ruby to a mirror in the hallway, grabbed a brush and some hair pins, holding them in her mouth as she worked. "Watch me so you can do it yourself next time."

Ruby hesitated. "Nothing that would make Mother upset, right?"

"She'll wish she looked this good."

Brush, brush, brush, back sweep it this way. There, finished. Ruby's guy wouldn't be able to take his eyes off her.

Ruby stared at her reflection. "Is this really me? You made me look so good."

"That's the idea. This guy of yours –"

"Tadashi."

She'd heard the name but couldn't place him. "This Tadashi guy, he won't know what hit him."

Ruby hugged her. "How can I ever repay you?"

As if seeing her smile a mile wide was enough. But Ruby knew so many things about keeping healthy. "There is one thing you can do." She lowered her voice. "Lillian? She has acne. Can't seem to keep her skin clear."

"It's not that bad, but let me take a look."

"Be casual. She gets a little defensive sometimes."

Ruby nodded and they returned to the kitchen. She leaned against the doorjamb. How in the world was Ruby going to approach this topic?

Ruby twirled around. "Look at what Anastasia did for me."

"The poof. A good look for you."

"I want to do something for you girls in return. Can I show you my regime for perfect skin? Lillian, you're wearing makeup, so let me use you for my example."

That was a good way to suggest it, no way could Lillian get defensive about this.

Ruby looked her way. "I'll need a pan with water. And a towel."

"Aye, aye, captain." She scrounged around the little kitchen and handed Ruby the items she needed.

Ruby began boiling the water. "Let's see what you have in your pantry." She opened it and peered around. "Ah, cucumber. Perfect." She grabbed it began mashing it up. "Do you know that the cucumber is the only plant you can eat that uses more energy to process than it puts in your body?" She had Lillian stand pressed against the sink, scooped up the mashed cucumber and smeared it on. "Use your hands to rub it around. "Give it a good five minutes and keep rubbing."

Lillian made a face. "It feels weird."

It looked weird, too. But Ruby had never steered them wrong before. "Why does she have to keep moving it around?"

"This will remove her makeup but the seeds are gentle yet abrasive enough to remove dead skin, too." She reached out and caught areas Lillian had missed, using circular motions. "You don't have to press real hard, do it like this. Do it for a minute."

"It's been five hours," Lillian complained. "Now what, Ruby?"

"Rinse it off, then we'll go over to the boiling water."

Lillian followed orders, rinsed off and went over to the stove where Ruby had her lean over the boiling water and set the towel, tent style, over her head and face.

"This will open your pores so all the junk can get out," Ruby said. "You can do this two times a day if you want, but *always* do it before you go to bed at night so you're not sleeping with clogged pores."

That made sense. But it was a lot for Lillian to do and the girl was not known for committing to things that took effort. Better speak up. "We're tired at the end of the day. What if we just don't have time to do this?"

Ruby thought for a moment. "You can dip a wash cloth in hot water, wring it out and press it against your face. That'll open the pores, too."

Lillian would be more apt to do that. Quick and simple, that was her style.

"You can follow it up with rubbing a lemon over your face to kill the germation."

"Germ –what?"

"That's what Louis Pasteur, a scientist in France, calls it. Just think of it as the bad stuff. I just read about his discovery."

Lillian peeked out of the towel tent. She looked like she was on board. "Let's try the lemon, too."

Anastasia hid a smile. It was good to see her enthused about something. "I think we have one. Give me a sec." She ducked into the root cellar. It was much cooler here. Lemon, lemon, she was sure she'd seen one. Ah, here it was. She hurried up the stairs, holding it up like a prize. "Now what?"

Ruby gestured. "Slice a small wedge and give it to me." She had Lillian stop steaming, take a seat and dry off her face. "Anastasia, find me some apple cider vinegar, too."

"Right here." She reached into the cupboard and set the bottle on the table.

Ruby took the lemon wedge and ran it over Lillian's face, now pink from the heat treatment. "Now, this is strong stuff, so you always follow it immediately with apple cider vinegar," she said.

"Why?" Lillian asked.

Ruby set the wedge aside. "How does your skin feel with the lemon juice on it?"

"Kind of tight."

"That's why. It's not the proper balance for your face. But it only needs to be on for a second to do its job. Now, tip your chin up to me." Ruby finished off with a cotton cloth dipped in the apple cider vinegar and ran it over Lillian's face.

"The tight feeling is gone," Lillian said. "Will this really give me clear skin?"

"Part of what causes skin blemishes is what we eat. But, yeah, pretty much, it'll do the job."

Anastasia escorted Ruby to the door. "I can't thank you enough, sugar." The herbal formula for their monthly cycles, the tips she'd given Lillian just now, the girl was a godsend.

Ruby waved away her words. "When Tadashi gets back to town, I'll let you know how he likes my new look."

Phillip sat at his desk in the room just off his bedroom and sighed. He had to get Cradshaw to agree to let the railroad cross his land. It was just a sliver of his parcel, rocky as heck and nothing that the man could use for farming, so what was the big deal? The man was holding up the whole project.

There was talking outside. It sounded like a crowd.

What the devil was going on? Maybe Felicia was throwing a garden party and had forgotten to tell him.

He stepped over to the window and moved the lace curtain aside. Good Lord, there were people lined up on their front walk.

What the devil was going on?

He'd better find out and fast. He hurried down the hall and took the main stairs, stopping halfway down.

Amelda was manning the front door, ushering in a woman and her two children, both of whom had red noses and watery eyes. "Right this way, Mrs. Fields," she said.

They crossed the foyer and entered the front parlor.

He got to the first floor and hurried across the foyer after them.

Amelda threw out her arm, barring him. "They need their privacy, sir," she said.

Their maid was keeping him out of part of his own house? This was too much. Gone for three weeks and now his home was turned into some kind of boarding house? "What is going on here? Where's Felicia? Does she know about this, this ... mob? Who are those people in there, anyway?"

"It's Mrs. Fields. She lives a few blocks east of here. Her children are sick, sir."

That still didn't tell him why they were here. "And all those other people on our front walk? Who are they?"

"Everyone's here to see Miss Ruby," Amelda said. "They can't wait for her to go to the community garden to tend to them, so –" she made a can't-fight-city-hall gesture "– they've started coming here."

He crossed the floor and stared out the front window.

There had to be thirty people in a line that snaked around the block.

He turned back to Amelda. "How long has this been going on?"

The maid thought. "For a good week, now, sir. If Miss Ruby can't help them, she runs things past Miss Meifeng, that or she lets her dreams tell her what to do. Then they come back again the following day and she gives them their medicine."

His daughter was gaining a following in the community. "Well, I'll be damned."

Amelda bit her lip. "Begging your pardon, sir, but best not to tell Miss Felicia about this. She thinks Ruby is purely focused on reading and arithmetic while she's here."

Sure, like they could keep it from Ruby's mother for long. Lord knew, there'd be hell to pay once she found out.

Ruby rushed into the cabin and pulled the pouch off her shoulder. Was he here? Was he here? Yes, Tadashi was sitting on the floor. "I'm ready for my lesson."

"You seem happy."

That smile. She loved that smile. That tingle she always felt whenever she spotted him shot through her. Did he like her new look? "I brought you some presents." She pulled the ink bottles and a ream of paper out of the pouch. "Ta dah." She handed him the bottles, then the paper.

He looked puzzled. "Did you rob a store?"

"You're funny." She took the spot beside him and sat cross-legged. "Father has oodles of paper in his desk, I helped myself to some. He won't even notice." She waved away the notion. "Besides, if he does, I'll just buy him more. And ink is insanely cheap. I brought four bottles. Two for here at the cabin and two for you to keep in your tent. If you need any more than that, just let me know."

"I see." He set the gifts aside. "Let's get started."

Started? She was way ahead of him. She pulled out another sheath of papers, Chinese characters covered page after page. She flipped through them so he could see for himself how busy she'd been. "I've been practicing." More like forcing herself to commit the characters to memory so she would never embarrass herself in front of him again. "Go ahead, ask me to draw any of these characters."

"*Write* any of the characters," he said stiffly, correcting her. "This isn't an art class."

OK, write them. He sure was acting stuffy all of a sudden. She grabbed a quill and dipped it in the ink bottle. "Watch this."

She wrote out the symbols he'd shown her, one letter on each sheet of paper, finishing with a flourish. Ten characters. Ten sheets of paper. She dashed off one after another, flinging the paper at his chest as soon as she finished. This was fun. He had to be impressed. Finished, she looked up at him. *There, go ahead, congratulate me.*

"Impressive." But he wasn't smiling. "It's impressive that you get anything your heart desires."

Not everything. Not you.

He looked at the papers strewn around him and scoffed.

There was a pang in her heart. Something was wrong here, but what? Maybe ten characters wasn't enough. Maybe kindergarten kids in China picked up writing these things twenty at a time. "I can learn ten more by tomorrow," she said and instantly wished she could take it back. These had been tough. She'd convinced Grace to throw out two days of lesson plans so she could concentrate on doing these, even give her a quiz. But if she really concentra -

"Is it always this way?"

"What way?"

"You waltz into any shop in town and buy whatever you want? For you, it must be Christmas every day. Then you come here loaded with supplies and hand things out."

Now she got it. He was talking about the ten pots she'd purchased. "The men needed the cooking pots for their witch hazel treatments. It was the least I could do."

"And this?" Tadashi said sharply and held up one of the ink bottles.

"I told you, it was ridiculously cheap." And a heck of a lot easier than explaining the bill for the pots to Mother. "You said your ink bottle was almost out, remember?"

He scowled. "This paper, so much paper." He jumped to his feet and pointed at her. "You throw money around like you threw these pages at my face."

It wasn't at his face. "I thought you'd be pleased that I learned the symbols."

"Maybe you should think again. We're not American but we're proud people. We don't need some spoiled little rich brat coming here, handing out gifts and expecting us to praise her, to honor her. Yes, the men accepted your precious pots. They had to. They had no choice. They needed those pots. But praise? Honor? Keep waiting, little brat. Those things have to be earned." He stormed out.

Ruby waited in the lobby of the city council office. Would he believe her? Or would he throw her out? The dream had been so specific, she had to try.

Ross Wallace stepped through the door carrying a leather satchel. He nodded to the receptionist. "Good morning."

"Here's your mail, sir. And this young lady has been waiting for you."

He turned and spotted her. "Well, well, you're Phillip Fontinello's daughter. Did he send you?"

This wasn't the place for what she had to say. "If we could talk in your office?"

He escorted her down the hall, unlocked his office and ushered her inside. He set down his satchel and took his seat. "Have a seat. Coffee?"

"I'm here about your health, sir."

"Oh, that's right, you're the one who hands out treatments for people on the far side of the tracks."

And upper class people too.

"Admirable work, helping those kinds of people. I'm sure they appreciate it. So, how can I help you?"

"You have sores on your penis."

He jerked and his face became red. "I beg your pardon," he said, indignantly.

"Don't be ashamed."

"Young women shouldn't talk of such things."

"If you ate a better diet, your body could fight it off and eliminate it." But he was not one to follow the strict regime that her guides had shown her that last night. No, she would have to take another course of action with him. "They're painful, these sores, yes?"

"Young women shouldn't even *know* of such things. And to accuse me, of all people." He snapped his lapel. "You speak of indecent things."

There was nothing indecent about two people who were in love sharing that love in an intimate way. "I'm not here to judge you. I'm here as a healer. I can tell you how to keep it at bay, but you must do what I tell you every day and every night."

Wallace blinked quickly, reached in his drawer and pulled out a sweet, yanking off the shiny wrapper without taking his eyes off of her. "And I won't be bothered by it again?"

"You'll have to stop eating those." Sugar was the enemy here. "Things like that, and stress, will cause a flare up."

"I've heard you hand out herbs. Is it going to require tramping through the woods for miles to find some obscure plant that's about to go extinct?"

"It's actually right in your neighborhood apothecary. It's called hydrogen peroxide."

He scribbled it down and looked up with fear in his eyes. "If I ask for it, they'll know why. I'm a city councilman. I can't have people snickering behind my back."

"No, it can be used for many things," she assured him. "No one will know. Soak a small piece of cotton with the hydrogen peroxide and lie face down. Let the cotton sit for two minutes on the spot at the bottom of your spine, right where your butt cheeks start. There's a tangle of nerves there and that's how this disease travels. Let it soak into the skin for two minutes every morning when you get up and two minutes just before you go to bed at night. You can use it on the sores you have now to help heal them, too. But afterwards, keep them dry."

Wallace scribbled some more. "That's it?"

"That's it."

He eyed her and hesitated. "How much do I owe you for this advice?"

"I have no need for money. If you want, make a donation to feed the poor." She got up from her seat.

"And in two days I'll receive a letter demanding hush money. Is that what this is about?"

He did not understand. The world she knew didn't work that way. "There will be no letter, no demands, Mr. Wallace. I came here only to help you. Have a good day." She turned and left.

Ruby eyed the basket. They were running low on herbs. It had been a busy afternoon.

Beside her, Meifeng gestured for the last woman to come forward. She nodded with her usual wide smile. "How help you?"

One of these days, the Chinese doctor would drop her "me just China woman" act and surprise everyone with her ability to discuss politics and anything else in numerous languages, but it was her decision.

"Not you. I want to talk to her." Penelope Fitzgerald pointed.

Me? "Yes, Mrs. Fitzgerald?"

"You said my Jerry had whooping cough. But the doctor said it was croup."

"He did have whooping cough." She'd heard the distinctive intake of breath after he'd suffered coughing fit in front of her, she was sure of it. She'd prescribed taking garlic juice three times a day, but the boy had balked at the taste, so she'd switched him to a syrup of hot water with ginger and fenugreek with a dash of honey to make it sweet.

"He didn't get better under your care. The poor thing barely slept a wink, the phlegm was constricting his throat."

"How high did you have him propped up with pillows?"

"How was he supposed to sleep if he was sitting up? That's the silliest thing I ever heard of."

Silly? It was vital. "Mrs. Fitzgerald, that was to keep the phlegm from collecting in his throat while he slept."

Meifeng nodded. "She right."

Penelope put her arms akimbo. "He was so miserable, I had to give him ice cream every day to stop his crying."

It was the last thing she should have given him. "Mrs. Fitzgerald, dairy products are counter-intuitive with something like whooping cough."

"I told you, it wasn't whopping couch."

No, it had probably progressed to something far worse thanks to her faulty maternal instincts. But Penelope was a lost cause. Best to move this conversation forward. "How's little Jerry doing now?"

"Thanks to the doctor, he's recovered."

That was good news. "I'm confused. Is it *you* who needs to be seen today?"

"You're confused all right. No, there's nothing wrong with me. But if there was, I wouldn't come back to you people, not even if I was on my death bed. No, I only came to tell you that I contacted a reporter. I told them the whole story. The newspaper will have a feature on what a quack you are."

And the reporter hadn't contacted her to get her side of the story? Great.

Penelope Fitzgerald flounced off.

This whole fiasco could have been avoided and little Jerry would not have had to suffer more than was necessary. Ice cream. The woman was certifiable, giving it to a child with whooping cough, or with any cough, for that matter.

Meifeng eyed the line of people at the garden. There weren't that many today and it looked like all of them were from the slums. She watched Ruby as each person approached, half listening to what was said. Ruby knew what she was doing and when she wasn't sure, she would ask for a second opinion. Good thing her Chinese language skills were coming along, but, with so many medical terms, it could get iffy, so they still whispered to each other in English.

A high society lady was working in the garden. Another woman joined her. They both sent surly looks their way, threw their shoulders back, turned and left.

Something strange was going on here.

A newspaper page fluttered on the breeze. She snatched it before it flew away.

The headline screamed in large letters: So-called Intuit's Cure More Apt to Cause Harm: Misdiagnosed Whooping Cough Nearly Caused Innocent Child His Life – The Update.

How dare they, how dare they disparage Ruby in this way. Penelope Fitzgerald was behind this smear campaign, she had to be.

"I'll be back," she whispered.

Ruby stared at her. "Where are you going?"

She strode down the street, the paper in hand. She'd get to the bottom of this.

The horse-drawn trolley car got her downtown. She checked the masthead for the address and found the newspaper office.

Sacramento Star Register.

Sacramento Smear Register, if you asked her.

She stepped inside. It smelled of ink. There was a long counter.

A man in spectacles was sitting at a desk on the far side of it. He looked up quizzically, stood up and came over, a big man. He pulled off his spectacles. "Yes?"

"I'm here about this article." She jabbed the disgraceful piece of trash. "How could you print such a disgraceful piece?"

"I beg your pardon? Who are you, anyway?"

"This casts dispersions at a young woman who is years beyond your American so-called medical doctors. She is healing numerous people in the community and you take the word of one woman, one despicable, mean-tempered person, who wants nothing except to ruin Ruby Fontinello's reputation."

His eyes had a steely look. "We wrote her account as she stated it."

"Without covering the other side."

"What side?"

Ruby's side, you dumb ass. The side that knows the truth. "You never contacted the person who the article accuses of wrongdoing." She gestured at this disgrace they had the audacity to call a newspaper. "Doesn't she have the right to defend herself against this, this ... sleaze?"

The man drew himself taller and scoffed, waving her off like she was a pesky fly at a picnic. "Go away, old Chinese woman. We're busy here."

"You're not going to retract this? Not going to give Ruby a chance to redeem her name?"

He glared at her. "Get out or I'll throw you out." He leaned over the counter to be face to face with her. "And I promise you, it won't be pretty."

Meifeng glanced over at Ruby, who was across the cabin mixing herbs for their next visit to the garden. It would be getting cooler soon and their access to local plants would be cut off. They'd have to rely on her contacts overseas to ship them the proper ones. Odd that Ruby had known of apothecaries here and in San Francisco, using them for her own simple remedies, before the two of them had even met. And that talent of hers, dreaming of how to help people, a person like that didn't come along often.

They had a lot of work to do. Best to get going. "Ruby, you can do that later. Let's go collect herbs."

Ruby put away her work. The teen sure was being quiet lately. She did not look well. All weeklong she'd been listless, subdued. Her exchange with Penelope Fitzgerald was likely weighing on her mind.

"You feeling all right?"

Ruby didn't look up. "Yes."

The recent change in herbal formulas for the girl's mental issues could be at play here.

Aristolochia fangci was good for cell growth but it was a tricky herb to regulate. And it could cause complications of its own, severe ones, down the road. She'd hesitated to use it on Ruby, pondered it for days, especially considering her age. But the teen was past detoxifying and her brain needed a kick to start regenerating those brain cells. "Are you experiencing any stomach issues with this latest switch in herbs?"

"None."

"Sleeping well at night?"

"Yes."

That was a lie. She'd awaken to quiet sobbing in the middle of the night. It could be her parents were pressing her to return home. She could hear Felicia Fontinello now – "Quit this silly notion of learning Chinese herbs, where will it get you in life?" or, more likely, "Stop this childish notion that you can heal people without a proper education. Everyone knows medical school is only for men. Find yourself a husband and then you can dabble in this little hobby of yours." It had to be tough, being pulled in two directions, one way by her heart, the other way by her parents. "Let's head to the north meadow and gather herbs before there's a frost."

Ruby stepped on the porch and pulled on her boots. She was so pretty since she's begun adding a bump to her hair. It only added to her fresh, innocent appearance. Too bad there was no light in her eyes like before.

They had a good four hours of sunlight left. The meadow was a half hour's hike away. She grabbed her walking stick. "Let's go."

Meifeng cursed her age. Ruby may be subdued of late, but even though she hung her head, she tramped along automatically, her step was as quick as ever. It was hard to keep up. Thank goodness for her walking stick.

The meadow was just up a head. Finally.

There was a sound in the brush off to the side. The leaves of the undergrowth were moving, a squirrel or a chipmunk causing it, most likely.

The skunk waddled out. He was scrawny and his head moved from side to side as though searching for something. They weren't often spotted, tended to shy away from humans. Not this one.

"Go away, go on, shoo."

Ruby stopped. She turned. "What did you say?" She'd been so preoccupied with her thoughts, she'd probably never heard the brush move.

"It's a skunk."

"Let me see." Ruby came back to her. "Wow. I've never seen one before."

"Me, either." The last thing she wanted was to get sprayed. If they just let it pass, they'd be fine.

There was something wrong with this skunk. It had something in its mouth. It was moving its head side to side and panting as though it had been running.

She peered closer. That wasn't prey in its mouth, it was thick spittle hanging from its lips. The animal was frothing at the mouth. That meant -

Rabies.

"Ruby, stay away from it." She backed up, her back hit a tree trunk.

There was so little room for maneuvering here.

The animal snarled, it lurched closer, turning to look at one, then the other. It jerked as it tried to move. It was only four feet away.

Oh, no. It was going to attack.

The rabid skunk snarled. It found its target, locked on it and launched itself, teeth bared.

No!

CHAPTER SEVEN

There was light. It was so bright that it hurt.

Her head swam. Where was she? Why couldn't she focus?

"There, there." The voice was sluggish and the words were slow and drawn out, barely sounding human.

"Take it easy."

She knew that voice. At least, she should know it. But she couldn't place it, couldn't quite put her finger on it. Was it male or female?

She replayed it in her head.

It was neither.

There was movement. Everything looked white and distorted. Why couldn't she make anything out? It was like looking through milk. She squinted, trying to make out something, anything. There was a form swimming in front of her.

There were voices. She caught a word.

"Rabies."

Rabies? Someone had rabies and needed her help.

She thought back to her training. Rabies, rabies, what to use?

Skullcap. Yes, it had been used for centuries in China.

There were other herbs. Think, think. She had to help this person. If only her brain wasn't so befuddled.

Cumin. Peppercorns. Echinacea.

But ... in what measurements? In what order?

There was sound again. It seemed directed towards her. Those slow, drawn out words again. It took every bit of her strength to make them out.

"Just ...rest."

Yes, if she could just rest, perhaps she'd make sense of this and then she could help the person, whoever they were, who had contracted rabies.

She closed her eyes and let the nothingness engulf her.

Tadashi turned over so he was face down, trying to get comfortable. But he was in San Francisco again, acting as Mr. Fontinello's translator and this mattress was thin at best. He could feel the planks of the floor underneath it.

More workers for the railroad, that was all the man thought about. That's why he was here, so he could act as the man's assistant.

Too bad he wasn't allowed in the fancy hotels that Mr. Fontinello frequented. No, he always had to sit outside, watching the front entrance so he didn't miss Ruby's father, always from a hidden spot so the police didn't tell him to move along. Move along or prepare to get whacked with a baton. He'd learned that lesson a long time ago. Not that it helped last week. He'd been in Sacramento, waiting outside the Belmont Hotel when he'd fallen asleep.

The policeman had struck him in the arm with his baton. Hard.

Worse, Ruby had been coming around the corner and seen it. She'd stopped and thrown her hand to her chest.

He'd sported a nice welt from the baton. Worse than that was having Ruby witness his treatment at the hands of other whites. He'd felt her eyes on his back as he'd scurried away, red-faced. Of all the people to have witness his shame.

Tadashi ran a hand down his face. Yeah, it would have to be her.

He tried again to get comfortable. This was impossible.

Ruby. Every time he tried to close his eyes and go to sleep, he saw her face, saw those big eyes with those long lashes and ...that mouth. He wanted to kiss that mouth so badly.

He scoffed. He was only kidding himself. She probably never wanted to see him again.

He shouldn't have lashed out at her. The hurt had been evident in her face, the look of shock she'd had at his words. He'd regretted it immediately.

He'd called her a brat. Like she was a little kid.

Ruby was no little kid. Far from it.

He'd noticed the jutting peaks of her breasts as they pressed against her tunic, seen the curve of her hip when she'd bent over to tend one of the men in the encampment.

What she must look like naked.

There was a sudden twinge in his loins at the thought.

It was unlikely he'd ever know, not after the way he'd treated her. And the worst part was, he wasn't sure why he'd done it. She'd studied hard, learning the characters fairly quickly, especially for a Westerner. She'd come to show him what she'd learned, looking for his approval.

But had he complimented her? No.

Now, he was here in San Francisco trying to round up more workers for her father, and he couldn't even get word to her to say he was sorry.

She'd brought him paper and ink. They were precious in his world, hard to come by and to be used sparingly.

But not by Ruby. No, Ruby had slapped the ink on one sheet of paper after another and then flung them at him, practically laughing, like wasting paper was a joke.

His blood had boiled at ...

... at her? Not, not her. He'd been mad at her impudence, yes, but he didn't think he could never be mad at her.

Maybe, his anger wasn't do much about Ruby as what she represented. She had wealth, status, prestige. Those were things he could never achieve, not here in America, not in China. He belonged nowhere.

Ruby belonged everywhere.

He tossed in his bed. "She belongs here with me."

His hand slid down his flat stomach and between his legs to his penis. It was growing erect.

He stroked it, seeing her eyes, her lips. Those lips that he wanted to consume from the moment he'd first laid eyes on her.

He stroked it harder.

He saw her body. What would it be like to be tangled up with her? Rolling over a bed with her in his arms?

He stroked it harder.

Why did Ruby have to be so far away?

She belonged ....right ....here.

Felicia heard the voices. Something was going on outside.

She got up and stepped over the second story window. There were a few people coming up the walk. They were carrying things. A couple more people joined them, then more, until there was a line.

It had something to do with Ruby, she just knew it.

She hurried out into the hall and down the grand staircase. "Amelda, whatever do those people want?"

"Let me find out, Ma'am," the maid said. She opened the door and had a muffled conversation. She let two people inside.

Inept. Her entire household staff was inept. Letting just anyone inside like that. It looked like it was up to her to maintain the peace. Felicia stormed down the stairs. "And who are you, pray tell?"

The couple looked up. The woman was petite and in a shoddy dress. The man was in a suit that hung off him, obviously tailored for a man much larger.

He stepped forward. "We're the Abrams. Miss Ruby tended our little Charles when he had scarlet fever."

The woman pressed a basket into her hands. "Cookies for Miss Ruby. How is she doing?"

"She's still comatose. Meifeng is tending to her."

"Then she's in good hands."

Devoted hands, for sure. The Chinese woman was upstairs now, hadn't left Ruby's side since the Chinese men had carried her all the way from the far side of the mountain yesterday.

Ruby had been in a coma by then. Meifeng had said to expect it. It was the body's way of handling things such as this, she'd said.

But Meifeng was on her turf now and it didn't hurt to have an American doctor's opinion. She'd sent word with her housemaid right way for Dr. Smith, insisted that he come at once.

His two-horse carriage had pulled up an hour later and he'd hurried up the stairs.

Seeing Ruby lying on the bed, he'd opened her eyelids, shaken his head and made some tsk, tsk kind of noises. "She shouldn't have been out in the woods," he muttered.

"It's a little late for that kind of wisdom now, isn't it?" she'd nearly screamed at him. Instead, she'd bit her tongue and asked his prognosis.

"Not good, I'm afraid," Dr. Smith said. "You'd best make funeral arrangements."

Like hell. This was her only child.

Now, Meifeng was their only hope.

Her guides were showing her something. They took her down a hall. It was a very long hall with a perfectly arched ceiling. There were no lanterns, no windows, but somehow there was light everywhere. It was as though the air itself was infused with it.

The walls were cream colored and smooth. They and the arch were filled with markings.

Ruby stepped over to the wall on her left and peered closer.

Oh, they were Chinese characters. There were many, many characters, rows and rows of them.

This one called to her. It was beautiful in its simplicity with strong bold strokes and flourishes sprouting off of it.

Her arm automatically lifted, poised as though she had a quill in hand. She began drawing the symbol for herself in the air. One bold stroke down, then this one over here. It was suddenly so easy to write it, to embrace it. Nothing like when she'd struggled to learn the ten characters to impress Tadashi. One would have thought she'd encountered the symbol before, knew it to her very core.

She finished mimicking the strokes of the character.

A word suddenly blazed into her consciousness.

Cancer.

Ruby gasped and turned to her guides. "Is this symbol is for cancer?"

They nodded.

Had they told her or had the symbol itself told her? This was so strange. She looked at it again – cancer. She could see it, write it and speak it. She could understand it as though this were her native language.

She moved to another one and began writing it automatically in the air. The voice, no, not a voice, more of a realization, shot through her mind.

Bronchitis.

It could have been thunder booming, it was so startling, so commanding. And the comprehension of it was compelling in its naked truth. It was so complete that she didn't doubt for an instant what she was learning.

"Do you understand?" her guides asked.

"Yes. I want to learn more." She wanted to learn everything.

"You have time," they said and left her, disappearing as though they'd never been there.

Ruby turned back eagerly to the wall. There had to be tens of thousands of Chinese characters here for her to learn, stretching as far as the eye could see, just waiting for her to make them her own. It was a library of knowledge. Knowledge that came to her if she only paused before the symbols.

She wasn't thirsty. She wasn't hungry. She wasn't sleepy.

All she wanted to do was stay here and tackle this task, to soak in the meaning of every single symbol until she had them all absorbed.

Meifeng lifted her head off her arms and her eyes popped open. What was that sound? "Ruby?"

"How long have I been out?"

"Nine days."

"I learned so much." She sat up, smiling, looking peaceful. "Ask me anything."

The girl was obviously delirious. She needed to be checked out – her vision, her blood pressure. "How do you feel?"

"I mean it. Ask me anything, Meifeng. Ask me how to write 'heart attack' in Chinese."

She had no idea what Ruby was talking about. The girl only knew ten characters, simple words, every day words. None of them were medical.

Ruby threw the bed clothes aside, jumped out of bed and ran across the room.

Surely this was not the way normal rabies victims acted. "Slow down. Don't exert yourself."

Ruby waved away her concern, grabbed a sheet of paper from her desk and wrote quickly on it. She held up the sheet to show her handiwork. "See?"

It was the Chinese symbol for "heart attack."

And it was perfect.

Perfect in its execution. Perfect in its symmetry.

Meifeng stumbled over. "How do you know this?" Something had happened while Ruby was out. Something strange. And now Ruby was babbling excitely. Guides. Hallway. Characters everywhere. And instantly *understanding* every one of them.

Ruby laughed. "I know how to pronounce them. I know how to write them." She threw out her arms. "It's like the whole world has opened up for me. Your language is imprinted in my brain. More than that, I know everything there is to know about them. Noun phrasing. Relative clauses. Time principles. Serial verb constructions in sentences." She caught Meifeng by the shoulders and hugged her. "Do you know what this means for me?"

That you're truly The Healer.

Tadashi burst into the cabin and stopped.

Ruby turned. She looked as though nothing had happened to her.

He panted, trying to catch his breath from hauling-ass up the mountain as soon as he'd heard. "You're all right." He'd expected her to be restricted to her cot, a poultice on her chest, compress on her forehead, looking pale and sickly as though she was on death's doorstep. But from here she looked refreshed, bright-eyed and, damn, more beautiful than ever. "When your father got word you had rabies, we both thought –"

"That I was dead?" She shook her head. "Far from it."

Thank goodness. He crossed the room, had to see for himself. "We rushed to get here. Thank goodness your father has a stake in the railroad. We both got seats." It was the first time he hadn't had to ride standing up.

"He's back in town, then? He's probably worried silly." She shelved the book she'd been reading. "I'll have to hike down the mountain to see him."

Her perfume smelled heavenly. "I'm so glad you're OK."

"You are? But I thought –" She looked into his eyes.

Those lashes. He reached out to her and took her in his arms. "I have to apologize to you, Ruby."

She was pressed up against him. She fit perfectly.

"You're not a brat," he said. "I called you that. I didn't mean to. It just slipped out. I said it because I was mad." Oh, no, she might take that wrong. "Not at you," he hurried to say, "but what you have, how easy things must be for you."

"Easy?"

"You have money. You have status. I'm nothing more than your father's lackey, a mere employee, only useful because I speak English and can relay his orders to the men. I have no right to think you'd ever look twice at me, that you might consider me your equal or –"

"Stop." Ruby slipped a hand up between them.

Oh, no. She was going to push him away.

She pressed one finger to his lips and locked eyes with him. "Shhh." She tipped her face up and leaned in until her lips were pressed to his.

Her kiss was soft, searching.

He groaned and pulled her closer. This kiss, this kiss. He came up for air. "Oh, Ruby, I've wanted to do this with you for so long."

She blinked up at him. "I was miserable, thinking that you were angry with me."

Really? What a fool he'd been. He bent his head down, covered her lips with his. He explored her mouth with his tongue and never wanted to stop.

Ruby hurried down the street. Anastasia had sent word that Lillian was in a bad way, whatever that meant.

She rounded the corner and almost ran into a woman with a little tyke of about three in tow. "Oh, I'm sorry."

"Mommy, quit pulling me," he whined. The little boy's eyes were red. So was his nose.

A cold, maybe? No, his voice had not sounded scratchy. Allergies, more likely. "How long has he been like this?"

The woman jerked him closer, hiding him behind her skirt. "I beg your pardon."

"I can help."

"What are you talking about?" she demanded.

"Your child. He's got allergies. There are natural ways to achieve –"

"I know who you are. You're that weirdo." She pushed her boy farther behind her. "I read about you. Whooping cough, really? That was your diagnosis. A lot you know. Get away from us." She gave a snort. "You're a fake." She stormed off.

Ruby watched her leave. Stinging nettle would have helped. Or butterbur. But, no, her son would have to suffer needlessly. "Have it your way," she muttered.

That darned newspaper story. It was so unfair.

She got to Anastasia's house.

The door opened before she even knocked.

Anastasia grabbed her arm and pulled her in. She winced. "Lillian spent four days with a client and didn't have a chance to do her facial routine."

Not good. Someone like Lillian really couldn't afford to go even a day without cleansing her skin.

"To tell you the truth, I was afraid she wouldn't return." She shivered. "I heard from the place I used to work. They lost one of their girls."

What exactly did "lost" mean? "She went missing, you mean?"

"They found her body a week later."

She was killed. "Oh, my god." She'd never thought about how dangerous Anastasia's profession could be.

"She was a sweetheart."

So, she knew her. "Anastasia, I'm so sorry."

"But you're here about Lillian."

That's right. "Where is she?"

"Upstairs."

Lillian was in her room. She was sitting on her bed, head down. "Thanks for coming."

Ruby went up to her. "Let me see."

Lillian tipped up her chin.

Ouch. Not just acne. Cystic acne. It was bad, on both cheeks and her chin. She hoped the four days was worth it because Lillian wouldn't be seeing customers any time soon. The girl had full-on cysts and there was no hiding it. Cystic acne went deep and this was a bad case. "Let me guess. They started as regular pimples, then you poked and prodded them, didn't you?"

"Yes."

Lesson learned, this was what could happen if someone picked at their acne. "It'll take a few days, but everything you need to clear it up is here in the house."

Lillian brightened. "Really?"

Ruby turned to Anastasia. "I'll need a teaspoon of baking soda, a teaspoon of sea salt and two teaspoons of lemon juice in a small dish. Don't let the juice touch the other ingredients until you bring it here."

"Got it. Be right back." Anastasia hurried out.

Lillian eyed her suspiciously. "Will this really work?"

"Trust me." She patted her on the shoulder. "It's like the cucumber scrub, only this will attack the germs *under* the skin. Just be sure and keep it away from your eyes. Oh, and away from the under-eye area, too, unless you want to look like an old woman for the next couple of weeks."

Anastasia returned and set out the ingredients on the dresser.

Ruby mixed the first two ingredients then added the lemon juice.

"Look, it's fizzing," Lillian said. She dug in and rubbed it on her face. "I don't feel anything. You sure this will work?"

"Leave it on for about a minute and press it in. Then rinse it off with water."

Lillian nodded. "Follow it with the apple cider vinegar, right? How often should I apply this stuff?"

"Three times a day ought to do it."

She could whip up a tincture with zinc in it tomorrow and bring it by. Zinc could zap a zit overnight if you caught it early. She went to leave.

Anastasia stopped her just as she got to the door. "You sure it's nothing more serious?" she whispered. "I mean, nothing from ...you know, our profession?"

"Relax. It's just extreme acne. Nothing more."

Tadashi led Ruby through the trees. The stream with its little bubbling waterfall was just up ahead. He'd promised her a picnic at a special spot. Hopefully, she'd like it.

"Where are we going?"

"You'll see. Only a little farther."

They got to the clearing and he stopped.

Beside him, Ruby looked around in wonder. "This is so beautiful. How did you ever find it?"

So, she *did* like it. Good. "We can call it 'our' spot."

"No one else knows about this?"

"I stumbled across it. There doesn't seem to be a trail to it."

Ruby looked around. "Then, 'our' spot it is." She sat on a boulder. "Let's eat. I'm famished."

He pulled out the food. It wasn't much, not like the big meals she probably had in that big fancy house of hers in town. "What's it like to be rich?" he blurted. Oh gosh, that was rude.

"I don't really know. Mother likes being rich, She buys dresses and hats and all kinds of jewelry. Me, I just like simple things."

"Not hats and jewelry?"

"I'm not like most girls, Tadashi." She played with a leaf. "When I was little, I was kicked out of school. I always had tutors after that. They came to the house. Grace is my latest one. So, I never got out, well, not 'never'. I went to church of course, but I never had playmates, never had friends."

It sounded as though her upbringing wasn't all that different from his. "Meifeng pulled me off the streets of China when I was like, five," he said. "She tried to get me involved with school programs, but all the other boys picked on me."

"Why?"

With a face like this, you have to ask why? "It was obvious I wasn't Chinese, not even half Chinese. So, I had two strikes against me from Day One." No one had sat with him at lunch. No one had volunteered to be his buddy for team sports. "I looked different from everyone else. It was only when I took martial arts that I started earning respect." Respect, but not friends.

Ruby came over and ran her hand through his hair.

He loved it when she did that. She was so perfect, could it be that they were meant to be together?

She kissed him on his lips. "You're not alone anymore, Tadashi Moro."

Ruby was let in by Estelle Krofton's housekeeper.

"I'll go announce you."

The house was certainly well appointed. Mother had mentioned the Edwardian couch the Kroftons had ordered from that new business, Sears Roebuck and Company. That must be it in that room over there.

There were footsteps above her. Estelle appeared at the top of the staircase. "Ruby, forgive me, but can you come up here instead? I'm not feeling well enough to handle the steps."

"Of course." She hiked up the stairs two at a time. It was like climbing the mountain trail. She took the woman's arm near her wrist. Estelle's pulse felt fine, a little fast, but that wasn't a concern. "Let me help you back to your room. Which way is it? This room?" She stopped. "Oh, dear."

There vase was on the floor, broken into small pieces.

Estelle made a gesture. "I stumbled."

Charity appeared near them. She was a chubby little girl now, the choke cherry incident most likely a faded memory. "No, you didn't, Mommy. It was –"

"Never mind, go play."

Ruby got the woman to her bedroom, tucked her in and pulled up a chair. "Just why did you need to see me?" The note she'd received merely said, "Urgent."

"I have malaise."

"Can you be more specific?"

"I have no energy, can't seem to wrap my mind around things."

"What have you been eating lately?"

"Why would that have anything to do with it?"

"Humor me, Mrs. Krofton. What would be a normal day's intake for you?"

"The usual. Let's see, fried potatoes, bacon and eggs for breakfast, something like fried chicken for lunch, beef brisket for dinner. My cook makes *the* best beef ribs and her apple pie, oh, my, it's delicious. But then, that's why I hired her. She won a blue ribbon at the state fair for her pie, you know."

That was a reason to hire the woman, all right. As long as you didn't indulge in that pie often. "So, how's your appetite been?"

"No issues there."

She looked about fifty pounds overweight, maybe more. "How much water are you drinking?"

"I have coffee all day long."

"It doesn't affect your sleep?"

"Not if I stop by five in the evening."

"Bowel movements?"

She threw a hand to her chest. "I beg your pardon, young lady. We don't discuss such things in polite company."

"I'm not here on a social visit, Mrs. Krofton. You requested that I come to help you, remember?"

"Well, I guess. I, um, don't 'eliminate' as properly as I should."

"Meaning?"

"They're very loose."

Not good. "Stick out your tongue. OK, now move it right then left." The sides were affected, indicating the gallbladder, spleen and kidneys were not functioning fully. The back of the tongue was also showing distortion. That meant the liver was in trouble.

There was a rash on her arms. With all that waste trying to make its way through her system, and not enough hydration to help it move along, the rash was no big surprise. She could treat the symptom with a skin-soothing remedy but it would have no effect on the underlying cause. What else was going on here? "Look out the window, please," she said.

There was a light blue ring around the iris of the eye where it met the white part, the sclera, Meifeng had called it. Estelle Krofton's blood was being clogged with cholesterol, first discovered in the late 1830s. The skin under both eyes had tiny white masses noticeable just below the skin. "Have you developed any moles?"

"Now that you mention it, yes."

"Do you have heart palpitations?"

"How did you know?"

"Extended stomach?"

"Yes, and I just can't imagine why."

It was another classic symptom.

There was a bowl of candies on the nightstand. No wonder her breath smelled so sweet.

"What did your doctor say was the problem?"

She hesitated. "I only sent word for you to come."

That was bending the truth. Everyone knew Estelle Krofton had travelled to see every doctor in the county.

She could give the woman a mix of peppermint, chamomile and ginger, but that didn't address the underlying reason for her distress – Estelle's daily diet. The woman was sending herself to an early grave and making each day miserable for herself. Ginseng would help her energy level. She reached in her pouch, measured out the herbs in the right proportions and mixed them together. "Make a tea using one tablespoon. Drink this three times a day. Cut out the fried foods and the dessert."

"No pie?"

All right, she'd cut her some slack. "Once on the weekend is fine. Think of it as a reward for being good the rest of the week." She'd given her enough herbs to last two weeks. "Come see me when this runs out." More likely the woman would call her to her home again. High society people didn't want to come to the community garden and be seen consulting with someone who was not an American-trained doctor, especially not after that newspaper article. "I'll let myself out."

Ruby stepped onto the Kroftons' wide porch.

Charity was there on the swing.

"You doing OK? Worried about your mom?"

"Yeah."

Here was a chance to find out a little more. "Your mother said she drinks coffee all day. *All* day, really?"

"That's not what she has. She fills her coffee cup from a wine bottle."

Things made more sense now.

Ruby sat up and stretched her back. She'd been leaning against the cabin wall and her shoulders were killing her.

The light was fading. She must have been reading for hours.

She read the final words and closed the medical book with its embossed and stylized caduceus on the cover. The wall of books loomed above her. One book down. Only a gazillion more to go. Her guides may have taught her to read and speak Chinese, but it was up to her to learn medical techniques and how to apply them.

Hold on a moment. Meifeng had her on a new set of herbs, but from what she'd just read, maybe there was a way to speed up the process. Where was that book? The one Meifeng had said dealt with brain issues?

She scanned the shelves. No, not that. Not that one.

There it was, way up there. She got out the ladder and climbed it. She pulled the book off the shelf and read through the introduction.

Yes. This was it, this one right here.

She climbed down and began flipping through the pages. This part sounded like it addressed brain cell regeneration. No, better not jump to that part. What if there was something in the chapters before that, things that warned of what *not* to do? She'd better read it cover to cover, just to be sure.

She went back to her reading spot, lit a lantern and hunkered down.

Chapter One. The Amazing Human Brain. Here we go.

She began reading.

The door opened.

Now it was completely dark outside. She must have been reading this new book for at least two hours.

Meifeng came in. "What are you doing?"

Ruby marked her place and set the book aside. "I'm going to cure myself."

"You mean, be your own doctor?" she paused. "Do you think that's wise?"

"Don't worry, Meifeng, I'm not going to do anything without consulting you. But I just wonder if there's a cure in one of these books, something that applies to me." She looked up at the wall of tomes. Maybe that one on acupressure. She'd have to read it. "If there is, then I'm going to find it." The answer *was* there, she could feel it.

Tadashi tiptoed into the inner office and spotted paperwork on Philip Fontinello's desk. This was what he'd hoped to find, right here.

He scanned the order. Another weekend that the men would have to work, was Mr. Fontinello serious? They hadn't had a day off in three weeks. This couldn't continue. The men were near revolt already.

There were voices. Someone was coming.

He dropped the order, dashed out of the office and pulled up a chair by the secretary's desk. He struck a pose of boredom as though he'd been waiting all this time. Maybe he should whistle under his breath. No, that would be over doing it.

The secretary, Jerold Fulcom, stepped in from the hall and spotted him. The man hated his guts. "Where did *you* come from?" he said with a sneer.

"Mr. Fontinello sent me to get the surveyor's plans for the north corridor."

"I doubt that very much. The only one who gets to see those is me and I won't let them out of my sight."

He pushed off the desk. "The order came from the top."

"Get out."

The man was a major thorn in his side. He was preventing him from carrying out the orders of his boss. "He won't be happy when I return empty handed."

"That's your problem."

"I'm telling you, Mr. Fontinello won't like this. He wants those plans."

"Scram."

This was ridiculous. Phillip Fontinello needed those plans. "I'll get them myself." He strode across the room and opened the cabinet. They were in here somewhere.

"Oh, no you don't." Fulcom hurried over. "I said, 'Scram.'" He slammed the cabinet door closed.

"Ouch, my hand!"

"Too bad. Leave right now or I'll have you arrested."

"For what? I'm just doing my job."

Fulcom smiled. "I'll think of something. Assault or robbery, maybe. Whatever I decide, it'll be my word against yours. Who are they going to believe?"

So, that was how it was going to be, huh? "Fine, I'm leaving." He turned and walked out. He stood on the sidewalk thinking. Shoot, now what was he going to do, go face Ruby's father and admit he couldn't complete a simple task? The man would fire him on the spot.

He hated this, hated the way he was treated by some people as less than the man he was. He was educated. He had brains. But the color of his skin and his features branded him as an outsider, someone to be distrusted. Stupid Americans. Sometimes he hated it here.

Someone was coming up behind him. It was probably that damned Fulcom. He wanted a fight? He'd show him a fight.

Tadashi swung around.

It was Ruby.

"Oh, it's you." He checked the forward momentum of his fists and quickly lowered them. "Sorry. I didn't know who was there."

"Is everything OK?"

Now that you're here, it is. "You're father's not here."

"It's not my father I wanted to see." She beamed. "What are you doing here?"

"I came to get something to take to your father. But it looks like I'm going back empty handed." He told her about Fulcom stopping him from getting the surveyor's plans. "He nearly smashed my hand, too."

She reached out, took his sore hand and soothed it with hers.

Such a gentle touch. He could get used to this.

"Better?"

"Much."

"For the north corridor you said? Wait here." She stepped inside.

"Ruby, don't –" Too late. She was gone. Great, she'd tell Fulcom he was being mean and that she was going to tell her father on him. He could hear it now.

He paced the sidewalk, eyes on his feet. If he couldn't get those plans, he'd be in big troubled.

Ruby came back outside. She had the plans. "Here you go."

He took them. "What did you say?"

"I asked him to fetch me a newspaper from down the street." She smiled at him. "Fulcom's always been a little afraid of me. I knew he wouldn't refuse."

So, she'd set him off on an errand while she filched the plans. Brilliant. "I don't know how to thank you."

"Let's hurry to the train station before Fulcom figures things out." She pulled him away and they scampered off. When they got around the corner, she slowed down.

He liked walking beside her. If only they could hold hands. It would scandalize the whole town and everyone would be talking about it. Ruby would get the brunt of it.

"Want to know why Daddy's secretary is afraid of me?" Her eyes were bright. "When I was, like six years old, I walked up to him and point blank asked him why he was peeing blood. Scared the hell out of him."

That's right, Meifeng had said Ruby "knew" things about others' health. "He was peeing blood? That would scare me, too."

"It wasn't blood. Turns out he was drinking this juice blend made in some factory and whatever dye they were using was coming out in the urinary tract."

Tadashi hid a grin. "Guess he didn't appreciate being told that, huh?"

"Not in front of the preacher, he didn't."

He chuckled. Somehow, just being with Ruby always made him feel better.

"I really didn't fit in as a kid." She lost her smile. "That's why Mother insisted I have tutors. I'd be doing my studies, hear other kids outside playing and I'd hurry over to look out the window. I wanted to play, too, you know? But I never could."

No one had wanted to play with him when he was growing up. He wasn't Chinese. He wasn't Japanese. He wasn't American. He was this weird foreign mix they'd never encountered before.

"And then, for the longest time, Mother made me wear these gloves."

"Like, to church, you mean?"

"No, all the time. Day and night. Finally one of my tutors put her foot down, said they were interfering with my lessons and I finally got to take them off. But I was, what, eight or nine by then. Still, it was heaven being free of them."

Now she that she was a teen, she was an outsider for preferring to wear a tunic and cut-off pants and for learning healing ways from Meifeng.

Ruby, this beautiful girl walking beside him, was probably the only person on the earth who could truly understand who he was.

Ruby looked up from reading her medical text.

Meifeng was stirring a tiny pot, staring into it as though she was about to fall asleep.

She set the book aside and went over to her. "Are you feeling all right?"

"Tired, is all."

"Sit down. I can mix the herbal teas." She helped her to a floor mat. The Chinese doctor never had been one for chairs. Maybe that needed to change. The woman hadn't grown up in a Chinese slum, for goodness sake.

Ruby stirred the tea, then pulled it away from the flames. It smelled so different. "I don't recognize this fragrance. What is this?"

"Wormwood."

Her heart lurched. Wormwood was for cancer. She hid her reaction. "Maybe I'll have some with you."

"If you want, sure."

So, did that mean it *wasn't* for cancer? Or just that it was all right for anyone to drink? "Is it purely wormwood?"

"No, there's some astragalus and licorice root in there, too."

Ruby poured out two cups and handed one to Meifeng. She sat beside her on the floor. "You work too hard." And she'd been having coughing fits of late. "Let me take over mixing the formulas."

Meifeng nodded.

That in itself told her the old woman was feeling her age. "There's no need for you to go down to the garden three days a week, either. I can handle things."

"Two heads are better than one for discerning people's illnesses."

"I'm an intuitive, remember?"

"Even an intuitive may never know the full extent of an illness or how far along it is."

"Like your arthritis?"

"Yes, and you don't want to over treat someone. It's all about balance."

Good point. "How many intuitives have you trained to heal with Chinese medicine, Meifeng?"

She sighed. "Two. No, three others, besides you."

"But they were all Chinese, right?"

Meifeng nodded. "None of them went on to train with Bojing, though."

She'd never heard the name before. "Who is that?"

"Bojing? He lives in Shanghai. He is the Medicine Man Most High in all the land. Only the best get to train under him."

"Really?" *I want to train under him.*

"He takes intuits under his wing, if they're good enough, that is."

She drew her shoulders back. "I'm good enough."

"Are you?"

Of course she was. She'd cured old Mr. Finney's tinnitus, hadn't she? And Edith Sedgewater's arthritis was under control, thanks to her. "I'm as good as any of your former students."

Meifeng coughed. It sounded phlegmy.

Time to play doctor and help her patient. "Finish your tea, Meifeng, and then let's get you to bed. You need to rest."

Meifeng went to answer and suddenly jerked and clutched her chest.

She gasped for air.

Her eyes glazed over.

Meifeng collapsed to the floor.

CHAPTER EIGHT

Ruby jumped up. "Omigod, Omigod, what do I do? Meifeng, wake up. Meifeng!" She shook her shoulder.

No response.

This was bad, real bad. "Meifeng, wake up." She wrung her hands. "No, no, no, don't die."

Ruby stared at Meifeng's listless form. Was she dead?

She shook her again.

Nothing.

She shook her harder. "Meifeng!"

Still nothing.

The tears threatened. "Please wake up," she cried. "Please don't die on me."

Meifeng opened her eyes and sat up. She shook her head. "No, you're not good enough. Not yet, anyway."

Ruby swung by Anastasia's. She knocked.

The door swung open. A girl in a silky robe that barely covered her thighs eyed her. She'd come to the garden a couple of times.

"You're not my Paulie-poo." She stretched her neck out, trying to see down the street without stepping outside. "Is there a man coming this way?"

"I didn't see anyone, sorry. Is Anastasia here? Or Lillian?" She wanted to see how the tincture was doing. If she'd made it too strong, it could cause dry skin and peeling.

The girl went to the bottom of the stairs and hollered up, "Lillian. That herbal gal is here."

Lillian came down in a similar outfit. Her face looked clear. "Ruby, you can't stay here, the train workers usually pull in about now. They're due any minute."

"I brought you more zinc tincture," she said and pulled out a small jar. "It's working, yes?"

"I'll say, except the other girls keep stealing it from my dresser top."

There was a wailing sound from the kitchen.

They all hurried over.

Anastasia was carrying Buster. He was limp in her arms. There was blood coming from his mouth.

It was a sign of internal bleeding. Her heart lurched. "What happened?"

Anastasia cuddled him. "He got away from me. The trolley cart ran over him." She began sobbing. "He's hurt bad."

Worse than bad. She had to have a look. Ruby reached out. "Give him to me."

He weighed seven or eight pounds, he was so tiny. His eyes were closed. He wasn't breathing. She pressed her ear to his chest. No heartbeat. "I'm sorry, Anastasia, he's dead."

Her friend wailed as Lillian wrapped her arms around her. "He was such a cute little guy."

"I know and you loved him," Ruby said. "I can bury him in the woods, lay him to rest there." That's where he belonged, not in some house, stuck in a cage.

Anastasia nodded. "You'll show me where his grave is so I can visit him?"

"Of course."

Lillian gave Anastasia a hankie. "Wipe your tears. Our guests will be arriving soon."

Ruby bade them goodbye and went out the back door. She carried the little monkey up the mountain. The poor thing had been captured, probably stripped from its mother's arms and sold, winding up on some dock in San Francisco. Then someone had bought it, or won it in a poker game, more likely, and ended up at Anastasia's house of prostitution. She wondered how long a life it had led. Probably only a few years by the looks of him. But, what did she know about monkeys?

She left the carcass on the porch, removed her shoes and went inside.

Meifeng was there, treating one of the Chinese railroad workers.

Ruby waited until they were done and when he left, said, "Do we have a shovel?"

The doctor paused. "Somewhere. Why?"

She explained about the monkey. "I thought overlooking the meadow would be a nice spot to bury him."

"Did the sight of his blood bother you?"

What a strange question. "No."

"Do you know monkey bodies are, basically, ninety-five percent similar to ours?"

Maybe she thought there had been a way to save Buster's life, that she should have used her medical knowledge of the human body to patch him up. "You don't understand. He was already dead by the time I saw him."

"Really? All the better then." Meifeng stepped outside, retrieved the body and placed it on the kitchen counter. "Watch and learn." She went to a cupboard and brought down a thin case. When she opened it, eight shiny little knives, sheathed against the felt that lined the interior, glistened in the light.

They were scalpels.

Ruby stepped closer and brought the lantern. "Show me what to do."

Ruby peered closer at the body of the little monkey.

Meifeng had the body cavity opened up.

"How do you know all this?"

"I did autopsies in China." She stopped and hurried to say, "You must never tell anyone."

"Surely, it was part of your education."

"It's forbidden in China," Meifeng said. "Some of us thought that books are fine but working hands-on style is better for learning."

So, her mentor had bucked convention by secretly learning more than her counterparts. Good for her.

Meifeng began identifying the organs. "Heart, see how small? And lungs. Only the left lung has an upper and lower lobe." She pointed. "See the delineation?"

"Yes. Fascinating."

"This is the liver." She frowned. "Oh dear, this little guy digested a lot of bad food." She used the point of her knife to draw a line along the skin where she'd cut open its belly. "Look right here. Look at all this fat."

It was noticeable, and right there, sandwiched between the outer layer of skin and the white, inner membrane that separated it from the muscle.

"The thyroid is swollen," Meifeng said, pointing with her scalpel. "See here? It's probably a third larger than it should be."

"Meaning, what?"

"Iodine deficiency, possibly. Iodine helps the thyroid function. Sea kelp is a very good source of iodine used my country, so are fishes, but it's not likely he got any here in Sacramento. Do you know what it was fed?"

Human food, from what she'd seen. "Whatever the girls were having. I know it craved eggs." But Anastasia had refused to give him any more after the food had made for a rather gaseous atmosphere.

"Eggs are high in iodine, so that makes sense. The body naturally craves what it needs." Meifeng sighed. "It would have eaten bananas if the poor thing were living in the wild, another food with iodine."

But bananas were a delicacy here, pretty much only available in San Francisco. By the time they were transported inland, they were so spoiled as to be inedible. No, poor Buster never got to eat a banana once his life's path brought him to Sacramento.

The organs were fascinating to see, this was so much better than just reading about them in the medicals books. The drawings didn't allow her to get a full understanding of them. But this was up close and personal. Something was drawing her to look at one in particular, as though a big arrow was getting her attention. "That's the pancreas, right?"

"Yes."

"For some reason, I want to say it has issues. Like, it's too small." It was all she could do to keep from taking the knife out of her mentor's hands and dissecting it on the spot. It was as though her guides were standing behind her, watching over her shoulder. She could feel them there, urging her on.

Meifeng prodded the organ. "You know, I think you're right. And it appears inflamed, too."

"Cut it open."

"Why?"

Because my guides say to. "Just do it."

Meifeng drew a line down the organ and spread it apart.

There were gall stones.

But that wasn't all they were telling her was wrong. "Now cut here and here," she said, pointing.

Meifeng cut and drew back. "Oh, my." She looked at Ruby. "Cancer." She prodded at the mass. "Look how deep it's hidden."

So *that's* what cancer looked like, a mass that was red and ugly and taking over the body's tissues as it grew out of control. She wouldn't wish it on anyone, not even her worst enemy.

Poor little Buster. How he must have suffered.

The killer entered slipped back to his house. He'd been a bad boy again. He'd been to the whorehouse, the one with the pretty girl.

She'd been so soft, so enticing. A thrill courses through him, remembering all the things she'd done to him.

You were with that filthy whore again.

The voice. It was back.

You're a bad, bad boy. She's a bitch and you let her lure you into her lair. You for it, hook line and sinker.

He felt shame. The vice was right. What had he done?

He'd debased himself so sinful pleasure. He'd tried to resist. Honest he had.

But she pulled you in.

Yes, she did it. It was her fault. She made herself pretty on purpose. She put that rose-colored paint on her lips. She'd slipped out of her clothes like it was the easiest thing in the world. Like she enjoyed it.

It could only mean one thing: She was the devil.

All of them in those houses were devils.

That's right. You need to teach those whores a lesson.

He would, too. But they were cunning, appearing to be women when they were actually from Satan's lair. He'd have to be cunning. He'd have to outsmart them at their own game.

It would take some planning, but he would take them out.

Ruby hurried down the street. Daddy was having stomach problems again. He was working too hard. This mix of ginger and cinnamon should help. Lord knew, he'd balked at the taste of the dandelion brew she'd first given him.

She entered the railroad office building.

Jerold Fulcom was at his desk. He flinched when he noticed her. "Miss Ruby," he said, giving her a curt nod. He squirmed in his hard wooden chair.

Hemorrhoids.

She could tell him how to ease them – witch hazel compresses and applying jing wan hong –but after the way he'd treated Tadashi, he deserved to suffer. "Is Daddy here?"

"In his office."

She crossed the room and, giving a brief knock, entered.

Daddy had company. It was Tadashi. They were both standing before a map that was tacked on the far wall.

She ducked her head. "Sorry to interrupt. I'll just wait until you're done." She took a seat and tried to occupy herself but instead kept stealing glances at Tadashi's backside. He cut such a lean figure, so tall, so straight. At the encampment, he towered over the Chinese workers. Maybe that was partly why they respected him. No doubt, his education made them look up to him, too.

Daddy used a pencil to point to something on the map. "So, we need to complete this section on schedule. No excuses."

Tadashi marked something on his clipboard. "Understood. I'll increase the number of men we have there to ensure it's done on time. Twenty more ought to do it." He hesitated. "I need to bring your attention to something. There's a stretch of caliche in this area here." He pointed. "The men can chip through it but it's time consuming and, to my mind, unnecessary."

"Damn it." Daddy ran a hand down his face. "Are you suggesting that we route around it?"

"No, I want to move Liwei there, temporarily."

"One man? What will that do?"

"He's got explosives experience. He said he can rig it in two or three days and –"

"Why not one day?"

"You have to find the vein and follow it. Otherwise, you're wasting your resources. Find it, rig it and blast it and you don't have to go back and retrace your steps."

Daddy considered his words. "OK, go ahead and get him there. Make sure he has extra explosives on hand, in case another vein shows up."

Tasdashi made a note. "Now, you wanted me to order materials to build the bridge at Breakneck Forge. But according to this map, you also plan one built at Foster's Creek."

"Yes, that's at two or three months down the road."

"But if you order the materials for both at the same time, you'll get a better price. Get the estimate for the first one, then come back and say, 'I've got a second job for you if you work with me.' Use it as leverage to keep your costs low."

Good looking and smart. I knew it.

The two men seemed to be finished. Ruby stepped forward. "How is your stomach?"

"It's bothering me again."

Tadashi sent her a smile, took his paperwork and left.

Did he have to go? Maybe she'd see him later on the mountain. "I'm going to make you a tea, Daddy."

"Not that dandelion stuff again."

"You'll like the taste of this one, I promise. Take a seat." He smelled of rose water. Mother must have a new perfume and they'd pressed against each other to kiss goodbye. She let her hand hover over his abdomen. She felt nothing. *Thanks a lot, guides.*

Meifeng had warned her of treating her family and trying to ascertain things through her ability. It was like a barrier because one was too close to them emotionally, she'd said. She wondered how doctors diagnosed people without having the extra assistance of feeling issues with their hands, she'd come to rely on it so much.

"Does it come on at certain times?"

"Whenever I eat. It's like a slow burn."

"Let me get a cup of hot water." She took his mug and went down the hall to where a tea pot was on the stove. Excellent, it was boiling. Herbs and plants gave up their essence better when the water was super-hot.

"Psst."

She turned. It was Tadashi, tucked just around the corner like he was hiding from someone. She hurried over. "What are you doing?"

"I just wanted to see you."

I wanted to see you, too.

"Will you come to dinner tomorrow tonight at my tent?"

This was unexpected. "Yes, I'd love to."

"Can't claim to be the greatest cook, but I try." He gave her a quick kiss, turned and was gone.

Dinner. With Tadashi. Tomorrow night. And he'd just kissed her. A thrill coursed through her. She couldn't wait.

She hurried back to the stove and poured the boiling water into Daddy's cup.

There was something on the floor, a piece of paper. It was where Tadashi had stood. He must have dropped it because it hadn't been there when he'd first gotten her attention. Maybe it was important.

She snatched it up.

It was a telegraph request form. Orders from Daddy. "Reroute six cars of railroad ties to Kansas City."

To Kansas? That didn't make sense. Daddy had once said he'd never try to expand farther east than Nevada, that the market was too tight. She looked closer. It was from Daddy's desk. But that wasn't Daddy's signature. Close, but not quite.

This could only mean one thing.

Tadashi was purposely undermining Daddy's railroad business.

When she arrived at the garden, Ruby spotted her recent patients in line, there for checkups.

Charles Withers had sustained a broken arm from his work at the stables. She'd set it and given him ginkgo biloba to boost the oxygen levels in his blood and help promote healing. "Get plenty of rest," she'd told him. "Your body heals at night when the systems are at rest."

Little Caroline Duchesney had been stung by a bee. She'd crushed a clove of garlic and put it atop the site, then followed it with yellow dock mixed with baking soda.

Edna Vichellia had complained of thickening ankles. It was fluid retention. Fu ling was in order. It wasn't just a diuretic, it was good for the woman's insomnia.

Mable Pope was eighty, bless her heart, and had developed arthritis in her fingers and it was too painful for her to crochet anymore. For her, a careful mix of boswellia and cat's claw to ingest, with a topical approach of a eucalyptus compress and heat for the swelling.

Douglas Stubbins had asthma symptoms. Bishop's weed had been her good choice for him to help control it, with lobelia for when he experienced an attack.

Half of these people had come to her after modern medicine had proven ineffective. Perhaps now they understand that Mother Nature provided treatments for most anything that ailed them.

But the line was short again. Maybe people were getting a slow start to their day lately.

She took off her sling pouch and laid out her herbs. "Who's first?"

A woman stepped forward. "I've heard about you. They say you know things about people." She lifted her chin and stuck her arms akimbo. "Prove it."

Her first patient of the day and it would have to be someone who challenged her before she even got into the rhythm of her work. She hated people like this. They came looking for miracles and quick fixes and they went home and didn't follow her advice about eating plant-based meals or take her remedies on schedule.

Fine, you want a sideshow, you'll get a sideshow.

Ruby sighed, rubbed her hands together and calmed her mind. *Guides, help me with this one, please.*

Here went nothing.

She stepped forward and ran her palms slowly in front of the woman, about five inches away from her clothes. "You've given birth at least four times."

The woman flinched.

"Your eating habits are horrible, hardly any raw fruits, hardly any vegetables. Wow, you sure like pies and baked goods. You have them every day. You never get a good night's sleep and your breathing is labored by the time you've climb the stairs to the second floor."

The woman also had an inflamed liver and a long, snaking parasite living in her gut. But tell her that and she'd be accused of devil worship or some such thing.

The woman dropped her arms. "So ... what do I do?"

"For one thing, your eating habits have to change starting today."

She pouted. "But, but I love cream puffs and pies and turnovers."

"Cut your intake in half, then taper off over a month until it's only once a week."

"Once a week? Nooo."

She sounded like a petulant child. And the woman was, what, forty?

"Think of it as your Sunday treat for being good the other days of the week." No one she'd tended to could go cold turkey when it came to sweets. It was as though sugar was an addiction. "I'm going to give you items for a tea. Drink it twice a day, first thing in the morning before you have anything else, then again just before you go to bed."

She turned to her pouches. Let's see, the parasite could be killed with garlic, clove, thyme and black walnuts with both the meat and hull minced up. Oil of oregano was another kill-all for bacteria, fungus and viruses. If she added Chinese golden thread, it would take care of any yeast issues. The mixture would have to be just so or the woman could have an adverse reaction. She eyed the woman to judge her weight and measured out the herbs and gave her final instructions. "This should last you a month. Come back after that and we'll see how you're doing."

The woman hesitated. "You know, I read about you but I came anyway. This had better work."

Don't put it on me. "You're the one who will decide that. You didn't get this way overnight. Follow my instructions and it will. Slack off and it won't." She hated sounding harsh but she couldn't be there to babysit people.

The woman reminded her of Estelle Krofton. She'd been drinking daily. No wonder that the sides of her tongue had indicated distress in the liver. Drunks were notorious for their poor balance. That would explain the broken vase, though Charity had disputed exactly how it had happened. Not much she could do for the woman if she kept consuming the alcohol.

At least her other patients were doing well.

Another newbie, a woman, stepped up. "The newspaper said you misdiagnosed a boy." She held it out, the headline screaming from the front page.

Ruby stared. She swallowed away the sting of the words. "So, if you're a skeptic, why are you here?"

"Because you gave my grandmother things to take last year and now she claims she's cured, that she's never felt better."

Finally, a person who believed after seeing results. "Let's get to work. How can I help you?"

Tadashi set the lantern by his cot. No, maybe it should go over here. No, then it would be in the way. Perhaps over here. Yes, that was better. He wanted everything to be perfect for when Ruby arrived.

"Knock. Knock."

She was here. His heart sped up. He hurried over and yanked the flap aside, gesturing her in. "You found it. I was worried."

She looked so pretty. "Smells wonderful."

He'd only fussed over it, trying to decide on something he could pull off without making a mess of everything. "I warned you about my cooking." Where were his manners? "Can I offer you some tea?"

"Yes, thank you." She looked around.

Maybe she was judging him by what he owned. His belongings were few but maybe Ruby could appreciate how neat he kept his tent. He was the only one in the encampment without a roommate. He'd pushed his cot off to one side. It was where he slept. Naked. Thinking of her. His face heated up. "Here's your tea." He passed her the tiny cup with no handle.

Their hands touched.

Wow. Had she felt the shock, too?

She accepted the chamomile tea and sipped. "Tell me how you came to be here."

"Meifeng brought me with her from China. I thought you knew that."

She sat on the floor mat. "So, did you plan to come here first? I mean, there had to be other places she could have set down roots and practiced medicine."

He'd never really thought about it. "We were in San Francisco for a while, but then the railroad construction brought us here." The railroad workers had, actually. Meifeng was nothing if not obsessive about seeing to their health. Yet, the doctor also healed the townspeople. "So, how do you like it here?" Gosh, that sounded dumb.

She sent him a smile. "I like the company."

Him, she meant.

He scooped the meal out of a pan. Roots, mushrooms, carrots with a glaze. He added rice, eying her to see how much she wanted, then handed the plate to her. "Tell me what you think."

She took a bite. "Hmmm, teriyaki. Delicious."

It was the only dish he knew how to make. Thank goodness he'd pulled it off.

"A man who could cook, who knew?" she teased. "What do you like to do in your spare time?"

"When I have extra time, you mean?" There wasn't much of that, not the way the Fontinello company operated. He spooned out his own plate and took a seat on the mat opposite her. "Reading history, I guess. What about you?"

She ignored the question. "How did Daddy come to hire you?"

"He needed somebody who spoke both languages to act as a go between."

"But why you, why not someone else?"

So many questions. "I just happened to be in the right place at the right time."

"He's said you're invaluable to him. Why do you think he said that?"

"Well, because he trusts me." He looked down at his plate. He liked to think Phillip Fontinello could confide in him and teach him things about the business. His job could be a juggling act, trying to keep both sides happy. The men complained that they work hard, real hard. Truth be told, he didn't know how they could swing those heavy hammers, pounding in tie nails all day long.

But the company only looked at the bottom line. Work harder, faster, longer. It had ordered them to give up one of their two days off each week. Then, it had cut the finish date down to the bone. Like the men didn't already work at one hundred percent effort. What did they want? Blood? Phillip Fontinello was a good man, yes, but he answered to his investors and his investors wanted the rail lines up and running so goods could be moved and money could be made. He'd tried to impress on his boss how the men needed some slack. He'd agreed to take it under consideration, but then the investors had contacted him again, demanding results. He'd seen their telegrams, read the tone that underlined their clipped words. "I like to think I'm his best advisor."

Ruby lost her smile. "So, why are you sabotaging his plans?"

His head shot up. "What are you talking about?"

She pulled out a piece of paper. "This."

Crap. It was the order to reroute rail ties to Kansas City. His heart pounded.

He looked hurt. "You forgot this, Tadashi. You're a traitor." She dropped her plate to the floor, got to her feet and stormed out.

Ruby looked up from her spot at the community garden.

Anastasia was here, her final patient of the day. That's right, she and the girls were due for their monthly herbs to prevent pregnancy.

"Does Buster have a nice resting place?"

Now that Meifeng had shown her how to stitch him back up, yes. "The view is lovely. You should hike up the mountain to see it." She'd marked it with a tiny cross.

Ruby measured out the main herbs – thyme, rosemary and sage. "Here, hold this open for me while I add the other stuff and mix it." What was that mark on Anastasia's arm? "Are those fingers marks?"

"A new client got upset when he couldn't perform and he blamed the girl for it."

There was probably an herb for men who encountered that. She'd have to meditate on it.

"Anyway, no matter which girl I send in, he couldn't keep it up. He went through four girls last night and never got off."

"What happened?"

"I refunded his money and told him not to return."

"No, I mean when he got physical." Something must have occurred for Anastasia to have such obvious marks. A girl, in a room alone, with a male stranger. She worried about the prostitutes sometimes.

"He turned real mean and started hitting Rosemary. I had to pull him off of her."

"You? You're a little slip of a thing."

"Not just me but also the guy I was with. He stepped in, thank goodness." She beamed. "I gave him a freebie after that."

"You girls put yourself in danger. Aren't you ever afraid?"

"Sometimes I am." Anastasia was quiet for a moment, then waved the thought away. "Occupational hazard. How else am I supposed to make a living?"

Yeung watched as Ruby administered to the gash in his right forearm. It hurt like hell but he wasn't about to let her know that. "What's that?"

"A wash of white sage and lavender. It'll disinfect it," she said, dabbing at the wound. "And numb the pain, too."

Not soon enough, it wouldn't. He should have been more careful, but time was money when you worked for Phillip Fontinello. Odd that his daughter was more inclined to help people instead of sticking it to them. "You like being our nurse?"

Ruby looked at him, amused. "Is that what I am?"

Sure it was. She'd been prescribing for everything from the sniffles to stomach aches. Now that she spoke Chinese, Meifeng didn't even need to be there to act as her interpreter. "Meifeng is the doctor. You're the nurse. How long before it's healed?"

"That deep? Maybe a week." She paused, eying it. "I'm tempted to stitch this up."

Like, with a needle? Yeung shuddered. He didn't know if he could handle that right now.

"But let's see if we can get away with just this."

Thank you, Buddha.

Ruby tore a bandage to size and wrapped it securely around his forearm. "Don't get this wet or it might become infected."

"Understood."

"Your wife will need to change this bandage every day."

What was she talking about? "My wife isn't here."

"Well, not here at the encampment, but wherever she stays."

"She stays in China."

Ruby blinked. "I always assumed the wives stayed somewhere outside of town. No?"

"I haven't seen her in three years since I sailed here."

"Why didn't you bring her along?"

Such a question. The girl truly had no idea. "I can't. The rules of your country," he said and made a gesture of hopelessness. "I saved every penny, wrote her that I would bring her here soon. Then, when I had enough, I went to buy her a ticket and was told, 'No. You are Chinese. You are barred from bringing family to America. It's the law.' I thought the man was lying. So, I checked it out. He was correct."

"That's horrible."

"Land of free is not so free if you're Chinese."

Ruby arrived at the address on the note from a Mr. Atwater, walked up on the front porch and rang the bell. The dinner with Tadashi still weighed on her mind. Had she been right to confront him? To judge him?

The door opened and a young woman in an apron stood there. "Yes? Oh, you're that girl at the garden." She held the door open. "This way, please." The housekeeper led her to the parlor.

A large man was seated there. He got up as soon as he saw her.

"Hello, Mr. Atwater. You said it was urgent."

"Yes, I –" He paused. "Rosa, close the doors."

The housekeeper complied.

This must be rather personal if he wanted the doors closed. A sexual problem, perhaps? "Just how can I help you?"

He winced. "I've been having this 'issue' of sorts." He paused and his face turned red. "Of an ...elimination nature, you might say."

Now she understood. "Urine or solid matter?"

"So solid nothing that is happening."

"How long has this been a problem?"

"I haven't gone in more than a week."

Not good. "Does this happen to you often?"

He nodded. "But this is longest I've gone without, you know, anything happening."

It was likely his diet. But she had to be sure. "Let me check a few things. Look into the light, please. OK, stick out your tongue."

She passed a hand over his abdomen. This was not good. The blockage was obvious, way up his gut. "If I may ask, what kind of work do you do?"

"I'm the regional supervisor for the mining coalition."

"So, can you take a day off?"

"I suppose. Why?"

Because by tomorrow you'll be sitting on the toilet more than you ever have. "I need to go get some materials and will be back."

An hour later, she was at his stove. She found virgin olive oil in the pantry and sniffed it. Yup, it was on the verge of going bad. Perfect.

Now, she poured it into a fry pan. She added the garlic she'd minced, added it to the pan and let it heat, hot but not too hot. Next up, bok choy.

Rosa peered over her shoulder. "What is that?"

Only the key to this whole thing. "Pass me those broccoli pieces, would you?"

She let it cook, added some mushrooms slices and Chinese pea pods, let them simmer and then stirred in some teriyaki flavor.

She pulled the skillet off the heat and scraped the meal into a bowl. Yes, that should be enough. Mr. Atwater was a large man but his bowels would thank him for this dose of real food. She grabbed a fork, took it to him and handed everything over. "Here's your dinner."

"What is this stuff?"

"Real food. The kind of stuff you should be eating on a regular basis."

He didn't look convinced but he took a bite. He cocked his head, considering it as he chewed. "It's not bad." He took another bite. "In fact, it's pretty tasty."

She sat back and watched. He was plowing through it. His stomach was probably amazed to have plant food at last. That's what the human body was meant to mainly eat.

Ruby waited until he finished.

He wiped his face with a napkin and patted his belly. "Quite delicious."

And quite effective, as he'd soon learn. "In about twelve hours you'll need to be near a toilet," she warned. "In fact, I wouldn't go into the office if I were you."

Ruby closed the textbook and stretched her neck. The Chinese sure took a different approach to medicine than the English textbooks she'd read. A whole body approach, not just addressing the symptoms.

There were shouts from outside.

She and Meifeng rushed to the window. Two men were carrying another Chinese worker on a stretcher. He was injured, wincing as he was jostled. There was blood.

Meifeng grabbed her shawl.

Ruby turned toward the apothecary jars with their medicines. "I'll get some white birch to help ease the pain," she called after her and got to work.

"And arnica as a topical," Meifeng called over her shoulder as she stepped outside.

Of course, she should have thought of that. It was one of the herbs they used on the men when the witch hazel treatments weren't enough.

The two men maneuvered the litter with the man into the cabin and set him on the floor. It was Renshu. She'd treated him for a sore throat just a couple weeks ago. His lower left leg was broken, the bone poking out of the skin about five inches above the ankle.

Ruby handed him a piece of bark. "Chew on it," she said in Chinese. It was not as good at pain relief as the tea would be but the water, while warm, had yet to boil. "What happened?" she asked in Chinese as she washed the wound, taking care not to cause any more pain.

"Stepped in a hole and it snapped."

Renshu was lying. The bone was jagged. This had not snapped. She lifted a single eyebrow. "So ...what really happened?"

"Everyone was swinging hammers, trying to finish on time, like the company wants." He made a gesture of hopelessness. "I didn't get out of the way in time."

Meifeng handed her a pan of shallow water – the warm arnica wash – and a cloth, then began gathering the material for setting the leg. "I only have kindling wood," she said.

It would have to do. Ruby wet the cloth, rung it out and pressed it gently to the wound. She switched to English. "How are we going to get the bone back in place?"

Meifeng assessed the break. "We push and pull. How else?"

Instead of chewing on the bark, Renshu would have to bite on a branch. No amount of arnica could numb the pain he was about to endure. "I'll be back in a minute," she told him.

She searched the area. Branch, branch, not too dry, not too thick.

There was a sound. Someone was vomiting.

She glanced through the trees that surrounded her.

There was a figure. It was Meifeng. This was the second time in a week. Something was wrong with her mentor, but she couldn't put her finger on it. Whatever it was, Meifeng wasn't saying.

CHAPTER NINE

Ruby arrived late to church. It was crowded but there was a spot next to Charity Krofton. "Where's your mother?"

"She's not feeling so good."

Last time she'd seen Estelle, the woman had had a number of complaints. Maybe she'd better swing by after church.

The service concluded with announcements. "And we should all pray for the soul of the poor young woman who was found yesterday."

She hadn't heard anything, but then, no news traveled up the mountain unless it was spoken in Chinese.

Everyone filed out. "I'll walk you home, Charity, I want to check on your mother." They waited until things cleared before descending the steps to the outdoors.

The girl tugged on her sleeve. "That guy is staring at you."

Tadashi. He was across the street, shifting from one foot to the other.

The turncoat. She was lucky she hadn't informed Daddy of what she'd learned. She turned up her nose and strode off, Charity in tow. "Let him stare."

They reached the Krofton mansion but the housekeeper was apologetic. "Miss Estelle is in bed feeling poorly and does not want to be disturbed."

"That's exactly why I need to see her." She brushed past the woman and took the stairs two at a time, outpacing the housekeeper. She got to Estelle's room, gave a brief knock and opened the door.

Estelle had a whopper of a black eye.

Up close it looked even worse. Cold packs to discourage swelling on Day One. Warm packs to encourage healing on Day Two. "What happened?"

The housekeeper hovered. "I'm sorry, Miss Estelle, she just barged –"

"I bolted past her." She'd take the blame on this one. She turned and addressed the housekeeper. "Listen, you can help. I want her to eat oranges, strawberries, broccoli and cauliflower. Do you have pineapple?"

"I think so."

"Give her that, too. But mash up some of it and apply it to the affected skin."

"Yes, Miss Ruby." The woman hurried away.

"So, Estelle, how did this happen?"

"I tripped and fell."

No, there was more to this story, she could feel it.

The woman was up to her neck in bedcovers. And there was a scarf around her neck. On a beautiful day like today? She must be suffering from the chills.

But, no, her forehead felt the normal temperature. "It's a gorgeous day. You don't need all these bedclothes." She unwrapped the scarf.

"No, don't, I –"

The scarf fell away.

Those marks on her neck, they'd been made by giant hands. Estelle's face wasn't the only thing that was black and blue. Someone had tried to choke her to death.

"Who did this to you?"

Estelle looked miserable. "Winslow."

"Your husband?" She ran her palms above Estelle's body. There was pain radiating from the left shoulder, both arms and the abdomen. Estelle had taken one hell of a beating. "You two had an argument and things, um, escalated?"

"No, he just came home. I asked him how his day was and he just blew up." She hugged herself. "At first it was just once in a while. I thought it was my fault, something I'd done to displease him and blamed myself. But it kept happening. Nowadays, I never know what will set him off. He has a terrible temper. I hate him."

"Well, I hope he has a black eye of his own, courtesy of *your* fist."

The woman threw a hand to her chest. "No, no, no." She shook her head rapidly. "If I did that. He'd hurt me worse." She grabbed Ruby's arm and said, "You don't know what it's like living here with him." She began sobbing. "I'm afraid he'll start taking things out on Charity."

This guy sounded like a monster. And yet, meet him on the street and Winslow Krofton was a fine, upstanding citizen. The broken vase from her other visit had not been an accident, after all. "There, there. We'll think of something."

The housekeeper returned with fruit. "I gave her an ice pack. She had it on the eye all last night."

So, this was Day Two. "That's good. You did the right thing. Now, I want you to boil an egg, peel it and while it's still warm, rub it gently on the eye. Keep dipping it in the water to keep it warm."

"Yes, Miss Ruby. I'll see to it. We'll get her back to looking pretty in no time."

That still didn't solve the problem of keeping her away from her husband and his temper. No one deserved to live in a house where they feared for their personal safety day in and day out. It was time to fight fire with fire.

Ruby turned to Estelle. "I think I know a way to make this stop. For good."

Ruby swung by Anastasia's before heading up the mountain. Better see if the girls needed anything.

Lillian let her in. "Hi, Ruby," she said quietly.

All the girls were seated in the parlor. They looked miserable.

"Why the long faces?"

"It's Tina," Anastasia said. "She's gone."

To work in San Fran? Or Chicago maybe? "Needed a change of scenery?"

"She's dead."

Her knees felt weak. She plopped down on an empty chair. Tina was the "young woman" that the preacher had mentioned, had to be. No wonder the congregation had not responded favorably to being asked to keep her in their prayers. Prostitutes were not considered by most to be respectable people. "What happened?"

Anastasia was on the sofa and sobbed softly. "She went off with a client. I hate letting my girls do that, but the man pays extra for it, so I can't very well say, 'No.' I wish I had though." Her chin quivered. "It's all my fault."

The girl next to Anastasia on the sofa slid over and pulled the young madam into her arms. "It's OK, it's OK."

Lillian turned to her. "They found her body in a ditch, about half a mile past Woodman's Bridge. You know, where that sharp turn is?"

"Of course." Everyone knew it. It was the site of at least one carriage collision a year.

"He beat her up pretty bad, head to toe." Lillian shook her head. "There were rope marks around her wrists and ankles. Tina didn't stand a chance." Lillian clasped her hands around her own neck as though protecting it. She shivered. "He strangled her. The sheriff said that by the looks of things, it was a man with big hands."

"Has the client been arrested?"

Anastasia dried her tears. "That's just it. We never saw him, don't know who he is. The request for a girl came by post."

"Local post?"

"Yes, but there was no name, no address, no signature."

She felt stupid for asking but, "Is that usually how things are done?"

"If a man is from out of town or if he doesn't want to be spotted entering a cat house," Anastasia said, "they'll resort to things like that. But the envelope contained the money, over and above the regular rate, so there was no reason not to send her."

"There wasn't even a signature?"

"No. It could have been sent by anyone."

Not anyone. Someone who had an anger problem and who took it out on the weaker sex.

Tadashi saw Ruby enter the cabin. She was home.

He hurried past the other tents and stepped on the porch.

Calm down, straighten your tunic, do this right.

He knocked on the cabin door.

There was movement inside. The door opened a few inches.

Meifeng stood there. She shook her head. "She doesn't want to see you, son."

"I just want to talk –"

"No," she said gently. "She's hurting. Stay away from her." Meifeng closed the door.

Tadashi hung his head, turned and shuffled off.

Nothing was the same without Ruby's smile or her laughter in his world.

He kicked a stone. If only Ruby would talk to him, he could explain. There were a lot of "if onlys" he wished he could fix.

If only she hadn't found his surreptitious order to send the rail ties to Kansas City.

If only she hadn't pulled out the order and confronted him with it.

If only he'd been able to explain.

If only she didn't put her father on a pedestal as though he could do no wrong.

Stop it. Ruby isn't at fault here and you know it.

He groaned.

His inner voice was right. He was blaming the wrong person and he knew it. He was the one at fault, him and only him.

And now Ruby would never forgive him.

He sat down on a rock and held his head in his hands. He was a fool.

Ruby headed home from seeing the Unser twins. When one of them got sick, the other was sure to follow.

Good thing it was only pink eye. They'd each had a yellow discharge.

She'd added equal parts honey to warm water and used a dropper to administer it.

"Repeat this morning noon and night," she'd told the mother. *Good luck trying to get them to sit still so you don't poke an eye out.* But that was Mrs. Unser's problem.

Her own problem was what to do with the Kansas City order with Daddy's forged signature. It burned in her pocket. How could Tadashi have betrayed her father this way?

She hiked down the road and came to the area about a half-mile before Woodman's Bridge. This was where Tina's body had been found. Her steps slowed.

Who would want to kill her? What had she ever done but service men's needs in her effort to survive?

There was a patch off the side of the road where the dirt had been disturbed.

Like a struggle had taken place there.

Like a fight. A fight for life.

There were foot prints and a piece of rope. Was it the rope that had bound the poor girl?

She stepped off the road and made her way down to the ditch.

Tina's barefoot prints were evident over here. So was a spot where her body might have been.

There were lots of shoeprints, those made by a large foot, and those made by a small one.

Could the smaller ones be made by a woman? Ruby lined her own foot up with the smaller ones.

No, they were made by a male. If the attacker had large hands, like the sheriff had said, then it stood to reason he also had large feet. So, the smaller male footprint was likely the sheriff's.

There was dried blood on the dead leaves over here.

And there was something else, here in the shadow of a tree.

She peered closer. It was a tiny piece of paper, a gold foil wrapper. It had dried blood on it.

Ruby picked it up. She'd take it to the sheriff. Maybe if he could identify it, it would be a clue as to who murdered the poor prostitute.

Ruby sat beside Estelle in the Kroftons' carriage as the clip-clopping of the horse's hoofs sounded on the street's cobblestones. Charity's mother was dressed in dark clothes, a hat and a dark, heavy veil covering her face.

"You sure this will work?" Estelle asked.

Ruby patted her hand. "Trust me."

The carriage pulled into the alley and the driver reined the horse to a stopped.

Ruby jumped down and knocked on the back door of the business.

It opened and a man greeted her. "Is she here?"

"Yes, meet Estelle."

He stepped over to the open door of the carriage. "I'm William. Welcome to my studio." He extended his hand and helped her out.

Estelle looked up and down the alley. "No one's around to see me, right?"

"No one," Ruby assured her. "But let's get inside."

William's studio was one large room. He rolled down a backdrop. "You wanted a white background, right?"

"Yes." It would contrast with Estelle's bruises.

He positioned Estelle well in front of the fabric backdrop. "Stand right here."

"I've never had a daguerreotype taken before."

William said, "Don't be nervous." He checked things from the area where the camera sat. "All set. You need to remove the veil now."

Estelle hesitated. "Well, all right." She lifted the thick veil and revealed her black eye.

"The shawl, too, Estelle," Ruby reminded her.

The shawl was slipped off.

The bruises on her neck were readily apparent. "One more thing." Ruby stepped over and pushed up Estelle's sleeves. The full extent of her beating should be shown.

William got behind the camera, ducked under the black sheet. "Turn a little to your right, that's good. Hold it and don't breathe."

There was a flash from the stick he held high, just outside the sheet. Smoke drifted into the air off the end of it.

Ruby watched from the side. They only had today to do this, while Winslow was out of town and Estelle's bruises were still evident. "How much of a close-up are these?"

William switched plates. "I'm shooting full body and also from the collarbone up." He moved the camera closer and readjusted things. "Look straight at the camera this time, Estelle," he said. "That's it. Now, take a breath and hold it."

The flash went off.

Too bad daguerreotypes didn't have color, but Estelle's dark hair and clothes would cause her bruises to stand out in the black and white shots, making them all the more obvious for the judge in San Francisco. These pictures and the witness statements from the household servants would ensure Estelle was granted a divorce.

William stood up. "All done. You did fine, Estelle."

Ruby stepped over and helped her put her shawl back on and get the veil in place. "You took five different angles, right William?" she said over her shoulder.

"They'll be ready later today."

Perfect, then Estelle and Charity could take off for San Francisco and live at the second home they owned there. A thought struck her. Ruby hesitated. "You know what, William? Make a duplicate set of prints."

"Sure. I took several shots of the same pose."

Estelle cocked her head. "But I only need one set for the judge."

"Yes, but we need a second set for someone else." She smiled to herself. Winslow would be in for a big surprise when he returned to town – an empty bank account, a silent house and an unmarked envelope with damning photos on his desk at work.

Ruby climbed the ladder to the cabin's loft, careful not to spill anything.

Meifeng was in bed, covered in blankets.

"I made some miso soup. Thought you might like some." She brought it over.

The doctor waved it off. "Not now. Maybe later."

The woman had barely eaten anything for the past three days. She had to keep her strength up. "Is there something else you'd rather have? I can make whatever you want."

"I'm not hungry, child." Meifeng curled up in a ball. "I'm just cold and tired."

Ruby set down the bowl and adjusted the blankets around her. "Remember when you pretended to collapse?" *To teach me a lesson?*

Meifeng let out a little chuckle. "You had no idea what to do."

There was an understatement. "It got me thinking. I know how to help people with ailments, but not when they have urgent needs. Like, I wouldn't have known how to set Renshu's leg. If you hadn't been there, I would have been lost." What if she'd tried and done the wrong thing? Made it worse? Affected Renshu's ability to walk for the rest of his life?

"You would have figured it out."

No, that wasn't her point. When people had urgent need for care, she should be equipped to act fast and decisively. Her guides could only take her so far with stuff like that. "I should know these things."

Meifeng patted her hand. "Don't worry about it."

I worry about you.

Meifeng shifted, closed her eyes and began breathing softly.

She was asleep, good. Here was her chance.

Ruby rubbed her palms together and quieted her mind. She held out her hands, her palms above Meifeng's outline, and let them hover.

She sensed discord in the body, yes, but it was vague, nothing that was definitive, damn it.

She yanked her hands away in disgust.

This lack of information on her mentor's physical state, it vexed her to no end. "She deserves my help," she grumbled to her guides. "I would think you'd allow me to know what's wrong with her."

But they were silent.

Fine, be that way. Ruby withdrew. But she was still mad at herself for not honing-in on Meifeng's illness. She got to the bottom of the ladder, jumped off the last rung and looked back up.

Meifeng was out of sight, but still weighed on her mind. Let her sleep, it was the best thing for her at this point.

Phillip shoved away from the paperwork and pushed his desk chair back. He massaged his temples. This headache, would it ever ease up? It had plagued him for two days now. He eyed the ledger wearily. Not until this task was done, it wouldn't.

There was movement of white outside the window.

Ruby. She was rounding the building.

Good, she was carrying that pouch of goodies. Maybe she had something he could take for his head. He jumped up from his chair and crossed to the door.

Jerold Fulcom was in the outer office. He grinned, "I know the perfect solution to your headache, Phillip –a little levity."

"Let me guess. You pulled another prank on Tadashi?" The man seemed to enjoy testing the young man to no end.

"Not a prank, but I have a joke for you." He giggled. "You're going to love it."

It must be really good, the man could barely contain himself. "OK, let's hear it."

"Two Chinese people, Sum Lee and Tim Wong get married. A year later, she has a baby. But it's clearly half white. What do they decide to name it?" He paused for effect. "Sum Ting Wong." Jerold slapped his knees. "Get it? Sum Ting W –"

A voice rang out. "You think that's *funny*?"

They both turned.

Ruby stood in the doorway. Her face was livid. "That is so disrespectful, I don't even know where to start. You should be *ashamed* of yourself, Jerold Fulcom."

The secretary frowned. "It was just a joke."

"At the expense of someone else." Ruby threw up a hand to stop any response. "I don't even want to be around anyone who thinks that is *remotely* funny." She turned on her heel and huffed away.

Wait, don't go. My headache medicine. But if he knew Ruby, she wouldn't be back to help him. Damn that Fulcom and his stupid jokes.

Anastasia got off the bed, crossed to the wash basin and cleaned up between her legs.

Her client stayed put. Maybe the guy didn't get the hint that his time was up. *Get off my bed, close up your pants and get a move on, bud.* "You need a washcloth, sugar?"

He sighed and got up. "Nope." He straightened up his clothes and patted her on the behind on his way out. "Next time."

Yeah, next time it would cost you double, wasting my time with your senseless "Let's pretend you're my wife and I come home to find you pleasuring yourself" games.

Two hours he'd taken. What guy took two hours to reach climax? She could have made the same amount of money in fifteen minutes with any other guy.

Anastasia caught her reflection in the mirror, eying her high cheek bones, her blonde hair.

She was pretty, yes, but pretty only got you so far in this game.

She'd serviced lawyers and businessmen, investor types, even. They'd talked of finance. They'd mentioned their big business deals that were in the works, things to make them rich beyond imagination. A couple of them had said they'd like to have her for a wife. That was the phrase they always used: Have her for a wife. Yeah, right. More like, have her on the side for fun, besides having a proper, socially-acceptable wife.

They'd never actually proposed. And they were both naked when such talk had occurred, nothing she could take seriously.

But a girl needed more than what was between her legs to get her through life. And what would she do when she reached thirty and was over the hill?

Someday she was going to have a respectable profession. Someday she was going to find a way to make money not just for a night, but in a way where the money flowed in around the clock.

There was giggling on the other side of the wall. Lillian was finishing up with her customer. She was bringing in the lion's share of business lately. The girl sure was popular now that her skin was cleared up.

Maybe there was something to be said for Ruby's tincture.

Ruby clutched the pouch that hung across her body. It was weighted-down, chock full of new medicines that had come in from San Francisco. Maybe one of them could be the key to helping her mentor.

It was dark. She was tired. Hiking up the mountain on such an inky black night could get dicey. Maybe she'd better stay at the house tonight.

She hurried down the street, past the church, past the baker's, past the butcher's shop, giving a quick wave to those she knew. The farrier was outside, leading a horse.

"I'll bring by more medicine next week, Mr. Connors," she called out to him.

She headed behind the houses and began the climb up the knoll that led to their house. It was nice to have a view of the city, but it wasn't so nice if you were on foot and had to hike up to it.

Fifteen minutes later, she was breathing hard as she came up on the section where the trail tapered-off in its ascent. It was a short reprieve but enough to catch her breath. She shifted the pouch to her other shoulder. "Here we go."

A branch cracked underfoot somewhere below her.

She stopped, listening.

She hadn't seen anyone on the road when it switched back. But then, it was so dark, they'd be tough to spot.

Maybe it was a Chinese worker, hoping to catch up to her for some medical advice. "Hello? Is someone there?" she called out in Chinese.

Nothing.

She kept going. Her legs burned with the effort and she slowed down until the sensation eased.

A rock was dislodged and tumbled down the road behind her. Someone was definitely there and they were getting closer.

She tried again, in English and louder this time. "Who's there?"

Nothing.

But someone was there. They were getting closer, coming up behind her. *Danger. Danger.* She took off jogging.

There was a sound behind her, heavy footsteps taking the road fast.

Don't look back. Keep going.

She went faster, legs pumping uphill as fast as she could.

Go, go, go!

She was practically running. Her lungs were ready to burst.

She tripped – oh, no –and went flying.

Her head hit something –a rock –and the world began spinning wildly.

The footsteps caught up her.

He was big, a blur of heft. His hand grabbed her ankle. "I've got you now."

"No, please," Ruby winced.

He pinned her face down to the ground, sitting atop her. "You think you're so funny, don't you?"

She smelled dirt. *Have to stay conscious.* "Get off me."

"Ha."

Dirt and horse manure. "Let me go."

"Not until I'm done with you."

That voice. She knew it from somewhere.

He shifted, the weight of his knees now fully on her wrists, crushing them.

"Ouch. You're hurting me."

He snickered and shifted.

Oh God, he was undoing his belt.

The night swirled. The blackness closed in over her eyes.

No. No. Have to stay conscious.

She had only one chance. She had to be loud. She lifted her head.

Now or never. "Help!"

CHAPTER TEN

Ruby was pinned, helpless. "Help!"

The man slugged her on the side of her forehead. "Shut up."

There was a howl from behind them.

The guy rocked off, falling to the ground beside her with a groan.

Her wrists were free. Thank God.

Have to ...crawl ...away.

There were sounds of a fight. Grunts. Groans.

Her vision cleared. It was ...

"Tadashi?"

He was whipping his feet through the air, kicking the big man and following it up with punches to the stomach.

The big man doubled over.

Tadashi twirled on one foot and delivered an upward kick.

Her attacker's head snapped back.

He fell to the ground and didn't move.

Oh, no, he hadn't killed him, had he? "Tadashi, stop. He's out cold." She stood up, trying to maintain her balance on wobbly legs.

He turned to her. "Did he hurt you?"

She stared down at the man. "It's Mr. Atwater. He was a patient of mine." But why had he attacked her? All she'd done was help him. She listed to the side and stumbled.

Tadashi caught her around her waist. "Are you all right?"

Now that he was here to keep her safe, she was. "I'm fine."

He let his arms slip off her.

Atwater moaned. He was coming-to. After a few moments, he sat up.

She kept her distance. "Why?"

The mining official felt his jaw, eyeing Tadashi who stood between them. "You made a fool of me. That meal you fed me. All the next day I was running for the –"

"I warned you to expect that."

"Yes, but you didn't have to *tell* the whole world about it."

"Your condition was never discussed with anyone, I assure you."

"Well *someone* knew."

Gee, it couldn't be your household staff could it? But she couldn't say that, couldn't accuse them, not without knowing for sure.

Atwater gestured in frustration. "Everyone was snickering at me."

And so you physically attacked me? "Your home has neighbors on all sides, Mr. Atwater. Anyone could have looked out the window and seen you keep hightailing it through the backyard to the loo."

He hesitated. "Maybe …I guess."

Tadashi gestured as though he'd heard enough. "Get out of here and don't come back." He waited until Atwater got up and lurched away before he turned to her. "Are you going up to the encampment?"

And have to hike it with him? The man who'd crushed her heart? She didn't need the torture. "No."

"Then I'll see you home."

It was the sensible thing to do, though she really didn't see a need at this point. "All right."

They began walking the rest of the way to her house in silence. Thank goodness it wasn't far.

She stole a look at him. This was really awkward. The man was undermining her family's business. She couldn't ignore that. But he'd just saved her. This was so confusing.

They reached the porch. The house was dark except for the servant's quarters in back.

Tadashi looked around. "Where is everyone?"

"Mother's in San Francisco. Daddy's in L.A." She hesitated. "Thank you for –" saving me, coming to my rescue, being my hero "– what you did back there."

Tadashi stared at her. "You're hurt."

This throbbing on her forehead? It wasn't so bad. "It's nothing. You can get going."

He didn't move. "You're bleeding."

"I am?" She felt her face. It was wet. Well, gee, of course it was. The head was known for extensive bleeding. Wounds there always bled profusely. "I'll be fine."

He took her elbow. "Let's go inside where I can see it in the light."

She shook him off. "I don't need your help."

"Stop arguing. You make a terrible patient."

"I'm not your patient."

He crossed his arms. "Who stepped in when you were pinned to the ground?"

"You."

"Who took out your attacker?"

"You."

"Who's going to make sure you're really OK?"

"All right, you made your point." She opened the door and let him in.

There was movement in a far room. "Miss Ruby?"

"Yes, Amelda, it's me," she called out. "I'll be staying the night."

"Do you need dinner?"

"No, no, I'm fine. Go back to whatever you were doing."

The maid retreated.

The house was silent again.

She turned to Tadashi and whispered. "She had no idea you're here and I plan to keep it that way."

"Of course, we can't have the Fontinello name sullied."

"Stop joking." She led the way to the kitchen and put on the gas light. Their cook, Winifred, kept a mirror near the sink. She picked it up. So, how bad did she look, anyway?

Oh, that bad.

Tadashi stepped over, hands on her shoulders. He steered her to the table. "Sit down. Let me help you." He grabbed a cloth and wet it, then came over and dabbed at the side of her forehead.

She looked into her lap. Did he have to stand so close to her? Press into her shoulder this way? Gosh, but he smelled so good.

He paused.

Why was he stopping?

She looked up.

His face was inches away.

Those eyes.

Tadashi bent down closer. His lips hovered near hers.

No, she couldn't do this.

She turned away. He was a traitor. "Why, Tadashi? Why did you undermine my father's business?"

He straightened up. "This ends now," he said. "Where is your father's desk?"

What did that have to do with anything? "It's upstairs in his bedroom."

He took her hand. "Show me."

"Take you upstairs?" Where the bedrooms were? Where she'd fallen asleep wishing that he was naked in her arms? Her face heated up. "That's not proper."

"Time to forget proper." He led the way, pulling her upstairs.

They reached the landing. He looked right and left. "It's this way, isn't it?" He said it more than asked it.

He led her through the double doors and into Daddy's room ... with the big bed. "Ah, here's his desk." He turned up the gas light and began yanking out the drawers.

Those were Daddy's things. "What are you doing? Are you insane?"

He pulled out a ledger. "Here it is." He flipped the pages and pointed. "Here. Look right here."

She peered at the page. "What?"

"Labor costs. Right here."

She spotted the hourly wage – they made that little? – and did the math in her head. Most laborers earned $9 a week. The Chinese were being paid half that much.

Hold on. Maybe there was another factor here. Maybe they worked abbreviated hours.

She flipped pages and found the column with labor hours on it. She ran her finger down the column.

This was horrible. Daddy was having men work twelve-, fourteen-, even sixteen-hour days on a regular basis.

She turned to Tadashi. "I didn't know," she said. "But, certainly he compensated them for such arduous hours by paying them overtime."

"You think so?" Tadashi found the payroll page and pointed.

She looked at the entries. The Chinese men were only getting paid for eight hours a day. The entries were consistent, never deviating – eight hours, eight hours, eight hours.

If these numbers were correct, then Daddy was no better than a slave driver. No, it couldn't be true. "Someone is doing this behind my father's back." Had to be.

"All the entries are in your father's handwriting."

She looked. Oh, God, he was right.

"And look here," Tadashi said.

Ruby followed his finger. It was an entry for the purchase of work boots. Two hundred pair. Daddy had gotten them for a steal. She had no idea he could wrangle such a low price. "I don't see anything wrong here. So he scored a bargain price, so what?"

"Have you seen the men's boots?" Tadashi stepped back and scoffed. "They're square toed."

They were? She'd never noticed. No one wore square-toed footwear anymore, not since the War Between the States. In fact, the soldiers' difficulty with the loose fit of the wear-it-on-either-foot boots had led to cobblers designing shoes specific to each foot.

Her head spun. Daddy had scored a bargain because he'd located a warehouse with the obsolete boots taking up space and bought them for next to nothing. "That's disgraceful." *Oh, Daddy, what have you done?*

Tadashi took her shoulders and twisted her toward him. "Now do you understand why I rerouted the rail ties?"

"You were giving the workers a respite." *From my father's Draconian edicts.*

"You didn't know what was really going on."

But she should have. She hung her head. "I'm so ashamed."

He caught her chin. "Look at me."

She looked up into his eyes.

"Don't blame yourself, Ruby," he said. "How were you to know? You were busy helping others and learning to work with medicine. I only discovered what he was doing because the men would come to me with their grievances – too many hours, too little pay. I looked into what they were telling me and discovered that everything they said was true. Your father is building these rail lines – "

"– off the backs of poor immigrant workers," she said, finishing for him. And she'd blamed him for trying to derail the family business. This whole thing was a nightmare. "I misjudged you, Tadashi. I owe you an apology."

He drew her into his arms.

She didn't resist.

"Come to me, Ruby."

She laid her head on his chest and slipped her arms around him. It felt so right. She didn't want this moment to end.

Tadashi leaned into her. "I thought I'd lost you," he whispered, his lips in her hair.

"You never really lost me." All those nights, tossing and turning, longing for him, even when she'd considered him a traitor, all of it was for nothing. What a fool she'd been.

"One day, I want you to come live in my tent the way you live in my heart."

It was the sweetest thing she'd ever heard. She lifted her face to him. "Kiss me."

He caught his breath and bent down to take her mouth. And then he was kissing her.

Oh, those lips. She'd dreamed of those lips.

His kiss was soft as first, then more sensuous, more demanding.

She responded, knowing to her core that she could stay like this forever.

He broke away, pulling back to search her face. "You have no idea how long I've wanted to –" he bent down and those lips were on hers once again.

Yes, yes, yes. She slid her hands under his tunic. What hard muscles, what strength there was to him. And he'd tackled a man twice his size to protect her. He'd saved her.

She yanked back, breaking the kiss.

He blinked. "What?"

"My room," she breathed.

They shoved the ledger back into the desk, turned off the gas lamp and hightailed it out of there.

Ruby ran down the hall leading him by the hand, trying not to giggle.

"Keep it down," he warned.

She was so giddy with desire for this man, she didn't care if all the servants heard her. Ruby pointed. "This one's my room."

He stopped, yanked her to him and crushed her against him, his pull demanding and his touch like a spark.

His kiss was so hot, so heavy. She wanted to melt into him.

"You're in for a hell of a night," he breathed.

They crashed through her door with hungry kisses.

They yanked off each other's clothes.

God, he was an Adonis.

They ran to the bed, tumbling onto it.

He slid atop her, skin on skin, body heat on body heat, and smiled down on her. "I'll be gentle," Tadashi said.

Who wanted gentle? She wanted her man and she wanted him right now.

Ruby stretched in bed. The sun was just now dusting the night away. She looked to the side. There he was, her lover. "Wake up, sleepy head."

Tadashi popped an eye open. "Tell me that I'm dreaming."

"You're awake."

"Can't be," he said, reaching for her. "Not if I've got this vision in bed with me." He pulled her into his arms and kissed her.

Something in her stirred. "Again," she whispered, running a finger down his chest.

"You little vixen." He shifted to get on top of her and gestured between his legs. "You're going to wear him out at this rate."

"Seems to me he did just fine last night," she teased. Besides, she knew a couple of herbs that would come in handy should he ever have a problem. "Come on. Just a quickie."

He eased into her and let out a moan.

"Yes." Ruby arched her back. A flash of desire seared down to her loins. The man was a master. An urgency overtook her. She matched his rhythm and began bucking. "Yes, yes. Oh, yes." She was on fire for this man.

Tadashi closed his eyes, panting.

She grabbed his face, drew it toward her and planted a kiss on him, biting him, branding him.

Yes!

They came together and a moan escaped her. She couldn't get enough of him.

Tadashi rolled off her. His eyes suddenly widened. "I just realized."

That she was a virgin before last might? A towel had kept the sheets clean. "I'm fine." The servants would never know.

He shook his head. "What if we just made a baby?"

There was no way. "We didn't."

"You don't know for sure."

Yes, she did. She had a row of minuscule pimples within the crease of her chin. That meant her period was due any day. "Stop worrying. We didn't." But he had a valid point. She would have to start taking the same herbal mix that Anastasia and the girls took. It wouldn't do to have a baby out of wedlock. Mother would be aghast at the notion.

She slipped off the bed. "We installed a bathtub. How about we use it together?"

Ten minutes later, they were in the water.

"Good thing I didn't show Daddy the Kansas City order, huh?"

"I'll say." Tadashi let out a nervous laugh. "I wondered when you were going to, though. Spent a couple of nights stressing over when *that* altercation would come to a boil." He paused. "So, why didn't you?"

Good question. Maybe she hadn't wanted to believe he had a mean bone in his body. Maybe she'd wanted to believe there was an explanation. "Every time I went to tell him, something inside always stopped me." She made ripples in the water with her finger. "I figured you had a reason for doing it."

"So, you believe me?"

"It's not right, making the men work so hard."

"And without proper compensation."

Yes, the body needed to recuperate. It couldn't run at such a pace nonstop without consequences. Besides, it wasn't right to treat people that way. Her father just didn't realize how tough things were for the Chinese laborers. "I'll talk to Daddy about it."

"What?" Tadashi looked aghast. "No, you can't."

"He'll listen to me."

"He'll laugh at you."

"I'm his daughter."

"Who wears Chinese clothing," he pointed out.

Maybe he was right. Maybe Daddy would see her as a mere sympathizer and brush her concerns aside. "But, Tadashi, things have to change."

"I know they do, but let me handle it."

"How?"

"I'll figure something out." He didn't sound too sure.

There was a noise downstairs. The servants were up.

She lifted the drain plug and reached for the towels. "Get dressed. I'll show you the back way out so no one will see you."

He stopped her and pulled her back, eyes bright. "One more kiss."

How could she say no?

Ruby opened her eyes.

She breathed in the mountain air. It was morning, but barely.

Lying beside her on the mat of his tent, Tadashi shifted.

Let him sleep. She needed to tiptoe back to the cabin before Meifeng woke up.

She got up and pulled on her clothes. What a night they'd spent, wrapped in each other's arms. Sure, there had been sex, but they'd connected so completely on every level.

She slipped out of his tent and shivered in the morning chill. She picked her way past the other tents. There was dew on the grass.

Inside, the cabin was warm.

Hot tea sounded good right now. She stoked the stove and set the pot on top to boil.

She'd better check on Meifeng. The poor thing was still not feeling well.

Ruby climbed the ladder to the loft.

Her mentor was sound asleep, breathing softly.

It was what she needed. Sleep allowed the body to heal.

There was a tea cup nearby. Ruby picked it up and sniffed. Tumeric, ginger, and something else she couldn't identify.

Meifeng shifted. "Ruby?"

She hadn't meant to wake her. "How are you feeling?" She bent down and pressed her palm to her mentor's forehead. No fever.

"I'll survive."

"Glad to hear it." She gestured to the tea cup. "Ginger. Tumeric. What's the other ingredient you took?"

"Papaya. But only the inner lining of the bark."

"For?"

Meifeng made a wishy-washy gesture. "Discomfort."

Discomfort or more serious pain? What wasn't her mentor telling her? "I've never known you to prescribe that before."

"It's hard to come by."

And yet Meifeng had gone to the trouble to get it. Papaya, huh? She'd have to look it up in her medical books. "I want you to stay in bed, take things easy. You're not up to going to the garden today."

Meifeng nodded and snuggled deeper into her blankets.

"What can I make you before I leave? Miso soup? Sautéed zucchini?"

"Nothing. I'm fine."

Sure she was. For a powerhouse like Meifeng to take to her bed was a red flag. Ruby hurried down the ladder. She pulled out a medical book and flipped the pages as quietly as she could. No, not here.

She tried another book.

Papaya.

Papaya.

Here it was.

The milky inner lining was dried and beaten to a pulp, usually used topically but sometimes taken internally when indicated for severe pain.

Severe pain? This was bad.

She kept reading.

Side effects can be gastrointestinal distress if too much is taken. But it was proven effective, especially for treating pain in patients with –

No.

She slapped the book closed.

Felicia felt the carriage come to a halt. Good. She was home, finally. It was such a trek going from their second home in San Francisco to here in Sacramento. She grabbed her bag, opened the door and stepped out. "Bring my bags upstairs."

"Yes, Ma'am. As soon as I unhitch the horses."

"No, do it *before* you unhitch the horses." The beasts were sweaty. She wouldn't have horse lather sully her Italian leather travel bags. Honestly, did she have to tell her servants how to do *everything?*

She took the steps to the porch and strode across to the front door. She'd bet her last dime that no one had swept the porch in two days. Leave for a week and all hell broke loose around here.

She entered the house and put her arms akimbo. "Amelda, where are you?"

The maid came running up. "Right here, Missus. Sorry. I didn't hear you arrive."

"The porch is covered in dust. I will not have such a filthy house."

"I'll see to it right now, Missus." She turned to leave.

"Wait. Is my husband in town?" She removed her gloves.

Amelda hesitated. "We think he's due here later today."

"You *think*?"

"He wasn't certain."

"Well, tell the cook to make a roast. A man likes to have a hearty meal."

"Yes, Ma'am."

The driver came in with her bags and set them on the floor.

Idiot. Was she supposed to carry them up the stairs all by herself? "Take them up to my room, for goodness sake."

"Yes, Ma'am."

He hefted them and hurried upstairs with them.

Better make sure the house is in good shape. The basket had letters. She'd gotten one from her friend in New York. Lovely city. Maybe she should plan a trip to go see her, stay for a month or two and take in some shows. She'd heard there was a new art exhibit from Paris.

She peered into the parlor, the library, the dining room, the sun room. The downstairs was in decent shape, she supposed. Nothing that some dusting and fresh flowers couldn't help.

How did the upstairs look? She climbed the stairs and peeked into her husband's room. It smelled faintly of his cologne. She went down the hall and opened the door to Ruby's. That was odd. The bed had been made, but not very well. Something was off.

She ventured closer and threw back the covers.

The scent of sex assaulted her nose.

How dare their employees take their sick little trysts into the bedrooms of her family? "Amelda," she yelled. "Come up here this instant."

The maid's footsteps scurried closer. Amelda appeared in the doorway and shuffled in like a scared little mouse.

Let's see her try and explain this. She pointed to the bed. "What's the meaning of this?"

"It was made up this morning when I looked in."

She was a terrible liar. *"You* slept in it."

"No, Ma'am. I don't know what you're talking about."

Oh, she didn't, did she? The little tramp. "I will not tolerate this under my roof." Felicia pointed to the door. "You're fired. Pack your things and get out of my sight this instant."

Ruby swung by the photographer's studio and stepped inside. "William? Are you back there?"

He stuck his head out of the back. His nose was red and there were dark circles under his eyes. "Thank goodness you're here." He didn't sound himself.

"Your sinuses are clogged."

"You're telling me." He led her in back and collapsed on a stool, hanging his head. "I have zero energy."

It could be the flu, or it could be a severe cold. "How long has it been affecting you?"

"It began two nights ago. My throat is raw." He coughed.

"And it's tough to swallow," she finished for him. "Fever then the chills?"

He nodded.

It sure sounded like the flu. "OK, here's what you do. Put two tablespoons of apple cider vinegar and a squeeze of lemon in a cup of hot water." Hold on. He'd likely gag at the taste. Strange how women swallowed bitter things if they knew it was good for them but men, forget it. She'd better make it more palatable. "Stir in a couple teaspoons of honey. And hold your breath when you drink it."

William nodded. "OK."

"Drink a cup at least three times a day." She checked his eyes. "Four would be better."

"That many?"

Yes, that many. "You want to knock this thing out of your system, don't you?" He'd see his urine become clearer within a couple hours of drinking it and if he got a full night's sleep, could feel a difference as soon as the next day. Some people did, some didn't. "Are you coughing at night?"

"A lot."

"Sprinkle some of the apple cider vinegar on your pillow." If only curing Meifeng was so easy. But she didn't want to go there, didn't want to think about it. Back to the photographer's health. "Now, what have you been eating?"

He gave her a strange look. "What does that have to do with anything?"

"Humor me."

"Let's see, last night I had a thick rib eye steak, almost took up the whole plate, with fried potatoes, biscuits smothered in gravy and a big slice of lemon meringue pie."

So much for him feeling better by tomorrow. "Try to make half your plate be nothing but fresh vegetables."

William nodded as though he'd heard it all before. "Fresh vegetables, yeah, sure." He got up. "Thought you might want to see these." He pulled out some photos and handed them over. "I used the extra poses to made extras, just like you wanted."

There were the close-ups of Estelle, showing her neck injuries. The fingermarks around her throat where he'd choked her were obvious. Her husband's hands had to be huge. She thought back to what Anastasia had said about Tina's murderer – the sheriff thought he was a man with large hands.

Could Winslow Krofton be the man who'd beaten and killed her? But no, he was a married man. Why would he visit a prostitute?

Mr. Atwater had large hands too. Maybe it was him.

Two large men, both with obvious anger issues. It could be either of them.

Ruby let her mind slip into meditation mode. She returned to the hall with symbols written on the walls.

Her guides were there.

"I need your help."

"What can we do?" they said, telegraphing the words to her brain.

"It's Meifeng. Tell me how to help her."

Silence. They just stood there.

"How can I cure her?"

Silence.

All right, if they wouldn't give her the cure, maybe they'd just diagnose what it was. "Tell me what's wrong with her."

They turned and began gliding away.

"Oh, that's great. Turn your back on me. You were no help when I asked you how to cure myself of this brain deficiency. No, I had to diagnose myself and search through all those textbooks, looking for a cure. Fine. I did that. But now, I'm not asking for myself. I'm asking for someone else. Isn't that why you come to me? Isn't that why I have this ability? To help people?"

They were mere dots down the long hallway now.

"Why can't you tell me what to do for her?" she yelled after them.

They disappeared.

She wanted to break something, anything. "Damn you, what good are you two anyway?"

Tadashi eyed the men working the rail line as he carried the water bucket. They'd been going at it since early morning without a break. He stopped at the first man, scooped up some water in the ladle and held it out.

The man drank, nodded his thanks and went back to work.

Tadashi approached the next man. "Drink."

The man guzzled down the water.

This was no good. These men deserved an honest break. He cranked his neck and checked the track that led to Sacramento. The foreman and the supervisor had both been called back to town.

Now or never.

He set down the bucket. "Men, stop working," he yelled. "Listen up."

The sound of hammers, pickaxes and shovels stopped.

He jumped up on the flat rail car and gestured them over.

The men, dozens and dozens of them, gathered around. They were covered in dirt and dust, sweat dripping down their faces.

Tadashi raised his voice to be heard. "When is the last time you were asked to work late?" he asked in Chinese.

There was grumbling.

"When was the last time you had to work extra days?"

The grumbling was louder.

"Heck, when was the last time you were asked, make that *told* to work without lunch?"

"All the time, Tadashi, you know that," one man near the front called out.

Yeah, all the time. Day after day. Without the end in sight. "I see you busting your backs to put in this rail line but I don't see management taking into consideration *your* needs." He threw his arms out. "When has the Fontinello organization paid you overtime? How many times has it said to you, 'Good job, we made our goal this week so we'll make tomorrow a day off?"

"Never," The men grumbled.

"Never, that's right. That has to stop and it has to stop now."

"What can we do, say, 'Pretty please, don't work us so hard?'" someone called out in a sing-song voice.

The men jeered.

If only this were a laughing matter. "No, we get their attention the only way there is." This could work, this idea that had been bubbling in his brain. "There are, what, three hundred of us at the encampment? Let's show Fontinello what happens when he tries to mess with us."

The crowd cheered.

"Yes, but how?" someone called out.

"It has to be all of us doing the same thing. Our strength is in our numbers." It would be an uprising. He nodded to himself. This might just work.

Ruby headed toward the cabin.

The Chinese symbol for Meifeng's ailment, the one that the papaya lining tea addressed, burned in her brain.

No, not Meifeng. Not cancer. Anything but cancer.

She lost her shoes and stepped inside. "Meifeng? Are you up?"

"I'm in here." Her voice came from the kitchen.

Ruby rounded the corner.

Her mentor was at the sink, washing carrots. She looked better, was moving better, at least.

"Here, let me do that. Take a seat." She took over the washing. "How are you feeling?"

"I'm doing all right. Got a little of my strength back."

Yes, but for how long? They needed to be upfront with one another. "I read up on papyrus lining. Then I got to thinking, healers can't instinctively diagnose themselves. So, maybe you *don't* have cancer."

"You're right, we can't automatically know what ails us, but we can look up our symptoms and take an educated guess. Besides ..."

Her ears pricked up. Something was being unsaid here. She turned her back to the sink to face Meifeng. "Besides, what?"

"Besides, I had a case in China that had my same symptoms." She hesitated. "You must never tell anyone this."

"OK."

"No, not just 'OK.' You have to promise."

This had to be pretty big. "All right, I promise. I'll never tell a soul."

"In Chinese culture, cutting into a dead body is a moral and spiritual sin."

"You mean an autopsy? But you said –"

"That I'd done it before, yes. But it was done in secret. Only a few of us were in on it and we swore to never tell on one another, to never give up each other's names. We swore a binding oath. One that goes beyond the physical world. One that we'll take to the grave and into the next life, to affect us forever. Do you understand?"

This sounded pretty deep. "I think so."

"In order to do autopsies and gain better knowledge of human conditions, we formed a secret group – xunshao hwanyu – loose translation, the Seekers of the Universe. We were determined to learn everything we could about the human body so that we could prevent disease and cure it if it did occur. One of the ways we sought knowledge was by doing autopsies. But we had to select bodies carefully. They had to be ones that we were sure wouldn't be questioned when the family dressed the corpse and noticed the incisions. They had to think the incision had come from an operation."

"So, something that was done when the patient was still alive?"

"Yes. Now, remember the way we cut into Buster the monkey?"

It had been like a capital I, only the top serifs were flared, a headless "jumping jack" kind of shape. "I remember, yes."

"We could only do those kinds of incisions, big, obvious incisions, I mean, on those who had no family."

"Corpses where no one would be changing the clothes for their burial."

"And even then, I'd wake in a sweat for weeks on end, sure someone would eventually find us out."

"But no one did." Thank goodness. She could only imagine the uproar it would have caused.

"The other corpses, the ones with family, we expanded the incisions that were already there from surgery so we could peer into the body cavity and do exploratory work. The family would just assume the incision was from surgery. They couldn't tell an old cut from one where no blood circulation was involved."

That made sense. You sewed up the incision and made it look like a continuation of the former one. No one would be the wiser, well, unless they were a doctor.

"There's more."

"More?"

Meifeng sighed. "Sometimes, no, many times, we removed the diseased organ and kept it in a secret lab."

Her jaw dropped. "You sent someone go to their grave without all their parts? Isn't that a sin of immeasurable cosmic consequences in Chinese culture?"

"It was for the sake of science. To further our understanding of the human body."

That made sense but still...

Meifeng paused. "I did not take this action lightly. I prayed for their souls before I cut into their corpses, thanking them for the opportunity to learn, to grow as a doctor." Her eyes teared up. "And I prayed for mine, so I might not be judged too harshly for thirsting for knowledge that would, ultimately, serve others. In the process, I hope I did not damn my soul."

Ruby hurried over and hugged her. "You had a noble reason for doing the autopsies."

Meifeng clung to her for a long moment then pulled back, wiping her eyes. "But my country's government would not have seen it that way. It would have jailed me and executed me. How could I have helped the sick and dying if I wasn't there to minister to them?"

Ruby nodded. She could hear the pleading for understanding in the tone of her voice. Damned if you do, damned if you don't, in other words.

"I came this close –" she pinched two fingers together "– from not going forward with it."

"Then, why did you do it?"

Meifeng locked eyes with her, holding the look for a long time. "For the same reason you will. Because, as a doctor, it's your duty to find the truth so that the next patient doesn't suffer."

Anastasia waited her turn at the garden. Hurry up, folks, she didn't have all day.

Her turn. Finally.

She hurried up to where Ruby sat.

Ruby looked at her quizzically. "Are you girls out of monthly herbs already?"

She wasn't here about that. "That acne tincture you gave Lillian? I've got a great idea." She opened her hands in an abracadabra manner. "Imagine making more money than you ever thought possible with Ruby's Acne Cure."

"Whatever are you talking about?"

"Let's bottle it and sell it." Yes? Yes?

But her friend just shrugged. "It's only a tincture. Anyone can make it."

"Then let's be the first to bottle it and sell it."

"You don't bottle a tincture, silly. You put it in a squeeze tube."

The girl was not getting the message here. "Whatever you do to contain it, we'll sell it. Do you have any idea how many people have acne? Not just teenagers. Some people have it as adults."

"Like Lillian."

"Exactly."

"I give it to her for free."

Oh, that's right, the Fontinellos were set for life. Ruby was in line to inherit a gi-normous amount of money one day. She could afford to hand out cures for free. It must be nice. "Not everyone has wealthy parents to take care of them."

"Oh, I hadn't thought of that." She was quiet for a moment. "So, this is a joint venture? A partnership?"

"I'll take care of the manufacturing, the distribution, everything. All you have to do is make up the formula, put your name on it and we'll sell it."

"Anastasia, I hate to rain on your party, but you know nothing about manufacturing and distribution. You wouldn't know where to start."

Oh, but she did. She had clients who were barons of such things. All she had to do was crook her finger at them and they would get the ball rolling. "Leave that to me. Can you make up a recipe that can be duplicated by a factory?"

Ruby bit her lip. "I don't know about this. It just seems so ..."

"Lucrative?"

"...risky."

"Promise me you'll think about it." Anastasia walked away, thinking hard. She'd managed to get Ruby to consider it, but really convincing her, that would take some creative convincing. She just had to find the right tack to fill the sails of this venture and get moving on it.

Ruby finished her lessons with Grace. She pushed away from the dining room table. At last, she could get out of this dress and back into comfortable clothes.

Mother appeared at the door. There was a note in her hand. "Ruby, dear, Eloise Gardner needs you. She sent word by currier, said it's important."

The name didn't sound familiar but then Mother knew more people than God and she expected everyone to know immediately to whom she was referring. "I don't know anyone named Eloise."

Mother made a rolling-eyes face. "The governor's sister."

Of course. Eloise the Governor's Sister, that Eloise. "I'll change clothes and –"

"Don't you dare, young lady." Mother steered her to the foyer. "Grab your pouch of weird plant cures and go outside. The carriage is prepared and waiting for you. This card has the address."

She'd thought of everything. "I get to use the carriage?"

"It's in Dentonville."

Dentonville was a good two hour ride, no wonder Mother was being generous with the driver, horses and carriage. "I guess I'm on my way, then."

She left the house and greeted George, their stable man. "How's the gout?"

"Manageable," he said. "But what do I do when cherries aren't in season?"

"Beets will do the same." She passed the note up to him. "Looks like we're going to be on the road for a while."

"So I heard. Don't worry, I'll get you there and back before dark."

In his dreams. It was already three in the afternoon. She hopped inside.

The carriage started up and they were soon on the road to Dentonville. She settled back into the plush seat. Mother had gone all out when she'd had it reupholstered. This thing was like being cuddled in a baby carriage. She barely felt the road at all.

Ruby settled back. She closed her eyes and went into a meditative state.

The two guides appeared.

"Tell me about the client I'm going to see. How can I help them?"

A picture came into view. There was a child. He was about two years old and covered in spots. There was a bad one above his left eye that he kept trying to scratch. He was crying and fuzzing, clearly unhappy.

"Chicken pox, is that what's I'm seeing?"

They nodded. "Yes."

She could use calendula but it required soaking the flowers overnight then drying them out to crush into a powder. No time.

Ginger powder could be used in a soothing bath but it required a lot of the spice and had to be repeated throughout the day. The family could afford it but the supply was not available.

Jasmine tea would help by working from the inside. She would use that.

But she wanted something to complement it, something immediate to take away the itch and misery of the pox sores.

"I didn't bring any sandalwood oil, darn it," she told her guides. She could have mixed it with a little bit of turmeric powder and applied it. "Give me something else I can use."

"Look out your window."

She opened her eyes. They were passing a farmer's field.

Of course. The answer was right in front of her.

Ruby sat up and rapped on the carriage ceiling. "Stop, George."

The horses came to a halt.

She jumped out and picked some plants, gathering them in her skirt. She had enough for a full day's worth of soothing baths. Ruby climbed back in the carriage, sat down and closed her eyes. "Thank you," she whispered.

"There's more," they said.

CHAPTER ELEVEN

Eloise Gardner heard a carriage approach. Maybe it was that healer daughter of Felicia Fontinello's. She hoped so. Poor little Arthur was a handful when he was cranky. And who wouldn't be cranky with all those horrible pox marks all over him?

She peeked out through the lace curtains. Yes, it was the Fontinello carriage pulling up.

She hurried outside. "Thank goodness you're here."

A young woman emerged from the carriage.

This was the girl she'd heard so many promising things about? This mere slip of a girl? She didn't seem like anything special. Oh, well, no time to dwell on that now. "Thank you for coming. It's Ruby, isn't it?"

"Where's your little boy? He's covered in pox and that one just above his eye is particularly troublesome for him."

How did she know? "Um, this way." She led Ruby up the stairs to Arthur's nursery. The nanny was rocking him on her lap.

Ruby approached and pulled a fabric satchel off her shoulder. It looked so out of place next to her lace and satin dress. She knelt down by the side of the rocker. "Hi, little guy. Having a bad day?" She pulled out a kerchief full of green plant-looking things. "These are little soldiers who are going to do battle for you."

Soldiers? They were pea pods.

Ruby patted Arthur's hand. "We'll get you fixed up in no time." She reach out, gently lifted his left eyebrow and inspected the pox near the eye. "Yeah, we can cut your healing time in half and make it easier on you to boot. Say goodbye to the soldiers."

Arthur still pouted but he waved bye-bye. He was such a little trooper.

Ruby got up and came over to her. "Mrs. Gardner? Can you show me to your kitchen?"

"Of course, this way." She led her back down stairs. "I should tell you, I've had three doctors here already."

"That many?"

She didn't understand. "He's my only child. I'd call in twenty if I had to."

"No, I meant that many before you decided to get word to me." She dumped the pea pods on the counter. "There are about five cups worth here. You'll only need one for each treatment." She measured them out. "I'm going to show you what to do, so watch carefully."

"Should I take notes?" She had five pages worth from the doctors' visits.

"Nope. This is quick and simple, no need." Ruby selected a pan, dumped the cup of green pea pods in and added water. "Just enough to cover them, OK?" She set it on the stove. "We're going to use every part of this, so don't throw out the water. We'll use that later."

"All right."

"Now, when the water boils and these get soft, I'll scoop them out, mash them up and make a paste. Then I'll dab the paste onto the pox and let them dry for an hour."

"Then what?"

"Then –" Ruby said, pointing to the water "–you rinse it off."

"That's it?" And to think the three doctors had ordered her to jump through hoops to get him treatment.

"The Earth offers easy solutions, Mrs. Gardner."

"Wait. What about the water you said to save?"

"After it cools down from boiling the pods, you can use it for a warm sponge bath. It'll help the skin heal further and ensure there are no lasting scars."

Thank goodness. A Gardner couldn't walk around with pox scars on his face for the rest of his life.

"How often do I repeat this?"

"Three times a day until it's cleared up." The girl waggled a hand in a wishy-washy gesture. "Maybe three days from now."

"That's such a relief." She threw a hand to her chest. "I was so worried."

"Now, about you."

What? "Me?"

Ruby lowered her voice. "You're having dryness, um, down there, right?"

She knew about this? Her face felt warm. "Well, yes."

"It can be caused by stress, or the changes that come from having a child. It's nothing serious. I'm going to give you a mix of herbs – ginseng, dong quai, black cohosh and chasteberry. These are strong medicines and if mixed in the wrong proportions, could do harm. But, while I was on my way here, my guides told me how much to give you."

So, she was a spiritualist. Amazing. "I'd better write this down."

"It's imperative. Like I said, if measured wrong, they can be deadly."

Tadashi threw up his hands. He had to make this sound convincing. "I don't know what to tell you, Mr. Fontinello. The digging was hard. This isn't soft dirt, you know." He pointed to the map on the wall. "It's rock in this section. The men just couldn't make as much headway as usual."

"But only a tenth of a mile? This puts us behind schedule." His boss ran his fingers through his hair as he took in the news. "Can we dynamite it?"

He was prepared for this suggestion. Ever since he'd suggested Liwei be used to blast the caliche, Phillip Fontinello had been keen for the dynamite solution. He liked using it but he didn't seem to grasp that it came with clean-up measures. You simply couldn't blast and then expect the men to immediately begin laying track. If the man would only take the time to go out to the site and see things for himself, ... but that was like talking to a wall. "Dynamite it? Questionable. Blasting isn't as effective in a flat area."

Phillip Fontinello nodded in defeat. "Well, OK, I know you had the men do their best. Thanks for letting me know." He picked up his satchel.

Tadashi hadn't noticed it in the corner. "Going out of town?"

"Back to Los Angeles. Not sure what I'll tell the investors." He smiled in a "what are you going to do" kind of way. "Have to be there by morning. Half my life is spent away from home."

"Yes sir. Have a safe trip. If that's all ...?"

"Yes, go home. It's been a long day and you've got a long trek up that mountain."

He left the office and hurried across town to the trail head. The men would be gathered there, eager for news. He couldn't wait to tell them.

Twenty minutes later, all faces turned to him as soon as he approached.

Tadashi spread his arms open wide. "We did it," he said with a grin.

The men cheered, patting each other on the back before heading up the trail.

Tadashi followed behind. Yes, they'd done it, won a small slowdown. The trick would be maintaining the pace.

Ruby returned home, the horses pulling the carriage to a stop just in front of the house. It was dark and too late to take the trail to the encampment. They would have been home sooner if she hadn't insisted on finding the farmer and paying him for the pea pods. And then they'd stopped at a tavern to eat.

"Thanks, George," she said as she stepped out of the carriage.

The horses clopped away.

The house windows were dark. Mother must be in bed already.

Inside, she gathered her skirts and hurried up the stairs. It was so cumbersome wearing a dress. She'd forgotten how much material there was with which to contend. In the bathroom, she lit a candle, much more soothing than the gas lights, and filled the bath. It would be tepid water at this hour, but all she wanted was to wash away this road dust.

She peeled off the dress, leaving it in a heap on the floor, got naked and slipped into the water. Ahhh, this was so relaxing. She let her mind wander over the day's events. Little Arthur had responded well to the treatment and stopped trying to itch his pox marks. Mrs. Gardner had begun taking the tea Ruby had mixed up for her. So, those things were good, but the unexpected trip had taken up so much of her time. When she returned to the encampment tomorrow, she'd need to make up more herbal formulas. And check on Meifeng to see how she was doing. And then there was that crazy acne tincture idea of Anastasia's, sure, like they could become a household name. She chuckled. Utter nonsense.

There was a thump.

She cocked an ear.

A floorboard squeaked.

"Mother?"

There were footsteps coming down the hall. Stealthy ones.

Mother wouldn't need to tiptoe through her own home. No, this was someone else in their house and here she was, completely naked.

Every nerve was suddenly on edge. What to do? What to do?

Ruby blew out the candle quickly.

Now she had the darkness on her side.

The door handle jiggled.

Oh, no. The intruder knew she was in here.

Someone was in their house and right outside the bathroom door.

Her eyes adjusted to the dark and fixated on the door knob.

Please, please, please, make them go away. Don't let them know I'm here.

It began turning.

Ruby froze. Oh, God. Oh, God. Oh, God.

The door opened slowly with a crazy creak.

A shadow of a man was standing there.

He paused, then strode in, right up to the side of the tub, towering above her.

She cowered.

"Mind if I join you?"

Ruby let go of the breath she was holding. "Tadashi, you scared me."

He leaned down and kissed her. "I was climbing the trail when I looked back and saw you emerge from the carriage."

If he'd been able to see the house then he'd been at the quarter-way point. "So, you came back to see me. I'm glad."

He loosened his clothes and stepped out of them.

Those legs, that strong back. She made room for him in the tub.

"Ooh, it's cold."

Yeah, unless the cook had the stove fired up, the water could be less than inviting, but, "It's not so bad."

"You'll have to keep me warm."

She lifted one eyebrow. "My pleasure." She relit the candle – now she could see that Adonis-like body better –, took the sponge and began soaping him down.

Ruby ran a finger down his cheek, along his jaw and down his throat. She wanted to explore every inch of him. "What's this divot at the base of your neck? I've never seen anyone with one so pronounced before." She could stick a golf ball in there and it would probably stay.

"Meifeng says it's an anomaly, likely passed down from one of my parents. I have something to tell you." Tadashi's eyes sparkled. "You know how we talked about the way the workers are treated? Well, we did something about it today, a work slowdown." He explained how everyone had agreed to work a little slower, a little more carefully, so they weren't going at breakneck speed any longer.

"I see. So, a more humane pace means less injuries," she said. Goodness knew how she'd tended to more sprains and aches and bruises for the Chinese workers than any other group of people. Nice to know that their suffering would be ending.

"Your father didn't suspect a thing. By the time he returns from Los Angeles, we'll have established this pace as the norm."

She locked eyes with him and ran the sponge under the water, to that sensitive spot between his legs. "Do we *have* to talk about work right now, Tadashi?"

His member responded to her touch. "Not if you don't want to."

She moved closer until her lips were nearly on his. "I don't want to talk at all."

They stared into each other's eyes for a split second.

His kiss was sudden, eager, sensual, probing. His tongue parted her lips to explore her mouth.

She could spend all night kissing this man. She ran her fingers through his hair, turned her face to better access his mouth. She probed with her tongue, matching his energy.

He broke away. "I want to lick you all over," he moaned.

And vice versa. "Me, too."

They stepped out of the tub, grabbed towels and hightailed it to her room, trying to be quiet. Impossible.

They fell onto her bed giggling and she pulled him into her arms. "Anastasia told me a few things I should try with you." Not all her visits to the red-roofed house were strictly for medicinal purposes, after all. "You don't mind being my sexual playmate for the night, do you?" she teased.

"I'm liking the sound of that." He ducked his head and claimed a breast with his mouth, eagerly taking possession of it.

A streak of desire shot through her core to her loins. The man had no idea what that did to her. He wanted to lick her all night? She'd have to reciprocate. *Such a chore.*

The door slammed open.

"What's the meaning of this?"

It was Mother.

Tadashi froze.

Ruby grabbed the bed sheets to cover herself. She was in big trouble now.

CHAPTER TWELVE

Felicia stared. Her daughter was naked, in bed with some disgusting heathen.

This was beyond horrific. It was abominable, detestable, and so utterly base.

No self-respecting girl would ever willingly consent to such nauseating carnal desires.

And yet, here was her daughter, openly flaunting her nude body before this foreigner, this barbarian, and doing outrageous acts of– she shuddered –*sex*.

If word ever got out about this, the Fontinello name would be smeared forever. They'd be the laughing stock of the entire city. People would whisper and snicker behind her back. How *dare* Ruby put their family in this despicable positon!

Felicia let her eyes burn into Ruby's. "Get ...out ...of ...my ...house."

Ruby clutched the sheet to her body. "Mother, you don't understand. I love –"

No! "Don't ever utter those words in association with this, this, *infidel* in your bed. I told you to leave, now, go. You're no longer welcome here."

"But Mother –"

"Don't 'But Mother' me. I know what I just saw. I now know how base and disgusting you are, though I would never have suspected my own daughter of being a tart, a hussy. You're no better than some senseless animal, a dog in the street, looking for a quick lay. Well, you've made your bed, young lady, and now you can lie in it."

She shot a look at the young man, no, not a man. He was a foreigner. Look at those eyes, those features. Oh God, he wasn't even a pure bred foreigner. He was a half-breed. She pointed a finger at him. "And *you*. You tempted my daughter as though you were the devil himself."

"I didn't –"

"Luring her into showing her nakedness to you so you can have your way with her. For shame. Well, you want her? You can have her. She's no daughter of mine. Not anymore."

She went to leave the room but stopped and turned. She wanted to be perfectly clear here.

"Take whatever you want that you can carry on your back and leave with this, this, *man* that you've chosen. I don't ever want to see you in this house again young lady. Is that clear?"

Ruby stared at her. "You're kicking me out?"

"You forfeited your place as my daughter when you brought him here." She took one last look at the nasty scene and shook her head in disgust. "Be gone in ten minutes."

Ruby trudged up the trail with Tadashi. Her head was reeling.

Mother had kicked her out of the house. One day, she was a Fontinello with the whole world ahead of her. Now she was left to fend for herself.

Her patients. She could no longer treat them for free.

Her imported herbs. She could no longer say, "Put them on my bill," knowing Daddy would pay for them.

Daddy. She'd forgotten all about him.

What would he say when he came home and found her tossed out with nothing but these few belongings she'd managed to claim? Would he scold Mother for overreacting? Because that's what she'd done. Would he talk sense into her? Send word that everything was OK and she could come back?

Or would he agree that she wasn't worthy to bear the Fontinello name anymore?

"You OK?" Tadashi asked.

No. "I'm fine."

They reached the encampment.

Tadashi stopped her and cupped her face in his hands. "I want you to move into my tent with me."

It made sense. "Let me check on Meifeng first. I'm worried about her."

She left her belongings, just some footwear and a couple of jackets, with him and crossed the meadow to the cabin. It was pitch-black inside. "It's just me, Meifeng," she whispered in case she'd awaken the woman.

There was a soft moan from the loft.

Meifeng?

Ruby scrambled up the ladder. "Are you all right?" She leaned over the old woman's body. It was too dark to see much of anything. "Are you in pain?"

"Hurts bad."

"What can I do?"

"My tea."

The one with papyrus. "I'll get you more."

She went down to the main floor and fixed the tea. Meifeng really should be sleeping on the main floor. What if she had to use the toilet in the middle of the night? She could fall off the ladder and break her back. Now that she'd be sleeping in Tadashi's tent, the old medicine woman should be moved out of the loft. She'd ask some of the Chinese workers to help her.

Ruby went up to the loft with the tea. "Here you go. Sit up for me." She held it to her lips as Meifeng drank. The tea took care of the pain, yes, but it was the core problem that needed to be addressed. But what type of cancer did Meifeng have? She had no clue.

How could she help her mentor if she didn't know where the problem originated?

She felt so darned helpless.

Helpless and homeless. That was her.

Felicia yanked the dresses off their hangers. There had to be twenty of these things – frilly, lacey, and all commissioned for her daughter, the tramp. She pressed them into the arms of the cook, the new maid and George, the stable man, until they could barely see over top of the heap in their arms. "Get them out of here."

"Yes, Ma'am," they said in unison and left what had been Ruby's bedroom.

She followed, carrying two dresses herself, one draped over each arm. She couldn't very well ask her servants to haul away all these clothes without carrying her fair share.

Felicia eyed the two in her arms. They were ball gowns, custom made for Ruby's coming-out festivities. Well, there would be no coming-out party now, not with her daughter a proven slut. She may as well work at that house of ill repute she'd heard about, out near the train tracks. A job like that served her right for carousing with that low-bred bastard, a half-breed, no less. The thought made her shiver.

She reached the bottom floor and headed for the back door. Winifred's load was too wide to make it through the door and she bounced off the doorjamb.

"For goodness sake, turn sideways," Felicia instructed her, tapping her foot as she waited. The woman was a wonder in the kitchen but short on common sense.

Finally, they were all outside in the back yard.

Winifred dropped her load of dresses on the grass and stared at the barrel used to burn the household trash. "They won't fit in there," she warned. "Maybe one of them will, but not all these."

Really, genius? "Fine, then we'll burn them one at a time." She just wanted every vestige of Ruby out of the house so she'd never have to think about her again. She stuffed the cotillion dress down into the barrel. The satin billowed up but she batted it down again. "All right, let's get this started. Someone give me a match."

George had one.

Felicia struck it on the metal barrel and watched it burn for a moment. Perfect. She tossed it in the barrel and the gown began to burn. She pointed to the new maid. "Stay here until they're all burned to a crisp."

Ruby went down the mountain and headed toward Anastasia's.

She'd spent a week on the mountain as a permanent resident. At first, it had been tough to readjust, knowing she could never go home. But then, a sense of freedom had settled over her. It didn't hurt that she spent the nights wrapped up in Tadashi's arms. Pure bliss.

Now, she had herbs to distribute.

It was early enough that the girls should still be up. The red-roofed house was just up ahead.

The front door opened. A man stepped out.

It was Daddy.

She stopped and ducked behind a bush. Her *father* visited prostitutes?

She thought back.

How many times had he come home late, claiming work had kept him but looking chipper and unstressed? How many of those times had he smelled of rose water, Anastasia's perfume of choice? *Gee, Mother, looks like I'm not the only one who thinks sex is a normal part of life. You're the one forcing your own husband to seek it out elsewhere.*

She waited until he'd disappeared down the road before she resumed walking.

When she got there, Anastasia answered her knock.

"Come in, sugar. Coffee?"

A man straightened his tie as he trotted down the stairs.

It was the city councilman Daddy had taken her to visit. Him, too?

Anastasia saw him out the door, "Bye now." She closed the door and pressed her back to it with a rolling-eyes face. "He talks about closing me down to his constituents but he's here twice a week."

They took seats at the kitchen table. Anastasia poured her a hot steaming cup.

Ruby ignored it. "We need to talk. That acne tincture? I'm ready to move forward with it."

Anastasia burst into a big smile. "Fifty-fifty partners?"

"Yes." She pushed a sheet of paper across the table. "Here's the formula. I noted where the temperature has to be in order for the herbs to release their healing ingredients."

"I thought it was just zinc."

"Zinc is very drying. These herbs are almost like essential oils. They sooth the top layer of skin while the zinc infiltrates the pimple below."

"Another selling point I'll tell the manufacturing guy. I'll get right on this." She stood up.

Right now? "Should I go with you? I've got time."

Anastasia waved away the thought. "Honey, what I meant was, when I see my manufacturing client *tonight*, I'll get right on this." She winked and giggled. "If you get what I mean."

"I'd better get going."

She bade Anastasia goodbye and headed out.

Ruby took her spot at the garden, arranged her herbs and got ready to meet people in need of medical help. She closed her eyes and settled her mind. "Help me diagnose and treat whomever comes today so that I might make their lives better," she asked her guides.

There were footsteps. Someone was approaching.

It was Penelope Fitzgerald, just like her guides had told her last night as she slept.

Penelope stepped up and fidgeted. "You were right," she blurted.

"Not according to the story you told the newspaper."

"I said you were right," she snapped. "What do you want from me?"

She let the sentence hang in the air.

Penelope kicked a stone aside. "All right, I'm sorry."

Ruby picked up a pouch and handed it to her. "Once a night, once in the morning, as far into the vagina as you can insert it. And eat yogurt every day for the next two weeks to rebalance your system."

Tadashi signaled the men surreptitiously. "Slower."

The tempo of the clanging tools changed slightly.

A handcart, powered by two Chinse men, appeared in the distance. It surged along the line as the men pumped, coming closer to the site. The supervisor was aboard. He had someone standing beside him.

Would you look at that, Phillip Fontinello was on board. It was about time the man took an interest in what was happening out here instead of staying cooped-up in that office, throwing decisions at people.

He trotted over.

The handcart stopped. Phillip stepped off. "Tadashi, what's going on?"

"I'm glad you're here. We're trying some new tactics."

Phillip shared a startled look with the supervisor. "Tactics? We never talked about any new tactics."

He'd have to sell this carefully. "Instead of the men all taking lunch at once, we're staggering the men into three groups. Group One has lunch at eleven o'clock, Group Two at noon and Group Three at one p.m."

His boss scratched his head. "I don't know about this."

He was losing him. Phillip Fontinello needed to see the benefit to the company or he'd never agree to it. "This way, the work never fully stops."

"For how long did it stop the old way?"

"An hour." He paused. "Or, at least, it was *supposed* to stop for an hour."

"You're not making sense. Either the work stopped or it didn't."

"That's the point, sir. For weeks now, you've had the men work through their lunch hour. In fact, you worked them nonstop all day long."

"Because we need to get this line finished so it can be up and running."

"But the men need nourishment. They can't continue to work this way without having lunch."

Phillip threw his shoulders back. "They never complained."

"Not to you. They don't speak English."

"It can't be that hard, working through lunch."

Oh, really? Tadashi spotted a hammer with a fifteen-pound head off to the side, picked it up and carried it over to his boss. "Here, take this."

Phillip nearly dropped it.

Tadashi hid a smile. The boss man hadn't anticipated the weight. "Swing it at that rail tie nail right there, sir."

The Chinese workers stopped to watch.

Phillip held the hammer sideways to his body, bent over and tapped the flat-topped nail, barely lifting the hammer six inches above his target. He straightened up. "It's not going in."

Not if you use it like some girl, it wouldn't. "You're got to *swing* the hammer, sir, not tap with it."

"Like this?" He tried again. This time, he lifted the head of the hammer about a foot above the rail. "This hurts my back."

What a wimp. Tadashi signaled to Bingwen, one of his biggest men. He said in Chinese, "Come over here and show him how it's done."

Bingwen ambled over and handed Phillip his own hammer, a heavier one.

Phillip blinked in surprise at the additional weight.

At least he didn't nearly drop it. Tadashi pointed to it. "Most of the men are using this kind of hammer, the twenty-pound one, sir."

Bingwen took the lighter hammer, ensured he had everyone's attention, threw it up over his head and brought it down with force, striking the nail with a solid blow. When he lifted the hammer, the nail was a good three or four inches farther into the wooden tie.

The Chinaman exchanged hammers again and returned to his spot.

Phillip nodded. "OK, now, I understand how it's done." He eyed the target, hefted the fifteen-pound hammer up high and, red-facedd with the sudden effort, brought it crashing back down.

A clang resounded.

He'd missed, hitting the rail tie, not the nail.

Phillip waved Tadashi away, signaling him to stay back. "Let me try again." He spread his feet, got ready, lifted the hammer high and, with a mighty effort, swung it down again.

He hit the nail but it barely drove any farther in.

Phillip stared, disheartened, at his lack of progress.

Tadashi took the hammer from his boss's hands. He'd just proved that Phillip Fontinello had no idea what he was asking workers to do, not just now and then, but for hours on end. "Not so easy is it?"

Phillip dusted off his hands. He did not look happy. "All right, Tadashi. You win. They can get staggered lunch breaks, but the work never completely stops. Because if it does, they'll all be fired and I'll bring in a whole new set of workers to replace them."

"Yes, sir." It was a start.

Ruby sat beside Meifeng's bed, the cot that used to be hers. A couple of the workers had helped her and Tadashi move Meifeng to the main floor of the cabin two weeks ago. The poor woman was getting weaker by the day.

She brushed the stray locks off the doctor's forehead. Her hair had gone completely gray. She'd never really noticed it before.

Meifeng turned as she rested. "Ruby," she said softly without opening her eyes, "I have to tell you something."

"Anything."

Meifeng smiled. "I'm glad you and Tadashi are together."

Truly? It made her feel good inside to know that. "He's a wonderful man."

"My two favorite people." She shifted on the bed. "And I lied."

Meifeng? A liar? Couldn't be. "You were being nice when you said you liked my cooking?"

"That you weren't ready."

She meant the day that she'd pretended to have a heart attack, leaving her in a panic. "You certainly had me going."

"You're ready, believe me."

To study under that ultimate healer guy in Shanghai? It wasn't a priority right now. "You need to rest."

"Get out paper and pencil."

She got up, grabbed the items and a book for a hard surface. "Ready. Is it a letter you want to write? In English or Chinese?"

"It's a list of my symptoms, from when I first became aware something was wrong. I want you to know so if you ever encounter this, you can have a suspicion."

She hated hearing Meifeng talk of dying. But they both knew there was no way to reverse her course. All Ruby could do was make her comfortable at this point. "May I point out that there are only men on this mountain for me to tend?"

"You treat women in the city, too."

She had a point. "All right, what were your symptoms?"

"My toilet habits changed."

"In what way?"

"It seemed like I had to go more often, peeing, I mean. And it was urgent." She waggled a hand. "Nothing more specific that that I can point to."

"Next?"

"When I'd eat, I'd feel full more quickly than normal."

That was odd. Maybe the cancer was in her stomach.

"My vaginal discharge changed."

"How?"

"The color, the odor. It wasn't bad-smelling. It was just … different. Sometimes I'd feel this pressure in my pelvis. I kept thinking it was something I'd eaten that was the cause, but then it was food I've had before without that occurring."

Ruby jotted it down. "I know you had back pain. Do you think that was attributable to whatever type of cancer you have?"

"It's possible, I suppose," Meifeng said, "although I can't think of why that would be. I had that bloated feeling come on me, too."

"A lot of women get that. Depends on the time of the month."

"Yes, but do they get all the other symptoms as well?"

Ruby held the pencil poised. "Is that it?"

"That's all I can think of."

Ruby scanned the list. She didn't like this. The symptoms were too disjointed. Having to go pee more often –that could be a urinary tract infection. The change in discharge – women's bodies were in constant flux. Back pain – Meifeng could have arthritis in her spine.

There was a knock at the cabin door. "Anyone home?"

Tadashi stuck his head in. He was back from Frisco.

She got up and went over, sliding into his arms. "I missed you."

He kissed her. "I missed you more."

Ruby shook her head. "Not possible."

He left her to check on Meifeng, sitting beside her cot and reaching out to take her hand. "How is today going for you?"

She stepped outside to let the two of them have time together. It was touching to see how much he cared for his adoptive mother. If they ever decided to have a family, she knew he'd make a great dad.

Tadashi entered the tent. He looked tired.

Ruby looked up from reading her latest medical textbook. "Hi, sweetie." She went to get up.

"What are you doing?"

Wasn't it obvious? She lifted the book. "I'm ...reading."

"Why aren't you with Meifeng?"

Oh, was that what he meant. She walked over to him, slipping her arms around his neck. "I was with her all day. She's resting."

"But you should be beside her." He broke away from her and began pacing. "What if she wakes up and needs something?"

She'd never seen him like this, not in all their months living together. "Calm down. I gave her a sedative. She needs to rest."

"But not alone." He threw up his hands in disbelief. "What kind of medicine woman are you? You have a very sick patient. You should be there."

If Meifeng was in harm's way, she would be. But the woman was not about to die any minute now. Why was he badgering her this way? "Tell you what, let's walk across the encampment and check in on her together."

"No."

"No? You're so worried about her, but you won't go look in on her?" Surely he had to realize how contradictory that was.

He stopped and searched her eyes. "Don't you understand? If I don't go see her, then she'll have to stay alive until I get back."

"You're not making sense."

"I have to go away."

For a week? For a year? When did this come up? Where was he going?

"I want to ensure she'll be alive when I get back. If I tell her I'm going, then she'll have a chance to say goodbye to me." Tadashi looked down at his feet. "But if I leave without seeing her, she'll hang on just so we can talk one more time."

"Meifeng is not about to die."

His eyes looked wet. "She's the only mother I've ever known."

"Oh, Tadashi, she'll be here when you return. I promise." She pulled him into her arms. "Sweetie, I owe her a lot, too. If it wasn't for her, my brain would be still be dealing with life the way a ten year old does. Just like she pulled you off the streets to give you a home, she kind of saved my life, too. I'm looking out for her, don't worry. She's just resting. She's fine." She held him until the tension left his shoulders.

Tadashi pulled back and nodded sheepishly. "Thanks."

She was glad that was over. "So, what's this about a trip? Where are you going?"

"I've found my calling."

That's good.

"I'm quitting as your father's interpreter."

That was not good. "But, Tadashi, he needs you on-site as his go-between person."

"He'll find someone else. Me, I'm going to organize the Chinese workers up and down the coast. No more working those long hours. No more being forced to take on extra days of work or else face being fired."

"For railroad workers, you mean?"

"For all types of workers."

Hold on. He was going up against the dock owners, the shipping companies, the ice factories, the agricultural companies, transportation companies, manufacturing – every business sector that used manual labor? Was he insane? "They'll kill you."

"I have to do this, Ruby." His eyes flashed, dark and intense. "Don't try to stop me."

Meifeng opened her eyes. Was Ruby here? Where was that little bell? There it was.

She reached for it. Missed it. Why wasn't her hand moving the way she was commanding it? Damn, it sucked being ill.

"Ruby?" Listen to her. Even her voice was betraying her.

Ruby hurried over. "You're awake. How are you feeling?"

Like a dry lake bed. "Water."

"Of course." Ruby held the cup rim up to her lips.

She was such a dear, fussing over her this way. "Thank you."

Ruby looked so serious. Maybe she and Tadashi were out of sorts. He hadn't been around to visit lately. She hoped things were all right between them.

"I have to ask you something, Meifeng."

Yes, Tadashi loves you. I see it in his eyes when he looks at you. "Anything."

"What would you say to having an operation?"

"You'd do it? By yourself?"

"No, no, not me. I'm not qualified. We can transport you down off the mountain. Take you to the hospital in Sacramento. We can have the finest surgeons in San Francisco come here and get this, this, horrible *cancer* out of you." She spat out the word like it was venom.

"Operate? On what part?"

"On the part with the cancer."

"And what part is that? We don't know for sure." She tried to sit up, found it too difficult and gave up. Fine, she'd stay prone. "You can't go cutting up the body, opening up this organ or that one, trying to locate this thing. Remember Anastasia's little monkey?"

"Buster?"

"If he hadn't been run over by the carriage, he would have eventually succumbed to his cancer. But remember how it was hiding in his gall bladder? We cut into it and didn't see it at first."

"But I can't just let this thing consume you. We have to try something."

"One thing I know about cancer. It spreads, Ruby. Even if the surgeons do find it, chances are, it's traveled by now."

There were tears in Ruby's eyes. "You're giving up."

"I'm being a realist." She closed her eyes. "I'm tired. Just let me rest."

Ruby waited in the front pew. She hoped that the parishioners understood. They had to, just had to. She didn't know where else to turn. They *had* to help her.

The preacher looked down from the pulpit. "Before we begin our final hymn today, we have a special speaker. I hope you will give her your full attention."

He signaled her.

Ruby got to her feet, stepped up on the platform and approached the pulpit. All eyes were on her.

Oh, God, Mother was here. Just ignore her, don't look at her.

She cleared her throat. "You all know me." She clutched the sides of the lectern and sought out faces of those she'd administered. "I've been there when you've had the flu. I've tended to you when you've broken bones or busted a rib. What you may not know, is that I couldn't have done any of that if not for my mentor, Meifeng. For years, she would come to the community garden and tend to you. Well, she tended to me, too. I was born with a mental issue. Meifeng recognized it and treated me for a number of years to give me clarity. During that time, she also taught me to use the same skills that she employed to cure you all of your laryngitis, to fight your measles, stop your cough, fix help your injuries.

"Now, Meifeng is sick herself and she –" her voice cracked and she swallowed hard "– needs your help. She is battling cancer and I am trying to cure her. But I need your help."

The tears threatened. Her voice wobbled. "Please, everybody, pray for her."

The preacher took her elbow and helped her step off the platform. "Ruby spoke from her heart. Now, it's up to you to use the voice in your own heart to speak to God. Meifeng has done wonderful things for many of us. Praying for her is the least we can do."

The hymn began.

Mr. Sanders stood up and came over to her. "Thank you for taking care of my wife when she took ill. She said between you and Meifeng, she knew she was in good hands. I don't pray as much as I should, but I'll be sure to pray for her recovery."

Another parishioner, Dorothy Montgomery, approached. "Remember how my little girl had that tooth ache? You knew just what to do. She was smiling in just a couple minutes. You have no idea how it pains a mother to see her child suffer. We'll all pray for Meifeng tonight."

Another mother came over, taking her hand and patting it. "Rest assured we'll pray for Meifeng. You and she made our lives here so much more enjoyable, knowing if we needed anything, one of you could help us and never ask for a thing in return."

She moved away and Ruby spotted Mother. She was staring at her from across the room.

A couple stepped up blocking her view, the next in the line of people waiting to thank her. "Meifeng helped our older child, you help our younger one. Of course we'll pray for her."

Fifteen minutes later, the line ended and the church was cleared out.

Mother was nowhere to be seen.

Ruby tipped the cup up to Meifeng's lips. "Here. Drink all of it."

Meifeng nodded. She reached up to take the cup but her hands were shaking.

"No, no, let me hold it," Ruby said, pushing her hands down. If any of it spilled, she wouldn't be able to tell how much the doctor had ingested. She was in unchartered territory here. She'd waited two days to take this step, two days to go over and over the herbs to use, the exact measurements to make.

Meifeng finished the concoction and settled back down against her pillows.

Ruby checked her pulse and watched for any signs of distress. None.

Meifeng closed her eyes and began breathing easier.

So this was how it was to sedate someone into an intentional coma.

Ruby got up. She frowned, watching her patient. Had she done everything right? Had she given Meifeng too much? She'd gone to sleep so quickly, maybe that meant her body was too susceptible to the herbs. The woman weighed no more than ninety pounds.

Meifeng was breathing slower.

That slow?

Oh, gosh, what if she'd overdosed the woman? The medical texts had only specified amounts for male or female. Well, gee, there was a pretty big difference between a ninety-pound woman and a two hundred pound one. No, cancel that thought. The text was written in China. Most people were small over there, small and lithe. So maybe the amount was right for Meifeng after all.

Ruby ran a hand down her face. This was torture, putting someone under. If only she had someone with whom to confer on these things.

She checked her notes.

Three months ago, soon after Tadashi had left, she'd begun Meifeng on a bacterial treatment to blast it out of her body. She'd curtailed her time at the garden, missed meals to tend Meifeng.

When the patient hadn't gotten better, she'd switched to bombarding the body with a viral cure. Still no change.

Last month, soon after Tadashi left, Ruby had gone the mega-force tack next, giving Meifeng herbs and concoctions to boost her immune system into stellar fitness. She'd responded slightly. But it hadn't lasted. She'd slumped again.

Now, the idea was to put Meifeng into an induced coma so her body could put all its energy into fighting off this cancer.

She hoped this worked.

Tadashi went to lie down and tried to close his eyes. Sure, like he could sleep. All he could think about was Ruby – that smile, that skin and those long eyelashes. Some days he'd heard a girl talking or caught a hint of a giggle and turned, heat pounding, thinking it was her. His spirit had been crushed when it turned out to be someone else. Every day away from her had been torture.

He'd even begun to dream about Ruby, silly things like sailing around the world together on a raft of pillows, of all things, swimming underwater without needing to breathe and riding horses to the top of the world where, it turned out, the horses could fly, all of it purely logical in the world of dreams. He'd awakened, sure that they'd shared those adventures together, until he looked about and realized that she was not in his bed.

But she should have been. What was he thinking, leaving her to go around California, hopping trains and organizing the Chinese workers? It was important work, but she was important, too, too important to let her be snatched up by some other man.

Ruby. She was the yin to his yang. The perfect partner.

Tadashi smiled. He reached for his pants, pulled them closer and felt around the pocket. There it was, the ring he'd bought. He pulled it out.

The opal stone was barely discernable in the near darkness.

He hoped Ruby liked it. He hoped it was her size.

It was nothing fancy. Not as big as she deserved. Hopefully, she'd realize it was the best he could afford right now. Besides, it was the message that came with it that mattered. The message was: He loved her.

"Ruby?"
Ruby stirred from her sleep.
"Ruby?"
Meifeng? She shot up in bed.
She'd heard her name, sure that it had been called out.
She threw the cover off herself and darted across the room to the cot. "Did you call out my –?"
She was cold.
Blue.
Gone.
No.
No, no, no.
She grabbed a mirror and held it to Meifeng's mouth.
No fog, no breath.
No, no, no.
Meifeng was dead.
The tears flowed.
Ruby dropped to her knees. She heard wailing – hers –and couldn't help it. Meifeng was gone, the woman who had taken her in, taught her so much, treated her like a daughter, treated her like a colleague.
She was gone, just … gone. And it was her fault, all her fault.
"I tried so hard to save you," she blubbered. "I tried everything there was."
Except an operation. She should have insisted, should have overstepped Meifeng's objections and just arranged for it anyway. So what if she was cut off from her parents' wealth? She could have found some way to cover the cost. Why, oh why didn't she have the workers shuttle Meifeng down off the mountain to get that operation? The surgeons would have found the cancer, cut it out and

Meifeng would still be here, smiling and laughing and full of life.

There was an empty space in her heart. Empty, yet full of so much pain.

She gave in to the tears again, her body wracked with sobs. They came in waves and kept coming.

Finally, she lifted her head. She had no more tears to cry.

"I let you down." She smoothed the gray hair off her mentor's forehead. "I failed you. I'm so sorry."

She stepped out into the cold mountain air.

How could the sun still rise? How could the birds still sing?

Her mentor was gone, dead.

Life would never be the same again.

Ruby sat with the body. She'd observed all the traditions, dressing Meifeng in black, covering any deities in the cabin with red cloth. A white cloth had been draped over the doorway and a gong placed to the right of it. A yellow cloth covered Meifeng's face. A blue cloth was over her body. Her comb had been snapped in half, part of it placed in the coffin, the other part would be given to Tadashi when he returned. Word had been sent, though she was not sure where he was.

Incense burned at the foot of the coffin, with a white candle burning there, too. She'd burned funeral money – for Meifeng to spend in the afterlife – in its flame.

The workers had come and paid their respects.

If this were China, the body would be on display for forty-nine days. She'd been told seven was enough.

At the end of seven days, there was only one person who still hadn't come to the mountain.

The cabin door opened.

Tadashi.

Ruby turned. Her lip quivered. "I couldn't save her," she cried, gesturing helplessly.

Tadashi rushed over to her and caught her up in his arms. "Shhh, it's all right."

How could it be all right? She'd promised him that she'd take care of Meifeng. Promised him that she'd be alive when he returned. She was a failure.

Tadashi rocked her as she cried. "Shhh, I'm here now."

She composed herself and gestured for him to leave her and go pay his respects. He'd want time alone. "I'll wait outside."

Ruby closed the door softly behind her. The air was fresh out here, fresh and cold. She blinked at the brightness. Ruby hugged herself. Her stomach growled. When was the last time she'd eaten? Three days? Four? She couldn't remember.

Thirty minutes later, the door opened and Tadashi emerged. "Come to my tent," he said gently.

"I can't leave her."

"Just for a little while." He slipped his arm around her.

It felt so right. "I'm glad you're here."

They began walking.

She had to explain. "Her symptoms were not definitive. There was no way to draw a conclusion. I searched through all the books, wracked my brain." She'd pleaded with her guides for a cure. Nothing. Not that she'd expected them to make it easy on her, but a hint was all she would have needed.

"You sat by her side long enough. You did your duty. We'll bury her tomorrow."

That soon? "If you're sure."

"You're skin and bones."

Who had time to eat when you were focused on saving the life of someone you loved?

They reached the tent and he held the flap open for her. She hadn't been in it since he'd left. Had they really lived in this place together as little as three months ago? It seemed so small inside.

There was their bed. A flash of desire hit her. "Take me, Tadashi."

"My pleasure." Tadashi undressed her and slid into bed with her. He ran a finger down her neck to the spot between her breasts. "I missed you, Ruby."

Their lovemaking was tender, soothing and utterly perfect. It was as if they'd never been apart.

She basked in his kisses and, when it was over, looked into those incredible eyes. She grabbed him and kissed him. "You have to come home more often."

"I hate being away from you."

"Me, too." She lay her head on his chest, breathing in the scent of him. How she loved this man.

The killer left the whorehouse.

His inner voice kicked in.

Shame on him. He'd lain with a whore. Again. He hung his head.

But she'd been so pretty, so soft and so very willing. Anything he'd wanted her to do, she'd done. No questions asked. And it had felt –he blushed –amazing.

What a fool. She was willing only because she was a whore. And he'd been weak, weak and gullible. She'd told him he was handsome, virile, a catch for any woman. She'd built him up, made him feel alive.

It had been exhilarating.

They were lies. All her words were lies. She was the devil sent to entrap men, weak men. Like him.

How the devil could look so nice, be so special, he couldn't fathom. He'd seen no horns, smelled no rot.

But she was the devil, nonetheless. And it was up to him to get rid of the devil.

His little voice was right. It was his duty, his calling.

Ruby stirred in her sleep. Something was keeping her awake. Something she couldn't put her finger on. She stared at the peak of the tent's ceiling, but didn't really see it.

Meifeng would be buried tomorrow. She still didn't know what had killed her. Uterine cancer? Stomach cancer? Bladder? Liver? Ovarian? Intestinal? Cervical? Fallopian? They were all possibilities.

Their discussion came back to her, about ignoring Chinese societal mores. Dead bodies were to be handled in a strictly structured way according to custom. Doing otherwise would affect their chances of happiness on the other side. But Meifeng had bucked tradition in the quest to understand, to find a cure.

She could hear her mentor's voice now: "I prayed for their souls before I cut into their corpses, thanking them for the opportunity to learn, to grow as a doctor. And I prayed for mine, so I might not be judged too harshly for thirsting for knowledge that would, ultimately, serve others."

And when Ruby had asked why she had ultimately gone through with the secret autopsies, she'd said: "For the same reason you will. Because, as a doctor, it's your duty to find the truth so that the next patient doesn't suffer."

The words echoed in her brain.

It was her duty. Her *duty*. How could she help someone in the future with the same weird symptoms Meifeng had presented if she let this opportunity pass her by? She *had* to do it.

She slid out from between the bedclothes, felt around in the dark and found her clothes, Ruby slipped into them, shivering at their chill, and pulled on her shoes. Ruby paused at the flap and cast a look back at Tadashi. Sound asleep. Good.

The air was biting cold. She picked her way to the cabin and stepped inside.

Oh, God. She covered her nose. The cabin reeked with the stench of death. She'd get used to it in a couple of minutes, but for right now, it was like to gag her.

Funny how she hadn't noticed it when she'd sat with the body, but then, this was winter so cell deterioration was slowed.

She lit the kerosene lamp and a couple of candles. There, now she could see.

Meifeng's case with the set of scalpels was on the shelf. She pulled it down and opened it wide, setting it on the lid of the casket.

One more thing.

She knelt down and clasped her hands, eyes squeezed shut. "Forgive me for what I am about to do. I mean no disrespect. I do it only to learn, to grow so that I might help others."

She opened her eyes and stood up. OK, time to get to work.

The blue cloth across the body – gone.

The clothes on Meifeng – unbuttoned and moved out of the way.

There was no need to don an apron. The blood was well coagulated in the veins and arteries, never to flow again.

Ruby took the largest scalpel in hand and eyed the body. Right about … here.

She cut, going straight down in, and drew the blade down the center of the body, mimicking the path Meifeng had taken with Buster the monkey. Soon, she had one long line like an upper case I, with the serifs at either end winged out.

Rigor mortis had long passed.

She peeled the skin back and eyed the rib cage. She'd need a saw.

Hold on. Maybe she didn't need to go that route. Meifeng's complains had centered on her abdomen. Best to start there.

The uterus was easy to spot. But it was small, way smaller than she'd expected. Meifeng had never had children. Did that mean she was more apt to have cancer in her womb? Or less likely?

Ruby cut the organ open, making flaps and folding the flaps back. She brought the lantern closer. Nothing looked abnormal or out of place.

Buster's cancer had been hidden. She slit the uterus more, delving into the small pockets of each tunnel.

Nothing stood out.

Next up, the tubes that led to the ovaries. Meifeng had told her of women whose pregnancies grew here until the tube burst. "It always means death," she'd said.

Ruby sliced along the length of the tubes and spread the corridor open, first the right side, then the left. All the tissue looked the same. No cancer here.

She reached in the right side and found the ovary. So small, but so life giving. She cut it free from the surrounding tissue, held it in her hand, then took the scalpel and cut straight through it, slicing it in half like a cherry tomato.

She caught her breath.

This was it.

The cancer was a dark red mass, ugly and dangerous-looking. It had overtaken the organ to the point that the healthy tissue was so thin, so sparse, it barely stood a chance.

Wait. The Fallopian tube. Maybe the end, where it fanned out by the ovary, had been affected. She hadn't cut all the way to the end.

Ruby grabbed the smaller scalpel and cut farther into the end of the tube. Yes, look right there. She moved the light closer.

The cancer had metastasized, taken hold here, too. It had been in a fold, hidden from view when she'd first checked.

"If only I'd known."

Her shoulders eased. She had the answer. She knew what had killed Meifeng – ovarian cancer.

She glanced up at the shelves of medical textbooks towering above her.

Somewhere in them was the answer. Had to be. If not the answer, then an inkling, something that would lead to addressing this damned disease quickly, decisively, nipping it in the bud so no other woman had to suffer the way that Meifeng had.

She would read every single one of them three times over if that's what it took.

Ruby took the diseased ovary and, feeling around the body cavity, put it back in place. If the cancer had moved to the Fallopian tube, had it also traveled elsewhere?

The clock read an hour before sunrise. If she hurried, she could delve deeper and still have Meifeng sewn up and put back together before the encampment woke up.

Tadashi turned over in bed and reached for Ruby. Nothing.

He sat up. She wasn't in the tent. Maybe she'd slipped out to use the toilet.

He'd come back to Sacramento to find her tending Meifeng, so devoted to her patient that she'd neglected her own self. Ruby's eyes looked sunken, her arms were skinny. Maybe she hadn't eaten in days, she was so devoted to Meifeng's care. But when she'd died – he could kick himself for not being here –Ruby had also devoted herself to ensuring his mother had everything done properly.

Respectful –that was Ruby. Respectful of traditions that governed the Chinese way of life. Respectful of the old ways, of their culture, their values, their devotion to their elders. She'd laid out Meifeng the proper way, draped the cloths the correct way, and followed the many other traditions that honored the dead and that ensured Meifeng would rest in peace in the afterlife.

Ruby probably had no idea how important that was, what it meant to all the Chinese in the camp, and what it meant to him, as Meifeng's adopted son. And yet she'd sacrificed her time and effort and respected the old ways anyhow. What a wonderful girl. She'd make a wonderful wife, too.

He smiled at the thought.

Where was she, anyhow?

Tadashi got up, pulled on his clothes and slid his feet into his shoes. He ducked out in the cool morning air.

There was light, a lot of light, coming from the cabin.

She must be over there, wanting to say her final goodbyes in solitude, no doubt. But why she needed so much light, he couldn't fathom.

He padded across the encampment and reached the porch.

Tadashi opened the cabin door. "Ruby?"

He stopped.

What the hell?

Ruby was arm deep in Meifeng's split-open corpse.

Ruby froze.

Tadashi was standing in the open doorway, mouth agape.

Oh, no. No, no, no, no, no.

Her hand was mid grope, up near Meifeng's heart, elbow deep.

She yanked it out. Guilty.

Tadashi stared, eyes wide. He stumbled closer, gaze locked on the corpse and croaked, "What the hell are you doing?"

"I can explain."

"Explain this, this abomination of human decency?"

It was a medical procedure, for goodness sake. Yes, it was on a dead body, but that was how science moved forward. "You're blowing this out of proportion."

His raked his fingers through his hair. "You knew our customs. You knew how sacred the body is once a person dies."

"Relax, it's just –"

"Just? Just? Do you know what you've done?"

"Yes." Ruby drew herself up taller. He'd stop acting so huffy when he realized what she'd accomplished. "I've discovered what killed Meifeng."

"You've sentenced my mother to *eternal hell*."

"I have not." Her soul was in Heaven. That's where good people went.

"You've desecrated her body."

"I had to know what killed her." Didn't he understand? "Through this autopsy, by finding out what it was that was eating away at her, now other women can be saved."

"You have damned her forever," he yelled.

She had to calm him down, appease him. Maybe if Meifeng's corpse wasn't splayed open like this. She unclipped the abdominal skin and folded it across the body. "I can sew her up, make her look like this never happened, Tadashi. You'll see."

"You've denied her eternal happiness."

"No one will know."

"Oh, really?" He stopped, turned on his heel and pointed at Meifeng. "She knows."

"Tadashi, you don't understand. She wanted me to find out what was killing her."

"She didn't want you to do –" he gestured, helplessly "– this." He stared at her, eyes burning into her. "Do you realize what you've done?"

It was an autopsy. What was the big deal? "Calm down."

"Calm down?" He shook his head. "You've dishonored my mother. She's lost forever. There is no bringing her back."

The Chinese custom of revering the body, he meant. All those funeral traditions she'd been told to follow. Well, she'd followed them, done her best. She'd prayed to her own God, too. To her way of thinking, Meifeng got double coverage that way. "What do you care about all those customs? You're not even Chinese."

"*She* was."

"I told you, she practically *begged* me to find out what had killed her." Well, not in so many words.

"No." Tadashi shook his head. "Not this way."

But they'd discussed it, on a scientific level. Meifeng had admitted to conducting autopsies, told her about the secret circle of other doctors who had done them, too. She'd even put bodies in the ground without all their parts. There was no way she could tell him about that private conversation. He would just call her a liar. "I had to know."

"You can plead your mission to help people all you want, Ruby, but there's more to life than curing someone's cough."

Is that what he thought she did? Just cured people's coughs? "I was here at her side, day in and day out, nursing her for months, all the time administering to other people as well, while you were who-knows-where." She could have used his help.

"I was doing a job, one that seeks to help other people."

Not nearly on the level that she did. She turned away from him, found the thread and cut a length of it. "Where were you, anyway?"

"I wasn't cutting up bodies."

He wanted to be cute? Two could play this game. "You certainly weren't here helping to care for your mother." She threaded the needle.

He didn't reply.

Ruby glanced over her shoulder.

He was just standing there, his eyes boring into her. "This is it, the end."

Whatever that meant.

"I can never look at your face again –"

Ruby stopped. Her heart lurched.

"–without recalling what you did here."

No, Tadashi, don't say that.

He threw out an arm and pointed to the door. "Get out." His voice was like a growl.

"I still have to sew up –"

His face turned red. "Get out or I will wake up this entire camp and then you can plead your case to them."

If this was *his* reaction, she could only imagine what the Chinese men would be like. "Tadashi, no one else has to know –"

"You'll be lucky if they don't kill you." He clenched his fists, hanging at his side. "You're lucky that I didn't, the moment I saw what you'd done."

From the tone of his voice, there was no doubt he wanted to strangle her right now.

He turned and faced the wall. "Get out, now, before I change my mind." He shook his head. "I never want to see you again."

Ruby crossed the room, numb, and let herself out.

It was over. Her life with Tadashi, all those tender moments they'd shared – gone, finished.

The tears threatened.

She'd imagined herself with him forever. They were soulmates who'd found each other in this crazy world. They'd discovered that they matched on so many levels – the things they liked, the way they viewed the world, their early experiences as near-outcasts of society – him for being a half-breed, her for her weird, innate ability. But there was more. There had been that spark, that desire.

And when, just hours ago, he'd returned to see his mother one last time, they'd come together as one. She'd never felt closer to him than she had last night.

Now, it was gone. There was only this overwhelming emptiness deep in her gut.

He's said that he never wanted to see her again. Never.

She stumbled down the trail.

Where would she go? Who would have her? She'd left without even a toothbrush. There was only one place to go when life had kicked you this hard.

She trekked to the house and knocked on the door.

A woman she didn't recognize answered. "Yes? Can I help you?"

There was a voice behind the woman. "Who is it at this ungodly hour, Gertrude?" Mother appeared and stopped at the sight of her. "Oh, it's you. I'll handle this, Gertrude."

The new maid stepped away.

Mother's eyes were stern. "Why are you here?"

"I have nowhere else to go, Mother. Please help me." She reached out and touched her arm. "I'm pregnant."

CHAPTER THIRTEEN

Felicia grabbed Ruby's sleeve – what was that odor? – and yanked her inside. Maybe she wasn't too far along. Maybe they could fix this. She'd heard of people who could, though she'd need to ask around, discreetly of course, to find them. "How far along are you?"

"Three months."

And she looked like this? She was skin and bones, wasn't even showing. "You're sure?"

"I'm sure."

"Whose is it?"

Ruby shot her a baleful look.

Oh, that despicable half-breed's, the one she'd walked-in on while the two of them were ... yeah. "You need a bath. Let's go upstairs. You smell awful."

"I was doing an autopsy." Her voice was flat.

She'd had her hands inside a dead body? Lord help us. "Who died?"

"Meifeng."

"Who you asked the congregation to pray for." The service that had seen person after person going up to her daughter to thank her for all she'd done for them. The Chinese woman had taken Ruby in and, miracle of miracles, fixed her brain imbalance. Moreover, she'd given her a purpose in life. "I'm sorry to hear that." But that didn't explain why her daughter was suddenly on her own. "Did that boy throw you out because you're pregnant?"

"He doesn't know about the baby. He threw me out because I did the autopsy. The Chinese believe that's desecrating the body, relegating the person to eternal unhappiness."

Well, that would be a reason to toss someone out, all right. "You can never go back?"

"Never."

"Take your bath. I'll find you suitable clothes." Ruby couldn't very well wear these rags. They needed to be burned.

Felicia left Ruby at the bathroom. She hurried downstairs. Time was of the essence. "George?" she called out. "Where's George?"

The new maid, Gertrude, appeared. "He's tending the horses, ma'am."

"Tell him to hitch them up. We're leaving for San Francisco within the hour."

"Yes, Ma'am."

What else? Ruby would be starved. "Have the cook prepare a packed lunch."

Best let Phillip know what was happening, well, some of what was happening, at least. She grabbed a receiving note off the desk near the entry and scribbled on it. "Ruby is back. I'm taking her to San Fran for some R & R."

Her daughter needed a decent dress. Willifrid had a daughter about the same size. She hurried to the kitchen.

Willifrid was making up sandwiches.

Good. "Ruby needs a dress. Can she borrow one from your daughter, Mary?"

"Margie."

Whatever. "Here, tell her I'll buy her a new one." She tossed some money on the table. That ought to get her attention. It was more than enough. "Send someone quickly. We need it in the next half hour."

"Yes, Ma'am."

There was something else the cook could do for her. Felicia pulled out more money, slapped it on the table and held out her hand, palm up. "Your wedding ring. Give it to me."

Willifrid froze. "I've never taken it off. It means –"

Yeah, yeah, yeah. "Just hand it over. You can buy a new one."

"Yes, Ma'am." She twisted it off and passed it to her slowly.

Why the sad look? The cook had been well-compensated. Some people were so sentimental. And this ring – what a dismal looking thing, plain and dull and utterly without panache.

Felicia hurried upstairs. She needed to pack.

She trotted into her room and caught sight of herself in the mirror. She was going to be a grandmother.

She groaned. Grandmother to a half-breed's child. Not if she could help it.

Ruby sat back against the carriage cushions. It felt strange to be in a dress again. It was so constricting. Strange to be riding in a carriage too. "Why are we going to San Francisco?"

Mother, sitting across the carriage facing her, cocked a single brow.

"Oh." So she could have the baby where no one knew her. That was why.

"You're now married." Mother pulled a plain wedding band from her handbag.

It should be Tadashi who was presenting her with a ring. Tadashi – she'd never see that smile again. Never feel his hands on her body. What had she done? She winced internally.

"Put this on. Your husband died in a carriage accident."

Mother had thought of everything, even brought out new toiletries so she could brush her teeth, have underarm powder, not that it worked as well as her herbal formulas.

Her herbal formula – she'd let it lapse when she'd gotten so busy tending others. That's why she was pregnant. It must have been that last time before Tadashi left the encampment to organize the workers.

She'd only experienced minimal morning sickness, had mistaken it at first as an upset stomach from something she'd eaten. Then she'd blamed her missed periods on the stress and lack of sleep. But there had been no time to think of herself or dwell on her own possible condition, not when Meifeng had needed her on a near-constant basis.

Mother leaned forward and patted her hand. "I'll ask around, find a doctor who can take care of this."

She was trying to tell her something.

"He'll be discreet, of course," Mother said reassuringly.

Wait.

Abortion?

Mother was talking about aborting her child, as offhandedly as if they were discussing new shoes. Ruby threw a protective hand to her stomach. "I'm keeping the baby." Mother could toss her out of the house again, her and the baby both, but there was no way she was going to end this pregnancy.

"We'll see, dear."

"No, there is no 'seeing,' nothing to discuss. I am having this baby." Tadashi's baby. No matter what he thought of her now, their child had been conceived in love. She wouldn't dishonor that love, that bond that they'd shared.

"Fine, then we'll see it gets a decent home." Mother turned to the window and muttered, "Though who will want to take in a half-breed infant is beyond me."

How dare she even consider adopting-out this innocent little child? "I will be the one giving it a decent home, no one else." Ruby folded her arms across her chest. Mother thought she was going to get her way on this one, but she was sorely mistaken. There was no way she was giving up her baby.

Ruby looked out the front window.

There were ships coming into the harbor, far below her.

Her hands went automatically to the bump in her belly. She was showing now.

Tadashi should be here. He should be sharing in this wonderful moment with her.

But it could never be. She'd crossed the boundary as far as he was concerned. She'd cut open his mother to do an autopsy and he couldn't get past that. She'd condemned Meifeng to hell, he'd said.

It had changed everything between them. Now, she couldn't get it back. She'd never get it back. All those times in his arms, those intimate moments, they meant nothing now, not to him.

It felt as though half her world was missing. Would this heartache ever go away?

She looked down at the bulge under her dress. "But I have you, little one," she whispered. "You and I, we'll face this world together, no matter what comes our way."

There was a kick.

Maybe it had been her imagination.

Another kick.

This was amazing.

She pressed the spot. Yes, she could feel it, right there. It was a foot. A tiny, little, perfect foot.

Her baby had begun kicking. She had to share it with someone. "Mother, come quick," she called out. "The baby's kicking."

Surely this would melt Mother's cold heart.

Ruby sat at the kitchen table and sipped her morning tea.

"Scrambled or over easy?" the cook asked.

Now that she was here with them, Willifrid still insisted on making eggs and bacon for breakfast.

Like she would eat such things. "No thanks."

"Got to keep your strength up."

Yes, but not that way.

Willifrid twisted the plain, dull-looking wedding band on her third finger. "You sure, Miss Ruby? I worry about you."

"I'm sure." She picked up her cup, took it to the front of the house and finished it as she glanced out on the other homes in Pacific Heights. Maybe she'd go stroll the market place. Plenty to see there. One thing about being in a port city, she had access to all the herbs she needed.

Mother came down the stairs. "Ruby, there you are. You need to get out of this house, resume living. There's a concert in the park this afternoon. Shall we go?"

"I'm going out to stroll the market this morning. I can meet you there afterwards."

"Lovely."

Ruby set out for the market. She could take the trolley, but why should she when walking was so much more pleasant on a gorgeous day like today?

Mr. Dardario was on his porch, tending his flower pots. That herbal formula for his arthritis must be working well if he was using his pruning scissors. She gave him a wave.

Farther down the street, Susan Nibusky was putting little Andrew into to his stroller.

She hadn't seen him in a week. "How's the colic?" Ruby called out.

Susan looked up and nodded. "It did the trick."

"Glad to hear it." Pilosula root and astragalus mixed with those nine other herbs, one had to be careful with both the ratio and the amounts when it came to babies, so she'd taken the route that was least burdensome on the body first.

Ruby kept walking. She'd been here nearly a month and was just starting to show. Mother had had a seamstress come to the house and commissioned five maternity dresses with expandable sides. They were so much more comfortable than the dresses she'd been forced to wear in Sacramento. There had been no more talk of shuttling her baby off to some stranger, thank goodness. She would have walked out of the house and disappeared if that had been the case.

Maybe Mother was mellowing. Maybe she'd come around to accepting this baby and wanting to be a part of its upbringing, share in its care and celebrate its milestones, the way most women would.

She paused. Who was she kidding? Mother would never change her ways.

This baby in her belly – boy or girl? Would Tadashi ever come around to meeting him or her?

Ruby sighed. *Oh, Tadashi, what I wouldn't give for things to have turned out differently.* Maybe she should have asked permission to do the autopsy. After all, Meifeng had been his mother, adoptive mother, true, but he was her only family. She should have taken the time to explain why she wanted to do the autopsy.

But the body was going to be buried. There hadn't been time.

Still, you should have asked.

The look on his face had said it all. He'd been appalled, if not disgusted, with her.

She should have done the autopsy right after Meifeng died, done it in the middle of the night when all the men were asleep. Then she could have gotten away with it. No one would have known there were stitches under those clothes. It would have been her own little secret.

If she had only done it that way, then no one would be the wiser.

But she hadn't … and look at what had happened.

Stupid, stupid, stupid.

It had cost her the one true love of her life.

Ruby stopped. She didn't recognize this street. Perhaps she'd taken a wrong turn.

There was a book store. She loved books.

A tiny bell tinkled when she opened the door. It smelled of paper and dust and ink in here, books just waiting to be discovered. Her eyes adjusted to the dimmer light. There were so many books, crammed into every corner, every nook and cranny. Meifeng would have liked it here.

An older man peeked his head out. "Hello there." He stepped forward – tall, wide in the shoulders, balding – and wearing suspenders over a striped shirt. His eyes sparkled behind his spectacles when he smiled. "Would have dressed-up in a top coat if I'd known a pretty lady was stopping by." He pretended to tip a hat.

She liked this old man. "Do you mind if I look around?"

"Help yourself."

Where to start? "You have so many books. Are they in any kind of order?"

He tapped the side of his head. "I'm afraid it's all up in here. What are you looking for? No, let me guess. Poetry? Love stories?"

"Medical texts."

He blinked. "Like, books that doctors would study?"

"Exactly."

"Don't get much call for that." He looked around. "Let me think." He began walking down the aisle, turning at the corner wall and gesturing for her to follow. "You a nurse?"

Yes. No, not really. "It interests me."

"Watch your step."

There was a step down, right in the middle of the floor. How odd. This place was like an Old Mother Hubbard's house.

He stopped so fast that she almost bumped into him.

Her hand hovered near his side. There was something intangible there.

He waved at a wall of books. "There are some in here. You'll need a step ladder to reach the upper ones, of course." He suddenly noticed she was in maternity clothes. "Oh, dear. You can't go climbing a ladder. Tell you what. You just let me know if you need something that's topside."

"Thank you, Mr ...?"

"Hannagan. Orville Hannagan"

"I'm Ruby Fontinello."

"Nice to meet you, Mrs. Fontinello."

Mrs.? Oh, he'd seen the bright gold ring on her left hand, the one she'd bought to appease Mother. No reason Willifrid had to give up her wedding ring for this pretend marriage. She spotted a little chair in the corner. "Is it all right if I sit there and browse the books first?"

"Of course." He gestured to the upper shelves. "I'm just a holler away if you need anything. And, you can call me Orville." Orville Hannagan took his leave.

Ruby eyed the titles. These medical books were all written in English. No surprise there. She pulled out a couple and checked their indexes.

So far, so good.

She flipped through the pages to get an idea of how each presented information.

They were so much different than the ones Meifeng had owned. Western medicine took a "let's treat the symptoms" approach. It had its place, sure, but why continue to treat a symptom if it was just going to keep happening? Eastern medicine looked to why the ailment occurred in the first place.

She flipped more pages. Still, for things like broken bones and operations, she could see where this information, especially the illustrations, would be useful.

Ruby got comfortable and settled in with two of the books. "Let's see what they said about kidney disease," she muttered.

Ruby jerked.

Mr. Hannagan was standing in front of her.

She threw a hand to her throat. "Goodness. You startled me." Why was it so dark in here?

"Store closes in five minutes, Mrs. Fontinello."

It was that late? She'd missed the concert in the park. Mother would be furious. She got up and realized she was hungry. "I'll take these two books," she said.

He nodded. "Let me ring them up."

She followed him to the cash register and pulled out her money, well, Mother's money, really. "Are you open tomorrow, Mr. Hannagan?"

"Nine a.m."

"Fabulous." There was no other place she wanted to spend her free time.

Felicia peered out the window and sighed. Ruby was coming up the street. Finally. She'd been worried sick.

Ruby spotted her and sent her a little wave. She was carrying something. More herbs, most likely.

She met her at the door. "Where have you been, young lady?"

"I'm sorry." Ruby held up two impossibly huge books, grinning from ear to ear. "Look what I found. There's this weird old book store just crammed with things in every corner. Time got away from me."

Felicia checked the titles. Medical books. This again? Did Ruby never stop? First, she'd approached the neighbor down the street and offered to help ease his arthritis, then she'd struck up a conversation with someone on the trolley and offered to make them a medicinal concoction of some sort or another. And those were likely not the only people Ruby had approached. Medical books? Really? Too bad she didn't look up how to naturally discharge the half-breed's child that she was carrying. But look at that belly bump. Too late for that now. Darn it. "How wonderful."

"Oh come on, Mother, you should be happy I found such a place to occupy myself."

"Your father's here. He doesn't know about –" the bastard growing in your belly "– your condition."

"Oh." Ruby looked down at her feet. "Then it's time he knew."

"He's in the library."

Ruby set down the medical books and led the way.

Phillip jumped up and hurried over as soon as they entered the room. "Ruby, so happy you're back home with us, sweetie." He hugged his daughter and then held her shoulders as he stepped back to look at her. "You are absolutely radiant."

Because she's pregnant, you twit. Don't you see how her dress isn't fitted? Didn't you feel the bump in her belly just now?

"Daddy, I have something to tell you."

Felicia closed the double doors. No need for the servants to witness the family drama. She stayed back, ready to referee. For now, she'd let the two of them decide how this was to play out.

"You've met a young man? Is that why you're glowing?"

"Well, actually –"

"Who is he? I can't wait to meet him."

"You already have, Daddy."

"He's from Sacramento? Fenton? Crawford? Who?"

"Tadashi Moro."

"Tadash – my former interpreter?" His face turned white.

"I'm having his baby."

Phillip's knees gave away and he barely made it to the settee. "You're pregnant?"

"Going on four months along."

"You sure?"

Felicia scoffed. How like a man, to ask something like that. Of course Ruby was sure. "She's wearing a maternity gown, isn't she?"

Phillip drew a hand down his face. "Tadashi? You laid with that, that *bastard*?" He shuddered. "When I get my hands on him –" He came alive, jumping off the settee.

"Daddy, we're not a couple anymore."

"Damn right you're not. That bastard tried to ruin my company. Do you know he sent carloads of materials all across the country? Caused us numerous delays. Then he told me that I was working the laborers too hard. Oh really? How does he think railroads get built?" He shook his head. "And these work slowdowns that he orchestrated. We could be halfway to Seattle by now, but he keeps throwing a monkey wrench into the works. Lunch breaks, shorter work days, weekends off."

Yes, yes, you have work issues. We have a home issue. "Ruby needs our support right now, Phillip."

"Oh." He stopped ranting and nodded. "Sorry."

Phillip needed to know that she'd handled things while he'd been off overseeing this railroad of his. "I've told all the neighbors that Ruby's husband died in an accident."

"Oh, OK, good thinking."

"The servants know to stick to that story or be fired."

"Yes, yes, all right."

She turned to her daughter. "Ruby, why don't you go see when dinner will be ready?"

"Yes, Mother." She slipped out the door.

Felicia eyed her husband. "Listen up and listen well. I don't like that some *half-breed* got our daughter pregnant. God only knows what it's going to look like when she delivers it, so we have to be smart about this. Ruby thinks she'd going to keep it. We both know that would be a mistake. Once anyone looks at her child, they'll realize that she debased herself with a lowlife immigrant. It will ruin our good name. So, we can't let her keep it. "

"And how, pray tell, do you expect to stop her?"

"We'll take her to an orphanage, show her how happy the little children are there and how well they're being cared for." She threw her shoulders back and gave a snort. "Then she'll forget this silly notion of raising a child who will be the laughing stock of high society." At least, she hoped that was what would happen.

He nodded.

Then it was agreed.

Ruby strolled down the path in the park and breathed in the salt air. It was another gorgeous San Francisco day.

There was group of young women on the raised park shelter, laughing, chatting. They were all rather pudgy. She wandered closer. No, they were in maternity dresses.

Her hand went to her stomach. Just like her.

Ruby approached one woman who was just striding up to join the group. She was a blonde and could be Anastasia's sister, she was so pretty. "Hello. I'm Ruby and new to town. What's going on here?"

The girl glanced at her belly bump and smiled. "Hi, welcome. I'm Madeline. We're the Girls of Good Deeds. We first got together because we're all expecting, but it got boring just talking about morning sickness. So, now we're each doing our part to make the world a better place. Ladies, we have a new member. This is Ruby."

The women came at her all at once, greeting her and introducing themselves – Edith, Hester, Charlotte, Rowena, Nettie, Agnes, Theodosia, Phoebe.

So many introductions and one after the other. Ruby threw up her hands, laughing. "I'll never remember all your names."

Madeline waved away the concern. "It'll come as you get to know us. We've just organized so we're planning our get-togethers. We were thinking of a picnic for next week, then visiting the new Memorial Museum the following week. I went the day it opened. So many exhibits. I could go every day. Have you seen it yet? No? They don't charge admission."

"How nice."

"I like it because that means the masses can go. That's my cause. I look after the poor and needy. Did you know there's a whole community down by the wharf?"

No, she didn't. But she knew that Madeline was a magpie.

"And it's not just men who pick up odd jobs at the docks – carting away broken pallets, cleaning off the rollers. No, there are women and children living down there, too. Horrible conditions. Can you imagine?"

"So, how are you helping them?"

"I organize food pickups every Wednesday. If your cook bought, say, too many melons and some are going to go to waste, we come by and pick them up and deliver them to the wharf so they can be enjoyed by the poor. Or maybe you had a social and now you have too many petit-fours left over. We'll take those too." She pulled a notepad from her handbag. "Can I put your house on the list?"

What a great idea. "Please do." She gave her the address. "Tell me more about the people who live by the wharf. Who are they?"

"Immigrant families."

"From where?" Not China, she'd bet her last dollar on that.

Madeline thought for a second, scrunching up her face. "Mostly Europe, I'd say."

"Really poor, huh?"

"Hester goes there too. She teaches the children how to read."

"They don't go to school?"

"Maybe they did where they came from. I don't know," Madeline said. "When I'm there, I just smile and hand out the food."

She needed to speak with Hester. "Point her out to me."

"Dark hair, maroon dress, matching hat."

"Thanks." Ruby found Hester. "Madeline said you teach the poor children at the wharf."

"Twice a week. Took me forever to convince the mothers to let me organize my little class."

The language barrier, she probably meant. "How old are the children?"

"All ages."

"What language do they speak?"

Hester laughed and made a rolling-eyes face. "What language *don't* they speak? I'm picking up a few phrases but most of my communication is through gestures and pictures."

She could imagine. "Tell me about the living conditions."

"They're not the best. They live in one-room shacks made of discarded wood or sailcloth, whatever they can find. They cook outside their front doors so they don't burn down their structures. At night, the family sleeps together for warmth."

"How many people are we talking about?"

"More than a hundred. There's not much space. They live practically on top of one another."

There had to be a lot of disease. She'd need more herbs. "When are you going there next? I want to join you."

"Really?" Hester lowered her voice. "I'd appreciate that. The other girls are kind of standoff-ish about going down there because, well, it's not all that pleasant."

And because they probably listened to old wives' tales about how being pregnant meant one was more susceptible to catching something. Utter nonsense. "I don't care about that. These people need help."

Orville Hannagan heard the bell tinkle. Already? Someone was sure up early. He got up from his desk and peeked around the corner. Oh, it was that pretty young lady who'd found his store last week. "Good morning."

"Hi, Orville." Ruby came over and pressed a little canvas pouch into his hand.

"What's this?" He sniffed it. Strange.

"For your gout."

How did she know? He hadn't mentioned it to her.

"Use a pinch to make a cup of tea twice a day. No more." She gave him a stern look. "It can have serious side effects if you over do it."

Don't take too much. "All right."

"And you need to stop eating so much beef. That's the root of the problem."

She knew he had a soft spot for red meat? But ... how?

Ruby set her arms akimbo and scanned the upper shelves. "I'm looking for books written in Chinese. Would you have any?"

She spoke Chinese, really? He would never have guessed. What am unusual young woman. "Actually, I don't, Ruby. I'm sorry."

Her shoulders slumped. "Not even one?"

"If I recall, you bought medical texts the last time you were in." He'd expected to hold onto those books until the day he died, and then she'd walked in, and snatched them up and spent the whole day curled up in the corner reading. "Is that what you're interesting in?"

"Medicine, surgery, diagnosis."

"And in Chinese, yes?"

"I find the Eastern medicines to be more in tune with nature."

Even medical students who came in here didn't espouse such ideas. Who *was* this young lady, anyway? "I don't currently."

"Oh, well, if you don't have any Chinese books, I'll have to look else –"

"Wait, I uh, I'm not sure how to make this tea thing you're talking about." He had to keep her here, find out more about her. "My wife is usually in charge of those things but I'd like to start taking it now." He gestured to the back room. "I've got a pot-bellied stove in my office. Can you show me?"

"Of course," she said. She indicated the pouch. "The mixture I gave you contains meadow saffron. Some people mistake it for wild garlic. Now, like I said, it can be potent. Every person is different and this can have side effects, so if you get, say, diarrhea, or vomiting, stop immediately. That's your body telling you it can't handle it and you'll know you're taking too much."

She sounded like his friend, Jianyu.

They reached his office and she set the pot on to boil.

"Have you had meadow saffron before, Mr. Hannagan?"

Yes. "Never."

"Speaking of never, you never want to give it to a child or even someone who's like, my size. It's very potent." She held up a finger, getting his full attention. "It has the potential to poison a person."

Poison? What?

Jianyu had never mentioned that fact. "Maybe I shouldn't even try it."

"Don't be silly. I'll show you how much to take. Once it's controlled your gout, you should stop taking it."

He found a coffee mug and peeked into it. Clean enough. "Tell me, how did you come to learn all this Chinese herbal medicine stuff?"

Ruby gestured away the question. "Long story."

No, no, he wasn't going to let her get away with brushing it off.

He gestured for her to take a seat. "I've got time." This was going to be interesting.

Ruby jumped down from Hester's carriage. There was a stench in the air – fish, rot, human excrement. It told her that those living at Wharf Village, as her new Girls of Good Deeds friends called it, were facing a number of diseases.

Madeline's blonde locks bounced as she alighted from her carriage behind them. "Help me carry these trays of food, girls," she called over.

No need for that. Women were pouring out of the tent city, coming over and surrounding them. There were so many of them.

Ruby joined her friend and handed out the food.

The women from Wharf Village jostled themselves into a line of sorts.

One had jaundice, her skin so yellow it was unnerving. Another's arm hug awkwardly, likely set wrong after being broken. Another woman coughed nonstop into a handkerchief. Another scratched her head every few seconds. Head lice, maybe? That was a condition sure to be passed around if families huddled together for warmth at night as she'd been told. This was not good.

Beside her, Hester leaned in and whispered. "You've got to smile, Ruby."

Right. Smile. Smile at all this disease around her.

The women of Wharf Village began taking the food and heading back to their shelters, loaded up with armloads of it.

No, don't go. I've got medicine for you to take. Hold on. If these women didn't speak English, how was she going to tell them how much to take, when to take it, and whether it should be with or without food? If their children were ill, the amounts to be taken were even more critical. Small bodies needed less medicine, yes, but there was also their level of development with which to contend. An eight year old's physiology was not the same as a ten year old's. Their bodies had different needs. Meifeng's books had taught her that.

The food was gone.

A couple women, latecomers, hurried up, then stopped as they saw the empty trays. Their smiles disappeared.

Madeline gestured for the women to hold on a second. She ducked into her carriage and came out with two more boxes of food, giving it to them. She sighed. "This happened before, and usually to the mothers with extra children. They have their hands full and can't step away as quickly, so now I hold back some food so everybody gets some."

Smart.

"Come on," Hester said. "Let's go to where I teach the children."

Ruby picked up some of the books, charcoal pencils and paper that they'd brought and followed her to a clearing just past the tent city. Some children were already there, about a dozen, smiling from ear to ear. Cute kids. This must be the highlight of their day.

She and Hester set down the supplies. Now what?

Hester held up a drawing she'd done – a girl, hands clasped in prayer, looking into a window that had a cat. The word "cat" was written in uppercase letters below.

Hester pointed to herself. "I want a cat," she said, pointing to the word "cat" as she spoke it.

"I want a cat," the children repeated.

Hester smiled. "Good! You remembered. Again. 'I want a cat.'"

They repeated the sentence.

Ruby peeked at the pile of drawings Hester had made. The next one showed the figure holding the cat.

Oh, she got it. Want a cat. Have a cat.

The next ones were similar, just with a dog in the window instead of a cat, "dog" written underneath, then the dog on a leash. Want a dog. Have a dog. Simple and she was a pretty good artist.

Ruby checked more pages. The items the figure desired changed to food –a loaf of bread, a carrot, an egg being fried in a skillet, a turkey drumstick. Hester had taken the lesson a step further and chosen sensible words the children were likely to encounter. What she'd do when she got to conjugated verbs was a mystery, but reading and learned to spell "cat" were not why she'd come here.

"You've got this under control. I'll be in the village," she whispered to Hester and took her leave.

Her herbs were in a basket, still in the carriage. She grabbed them and hurried into Wharf Village.

The stench was suddenly stronger.

She looked around.

Dear lord, the toilets were right next to the first tents. Liquid was leaking out from under the makeshift doors and pooling in front.

And they lived just a few feet away? What were these people thinking? Surely they hadn't lived so close to the facilities in their homeland.

She hurried past and ventured farther in Wharf Village. There had to be at least a thousand people living here.

Mothers and little children lingered about, they stopped talking to stare at her as she passed. Some of the women were at their fire pits, already preparing the food that Madeline had collected.

Smile, show them you're friendly. "Hi, hello."

The women nodded in return.

Ruby passed tent after tent, checking every open space. Where was the woman with the jaundiced skin? Her liver was screaming out for help. Bitter luffa, radish leaves and eating tomatoes could help.

A little boy ran past her. He had a pink eye. She could tell the mother about chamomile compresses and what foods to feed him, but not if she didn't speak the language. This was so frustrating.

She turned in a circle and raised her voice. "Does anyone here speak English? Anyone?"

People stared at her, looking puzzled. No one came forward.

Great.

She retraced her steps and left the village, tossing her basket of herbs in the carriage. She looked back and frowned. *I could help so many of you if we could just communicate.*

Phillip Fontinello heard the front door open. Ruby and Felicia must be back. "How was church?" he called out.

Ruby appeared in the doorway of the library, leaning on the door jab as she pulled off her gloves. "You should have come, Daddy."

Too much work to do, no thanks to that scoundrel whose baby you're carrying. She was definitely looking pregnant of late. It was like having Tadashi Moro in his home every day, laughing in his face and saying, "Screwed your company while I enjoy screwing your daughter, too." That dirty bastard.

"You work too hard, Daddy."

"Wouldn't have to, if the rail line's progress wasn't being disrupted all the time." Like she cared. No, she'd only cared about getting her jollies in bed with the man bent on ruining him.

"There was a telegraph for you." She crossed the room and handed it to him.

It was from the operation in Sacramento. Now what?

He scanned the lines. No, it couldn't be. A whole day? Nothing got done? This took the cake.

"Is everything all right, Daddy?"

No, everything was not all right. "Your boyfriend has been busy."

Ruby sent him a look. "He's not my boyfriend."

"Really? Well, I can't very well refer to him as your 'husband,' seeing as he didn't have the decency to do right by you." Not that he wanted the half-breed legally linked to his family.

"I already told you, Daddy. Tadashi doesn't know I'm pregnant."

"Want to hear his latest escapade?" Phillip held up the telegram he'd just read, waving it at her. "Tadashi apparently ordered a 'sickout', claimed the entire encampment got hold of bad food. No one showed up for work today. Not. One. Man." He shook his head in disgust. "Your boyfriend has some nerve."

"I told you, he's not my boyfriend." She scoffed, turned on her heel and left in a huff.

Yeah, leave. Leave me to handle the mess you made.

Listen to him. It wasn't Ruby he should be mad at, it was that damned half-Japanese, union-loving organizer who deserved his wrath.

Phillip bit his lip. There had to be a way to combat these little tricks Tadashi was pulling.

A plan began forming in his brain. Fight fire with fire, show him who's boss, that's what he needed to do. Yes, it just might work.

A smile spread across his lips. "I'll destroy him."

Ruby entered the bookstore. It looked empty. "Mr. Hannagan?" she called out.

He appeared around a corner in the back. "Ah, Ruby, there you are."

"I got your message."

Another older man, a small Chinese one who walked with a cane, stepped around the corner and joined him. He was in American clothes, but his manner said pure Eastern culture. Both approached her.

Orville Hannagan gestured to him. "Meet my friend Jianyu."

It was a common name. One of the workers at the encampment had been called that. She greeted him in Chinese. "Very nice to meet you."

He responded in his native language and held out his hand. There was an embroidered symbol on the cuff of his sleeve, two intertwined snakes. "Unusual to meet an American who speaks the language. But then, Orville said you are an unusual woman. He said you seek to cure people of their ills."

"I studied under a doctor trained in China. She was from a prominent family and highly educated."

Jianyu nodded. "So he told me. He also said you were interested in Chinese medical texts. Have you read, 'Healing From Nature?'"

Had she. It was the first book she'd ever studied once she learned Chinese. She could practically recite it. She should have taken it when she left the cabin. Ruby sighed internally. She should have taken a lot of books. "Yes, but I don't have my own copy."

"I have books."

Her heart beat a little faster. "What books?"

He smiled. "Books that your doctor friend likely used in her medical school days."

Orville said, "I'll let you two talk." He withdrew.

Ruby touched Jianyu's sleeve. "Please, could I see these books? I need to learn so much more." In the past five years she'd only had the chance to read about half of the books on Meifeng's shelves. "I'll be happy to buy them from you."

Jianyu shook his head. "I cannot let them go. You see, mine is more of a studying library. My home is not far from here. Let me show you what I've got and we'll see if we can work something out."

They walked to his house.

She had to know more. "How many books do you own?"

"Medical textbooks?" He considered the question and waggled his hand. Perhaps thir –"

"Thirteen?" That would be enough.

"– thirty thousand."

Holy cow. That many? "Any particular specialty?"

"General knowledge, I would venture to say, everything from childhood illnesses to adult ailments from A to Z, though there are some specific to surgery."

Surgery, now that would be interesting. Most of the American medical history involved amputation, the result of the War Between the States. It was basic stuff. Cut and cauterize, that was about the only instruction. "How much surgery have the Chinese done?"

"More than one might suppose," Jianyu said. He stopped and pointed with his cane. "That's my home."

It was set into the hill and even bigger than her parents' mansion.

They began climbing the steps to the front of the house.

"How did you come to have a library with that many medical books?"

"I'm a collector. You'll see."

He opened the door for her. A servant girl greeted them with a bow. "Can I get you some tea?"

She was here for way more than tea. She was here for knowledge. "No, thank you."

Jianyu sent the girl away. "This way, Ruby. I think you'll appreciate this." He led her the length of the house and threw open a set of double doors.

It was a massive room.

This had to be a dream.

He led her to the railing at the edge of the landing to look out over this part of his house, obviously a special addition.

In front of her was a sunken room so colossal, it could be a whole other house. It measured at least one hundred feet long and sixty feet wide. Everything was done in white. Doric pillars held up the expanse of the two-story ceiling. But the best part was what it contained.

Cases chock full of books lined the walls, tall movable ladders allowed access to the highest shelves. Seated at a dozen long, white tables were about at least twenty people reading thick tomes. Some of them had notepads and paused to scribble on them.

"What *is* this place?" she breathed.

Jianyu gestured. "It's my library, free for your use."

She felt the need to whisper. "I've never seen so many books." He really *did* have thirty thousand.

He led her down the stairs to the main floor and briefly studied the shelves. "Ah, here it is." He pulled one off the shelf and handed it to her. "Look familiar?"

Healing From Nature.

She took it and held it tight. "I thought I'd never see it again." It felt so right in her hands, almost like a long-lost friend.

"It's safe and sound right here." He took it from her, re-shelved it and gestured around the room with his cane to the people sitting at the long desks, quietly reading or taking notes. "These are medical students. They come here to do research."

"They all speak Chinese?"

"No, no, my dear. They're from all over. They speak all different languages. I have books in numerous languages – Italian, German, Russian, Swahili – you name it. If someone published a medical book, chances are, I have it."

She didn't doubt it.

Jianyu indicated the shelves closest to him. "In this section are the ones written in Chinese."

It had to be fifty feet worth of the wall. The Chinese characters were written on their spines. This place was incredible. "And you'll allow me to come here and read any book I want?"

"Of course."

Ruby could have hugged him. "No wonder you painted your library white."

"Excuse me?"

"It's heaven to someone like me."

Tadashi headed toward the train yard. This was odd, someone had erected a fence. It had to been done in the last couple of days. He followed it around to where he could see the entry to the workers' area.

There was a sign with big, red lettering.

Restricted Area. Badges Required.

There were guards about fifty feet farther, standing at the entry point. They held rifles.

What the hell?

He passed the sign and strode up to the closest guard. "What's the meaning of this?" His men were due here any minute, a triumphant return to work after giving themselves a much needed two-day weekend free from busting their backs with shovels and pickaxes. He knew for a fact that none of them had these so-called badges.

"You need a badge to go any farther."

"What badge?"

"Issued by the Fontinello Company."

Now things were making sense. "When did this change occur?"

The guard looked him up and down. "I can't answer any more questions. You'll have to speak with someone in charge." He jutted his chin toward the main platform three hundred yards away, where passengers were milling around, waiting for the next train. "They're all over there."

He hurried around to the train station and jumped on the platform. He brushed past men in three-piece suits and ladies in their travel coats.

The train was just pulling in, slowing to a stop.

At the very end of the train, Chinese men in work clothes hopped off the flat cars.

A voice called out, "Huizhang, huizang." Badges, badges.

The crowd parted enough for him to see.

It was Jerold Fulcom.

That scumbag. Wait until he got his hands on him. He trotted down to where the Chinese men were gathering.

"Fulcom, what's the meaning of this?"

"Oh, look who's here. Tadashi Moro. Oh, gee, I can't seem to find a badge for you." He raised his hands in a "just following orders" kind of way and smirked. "So sorry."

What a butthead this guy was. He leaned in close. "I ought to beat your ass right here." But he knew he wouldn't. He had to stay out of jail in order to keep organizing the laborers.

The laborers. He had to warn them.

Tadashi turned away and addressed the new workers who had been transported in. "You men," he yelled in Chinese, "listen up. This company will work you to death and the only way to beat them is to organize and stand up to them. That's what the men you're replacing are doing. If you take their place, you'll need to organize, too. But if you force them to take you back to where you come from, you'll help us defeat Fontinello and his kind. You have to decide right now. Do you want to be worked as hard as mules? Or do you want to support your brothers who are standing up for their rights?"

The men paused, then turned away from him as one.

Fine, just wait until Fontinello works you to near-death. Then you'll start to listen and when you do, you'll join our united front. He bit his lip and headed back down the platform. He'd best tell the men they were out of a job before they found out on their own and did something stupid.

"Bye, bye, Tadashi," Fulcom called after him in a taunting, sing-song way.

Yours is coming, just wait.

CHAPTER FOURTEEN

Ruby read Madeline's note. "I need your help. Most urgent. Please come quickly."

She grabbed her scarf and hurried out the door. "I'll be back as soon as I can."

The address given meant that Madeline only lived a few blocks away. She strode along. What could Madeline possibly need? Number four thirty-two, here it was.

She rang the chime.

A stiff-looking woman answered.

"I'm Ruby Fontinello, a friend of Madeline's. Is she here?"

The woman nodded. "This way."

Madeline appeared at the top of the grand stairway that was shaped like a wishbone. "Ruby? Is that you? Oh, thank goodness you're here."

The woman gestured for her to go up.

Ruby gathered her skirts. "Is everything all right?"

"No, the world is going to end. My world is, anyway." She pointed to her face and quietly wailed, "Look at these. I heard you know how to address this kind of stuff. Can you help me? Please?"

Acne cysts. Someone had been obsessing with a few pimples and now her face was erupting. It wasn't only prostitutes who needed to learn skin care. "I think I can help. Let me get a few things from your kitchen."

Within a few minutes, Madeline was rinsing the sea salt, lemon, baking soda mixture off her face. "You sure this will work? We have a gala to attend in three days."

"If you don't pinch it and just leave it alone, it should be fine." She'd better whip up some of that zinc tincture, just to be sure. "I'll come by in the morning with something else you can use to speed the healing." Odd that Madeline had known of her sideline. She didn't recall telling her anything. "Madeline, I can't help wondering how you knew to call me for this condition of yours."

"It was something someone mentioned in passing. That you know about healing ways."

"And who was that?"

"Let me think." She paused for a moment, then brightened. "Estelle."

"Estelle Krofton?" Small world.

"She lives in the next neighborhood over." Madeline frowned. "But I think her last name is Williams."

Williams was probably her maiden name. "She has a little girl named Charity, yes?"

"Yes, that's right."

"I haven't seen her in a while. Can you give me her address? I really should call on her." Maybe those hand prints on her neck had left some lasting marks.

Felicia heard the front door close. She peeked out the window and watched Ruby make her way down the sidewalk. There she went again, walking all over the city. Ruby was definitely showing now, no one who saw her could ignore the fact. She'd ruin her figure this way, stretch everything out with the baby bouncing so much as she walked.

Ruby seldom took the trolley. She refused the use of the family carriage. No, she took to the city using her own two feet. Who walked this much when they were pregnant? It wasn't right. It wasn't healthy. She was going to strain herself, probably end up ordered to bed rest with all this exercise.

And this idea of hers to tend to sick poor people down at the wharf. Good Lord, whose idea was *that*?

When Ruby had told her of the plan, it had taken all her might not to recoil in disgust. Who would *willingly* go be around those people, talk to them, reach out and *touch* them for goodness sake?

It wasn't natural. It certainly wasn't wise. The germs. The disease. The place had to be a cesspool of horrible –

Wait. Maybe that was the answer. Maybe Ruby would pick up some disease so infectious, so nasty that it would cause her to spontaneously abort.

No more baby, no more problem.

It was the perfect situation.

Of course, if Ruby didn't pick up some horrible germs at the wharf and make herself abort, it would be wise to have a backup plan.

Felicia thought. It would have to be foolproof, foolproof and ingenious. She caught her reflection in the mirror. Ingenious was her middle name.

Ruby sat down in the rocking chair. Her hands slipped to her belly. The baby was kicking. "Somebody's awake. Are you swimming in there, little one?"

There was another kick. Wow. So strong.

She began rocking and singing a lullaby under her breath.

This was amazing. In all her twenty years, she would never have believed she could feel this much love.

"I can't wait for you to arrive so I can hold you in my arms. I'm going to take you to so many places, teach you so many things."

If it was a girl, she would be named Meifeng, no question. It was only right.

If it was a boy, she'd honor his father. Tadashi meant correct, righteous and loyal. And he'd been all that, no question.

She sighed.

Tadashi – where was he? What was he doing right now? Did he think of her? Did he wonder how her pregnancy was going?

Wait, he didn't know.

Maybe it was better this way. Maybe one day she'd seek him out, bring their child along, introduce them and his heart would melt.

Maybe he'd say that he'd reacted brashly, been wrong to send her away.

They could get back together, be a real family.

She stopped rocking.

Who was she kidding? He never wanted to see her again.

Ruby arrived at Jianyu's library. She pulled out the key he'd given her and slid it in the lock of the private entrance. It was so nice to be able to come and go any time she pleased.

She let herself in.

There were a few other people already here, all men, hunkered over books. One of them looked up when she passed and nodded hello to her.

Ruby strode over to the area with the Chinese texts and scanned the titles.

This one, this one and ... this one.

She pulled them off the shelves and carried them to the nearest table.

She opened the first one. The children at Wharf Village had numerous illnesses, mostly due to the horrible conditions in which they lived. Now, she needed to look up the diseases that came with unsanitary conditions and lack of hygiene – hookworm, jaundice, threadworm and diarrhea.

It was all new territory. She'd never had to treat any of those diseases. Meifeng had never even bothered to instruct her in any of them, there had been no need.

There was probably no consumption at Wharf Village, not yet at least. It was highly contagious. Very aggressive. She'd seen no one with a persistent cough, no one coughing up blood and no one suffering from the sweats.

No, there wasn't any consumption. There couldn't be. In that close of quarters, living on top of one another, one case and the entire village would be down with it.

Ruby put a protective hand to her belly. She wouldn't expose herself by going there if she *had* seen any sign of it. Not in her condition.

Ruby ran her finger down the index. Threadworm, threadworm.

There it was.

She flipped to the page number and began reading.

Someone came over near her and lit a lamp at her elbow.

Ruby looked up, startled. "Is it that late already? I hadn't noticed."

"You were so involved in your book." It was the same man who had nodded hello to her.

"Are you a doctor?"

"At Merciful Hospital. I'm James Finnegan." He was only a few years older than her, tall, thin, brown hair and blue eyes.

She introduced herself.

"So, Ruby, are you training as a doctor, too?"

Was she? "I lean toward Eastern medicine but I'm also interested in surgery." Why had she said that? It was true but not something she'd given voice to before.

"Surgery? Perfect. Come to Saint Raphael Merciful Hospital Monday morning. I can give you a tour. Maybe there's a place there for you."

A hospital? Really? Books would take her only so far. Being in a hospital ... yes, she needed that setting to reignite her abilities. "I'd like that."

Phillip entered the pub and waited for his eyes to adjust to the darkness. He grimaced. What a shady place this was. But this was where deals like this got done. He walked up to the bartender and gave the order he'd been told say. "Two fingers of Iron Fist whisky."

The bartender poured his drink.

He paid for it.

Now what? He'd never done anything like this before.

A man was sitting at the bar, caught his eye and flicked his chin to one of the booths.

Phillip removed his hat and headed that way.

There was one man in the booth. He smiled, showing a wide gap between his front teeth.

This was his man. "Mr. Crockett, I presume?"

The man gestured. "Have a seat." He looked about, leaned in close and kept his voice low. "I hear you have a problem, Mr. Fontinello."

He had about three hundred problems. The out-of-work Chinese were standing shoulder to shoulder to intimidate the new workers, daring them to cross the picket line on their way to work. Only about six workers had made it past. Six. Hardly enough to get any work done. "I need to have a certain person 'persuaded' not to mess with my railroad operations."

"Only one person?" Crockett raised a single eyebrow and gestured. "I heard you had dozens who needed to be taught a lesson."

"Just one for now." Hurting Tadashi would send a message to the others. He was the one who had riled up the others, told them to organize. He was the one who had betrayed his trust. He pulled the envelope with the money out of his inner coat pocket and pushed it across the table. "And when you do it, make sure he knows it's on my orders." Nobody messed with the Fontinellos.

Ruby arrived home. What she wouldn't give for a cup of miso soup.

The maid appeared. "A letter came for you, Miss Ruby."

The receiving basket held it. It was from Sacramento, a woman's handwriting. She had no idea who would be writing to her. A mother with a question on her child's sickness, perhaps?

Ruby slit it open and pulled out the letter. Pretty stationery.

"Ruby; I have the most exciting news. Go to the apothecary shop and look in their skin cream section. We're in business – yea! Told you I met a lot of people in my profession (wink wink) who could help get this business up and running. I've got ads running in the newspapers – another 'favor' from my client list – and we ship to Los Angeles this week. So, things are really moving along."

She'd done it, she'd really done it. And here she'd thought it was a passing fancy of Anastasia's. She'd have to show the letter to Mother, well, maybe not. She kept reading.

"Lillian says 'Hi' and that we owe her a lifetime's supply for being our test guinea pig. Heck, all the girls say hi. We've had some weird customer requests lately. Mr. Porter couldn't get off until had his girl pee on him – I kid you not. That did the trick. We all laughed about it later.

"Mr. Wallace wanted to tie up Penelope's wrists and have her call out 'Help' while he did her. Crazy, huh? I posted a bouncer outside her door just in case. Anyway, he complained that was too much of a distraction, having a guy listen in, that he couldn't get off because of it and demanded his money back. After two hours in there with Penelope? Hell, no.

"Oh, and that clerk of your father's? Mr. Fulcom?"

Tadashi's tormentor, yes, she remembered.

"He was in. What a pip squeak. He wanted our biggest girl, to 'smother' him he said, so I gave him Jasmine. She's, what, six feet tall. Turns out he didn't want to do her, didn't even want her naked. None of that. No, he had her rock him in a rocking chair while he wore nothing but a diaper and jacked himself off. I tell you, some of these people are just plain crazy.

"Of course, then we had the father come in with his teenage son and asked us to show the kid the ropes. The boy got so red-facedd, it was adorable. I took him on myself and ended up giving him a freebie coupon if he visited us one more time. Three for the price of two. Hey, maybe we should do that to build up sales with our skin cream line."

They had one product, not a skin cream "line." But, perhaps Anastasia had the right idea. If she could get one item on store shelves, why not two or three?

"Maybe our skin care products will take off and I can quit this business and make a new life for myself. If it does, then I know I owe it all to you. Love ya, Anastasia."

Ruby slid the letter into her pocket. No way was she letting Mother see *this* correspondence.

Ruby patted her pockets and ran down her mental checklist.

Notebook. Yes.

Pencil. Yes.

Peter's business card. Yes.

Money. Yes.

Better wear a cloak. It looked to be a blustery day. She pulled it out of the closet.

Mother appeared and crossed her arms. "Do you have to go out? You might catch a chill. We don't want anything to happen to the baby, after all."

"I told you. I'm taking a tour of the hospital." It was James' day off, yet he'd agreed to show her the ins and outs of Saint Raphael Merciful Hospital.

"You and your 'need' that you feel to help people," she muttered under her breath.

"I'll take the trolley if it makes you feel better."

"Yes, please, do. I worry about you."

Sure, she did. "Bye, Mother."

Thirty minutes later, she was at the hospital check-in desk. She produced the business card. "I'm here to see James Finnegan, please."

He appeared a couple minutes later, this time wearing a butcher's apron over his street clothes. There was a smattering of blood on it. "Ruby, welcome to Saint Raphael Merciful Hospital. Ready for your tour?"

He led her down the hall to the main room. People, dozens of them, sat on chairs, each one looking more miserable than the last. One held his jaw as though his tooth ached. Another massaged his stomach and moaned. Two men were in the corner. One of them had dried blood on his pant leg and leaned on the other for assistance. A mother held a crying child.

Their ailments flashed through her mind.

The child was burning up with fever.

The groaning man had eaten a meal past its due the night before and basically poisoned himself.

The leaning man had suffered a laborer's injury and gashed his leg.

It was all she could do not to hurry over and help each and every one of them. They needed help and they needed it now. "How long before they're seen by a physician?"

James looked grim. "The doctors are tending those with life-or-death situations. These people can wait."

No, they couldn't. If only she had her herbs with her.

"Come this way."

He escorted her to an infirmary, a huge, long room. Men and women were in beds lined up in rows facing one another. Their beds were parked so close that there was hardly any room to walk between them. Nurses tended to them but there were too few – she could count them on one hand –to handle that many people. And this was touted as San Francisco's premier hospital? Really?

"We have six halls like this."

Six? "All full like this one?'

"Every day."

Lordie.

He gestured. "Down here is our pharmacy."

She forgot all about the infirmary. "Show me."

The pharmacy had a cut-out window for dispensing the drugs. A man was filling a vial. She peeked inside. It was small, no bigger than their maid's room.

"We even have that new medicine, iodine."

Ruby scanned the shelves. There was not a single herb to be found. Not that she'd honestly expected to see the shelves crammed with them, but still, just the basics would have been nice.

James took her elbow. "The solarium is this way."

They passed a section with no signage.

She felt a tugging in the core of her body and stopped. "What about that door, there?"

"That? It goes down to the basement. We refer to it as the Gateway to Hell," he chuckled at his little joke. "Leads to the morgue. You don't want to see that."

Oh, but she did. Meifeng's autopsy still haunted her. Had she done it right? What had she missed? Maybe someone at the hospital could tell her. "Does the hospital ever do, you know, autopsies?"

James shook his head. "No, never."

Not even to determine if they'd done everything possible to help someone?

"That's police work, besides, there's no time with all the patients we see each day. We're not concerned with the dead. We're here to *save* lives."

They continued with the tour, seeing all four floors. The top one was where the children's ward was. Like the adults, boys and girls were in beds in a long room. They looked bored. Poor things. Maybe she could bring them books to read and paper and crayons for drawing. But there was still one area they hadn't visited. "Can I see the surgery room?"

"Rooms," he corrected her. "We have four."

Four? Amazing.

The operating rooms had windows in the doors. They peeked in. The rooms were empty save for one. This was so exciting. She was going to witness an actual operation.

James checked the paperwork tacked to the door. "Gall bladder removal," he said.

They stepped inside. Four men were huddled over a body. They'd already opened the abdomen and their arms were bloodied.

"Sponge," one of the doctors said, holding out his hand, palm up.

A tool with a sponge on the end was slapped into his hand.

A surge of energy shot through her. This was exciting, going in and fixing the body. She'd only begun reading about operations and what one had to be aware of before cutting into the body cavity. Fascinating stuff. Clamping off the blood vessels, she wanted to see how exactly that was done.

James caught her arm. "We have to stay back here, out of the way."

Oh, well, of course. They couldn't hinder the surgeons' work. But, darn, it sure was hard to see anything from here.

They exited the surgery room after a few minutes.

James turned to her. "Well, what do you think?"

"Impressive." Nothing like seeing people at the garden. This was far more sophisticated. One thing was for sure, she'd be back here tomorrow. "I want to donate my time."

He looked surprised. "Well, now. I'm sure the patients would appreciate another pretty face seeing to their needs. But –" he gestured to her belly "– in your condition, are you sure?"

She was due in about a month. She had time to help before then. It was the least she could do for these poor souls. Mornings at the hospital. Afternoons at the library. Wharf Village on the weekends. It was doable. "Yes, I'm sure."

"I'll introduce you to our administrator and we'll get the ball rolling."

Ruby greeted the young couple. The woman was carrying a newborn, maybe two or three weeks old. She seemed listless, her eyes dull. "Welcome to Saint Raphael Merciful Hospital.

"What seems to be the problem?"

"My wife is bleeding, you know," the man said awkwardly, keeping his voice low. "Down there."

He was too uncomfortable with the topic to be of much help. "You can have a seat, sir. Let me talk to your wife alone."

He took the baby and stepped away.

She gestured for the woman to come behind the desk. "What's your name?"

"Patricia."

"Let's see what we can do to get you straightened out. Bleeding after the birth is natural but you're pretty pale." She took the mother's pulse, checked her eyes. "Open your mouth and let me see your tongue." Ruby ran her hands above the woman's abdomen. There was a heaviness, almost like a wall stopping her hand. Whoa.

She moved her hand to the right, then to the left.

Right ...there.

A mass.

Uterine.

Not good.

Ruby smiled reassuringly. "Is this your first child?"

Patricia beamed, suddenly coming alive a little. "Yes. James Joseph."

Named after the father, no doubt. That was good because James Joseph would not be having any brothers or sisters. "Listen carefully, Patricia. You have a tumor."

"What?" Patricia squinted in confusion. "How could you tell?"

"We can take care of this and get you feeling better but we need to get you into surgery and pretty soon." She couldn't continue losing blood at this rate.

"Surgery?" Patricia looked over to where her husband sat. "James Joseph, come here."

Yes, call your husband over so he can hear this, too.

He hurried over, the baby in his arms.

Ruby addressed the couple. "While your child was growing in your wife's womb, something else was growing there too. There's a mass –"

"A mass," the husband gulped.

" –that's in the top part of the uterus and needs to come out." It was likely the growing fetus or the trauma of birth had caused the tumor to be ruptured. "This bleeding that you've been experiencing is a blessing, actually. It alerted you that something was wrong and brought you here."

The couple shared a look.

She took down their information, made sure there were no past issues with uncontrolled bleeding and marked Patricia as a priority case. "I'll walk you to intake and they'll schedule the surgery. They may not be able to take you for a couple of days," she warned. Ruby reached behind her and pulled out her basket. She found the herbs she wanted and measured them out. "For right now, I want you to make a tea of this and drink it three times a day. Make it strong. Take it right up to the day of surgery, understand?"

Patricia nodded. "OK. What's it for?"

"It'll boost your red blood cells and bring more oxygen to your cells so you feel better." It would do a bunch of other things, but she didn't have all day to explain them or how it worked. "Trust me."

After she handed off the couple to intake, Ruby returned to the information desk.

A woman was waiting with a child, a boy, of about nine. She was wringing her hands. He was looking down at his feet.

"Hello. Sorry to keep you waiting. What seems to be the problem?"

The mother looked fearful. "Slingshot fight." She nudged the boy. "Show her, Irving."

Irving looked up. His left eye was swollen shut, puffed up like a tomato.

Oh dear. From the color of it, it wasn't fresh. Ruby smiled at Irving. "You've got one heck of a shiner. Looks like it happened yesterday. Am I right?"

The mother nodded.

"Close range, too. Maybe five feet away?"

Irving nodded. "He suckered me."

"But not with anything small. This had to be, what, the size of an orange?"

He nodded. "It was a grapefruit."

Waste of a perfectly good grapefruit. But likely that the eye socket kept it from doing much damage to the eye itself.

"How did you know?" the mother asked.

Ruby reached into her basket of herbal treatments. "For right now, we need to get the swelling down. I'm going to give you something for making a compress, mom. I'll write down the instructions because the composition will change each day and this will take about three days. After that, come back here so we can reassess the eye."

At noon she finished her first shift at the hospital. She'd seen six to eight patients every hour, everything from a girl with appendicitis to an old man who saw devils lurking around the corner. Some she'd sent home with herbs. Others she'd had admitted to the hospital.

Now, she took off her hospital apron and set it in her locker. The cook had packed her a lunch. She'd take it to the park that overlooked the harbor, then head off to Jianyu's library.

Ruby ran a hand over her belly. "Soon little one. Soon I'll hold you in my arms."

She couldn't wait.

Tadashi hurried down the dark street. Phillip Fontinello may have tried to stop work out of Sacramento, but he'd been in for a surprise. He'd made sure none of the new workers made it to work. Yeah, they'd had to use strong-arm tactics, not something that set well with him, but it couldn't be helped.

His efforts had shut down the operation for weeks.

Now, he was off to organize more workers in the Lake Tahoe area where more rail spurs were going in. Sacramento, Tahoe, Ely, if this movement kept going, all Chinese workers would pose a united front and the rail operators would have to give in to their demands.

If only Fontinello had listened to them, met them halfway. But he didn't understand the Eastern ways of mixing the spiritual side of life with the everyday workaday life, not like Ruby. A pang hit his heart. Ruby – where was she, what was she doing? If only he could see her again, hold her again.

A man stepped out of the shadows.

Tadashi swerved automatically to avoid him.

The man advanced. He was almost on top of him.

What the heck? Tadashi dodged again, trying to avoid him.

No good.

He stopped. This was intentional intimidation.

The man stopped.

They were only three feet apart.

"Let me pass."

The man scoffed.

Oh, really? He feinted left.

The man lurched left. His fist shot out.

Tadashi ducked. Too easy. This guy was beer-belly bloated. Sluggish, too. "Let me pass, fat man."

"Not going to happen." He produced a knife and waved it.

Whoa. This guy meant business.

The man grinned. "Now what are you going to do, huh?" He lunged with it.

Not so fast. Tadashi caught his arm, bent it and swiped down with the blade.

"Ah, you cut me!" His free hand went to his face. Blood was running down his cheek.

"Who's the one holding the knife? You cut yourself." Tadashi twisted the man's arm around and wrenched it up behind his assailant's back.

The knife clattered to the sidewalk.

"Stop, stop, stop. You're breaking my arm."

"Who sent you?"

He shot a look over his shoulder and sneered. "Wouldn't you like to know?"

Two could play this game. Tadashi increased the pressure. Any harder and the shoulder would pop out of its socket. "Who sent you?"

The man lifted up on his tippy-toes. "Crockett."

Crockett. Crockett. He didn't know the name. "And who does he work for?"

"Some railroad guy. Fountain something."

Fontinello, that bastard. Now things made sense. "Tell him you met your match." He planted his foot in the man's derriere and pushed him away.

The man went sprawling.

What a tub of lard. Tadashi reached down and snatched up the weapon. "Thanks for the knife." *And, yes, besides being able to protect myself, I also know how to use a blade, so don't try anything stupid.* But he didn't say that. If the man wanted to find out, he'd be in for a hard-learned lesson.

The man, still holding the gash in his face, scrambled to his feet and stumbled off into the night.

"My daughter's due soon," Felicia said, sipping her tea. "She's carrying so big and yet she's so small-boned, it's a wonder a baby's head can fit through the skeletal structure in the hip area." *There, Ruby, you're not the only one who can read a medical book. Well, one page of it, anyway.* "I'm sure you understand my concern."

Dr. Welliman nodded. "Of course, of course. The female body is so fragile, women die every week from childbirth. I will give your daughter, Ruby, my highest standard of care to avoid such a tragedy."

"Excellent."

"Will you want to be in attendance?"

It was an unexpected question. Be in the room when the baby came? Did she really want to see all that blood? Yuck. But if anything were to go wrong, things could get dicey. "Yes, I'll be in attendance."

"And the husband?" He took a sip from his cup.

"He, um, died in a carriage accident before Ruby even knew she was with child."

"I'm sorry to hear that."

"Yes, well, these things happen. And dear Ruby, as stricken with grief as she was, she powered on despite the tragedy."

"It's a good thing the shock didn't cause her to abort." The doctor nodded as though he'd seen it happen time and again. "She's lucky. She must have a strong constitution."

She'd better warn him. "Now, Ruby has a ... hobby, shall we say?"

"How nice. Some diversion to keep her occupied during her pregnancy? Embroidery, perhaps? Painting? Flower arranging?"

If only. "She dabbles in Eastern medicine."

He nearly dropped his tea cup. "You mean, Chinese medicine?" Dr. Welliman scoffed. "Barbaric stuff."

"She has all these herbs, makes teas and concoctions." She waved her hands in the air. "She thinks it's the end-all for curing whatever ails you."

The doctor shook his head emphatically. "No basis to it. Completely unscientific."

That's what she wanted to hear. "So, you see no value in it, whatsoever?"

"Why, if I had my way, all those books on Chinese so-called medicine would be burned and good riddance to them."

She liked this man's style. "I understand you only use the most modern of ways to ensure a woman feels no pain whatsoever."

"Yes, I make sure she's rendered completely unconscious with the most current methods, so that she doesn't have to endure the agony of childbirth."

"And you can do that, here at our house?"

"I'll bring some of my equipment to ensure I can put your daughter under properly."

Felicia reached in her handbag and fanned the money. "You *will* take good care of her, right, doctor?"

His eyes lit up and he reached for it. "Absolutely."

She was no fool. She held the bills back, separated them and handed him one portion. "Half now, the other half upon, shall we say, delivery?"

He smiled at her joke. "Of course."

She produced a paper. "Sign here."

He signed the receipt, got up and bowed. "A pleasure. I'll see myself out."

Now, she only had one other arrangement to make.

Ruby finished her shift at the hospital. She'd been here a week, had seen dozens of people. Her pregnancy was only a hindrance when she tried to bend over. She pushed away from the information desk.

"Mrs. Fontinello? May I have a word with you?" It was one of the doctors James had introduced her to, a Dr. Goodman, if she remembered correctly.

He drew her off to the side. "I've been hearing how you tend to our patients. Sometimes you send them home without them seeing a doctor."

Only when it was appropriate. "Am I doing something wrong?"

"I'm curious as to how you come to ascertain a person's condition."

"The same way you do, I'm sure." Except he likely didn't feel a person's energy the way she did.

"And your training is ...?"

"I'm not university-trained by any means, Dr. Goodman. I studied under a doctor from China who came here to America. She mostly used Eastern medicine to treat people." Oh gosh, that sounded snooty. "Not that Western medicine doesn't have its place," she hurried to say. "It does, if the natural approach is not effective." She smiled. "I'm amazed at what you can do in the operating room."

"Ah, yes, I see." He nodded. "Well, then, carry on."

She removed her apron, folded it and stuffed it in her locker. Time to head off to Jianyu's place. But, first there was something she needed to do. Her inner core had been urging her to pursue it all week. Now, she finally had the time.

She headed down the hall.

There it was, the unmarked door. No one was around to see her.

Ruby slipped in and descended the stone steps into the bowels of the hospital. It was dank in here. There was a door at the bottom. She pushed it open. Here it was, the mortuary. It was cold, probably because it was underground.

It was so quiet.

The bodies were shrouded in sheets, the feet sticking out, looking gray and lifeless. There had to be a dozen of them, stacked on shelves with rollers.

Meifeng's feet had looked like that during her viewing period. She'd stared at them for hours. A pang hit her. If only she'd been able to determine what was wrong with her mentor before it took Meifeng's life. She shook the thought away. Too late to dwell on that now.

There was another door at the far end. It has an S on it, hard to see in the dim light. There were voices on the other side of it, probably men from a funeral home, here to retrieve a body.

She cracked it open.

A body was on a table, a man. His chest cavity to his groin was opened up, the I-shaped cut held aside with clips.

Hospitals didn't do autopsies. Only coroners did.

Yet, here was a body, splayed open with two men digging around its insides. These men were not here to retrieve the body for the funeral home.

A man looked up. He jerked, startled. "Ruby? What are you doing here?" It was James Finnegan.

Phillip looked up from his desk. Crockett. What was he doing here? He jumped up, crossed the room and shut the door. "You come here to my office? Are you nuts?"

There was another man, a big man, with him. He was looking down at his feet like a whipped puppy.

Crockett gestured to him. "Thought you'd like to see what your 'boy' did to my guy."

The big guy looked up. His face had a long gash down one cheek, slicing it open.

Phillip shook his head. "Tadashi doesn't carry a knife."

"No, but my guy here, does," Crockett said.

"Did," the big guy corrected him.

Did? So Tadashi not only cut this huge slug, he disarmed him, too? What was the slug doing, pulling a knife in the first place? "All I wanted was for him to get beaten up. I didn't say to use a weapon." He stared at the gash. It was deep and caked with dried blood. The man would wear it for life. "What injuries did Tadashi sustain?"

The slug grunted. "Never touched him. Too fast." He looked down at his feet again.

Crockett patted the big guy on the back and waved him to the corner. "Put your bandage back on." He turned back to Phillip. "We did what you wanted. We sent a message. It's up to you if you want another message sent."

He'd arranged for a thug to beat up his former interpreter and assistant but the tables had been turned and Tadashi had emerged the victor. Some message *that* sent. "Send someone else. Someone one faster, who knows how to carry himself in a fight. Surely there's a bar bouncer somewhere in Sacramento who can take on Tadashi."

Crockett nodded. "I know a prizefighter. I'll be in touch." He gestured to the slug and the two men went to leave.

Not so fast. "One more thing. Don't ever come to my office again."

Ruby felt her stomach. Something was wrong. Something was definitely -

A massive hand inside of her smashed down on her internal organs. She raised up on her tippy-toes.

Damn, this hurt. This hurt bad.

Oh, hell, she was in labor.

The pain left as quickly as it had begun, but her body was still reeling from it. Her ears rang. Her pulse raced. She knew she was in shock.

She stumbled away from the autopsy – she must have walked in on a class – and rushed past the cadavers.

Someone was calling her name.

No time to answer. Have to get home. Have to get home.

She made it up the stairs and took a gulp of air.

This was better. Damn, that contraction had come out of nowhere. She needed to get home. Fast. After all, a hospital was no place to have a baby.

She hurried to the lockers, grabbed her handbag and headed outside.

Have to get home. Have to get home.

There was a carriage for hire. She hailed it. "Glen Oaks Drive."

"Yes, miss. Can I help you in?"

"No, I'm fine." She hoisted herself up into the carriage and called out, "Hurry please."

The carriage took off with a jolt. He was asking the horse to trot.

She pressed her hands to her belly. "So, you're coming, huh, little one? Nice of you to let me know." She steeled herself for another contraction. Damn, she should have looked at a clock. Oh well, she'd figure out how far apart they were soon enough. From all she'd read, early contractions could be an hour apart or they could be ten minutes apart. There was no set rule. Babies came when they wanted and so did contractions.

Ruby took stock of her situation. She'd need to make a tea and soak in a tub of warm water when she got home.

The carriage slowed. "Which house, madame?"

"At the top of the hill." The one with the best view, mother's edict for a second home in San Francisco.

The carriage pulled up. Finally. She paid him double the fare and hurried up the steps. She burst through the door. "Mother, the baby's coming."

A second pain hit and her knees buckled.

Damn, damn, damn, damn.

Breathe, breathe. How much more of this could she take?

Mother appeared, looking alarmed. "Are you all right? Oh dear God, you're panting." She helped her to a chair. "Did your water break?"

The contraction passed and she could breathe again. "No."

Mother called for the servants. "We need the rubber mattress cover."

"I need to drink a tea."

"I'll make it."

Mother? Make an herbal tea? For the first time in her life? No, not today. Too much of the herbs and the labor could be compromised. "Just draw me a hot bath."

"Surely there's a medicine you can take to –"

"The bath, Mother, just draw the bath."

"Well, if you insist." She hurried away.

Ruby got up and stumbled into the kitchen. Hot water, good, the teapot was already on the stove boiling. Herbs for relaxation. OK, got them. None for pain. They were counter -ntuitive for childbirth. She could do acupressure – behind the outside ankle bone and in the center of the sole of her foot – for the pain as things got more intense.

She stirred her tea with one hand and rubbed her belly with the other. For such a little thing, it sure was anxious to make itself known.

Ruby sighed. If only Tadashi were here to share this moment with her.

Ruby lay on the rubber sheet atop her bed and panted. This Dr. Welliman was all about modern medicine. He didn't know a thing. He was between her legs now, ruining this beautiful experience for her. What had Mother been thinking when she'd called him here? She stood there now, over in the corner, watching. She should be over here, holding her hand, breathing along with her, cooling her forehead with a wet cloth.

Shit, here came another one. Her contractions were five minutes apart now.

"Push, push," Dr. Welliman said.

She pushed, trying to sit up. Damn, this hurt. "Ahhhh," she cried out.

The contraction ended.

Ruby slumped back against her pillow.

Dr. Welliman pulled back and frowned. "Oh, dear."

Oh dear, what? What did that mean?

He walked over to Mother and they talked about something in whispered voices.

It was obviously about her, so, why wasn't she being included in this discussion?

They kept talking, eyes darting her way every so often.

Enough of this. "Hello? Can you tell me what's going on?"

Dr. Welliman came back to her and stood at her side. He was not smiling. "The baby is breech."

No. Couldn't be. She hadn't pushed for the last three hours, hadn't come this far, only to learn her baby was stuck. "Are you sure?"

"It's too far into the birth canal to try and turn it."

Mother came over. She looked grim. "Dr. Welliman will have to cut the baby out. It's a procedure called a Caesarean section."

"I *know* what it's called, Mother," she snapped. She just never thought she'd have to have one. It wasn't supposed to be this way. She was supposed to have a peaceful, beautiful delivery, the baby slipping out and being placed in her waiting arms for a much awaited face-to-face meeting. How could this happen? She'd done everything right, eaten healthy foods and gotten plenty of exercise. It wasn't fair. "Are you sure?" Couldn't he just reach in and turn the baby? It couldn't hurt any worse than these fucking contractions.

The doctor patted her shoulder. "I've done plenty of these. We'll put you out. It'll be a sweet sleep and we'll monitor you carefully."

Some sort of machine was being wheeled in.

"What's that?"

"The apparatus to administer nitrous oxide, the gas to make you go unconscious," the doctor said. "When you wake up, you'll be all sewn-up and your baby will be in your arms."

This was happening so fast. "Can't you just try to turn the baby?"

Dr. Welliman shook his head. "We're at the point of no return."

Mother took her hand and looked earnestly into her eyes. "It's to save your baby, Ruby. Dr. Welliman says it might be denied oxygen if this goes on any longer. It's got to come out now or it'll die."

If was the only way ... "All right, put me under."

The machine was hooked up. A mask was put over her face.

"Breathe deeply," Dr. Welliman told her.

Another contraction hit her.

The room started spinning. Things started going black.

"Here it comes," someone said, the voice far away.

She didn't know where she was. Everything was just beyond her reach, lost in the darkness.

There were sounds, words spoken so slowly that every syllable was drawn out.

The blackness caved in on her.

Somewhere far off, a baby cried out for -

Nothingness.

CHAPTER FIFTEEN

Ruby opened her eyes. Daytime. How long had she been out? "My baby."

Mother appeared and stared into her eyes. "How are you feeling, Ruby?" She gestured to someone. "She needs water.

The cook brought her a glass of water.

Ruby waved it away. "My baby. I want my baby." She sat up. She looked around. Where was the cradle that had been set up in her room? "Where's my baby, Mother?"

"I'm sorry, Ruby," Mother shook her head sadly.

No, no, no. "What happened?"

"It was born dead."

She felt as though she'd been stabbed. No, couldn't be. No, no, no. "What happened?" she repeated.

"I'm sorry, sweetie. I know how much you were looking forward to having it."

"This can't be. Tell me I'm dreaming."

"You're not dreaming. It died."

This was surreal. It couldn't be happening. And to top it off, Mother kept saying "it" like it was a thing when they were actually discussing a baby.

Her baby. Her dead baby. She had to know. "Was it a boy? A girl?"

The cook pressed the glass into her hand. "A boy."

Mother shot the woman a sharp look.

Stole your thunder, did she, Mother? That's what you get for not telling me as soon as I woke up.

The news struck her. She and Tadashi had created a boy, really? He would have had a son. To hold. To love. To dote upon. She would have named it after him. "I thought I heard a baby cry when I was going under."

"No, it was born dead," Mother said quickly. She gestured the cook to leave them. "You need to stay in bed for at least a week."

Because of the stitches, she meant. Ruby felt her abdomen. How odd to have it flat again. Wait. She had no pain, no bandages, either. But a Caesarian should have left her with a long scar. She pushed the bed clothes aside to look.

No bandages. No incision.

"Mother, what happened? He said he was going to cut the baby out. But ...I don't have a mark on me."

She sighed. "You had another contraction and the doctor was able to turn the baby to deliver it. So, you were saved, at least."

"So, he *did* deliver it."

"He delivered a dead baby, Ruby."

"No. No, you're lying." She looked about the room. "Where is he? You're hiding him." She slid out of bed, peeked behind the bed. "Where is he, Mother? Is he in the other room?"

Mother shook her head and wrung her hands. "I'm so sorry."

There was suddenly a hole where her heart should have been. The tears threatened. *No, this couldn't be. It just couldn't be.*

Ruby stared out the window as she rocked. How could the sun be shining? How could the birds be singing?

Tadashi, Dash for short. He hadn't had a chance. Her poor baby boy. Born dead. She'd felt him kick in her womb, had sung him songs and counted the days until he arrived. But he'd died before he ever saw this world. And she'd never even had the chance to hold him.

What was the sense of going on with life?

Daddy entered the room. "There's my girl. It's a beautiful day, isn't it?"

Who cared when your child was dead?

"Say, I've got an idea. I have to travel to Los Angeles for a couple days later this week. Why don't you and your mother come along?" He grinned like it was the greatest plan ever. "The two can go shopping, have lunch at the shore while I'm in those long, boring meetings. Then we'll take in a show one night."

Sure, like that would solve anything. She got up and left the room. "I want to be alone." She stepped out on the porch.

"Ruby, your shawl," Mother cried, running up behind her and throwing it over her shoulders.

If she didn't wear her shawl, maybe she'd catch a cold. Maybe it'd grow into a fever. Maybe she'd die. Then she could be with her Dash, her poor baby boy.

She started down the street, walking by rote.

People were out and about. Carriages clattered down the street. The world kept turning. How could that be?

"Ruby! Ruby!"

Someone was calling her name. She stopped and looked over.

It was Hester, of the Girls of Good Deeds. She was pushing a pram.

Her heart dropped. Oh, God, Hester had given birth to her baby.

Hester caught up with her. "Ruby, meet Francine. Isn't she gorgeous?"

The baby had a cherub face and gazed at the world with big blue eyes fanned by dark lashes.

"She's beautiful, Hester."

"She keeps us up at all hours, but I just love feeding her and then rocking her back to sleep. I've never been happier."

"Good for you. She's an angel, I'm sure."

"Look at you. You certainly got your figure back." She leaned into the pram and smoothed the cheek of her baby. She blew a kiss, straightened up and brought her attention back to Ruby. "Taking a break from playing Mommy, huh? Doing some shopping?"

"Actually," she stopped. *Oh hell, just lie about it.* "Yes, I needed a break."

Hester waved any guilt away. "I'm sure your mother is happy to watch the baby. Maybe we'll see you at the park. Well, got to go. Ta-tah, now."

Just let her die right now, be trampled by a runaway carriage, so she'd go to Heaven and meet Dash there. Then, one day, Tadashi would join them and they'd finally all be together.

Ruby turned and stumbled forward. Maybe if she just walked into the harbor and kept walking as the water rose past her chin and mouth and nose and over her head, maybe that was what she should do because living was pure hell.

Tadashi winced as he watched his men dig their shovels into the ground. He should be in there, working beside them, but an effort like that would kill him right now. But he was still nursing his ribs after that beating he'd taken two weeks ago.

His crew had to disassemble this length of track before the next train came through. They only had four hours.

Two men were arguing off to the side. They were just standing there.

"Hey." He got their attention. "Can't you guys work while you talk?"

They nodded and came over. The taller one yanked a thumb at his buddy. "He says Meifeng was a better healer than Ruby."

Ruby. It was hard to hear her name again.

"And I say Ruby was better because she incorporated more acupressure in her sessions." He rolled his shoulder blade around. "Ruby always hit that one spot of mine. I never even had to tell her where it hurt. It was like she already knew."

The other man gave a begrudging nod. "I forgot about that. Ruby *did* always have a knack for helping a body with exactly what was needed. Good thing we have her to take over, now that Meifeng is gone. Say, when is Ruby coming back, anyway?"

Never.

Tadashi bit his lip. He'd told them that she'd gone to help a relative get over a particularly bad, lingering illness. Where had he told them that she'd gone? That's right, Seattle. It seemed far enough away that they would forget all about her. So much for that plan. "I have no idea."

"All the guys wish she'd come back," the tall one said. "That Ruby, she has a real gift."

The two men wandered off and got to work.

Tadashi went back to overseeing the track removal.

Ruby's face came to mind. That beautiful face. Where was she? What was she doing? He knew she wasn't in Sacramento. He'd only found an excuse to go past her house a gazillion times. Was she in San Fran? Was she enjoying the high life? Going to high tea by day? Attending fancy balls by night?

Maybe she'd caught the eye of a dashing baron. Maybe she was more than a passing fancy for him. After all, girl like Ruby was a real catch. Was she being wooed by some rich, handsome man right now? Were they at the race track? Or playing croquette on the lawn of some sprawling estate?

Was she in that man's arms at night, the way she'd been with him? Her smooth skin, he could feel it now, pressed tight up against him. And her kisses, how he longed for -

Stop it.

Stop thinking about her.

You told her to leave and never come back.

Not just told, he'd ordered her to go away. And now he was miserable.

Ruby eyed the ship from atop the hill, watching as it steamed into the harbor. Maybe it was from South America, full of silver goods to be traded. Maybe it was from Russia, its hull filled with furs. Or perhaps it was from the Orient, bringing in spices and oils and nuts that she could use.

She stopped herself. Use on whom? The Chinese workers? They were miles away and she wasn't wanted there.

She scanned the city. Surely someone could make use of such things. Wharf Village, maybe.

Hold on, maybe that was the key. Her heart pounded.

She needed to pray, right now.

"Lord, if I go back to Wharf Village and save the children, will you bring my baby back? Will you let me meet him in my dreams? Or make it all one big mistake? That Dash is alive and well and this has all been a terrible misunderstanding? I promise you that I'll save a hundred lives if you only make it so. I beg you Lord, let my baby be alive and bring him back to me."

She gathered her things. She had to uphold her end of the bargain. She'd better hurry if she was to grab her herbs and get to Wharf Village before it got too late in the day.

Hold on. Her healing could only go so far. She needed to be able to communicate with the people at Wharf Village. She spoke Chinese, but there had been nationalities of all kinds – who did she know who spoke a dozen languages?

"I know who." She had to hurry.

Ruby took off down the hill.

Ruby burst into the house. "Willifrid? Where are you?"

The cook stepped out from kitchen and came down the hallway. "Right here, Miss Ruby. Is everything OK?"

"I need my herbs. Quick, where are they?"

"You told me to get rid of them."

Oh no. "But ...I need them."

Willifrid gestured for her to follow.

They entered the kitchen.

Willifrid pointed to the far door. "I set them in the pantry. Couldn't see why they should be tossed out for no good reason."

Ruby hurried over. They were all there, thank goodness, just as she'd left them a couple weeks ago. "You're a gem." She grabbed them, opened the lids and checked that the oils hadn't gone bad. No, they were fine. She popped them back in her basket.

There was no time to waste. She almost bumped into the cook on her way out. "I'm going to go save children's lives."

Willifrid smiled and nodded. "Fine, fine. I'll tell your mother."

Ruby rushed out and scooted down the street. Forget walking. The trolley would get her there faster.

It let her out just two blocks from her destination.

She scampered down the walk, pulled out the key Jianyu had given her and let herself into Jianyu's library. There were at least a dozen people, just as she'd hoped. She jumped onto a chair. "Everyone." She waved her arms. "If I could have your attention please."

They all looked up.

"I'm Ruby and I'm trained in Eastern medicine. I speak Chinese but I need medical people who speak a plethora of languages. People like you." She pointed to a young man with wild, dark hair. "What's your native language?"

"Romanian."

"I need you." She pointed to another with a swarthy complexion. "How about you? What language do you speak besides English?"

"Dutch."

"Good. I need you."

She pointed again. "What about you?"

"Greek."

"I need all of you," she told them. "You probably don't know this but there is an area of San Francisco where all the foreigners have hunkered down. They live in squalor, mothers with children, barely making it day-to-day. They have medical needs. You are medical people, sworn to cure the sick to the best of your ability. Will you come with me? Will you use your knowledge to help those who cannot help themselves?"

Four hours later, Ruby checked over the last child to be seen. He was a little Pacific Islander toddler at Wharf Village. Bowed legs. An oddly-shaped skull. Protruding breast bone. She nodded to the medical student who was squatted down beside her. She'd seen enough.

"Are you thinking what I'm thinking?" the medical student asked her.

"Rickets," she said.

He nodded.

The toddler's dark skin meant he didn't absorb the healing qualities of the sun. Plus, the mother had told the Polynesian medical student that they'd had no fish, no eggs, no milk to eat. Plant-based diets had their place, but not for developing babies. He needed to eat fish, liver and cheese.

But these families couldn't afford such things. They were likely getting by with one main meal a day. If only Madeline and the other Girls of Good Deeds were still helping these people. But they'd each dropped out as their pregnancies had ended and their babies had come into the world.

She couldn't blame them. Their responsibilities at home had grown to twenty-four/seven ones overnight. She sighed. Like hers should have.

Ruby stood up and stretched her back. The sun was starting to set. She had no idea it was that late.

But look at the progress they'd affected.

All the doctors in training who had been at the library had agreed to come with her. Each of them spoke a different language – Portuguese, Italian, Swahili, Japanese, Dutch, Slovak and whatever else. It was a real melting pot here.

They'd dispensed Western medicine. She'd supplemented that with her herbs and tonics.

One of the Russian medical students was packing up his medical kit and got her attention. "I didn't even know this was here. All these people –" he gestured helplessly "– there's so much need."

It could be overwhelming, for sure. But that was why she'd asked all of them to come. "But it's do-able," she said.

"We'll need more supplies."

These people needed better facilities. Those outhouses, they were utterly disgusting. "And food. I'm thinking that if we all pool our contacts, reach out to the community for help, I think we can help these people." She looked around at the filth and disease. "They deserve better than this."

Wendell Parcells signaled his fireman. "Add a couple more logs, Henry. We don't want to lose any steam for that stretch up a head." He stuck his head out the window and let the night air ruffle his hair. It felt good. Not many men enjoyed a life like his, riding the rails at the helm of a mighty iron horse.

This new length of track was a blessing. The farmers down south had been especially eager for it to open. Heck, the twenty rail cars he pulled were mostly produce. This was a far more efficient way to get the stuff to market. Those ladies in Stockton would have a field day picking through all this fruit, all these vegetables.

He checked his pocket watch. Eight o'clock. Right on time.

They'd be pulling into Stockton in less than an hour.

He could get a steak at that new place. It stayed open late for workers like him. They sure did them right, chargrilled just so and served up with a big side of fried potatoes. He could almost taste it now.

Wendell smiled to himself. They waitresses were pretty there and they wore their blouses cut low. Scandalous, some newspaper had called it. And then the steakhouse had posted the article on their wall, along with a note. "Maybe that's why the reporter patronizes us so often."

The place was packed every time he went. Maybe that one waitress would be there, the redhead.

What was her name? Marge. That's right. Marge the red head with the pair of big-

Something didn't look right about half a mile up ahead.

Wendell squinted to better see.

The train surged ahead at full speed.

What was that? Was there water over the tracks, was that why he couldn't see them?

Oh, no.

There were no tracks.

They were just ... gone.

He grabbed the brake and yanked it as hard as he could.

The iron wheels shrieked in protest.

"Brace yourself, Henry," he yelled. "We're going to crash!"

There was a yell.

Ruby woke up with a start. What in the world was going on?

Downstairs, Daddy was shouting. No, he was cursing.

Cursing? Something had to be very wrong.

She slipped out of bed. There was a daisy – what the heck? – caught in her hair. She pulled it out and tossed it aside.

There was more yelling. "I'll kill him. With my own bare hands, I'll kill that son of a bitch."

The front door slammed.

She hurried to the window.

Father was storming down the front walk, a young boy by his side. No doubt about it, Daddy was steaming mad at someone.

She grabbed a robe, pulled it on and hurried down the stairs.

Mother was staring out the window.

"What was that all about?"

Mother turned, wringing her hands. She gestured to the morning table in the little alcove. "That was just delivered."

Ruby stepped over and picked up the paper.

It was a telegramh, dropped next to Daddy's unfinished coffee. She picked it up.

"Urgent. Train Eighteen derailed. Sabotaged."

Sabotaged? She gasped. It could only mean one thing. Tadashi had organized the displaced Chinese men and they'd made good on their threat to retaliate.

So, Daddy had not met with them. He had not taken the time to listen to their demands. And now this had happened. "Train Eighteen? Where was this?"

"It was on its way to Stockton."

She dropped the telegram. "How bad was it? Was anyone hurt?"

It was too far away for her to be of any good but it was possible some people could eventually be moved to Saint Raphael Merciful Hospital. After all, everyone knew all the best surgeons were in San Francisco.

Mother lifted her shoulders in a gesture of uncertainty. She didn't know. "Don't expect your father to be in a good mood when he gets home tonight."

Ruby strode down the aisle of the farmers market. There was so much produce, surely not all of it got sold. She approached one stall and waited for the customer, someone's cook from the looks of her, to finish before she stepped up. "Hello there. Are you the owner?"

He smiled, a robust man with a thick mustache. "What can I offer you today? Fresh peaches? Or maybe a mango?"

"Actually, I'm here with a business proposition."

"A pretty thing like you?"

"I'm Ruby Fontinello."

"I'm Walter Turrell."

"What happens to the food you have left over at the end of the day, Mr. Turrell? The stuff that's about to go bad and isn't worth putting out again, I mean?"

He frowned. "I sell it to a pig farm if I can. Otherwise, I have it hauled out to the countryside and it gets dumped."

Just as she thought. Good food gone to waste. "What if I took it off your hands? The extra stuff that the pig farm doesn't buy, I mean."

He gave her a quizzical look. "Why would you want produce that's about to go bad?"

Because there were starving children who needed it so they could survive another day. "If I send someone by, say, every other day, could you have the produce set aside for pick up?"

"Sure, I guess so."

Guess so? She needed a stronger commitment than that or Mr. Turrell would surely forget to have a sack waiting for her volunteers. "May I remind you that the money you save by no longer paying someone to haul it away will now add up each week in your bank account?" There, that got his attention.

"Sure, sure, I'll see there's food ready for pick up every other day."

"Excellent." She shook his hand and smiled. "You're helping people in dire need."

Ruby pulled the sheet out of her handbag and marked down his name and the number of his produce stall. One down, many more to go.

Phillip Fontinello burst into the sheriff's office. "I need to see the sheriff. This can't wait."

The deputy jumped up from his desk, blocking him. "He's busy right now."

"I don't care if he's busy." Damn this pup of a guard dog, blocking him this way. He feinted left but the deputy mirrored him. Enough of this crap. He straightened up. "Do you know who I am?"

"No sir, and I don't care. You can see the sheriff when he's finished."

"Who's in there who's so all important, anyway?" Surely his stature in the community bested anyone else who might need the attention of the sheriff.

The inner office door opened. A smiling woman stepped out. A pretty blonde woman.

Phillip caught his breath. "Anastasia?"

She brightened. "Well, hi, sugar. Imagine meeting you here."

He grabbed her by her elbow and drew her aside. Her perfume was exquisite. That wasn't all that was exquisite about her. "What are you doing here in the sheriff's –" he stopped himself. Stupid question. "You're no longer in Sacramento?"

"I have acquaintances all over. I travel to see some of them."

And probably got well paid for it, too. He wouldn't be surprised if the sheriff considered her "visit" part of his expense account. "How long are you in town? I, ah, may be in need of your services."

Anastasia gave him a saucy look as she leaned in and straightened his tie. "Empire Hotel. I check out tomorrow morning."

Empire Hotel. Wherever it was, he'd find it. He escorted her to the door. "I'll see you later." He hesitated. This mess would take a while. "Tonight."

"Bye, bye, sugar."

He watched her sashay away. Nice.

"The sheriff will see you now."

Phillip collected his thoughts and strode into the inner office. He was here on business, serious business. "Sheriff Dunne, we have a situation and you need to do something about it."

The sheriff leaned back in his chair and laced his fingers across his giant lap. He raised a single eyebrow. "Do I now?"

You fat bastard, don't act all high and mighty with me. People like me pay your salary. Wait until he saw *this*. He tossed the telegram on the desk. "One of my trains. A derailment. A deliberate act of sabotage."

"Let's see here." The sheriff sat up and reached for the telegram and read it to himself. "How do we know that it was sabotage?"

"I received that first telegram this morning at my home. I got a second one after about a half hour ago at my office." He pulled it out. "See? Right here, 'Rails missing,'"

"You own the railroad, do you, Mr. ...?"

"Fontinello. Phillip Fontinello." Certainly the man had heard of him. He'd had a glowing newspaper article written about him just last month. "These disgruntled workers are taking revenge on me. They were lazy. They purposely delayed progress, so I fired them."

"And now they're getting back at you by pulling up the rails."

"I demand that you secure all the sites."

The sheriff chuckled and pushed the telegram back across the desk to him. "Post men along every inch of track, is that what you're proposing?"

OK, so that was unreasonable. But having mounted men patrolling the tracks? Certainly that was do-able. "I thought th –"

"I have thirty men, Mr. Fontinello. They patrol the streets. They break up fights in saloons. They see to it that the riff raff of society stay in the dock areas so that this fine city is safe for your wives and children to walk around unfettered. I do not have any men to spare who can stand around train tracks all day, twiddling their thumbs, waiting for some group of men who may or may not show up to dig up your precious rails."

"But, bu, you have to help me."

"Your company is actually based in Stockton, am I right? Not my jurisdiction."

"But I do business here, too."

"I suggest you hire a private company to do your bidding."

"Who? The Pinkertons?" he scoffed. That would cost an arm and a leg.

The sheriff stood up. He was not just fat. He was tall, real tall. "Good day, Mr. Fontinello."

Some help you are.

Ruby donned her apron and hurried to the hospital's information desk. She'd spent all morning securing food from the produce sellers. Tomorrow, she'd approach the dairy farmers. She'd need to borrow Mother's carriage for that.

There were two girls already working at the information desk. She'd never seen them before, but then, a lot of people volunteered at the hospital. She wasn't sure why they were there doing her job. Maybe she'd gotten her dates wrong. "Were you both scheduled for today?"

"You must be Ruby. There's a note for you from the administrator." One of the girls passed it to her.

She opened it and read it. Odd, she was being summoned to Mr. Wallace's office.

Ruby hurried to the administration area. Mr. Wallace was only someone she'd seen in passing. They'd never been introduced, so what could he possibly want from her?

His secretary was a thin man with a receding hairline. He spotted the note in her hand and smiled. "You must be Ruby." He gestured her toward a second door. "Mr. Wallace is waiting for you."

She stepped into his office. It was small, neat, lots of book cabinets. Mr. Wallace took a sip from a coffee mug and saluted her with it. "Have a seat, young lady. Nice to have you back. Sorry about your loss."

She slid into the chair facing his desk. "I'm not sure what this is about."

"I've been looking into you. Your talents are being wasted."

"I like being at the hospital."

"Yes, but you can be of more help in a position other than at the information desk."

This sounded intriguing. "In what capacity?"

"We want you to be a nurse. Do you think you could handle that?"

A child could handle that. It was little more than being a companion to invalids. "Cleaning bed pans? Spooning feeding people? Forgive my boldness, but I would hope you'd see more value in my capacity to help people."

He eyed her for a moment. "Just what are you proposing?"

This was her chance. She steeled herself. "Put me in the operating room."

He lost his smile. "Now wait just a minute, young lady. You're smart when it comes to practical medicine, yes, but you're no surgeon." He gestured. "We can't have you running in there and cutting open patients."

No, but they could have her in there close enough to observe, to learn. "I meant as a physician's assistant, sir."

Mr. Wallace paused. "We only have surgeons in the operating room."

And they put two, sometimes three in there, for each patient. It was a waste of resources if you asked her. "Only one person can operate at a time. Free up the other surgeon by having me in there as an assistant." She paused and played her trump card. "Then the extra surgeon can handle another patient in another operating room. It'll bring in more revenue for the hospital."

He cleared his throat. "Well, yes, there's that. Let me consider your proposal for a minute."

"I think you'll see the 'value' in it, sir." Value, as in money.

He was quiet for about two seconds, then nodded. "All right."

Good. She jumped up and turned to leave. "You won't be disappointed."

"Hold on."

Ruby stopped. "Yes?"

"There'll be a trial period to see how things go." He held up a warning finger. "I do not want to hear of a scalpel even *touching* your hand. Do I make myself clear?"

"Absolutely." She thanked him and let herself out, trying not to squeal or rub her hands together in glee. She was going to learn surgery. Finally, yes! She couldn't *wait* to get her hands on those scalpels.

Ruby hurried home. After speaking with the administrator, she'd spent all afternoon in the surgery room, yes, but she'd been relegated to handing the surgeon, Theodore Manchester, sponges, suture thread and dressings. Their patient had been an older man with a growth on his back.

Mr. Wallace had stepped in, not once but twice, to make sure she hadn't taken up a scalpel and tried to carve out the poor man's innards. Like she would do that when the growth was on his backside. Honestly, now, did he think she had no respect for the human body?

Dr. Manchester had commended her on her assistance, even thanked her when she'd pointed out that he'd left a sponge inside the man as he went to close things up. But it was obvious that the hospital administrator had spoken to the surgeon and repeated his edict about what she could and couldn't do. Ruby smiled to herself. Things would relax after a bit.

Theodore Manchester had also commented on her pretty eyes. Maybe she could use her feminine wiles to soften him up and let her try her hand at cutting out some mysterious blob.

She entered the house. "Hello, I'm home."

There was a newspaper lying open on the floor. That was odd.

She picked it up. Oh, dear.

Train Derailed Intentionally.

There was a sub headline: Two Men Injured. This is War, Says Rail Owner.

Daddy had said that? She scanned the story. "Tadashi Moro, head of the gang ..." He wasn't in a gang. The paper made him sound like a thug. "... vowed to continue the attacks until owners come to the table ...treated men like slaves ...Phillip Fontinello denies work conditions were oppressive ...matter at a standstill ...tickets sales falter ... people afraid to ride trains ...detrimental effect on railroad's bottom line. ...Moro vows to continue the fight."

Tadashi, what are you doing? Don't you know Father will do everything in his power to stop you?

There were voices in the library. She tiptoed closer and pushed the door open.

Daddy was pacing. "When I get my hands on him ..." He stopped and noticed her. He pointed to the newspaper, still in her hand. "Did you see that? Huh? Did you see what he's done?"

Tadashi, he meant.

Daddy strode over and slapped the paper out of her hand. He jabbed his finger at her. "I'd better not hear that you're seeing that, that, traitor." He was red-facedd.

"No, Daddy, I'm not."

"He's doing this to spite me." He paced some more. "He's going to continue doing theses sneak attacks. He's out to bankrupt our family, I tell you." He glanced at the clock. "Shoot. Is it that time already?" He grabbed his jacket. "I don't want to be late."

"Where are you going, Phillip?" Mother asked.

"What? Oh, I have a special meeting at the Empire. Can't say how long I'll be, but the way things are looking," he shook his head and groaned in frustration, "it might be an all-nighter."

Ruby stepped back to him pass.

The front door slammed.

She shared a look with Mother. "Daddy's really upset."

"Indeed." She folded her arms. "All because of that 'boyfriend' of yours."

So, they were back to this again? Well, guess what, she refused to be Mother's punching bag. "I'm going to bed." She climbed the stairs to her room and undressed.

The sheets felt cool against her skin. She put her palms together. "Let everyone at Wharf Village get better. Let Daddy see how he treats his workers. Let Tadashi be all right."

She felt the night close in on her and shut her eyes. Sleep came quickly.

Her guides were there. They were pointing to a bed. "Come see."

She moved closer.

It was a little boy. Maybe three years old. Golden curls and a dimple in his right cheek. There was a wet cloth pressed to his forehead. Fever.

Her guides showed her the inside of his body. A tumor. It was on the inside of his upper intestine.

"Yes, I see it," she told them. She went to pull away.

There was a tug, a force pulling her back.

"There's something more. I can feel it." She looked again. Her eye trekked along the course of the intestine about eighteen inches. There was a second one, smaller, but at a critical turn in the intestine. "It will grow just as big if it remains," they told her.

The tug was still there.

She followed the course of the intestine even farther. A third tumor.

This poor child. "Who is he?"

"You'll find out." They turned to leave.

"Wait." She needed to know something. Only they could tell her. "I never got to see my baby. I have to know: Did he –" she steadied herself for the answer "– suffer?" It would kill her if he had. It was the last thing she wanted.

Her guides gestured.

There were clouds, thick clouds. She peered into them. She could make out two forms, a man and a woman. They were holding hands. The wisps of cloud parted.

Oh, it was her. Her and Tadashi. They were both smiling. God, he looked so handsome.

A tiny form tottered into view between them. She knew him in an instant and her heart leapt. Her hand flew to her mouth. It was her baby, her little baby boy.

Dash, look how adorable you are.

His eyes were bright, his smile beamed out at the world. If only she could touch him, hold him, but her guides were allowing her to get only close enough to watch.

Little Dash, he looked to be about two, reached up to tug on his mother's skirt. His left hand – what was that? He had an extra little finger. How odd.

Ruby dismissed it. Who cared? Her guides were showing her that he was happy. The message was clear: There had been no pain to mark his passing.

What a relief. "Thank you for showing me this."

Her guides left her and the clouds folded back on the sight of her and Tadashi and the child they should be raising together. If only.

"I love you, Dash. I love you, too, Tadashi. I will always love you," she whispered before the clouds closed in completely and she was left with only the memory.

Ruby found her way to the hospital kitchen. Huge pots were steaming on the stove. A woman was stirring them. This must be the main cook. "Are you Mildred? I'm looking for Mildred."

The woman turned. She was big boned, solid and tall. She wore glasses. "Yes?"

Ruby introduced herself. "This is quite an operation you have here."

"We feed the whole hospital, patients and staff. Day in, day out."

"What a work load. I don't know how you do it."

"Been doing it for twelve years. You learn your way around a kitchen."

No doubt. It sounded like Mildred was a workaholic. "If I may ask, how do you decide the menu?"

Mildred thought for a moment. "I just see what the butcher has the most of and go from there."

"I've noticed the hospital meals are –" meat heavy, ripe with fatty muscle, smothered in gravy "– a little light on the vegetables."

"Not much you can do with vegetables. You just boil them."

Which meant tossing out their nutrients when you drain the water off them. "Kind of bland tasting, huh?"

"Never cared for vegetables myself."

"When I was little, I tried to hide them under the rim of my plate so my mother thought I'd eaten them.

Mildred smiled. "I should have thought of that."

"But then, I met a woman who showed me how to fix them so they taste amazing."

"Vegetables don't taste amazing, no matter what you do to them."

"If you have five minutes, I can show you."

"Can't hurt, I suppose."

Ruby found a carrot and mushrooms and an onion. She sliced them up set them aside and poured oil to a skillet. "Where's your garlic?"

"I never cook with garlic."

She'd suspected as much, so she'd come prepared. Ruby reached in her skirt pocket and held up the bulb. "This is the magic potion, Mildred. It not only makes things taste appealing, it has so many medicinal properties, I can't begin to tell you."

She broke off three cloves, chopped them up and added them to the warm oil. She leaned in and took a whiff. "Breathe this in, Mildred."

Ruby let the garlic cook for a minute, then added the vegetables. "You can add ginger or sesame."

"Ginger or ...what?"

The poor woman had never heard of sesame? And she was feeding hundreds? No wonder the American diet was so out of whack. "Different spices to change things up."

The vegetables were soft.

Ruby grabbed a fork, stabbed the different vegetables and fed them to Mildred. Here was the moment of truth. "Well, what do you think?"

"This is amazing." Mildred dug in the pan, scooping up more and eating it. "I had no idea vegetables could taste so good."

"And it's easy to prepare, yes?"

"Sure is."

"You know, doctors say we should have at least fifty percent of our diet as vegetables." OK, so they were Eastern doctors and she was stretching things. They actually supported a ninety percent plant-based diet. But Mildred wasn't ready for that lesson. "When you think about it, ancient man lived off the land. They ate mostly plants. They speared a deer now and then, but that didn't feed them but for a couple of days."

Mildred nodded. She sure was bent on finishing the pan of vegetables. She jabbed the fork at the last of the food even before she swallowed. "I bet our patients would like this."

Music to her ears. But Mildred needed to take this idea a step further. "So, Mildred, how much of your budget goes to buy meat?"

She scoffed. "Are you kidding? As much as seventy percent."

"And what's the price of vegetables?"

The light went on in Mildred's eyes, she could swear it did. Ruby smiled. Her work was done here. "Remember, Mildred, garlic. Garlic and a good olive oil. Don't be afraid to experiment."

A week later, Ruby handed the needle strung with suturing thread to Dr. Theodore Manchester.

He began sewing up the woman, a hysterectomy case. She'd had ten children. Number Ten had nearly killed her. Had the women truly wanted to have child after child after child?

The surgeon stabbed at the flesh and hunted for a place to attach it across the opened expanse of the groin. He stabbed again.

Ruby cringed.

He was not even close to being directly across from his initial entry point.

She couldn't let him massacre this poor woman's body. She grabbed the needle from his hand. "Here let me. It's obvious you never had to sew any clothes as a child." Not that she'd ever been in a position to make her own outfits, but it had been part of her upbringing as something girls did, no questions asked.

"Thanks." He stepped back and let her in. "I just haven't got the hang of it."

Obviously.

Ruby stitched up the incision, making small sutures and keeping the transition as flat as possible. Amazing how the skin didn't rip, but then the human body was a wonder of incredible parts that all worked together. She finished up and tied it off. There, that looked better. She hoped the woman appreciated her adept hand.

Theodore Manchester smiled and gave her the bandage to apply. "Thanks, I hate doing at that part."

"You have big hands, that's all." It was a wonder he'd been able to fit them inside the woman's body cavity. No doubt he'd pushed a few organs off kilter to root out the reproductive organ.

They pulled up the sheet, called for an orderly to move the woman, then went to the sink area and began washing up.

Dr. Manchester got her attention. "We have another hysterectomy scheduled for this afternoon." He looked around to make sure no one was nearby. "Could you help me with that one? The woman's really tiny and I know I won't be able to get in there properly."

Operate? Not just watch? You bet. "What time?"

"Three."

CHAPTER SIXTEEN

It was all she could do not to jump with joy. She was going to operate. Finally.

She had two hours before she was due in surgery. She could check up on the patients who were in post-op or she could do some operating on patients of her own.

Ruby headed down the hall and found the door she wanted. The Gateway to Hell. The stone steps led down into the basement.

She entered the morgue, tried to ignore the odor and passed the gray feet sticking out at her. The door with the S, gosh it was dark in this corner. She found the handle and peeked in. No one. Good.

There had been a cart just inside the main door. She got it and selected a body. It was an old woman. The toe tag had just one word. "Indigent." No one would be claiming this woman's body. Ruby tugged on it. It didn't move. She'd probably weighed only a hundred pounds in life.

Ruby was only ten pounds heavier. She hadn't anticipated the logistics of handling a body that weighed as much as she did. She looked around. Surely morticians and autopsy doctors had faced this problem.

Something moved. She tried again. Oh, the shelves had sliders. Thank goodness or she would never have been able to get the body out.

She got the body onto the cart and wheeled it through the door in the back. The cart and autopsy table were of a compatible height. She slid one end of the body onto the table, then the other end until it was straight.

There were scalpels to one side, rubber gloves, beakers and a measuring scale.

Ruby unwrapped the cotton sheet.

The woman had gray hair, a sunken face with a gaping mouth with only a few teeth.

"Hello, Edith." It seemed as good a name as any.

Her skin was mottled yellowish and blue and her bones stuck out. Edith appeared malnourished. She had a big bruise on her left hip. Falls could be fatal for old people. Edith had never had an operation.

Ruby took the scalpel and made a slice down the center of the body, then V-shaped cuts at each end. "Let's see what happened to you," she muttered.

She sliced open the stomach. Edith had eaten before she died. She pulled the light closer and moved pieces of stomach content aside with the scalpel. There was a clot of something she couldn't identify. It certainly wasn't anything organic. Bread maybe? What a mess for the body to try to digest. Still, the inside of the stomach showed no signs of disease.

She moved on to the liver. It had been squishy in life. Not anymore.

An hour later, she shoved Edith, once again wrapped in the cotton sheet, onto the shelf where she's been.

"Thank you for allowing me to do this, Edith," she said and slipped out the door.

Dr. Manchester was waiting for her just outside the operating room. He pulled back. "Good Lord, what's that awful odor, my dear?"

Darn, she'd picked up the scent of delaying bodies. If she lied about where she'd been, he'd know.

"A gentleman came to see a deceased relative and I accompanied him to the morgue."

"I should have recognized the odor from medical school. But it's so strong." He gave her a quizzical look. "You must have been down there a long time."

Think fast. "He didn't want to leave her side. We were down there at least an hour. I finally had to pull him away."

"Busted up over her death, huh? He must have really loved his – what, mother? Grandmother? Aunt?"

Time to move past this topic. "So, we get to do another hysterectomy, huh?"

"Yes, yes, the small-boned woman I mentioned." He leaned over and whispered, "Thanks in advance for helping me with this one."

"Any time," she said. She couldn't wait for the honor of operating on her first living person.

Tadashi propped himself up on his elbow in the grass and used his spy glass to scan the road below. No one was coming. Darn. He should be here by now.

He rolled onto his back and squinted up at the sky. Phillip Fontinello was not one to take the multiple derailments sitting down. No, he was the type who would take revenge and to hell with the law. He'd heard the boss boast of convincing families to sign over access to their land. There had always been an insincere tone to his voice whenever Fontinello mentioned it.

Only later had he learned exactly how that had been accomplished. Tadashi shook his head. Goons, what an underhanded way to force people to lease their land, perfectly good farming land, to the railroad.

So now, he was laying low, not eager to take a bullet in the back. His beating had left him black and blue. Every movement had been painful. Now, he was healed.

Tadashi rolled back onto his stomach and checked again.

There was a puff of dust. A rider was coming from the east.

He recognized him as Enlai, a young man not afraid of confrontation. He also understood some English.

Enlai approached and began looking about.

Tadashi stood up and whistled.

The rider hurried to him, handing down a bag of food before he dismounted.

Dried meat. Bread. Apples. Carrots. Not much variety, but if he snared a rabbit, he could make a stew. "Thanks."

Enlai hobbled the horse so it could graze but not run off. "Don't worry, no one followed me."

"What's the word in town?"

"The men liked the publicity from the newspaper. Some said the telegraph took the story all the way back to New York City. We're famous."

Famous, but not in negotiations. Not yet anyway. "Tell the men that they did a good job. I'm proud of them." He bit into the apple. "Any word from Fontinello?"

"He went to the law."

Not unexpected.

"He's reportedly fuming mad, wants you to hang for this."

"No word on him agreeing to negotiate?"

Eanlai scoffed. "Hardly."

Change was difficult for people who were always used to getting their way. Fontinello would have to come around, see that they were a force with which to be reckoned.

"So, what's the plan? Where do we hit next?"

"We already have."

"Huh? You pulled up tracks all by yourself?"

Tadashi smiled. "You might say that." This was a much more subtle move, one he'd instigated weeks ago, his ace in the hole. If only he could see Phillip Fontinello's face when the realization of what he'd done struck him.

Ruby alighted from the hired carriage at the warehouse near the harbor and spotted the young Persian doctor. "Baraz, why are we here? I thought you said you could get clothes for the children." This looked nothing like a clothing mercantile.

"The clothes are inside. I need a person who reads English better than me to look at the contract."

Contract? They wanted donations. "I don't understand."

"Humor me." He ushered her inside.

A man in overalls was inside. He quickly wiped his hand on his pants before extending it. "Didn't know a proper young lady was going to be here." He nodded. "Enos Farnsworth, at your service, miss."

He was sweet to act so clumsy around her. "I'm Ruby. I understand you have clothing for some needy children, yes?"

Enos shot a look at Baraz. "Well, some clothes, yes."

What was going on here? Did he have clothes or not? "Well, what do you have?"

"They're not children's clothes, miss."

That was what they needed. The children at Wharf Village were in nothing better than rags. But if this was a donation, then perhaps the mothers could cut the clothing down to size.

"Here, let me show you." Enos ushered them through a door.

It was a warehouse. Wooden crates were stacked everywhere, so high they went up to the two-story ceiling. They were marked with stenciled letters and she caught a glimpse as she passed – rum, tools, and paper. Their origins were marked, too – Tokyo. Australia. Russia. There was a slew of them from India. Who knew there was so much commerce going on in this one building?

Enos stopped. "It's this crate." He found a crow bar and pried the top off. He pulled out one-piece miner's overalls. The seams were doubled and held by rivets.

Oh dear. It would take someone with professional skills and steaming equipment to undo all the heavy duty stitching and cut them apart. Even then, the resulting pieces would be so small, they would have to be patched together to come up with anything a child could wear. Now, the pants, if you took out the waist – no, what was she thinking? Even that would be a conundrum to make any kind of a waistband. "They're all the same?"

Enos nodded. "Yes, miss."

Ruby gestured helplessly. "There's is nothing here with which our mothers can work. It's just –" she searched for the right word, one that would not insult Baraz who'd, no doubt, tried hard to find them a donation "–too involved." It seemed that this had been a wasted trip. Unless ... "Enos, I don't suppose you know of anyone who can supply us with children's clothes? Castoffs? An unfilled order, perhaps?" Something? Anything?

He shook his head. "We don't usually even deal with clothes. Too expensive. Most people make their own."

"Do you know where I might find such things?"

"Let me think on it."

They headed back to the office.

A crate was broken, sitting in the corner. It had some kind of clothing bulging out.

She threw a hand out and stopped everyone. "What's that?"

Enos made a rolling-eyes face. "A disaster, is what it is. It was a cash on delivery deal. The guy never showed up to claim it, just left it on the ship. We've had it here for eight, maybe nine months now, just taking up space."

Taking up space was right. It was twenty feet long and about ten feet wide. She peered closer. "But what's in it?"

"Beats me." He resumed walking to the office.

No, no, no, come back here, Enos. "Let's check." She cocked her head and smiled at him. "Could we, pretty please?"

His face turned pink. "Sure."

Two minutes later, the top of the busted crate was opened up.

Lordie, look at that. There were bolts of cloth inside, yards and yards of cloth in all different colors. This was perfect, even better than pre-made clothes. Children were always growing. The mothers could make their clothes to whatever size was needed. "Who owns this?"

"Some guy who never showed up. We went to his address and it was a boarding house. The mistress said she hadn't seen the guy for weeks."

"So, no one owns it, am I correct?"

"It's abandoned goods."

"And this has been taking up valuable space here in your warehouse for nearly a year, yes?"

"Yup."

She needed Enos to keep agreeing with her. "Wow, that's a long time to have to deal with an albatross like this."

"Sure is. We should have just dumped it in the harbor."

"So, it's no good to you."

"None at all."

"In fact, you don't know why you still hold onto it."

He nodded. "There's really no reason to."

"So, if someone were to take this 'junk' off your hands, you'd appreciate that, right?"

"You bet."

"Well, Enos, I think you and I can help one another."

Ruby left the warehouse ten minutes later. Enos was giving her the fabric for free. Just as great, he was delivering it for free, too.

All she needed was to get needles and thread and the Wharf Village mothers would be having sewing parties ad nauseam.

Phillip set the telegram aside. That was odd. The state was asking him to supply the surveyor's report for the Chico line they were putting in. "Fulcom," he called out. "Come in here."

He appeared instantly. "Yes, sir?"

"The Chico line." He tossed the telegram at his clerk who scanned it quickly. "Didn't we submit those plans two or three months ago?"

Jerold Fulcom nodded. "As I recall, yes."

"They say they never got them."

"Perhaps they misplaced them."

Good Lord, he hoped not. The damn thing had cost thousands of dollars. For what? Silly surveyor's plans. What a rip off. But the law said it had to be done. Was it right to stick it to the hard working business man who brought commerce to the area? Next thing you knew, they'd start taxing him for the water he drank. "We have a receipt, right?"

"It should be in the files. I'll go find it."

That would prove they'd followed orders and submitted the plans on time. If the plans were lost, then it was the state's fault, not his.

He got back to work. Right now, he had to find out if his steel supplier was charging him more per ton than the contract stipulated. Things weren't adding up. He ran over the figures again.

Jerold Fulcom popped his head back in. "Um, sir?" he squeaked.

What now? Don't stand there like a scared rabbit. "Come in."

"There's no receipt."

"You said you saw it."

"I said we should have it."

"Then why don't we?" Shoot, they needed that damned receipt.

Fulcom wrung his hands. "Our regular courier was out sick."

Spit it out, man. "And?"

"I had Tadashi do it."

Oh, crap. It had been when Tadashi was pushing him to be nicer to the Chinese laborers, asking him to consider cutting their work hours back. And Fulcom had handed him vital papers, papers that been the originals. He pressed his hands to his temples. What was worse, he'd foregone the cost of having a duplicate set made. Save some money. Who needed duplicates?

This was bad. The Chico line was a huge investment. Everything was ready to begin.

Correction: Everything *had* been ready. Now, there was this set back. It could take two months for another survey to be done. By then, all the other paperwork they'd would have been filed outside the time parameters and they'd have to start the whole process over again.

He slammed his fist on the desk. *Damn you, Tadashi Moro.*

Ruby hurried down the hospital hallway. She'd just finished another textbook from the Seekers of the Universe library. The information was amazing. If she could try out the surgery technique in the morgue, she could get a feel for how it should be done.

A doctor was coming down the hall. He spotted her and hurried over. "Just who I needed. I have a patient, a Mr. Young, I want you to look at."

"At intake?"

"No, he'd been admitted. Age forty-nine, a laborer. No history of illness. Came to us complaining of difficulty breathing. We ruled out consumption."

That was a relief.

"But I don't know what it could be."

The man was coughing phlegm into a kerchief. He pressed his hand to his chest. "It hurts so bad."

She checked his eyes and felt his glands. She had him stick out his tongue. So far, so good. "When did this start, Mr. Young?"

"It's been tough to breathe for a long time now, years even. But lately, I just can't seem to catch my breath. It seems to be getting worse."

She took a stethoscope and pressed it to his chest. "Breathe normally." Ah, there it was, a gurgling intake, gurgling return. Mr. Young's lungs were filled with mucus. He wasn't expelling air very efficiently, either. Ruby shot a look at the doctor. Had he heard it, too?

The doctor looked grim and nodded.

Yes, he had.

"Are you tired throughout the day?"

"All the time."

"You get headaches a lot?"

"How did you know?"

"And it's tough to go up a flight of stairs?"

He nodded. "I have to stop halfway up."

"You have trouble sleeping, am I right?"

"I toss and turn all night."

Things were adding up. Did he have swollen ankles? She threw back his bed cover and checked. Yup. His decreased lung function was affecting his circulation.

"What kind of labor do you do, Mr. Young?"

"I work in a coal plant, shoveling coal."

"For how long?"

"Thirty years."

So, he'd breathed in coal dust for hours and hours every day.

He had pout lines etched around his lips. "How long have you been a smoker?"

He grinned. "My pappy taught me when I was twelve. Been doing it ever since."

A double whammy, coal dust and cigarettes. His lungs didn't stand a chance.

She had the man lie back. "I want you to close your eyes and just relax, Mr. Young." Ruby took a moment and calmed herself. She let her hands hover over his chest. Tightness. Restricted air flow. Muscle thickening. Damaged alveoli. How was this man even alive?

He opened his eyes. "So, what is it?"

She could not diagnose him without being a licensed doctor. "I'm ...not sure." She gestured for the doctor to follow her out to the hall. When they were out of hearing, she turned to him. "His lungs are giving out. They're so damaged, I don't think he can ever recover. I would suggest herbs that are expectorants such as ginseng or lungwort. We should also give him licorice, comfrey and especially fenugreek. He needs to drink lemon juice. Garlic will help him, too." Garlic helped just about everything.

"These herbs, I have no idea where to get them."

Her supply was running low. "I have to get some. As soon as I do, I'll give them to him." She just hoped Mr. Young wasn't too far along to be helped.

Ruby hopped down from Mother's carriage. Look at this mass of people. All of Wharf Village had turned out, it seemed.

Off to one side, the fabric was being cut off the thick bolts and handed out. The needles and thread that had been donated by the manufacturer – all she'd had to do was ask – were being passed out nearby. Over there, people were being handed blankets, yes, some of them had minor imperfections or were stamped with the name of the closed mission from which they'd come, but they would keep the people warm at night.

The latest food delivery had been yesterday. People's bellies were full and it showed. She could see it in their smiles, in the spring in their step.

She grabbed her basket with her new supply of herbs.

Her group of doctors were starting to gather. She counted eleven. She'd need every one of them. This was the weekend, so the male adults in the families were here. It was a whole new crop of people to treat. She joined the doctors and greeted them. "Everybody ready? Let's go to work."

They found a place to set up. Things were more organized now. Placards written in different native languages directed people to the proper line. Couldn't read the card? Then that was not the line to get in. Stakes and ropes kept patients back until they were called forward. Sheets were hung so that those being examined had some semblance of privacy.

Her first patient was an Irishman with twinkling eyes. "If I were twenty years younger, lass, I'd take you out dancing."

He would, huh? He was quite the ladies' man.

The Irishman had a strained back, easy enough to treat. She handed him some herbs to relax him. When she told him about using warm compresses, Meifeng's face suddenly appeared in her head.

Meifeng. She was smiling, eyes bright, happy. It was as though her mentor was here, guiding her.

Next up was a young man. He had a swagger to his walk and he smoked a cigarette. He had a dirty bandage with dried blood wrapped around his arm.

She jutted her chin at it. "What's that for?"

He scoffed. "I got in a fight with this guy. I didn't know he had a friggin' knife."

She knew by the smell what she'd find. Ruby lifted the makeshift bandage. Sure enough, it was infected.

He crinkled his nose at the odor. "Bad, huh?"

Worse than bad. But she wasn't about to tell him that. "This is treatable."

"I knew that."

"But if you don't follow my instructions, it will get worse."

He didn't look concerned. "Worse, huh?"

Way worse. She had to impress upon this cocky young man the need to care for it daily. "Don't do what I tell you and you could lose the arm." She made a lightning quick chopping motion. "Understand?"

"Yeah, whatever you say."

Great. She'd likely be seeing him again and would learn if he'd taken her advice to heart.

Ten hours later, she packed up and went to leave. Her work was done.

Someone bumped into her.

It was a young woman, Japanese. She held a baby.

There was a pang in her heart.

The infant looked so beautiful. It was sleeping, tucked up in its mother's arms.

Like little Dash would be in mine if he were alive.

That hole in her heart was still there. It would never go away, never heal. How could it, when she was without the one thing that mattered most – her little baby boy.

Ruby heard the footsteps retreating and peeked around the corner at the hospital intake desk.

Empty.

Perfect. She ducked out and tiptoed down the hall. The hospital was quiet this time of night. Footsteps and other sounds echoed off the walls. The office she needed to access was locked but she knew where Bertha, the nighttime desk clerk, kept her keys. The woman was notorious or her long bathroom breaks. If it was a urinary tract infection, there were herbs to correct that.

But she wasn't about to treat Bertha until she had what she wanted from the records office.

The keys were in the drawer. Bertha, bless her, had even labeled them.

Ruby grabbed them and hurried off.

The records room was way in back. She slid the key in the lock, turned it and felt the tumblers give way. She was in. She had to risk a lamp, there was no other way. At least the room had only windows way up high so no one would see her.

She eyed the files. There were so many, aisle and aisles of them.

Indigent. Indigent.

There it was. Ruby opened the drawer and flicked through the papers. She needed to go back no farther than last week. More than that and the body would be too far decomposed. She grabbed a bunch about an inch thick, yanked them out and stashed them in her carryall.

She closed the drawers, put out the light and retreated. No one would know she'd even been here.

Back near the desk, Bertha was still missing.

Really? She'd expected to have to wait until the woman made rounds before she could return the keys. It seemed that luck was on her side.

Ruby dashed behind the desk, dropped the keys in the drawer and hurried away.

Now, for the real purpose of her visit.

She found a table and pulled out the files. Thank goodness she could read the doctor's handwriting.

Name: John Doremann

Age: Forty-nine

Height: Five feet, eight inches

Weight: One hundred and sixty pounds

There were plenty of boxes left empty such as address, next of kin, payments made.

If John Doremann was labeled an indigent, then it made sense that such information was missing.

Ah, here, down at the bottom, was a box she wanted to see.

Symptoms: Headache every day, stiff neck, vomiting, patient cannot tolerate loud noises or bright lights.

There was only one thing that came to mind with those symptoms –meningitis. But it was missing the main symptom, the most obvious one.

Ruby flipped the page.

There it was, under Symptoms Continued: Red sores covering the body. The medical books said that one could press a drinking glass to the skin and the sores would maintain their redness, indicating they were not that way from blood flow.

She took note of his tag number – Two Five Six – and closed the file.

"Let's go see if we can't find you, John Doremann."

She headed down to the unmarked door. She descended the stone steps and entered the morgue.

Ruby shivered. She'd forgotten how cold they kept it down here. She should have brought a sweater. She lit a lantern and checked the toe tags.

Two Five Six. Two Five Six.

Here he was.

She got the cart and rolled it over. "Let's go for a ride, Mr. Doremann." She slid him aboard, easier to do now that she'd figured out how to better leverage the body, and wheeled him into the other room.

Oh, now that she had the lantern up high, she could see that the "S" on the door wasn't a letter at all. It was an asp. Who knew?

"Up on the table you go." She rolled him over so that he was facedown. Bright lights and loud sounds – those things told her that the brain was affected by this disease. If the brain was affected then maybe the brain stem could have a clue to it.

She donned the rubber gloves as a precaution. There was no sense to infecting herself with a disease that had a ninety percent morbidity rate.

Ruby took the scalpel in hand. "This won't hurt a bit." She felt better when she was talking to the corpses. It seemed more respectful.

She cut into the back of the neck and pulled open the incision. The tissues here appeared swollen compared to other corpses', as though they'd been inflamed. They appeared to have been a deep, dark red when he'd been alive.

She pulled the lamp closer and sliced along the backbone. The spinal column was right ...there. Yup it looked as though it had been inflamed, too. Not good. "This thing was all through you."

The brain. She needed to check the brain. It would require using the hacksaw. Poor Mr. Doremann. He would have to suffer another indignity in the name of science.

"I'm just going to cut from here to back past your ear," she told him. She picked up the scalpel. She started her cut and found bone almost immediately. Her line was long and straight. Perfect. She peeled the skin back, exposing the underside of the dermis. Look at all those vessels. No wonder the smallest cut to the head resulted in maximum bleeding.

The skull was white. She grabbed the saw. It had deep teeth. If that's what it took, then, all right. Best get to it.

Two minutes later, she was making progress. "You're doing fine, Mr. Doremann. What's that you say? This doesn't hurt a bit? Glad to hear that."

A song had been stuck in her head all day. She began humming it as she worked.

She made three cuts for a triangular opening. It had certainly gone faster than she'd imagined. Guess she was getting the hang of this.

She removed the skull piece.

What the heck?

She peered closer. The brain was pressed hard against the skull. It shouldn't be like that. There should be space, some room for the brain to shift around. Poor Mr. Doremann. The tissue showed signs of having been inflamed and swollen when he was alive, just like his spinal cord, only the brain had nowhere to go. It was confined by the skull. The pressure must have been utterly incredible. No wonder he'd complained of constant headaches.

"We have the final determination of what caused you so much trouble. Your brain had swollen so much it could no longer function."

She'd have to investigate which herbs could affect swelling of the brain for when she encountered a living person with the same symptoms. This man, who'd been marked indigent by the hospital, may have just saved another person's life. "Thank for your valuable assistance. Who knows how many people your autopsy may have help?"

If she could talk to this man, perhaps he could talk to her, too.

"Why thank you, Ruby," she said in a deep voice. "You did a fine job."

"You did all the hard work, Mr. Doremann," she answered back.

There was a crash on the other side of the door.

Ruby froze. *Oh hell, someone was here. Quick, hide!*

She ducked behind the table and held her breath.

There was the sound of footsteps running away.

She had to get out of here. But she couldn't leave poor Mr. Doremann.

It was silent on the other side of the door. She crept toward it and pressed her ear to it.

Nothing.

She turned the handle, opened it a crack and peered out.

No one.

But there was a mop on the floor. That must have been the crash that she heard. Someone had almost walked in on her. They might be coming back. If she got caught, she'd lose her job, lose access to the surgeries and this morgue.

Ruby hurried back to Mr. Doremann and quickly wrapped him in the cotton sheeting. There was no time to put him back together and stitch poor man up. If he was an indigent, then no one was going to come claim the body anyway.

"I'm sorry, Mr. Doremann. There's no time."

She lid him on the wheeled cart and took him back to the shelf from which he'd come.

Got to go, got to go.

She tore off the gloves, grabbed her things, blew out the lantern and hightailed it up the stone steps. She peeked out the door at the top of the stairs.

No one was in the hall, good.

Ruby tiptoed down the corridor, found an egress door and slipped out of the hospital and into the night. Phew. That had been a close one.

Tadashi splashed water from the creek onto his face. What he wouldn't give for a nice, warm bath.

Warm bath.

He and Ruby had shared a nice, warm bath once. She'd giggled and soaped him up, eyes bright, then let her hand slip down to his –

Yeah, that had been an awesome night. That night and the many which came after it. No one had understood him like Ruby.

But that was in the past, over and done.

He filled his canteen and hiked back to his campsite. He had to get there before it got totally dark. It was in a different valley from before. He had to keep moving his location, couldn't risk Fontinello sending someone to follow the men who brought him food.

The railroad boss man, he could see his face now. How was he handling the disruption of the Chico line? Pacing the office, probably. The delay would cost thousands of dollars. Money. It was the only language Phillip Fontinello understood, so it was the only way to get his attention.

His next move would be less subtle and a lot more expensive. But Meifeng had left her inheritance to him. Where she had used its income to bring healing formulas to the sick who needed it, he would use that income to bring fair wages and labor laws to workers who needed it, who deserved it.

Tadashi reached his campsite, banked his fire and settled into his sleeping roll. The stars above him were amazing. His mother, Meifeng, was not up there, was not enjoying paradise. Hers was a lonely, frightful existence in a dark and sorrowful place. "I should be there to protect you." Instead, he said a prayer for her soul, just as he did every night.

The night closed in. He let his eyelids drop and shut out the world.

He was in a house. Someone was calling his name. He went from room to room, following it. But they were always just a glimpse of a form, a wisp of fabric rounding the corner. "Stop. Wait," he called out. "Who are you that you know my name?"

There was laughter.

He knew that laugh. "Mother? Is that you?"

He raced forward and rounded the corner.

Meifeng was riding a carousel in the middle of a field. The grass was thick and so tall around her that he had to wade his way to her.

"Mother, are you all right? I've been worried sick."

She laughed again and pointed. A squirrel appeared, jumping from carousel horse to carousel horse until it reached her, hopped on her shoulder and sat there. "My friend," she said, feeding it nuts. "All the animals are my friends."

There was a thud and the ground reverberated.

An elephant was tromping toward them. A bear followed and a tiger.

His heart beat faster. "Mother, we've got to get out of here. They'll eat us alive."

She shook her head. "I told you. They're my friends." Meifeng spun around, the carousel suddenly gone. Now they were sitting on a rooftop. The elephant was behind them, sniffing his ear with its nose.

Meifeng laughed and gently moved the snout aside. "He's young and hasn't learned his manners," she said by way of apology.

Yeah, whatever. He looked around. It was Sacramento. There was Ruby's house, high on the hill. He frowned and turned away from it. "She betrayed you, Mother. In a most egregious way."

Meifeng scoffed. "Look at me. Do I look unhappy?"

No, just the opposite. She seemed effusive and vibrant. In fact, she looked young, like she was no more than thirty years old. "You're not?"

"I'm free as a bird, no more pain, no more worries." She looked into his eyes. "Listen carefully. I can only come to you one more time. You will be tested like you've never been tested before. Forces are gathering against you. Be smart. Be ready. Prepare well." She hesitated. "Whatever happens, I'm proud of you, my son. No mother could be prouder."

She disappeared.

"No, don't go." There was so much he wanted to say to her.

Tadashi's eyes snapped open. He must have been dreaming but, despite the carousel in the middle of nowhere, the animals coming to be with Meifeng and the shift to the rooftop, it had seemed so *real*.

How late was it? The stars had moved so Orion was completely on the other side now. Three in the morning, most likely, the time Westerners called the witching hour.

She'd said he would be tested. Tested how? Tested when?

If only she'd stayed so he could talk to her longer. "I miss you, Mother."

Ruby hurried down the corridor of the hospital. She was due in surgery, an appendectomy. This could prove interesting.

Four nurses were huddled around the nurse's station. They were gossiping, most likely. The hospital was ripe for word getting around about extraordinary ailments, walnuts swallowed whole and a child with a tooth growing out of his cheek.

One of them noticed her. "Have you heard the latest, Ruby?"

Here it came, the gossip train in full operation. "Can't say I have." She pulled the roster closer, grabbed a pencil and signed in.

"We have a ghost."

Funny. "That's nice."

"No, I mean it. The morgue is haunted." She gestured, eyes wide. "Old Mr. Glasby went down there to get something and he heard them."

Them, plural. "I thought you said that we had 'a' ghost."

Another nurse stepped up. "He heard one, a woman, he said, who was singing."

All the nurses nodded in tandem.

She lifted a single eyebrow. "Singing? So, we have a talented ghost."

"Not just that. He heard two of them having a conversation, a man and a woman."

"When was this?"

"Two nights ago."

That was me, you idiot. But if a fictitious haunting kept people away from the morgue so she could work, fine with her. "Well, if we're going to have ghosts, I guess that's the place they'd be, all right." She strode away.

The conversation replayed in her mind. Old Mr. Glasby was in charge of the morgue, she'd learned. So, why had she walked in on two doctors the day she'd gone into labor?

Time to wash up before they opened their patient. She was working with Benjamin Crimwell today. The man had graduated at the top of his class. Some suspected he used his father's money to ensure his grades were better than anyone else's. He must have paid a mighty high sum. Med school was expensive enough. *Stop it, you're as bad as the gossiping nurses.*

Ruby finished washing her hands, shook them dry, pushed her back against the swinging door and entered the operating room.

Crimwell was already there. He looked up. "Did you read the case file?"

Ruby nodded. Male. Age twenty. Good health. Sudden onslaught of pain. Other causes ruled out. She glanced over at the operating table.

The anesthetist just about had the patient to sleep. The clock was ticking. She didn't like having a patient under for too long. She had to prod him to hurry. "Let's do this."

"I'm coming, I'm coming."

Crimwell had the body cavity open in no time. He pointed. "See? Right there."

It was inflamed, obvious even to a layman that it had to be removed. Good thing it hadn't burst.

The surgeon removed it and stepped back. "You can finish up."

Her? This was unusual. Crimwell usually liked all the glory for himself. Maybe he thought a mere appendectomy was beneath him.

He dismissed the anesthetist as he toweled off his hands. "No need for you to be here."

"Yes, sir." He left.

Ruby stepped in to take the surgeon's place. She reached in. No wonder the doctor didn't want to finish up, the support tissues for the appendix had shrunk back into the body cavity and now had to be fished out. He should have used a tool to prop it in view if he needed two hands to cut it out.

But it was her problem now. Surgeons were the gods of the hospital. You didn't argue with them.

She grabbed the suturing needle, set it nearby and started feeling around. Where had it –?

There was a push.

She caught herself from bending forward. What the heck?

Crimwell was behind her, pressing into her. "Ruby, you have the greatest ass."

How *dare* he. "Stop it."

He ground his crotch into her. "Oh, that ass."

They had an opened patient here and he wanted his jollies? "Get hold of yourself, doctor."

His hands grabbed her breasts.

"Get your hands off me!"

"You don't know how much I want you."

"Dr. Crimwell, stop. Now."

He moaned.

Oh, god, now he was reaching up under her skirt.

The needle.

She grabbed it off the table and rammed it into his side.

Crimwell stepped back a few feet. "All right, all right. I'll stop." He smiled a naughty smile. "For now at least."

Oh, no, you're not getting off that easily. Ruby took a step forward, needle in hand like a sword. "Get out of here."

"Now, now, Ruby, no need to get uppity. You should be honored that I want you."

Honored? Oh, really? "Get out of here."

He stayed put.

You asked for it, buster. She rushed him and jabbed the hand he threw up in defense.

"Ouch." He backed up and crashed through the swinging door.

Ruby followed, jabbing at him some more.

"Ouch, ouch, ouch." He nearly lost his footing but managed to regain his balance.

The nurses and doctors in the hallway turned to see what was happening.

Ruby delivered a couple more jabs.

The surgeon threw up his hands in surrender. "No more, no more."

"Get out of here."

Crimwell scurried away, blood oozing from the pricks she'd delivered.

"And if you *ever* try to touch me again, I will have your job," she yelled after him.

There, let the gossip train talk about *that* one.

Felicia folded the baby's blanket and added it to the pile on the dining room table. "Is that all there is, that's all you found?"

"Three outfits and the blankets, yes, ma'am," the maid replied. "They were in the back of the closet."

"Burn them. Burn them all."

"But Miss Ruby will wonder –"

The insolence of this woman. "I don't care what Miss Ruby wonders. She purchased things a long time ago for which she has no use." Though why she'd held onto them this long was a mystery. It wasn't like the girl was seeing anyone and would – a shudder hit her – succumb to that disgusting act again and make another baby. "Take them out and burn them."

She needed to rest. All this decision-making was sapping her strength.

Felicia headed up the stairs. She'd loved this house when she'd bought it, loved the pseudo turret accents that flanked the entry and the cupula at the top. Loved the wishbone staircase that highlighted the high ceilings. Loved the chandelier that hung over the entry. Loved the separate bedroom off the master so she didn't have to sleep with Phillip.

Now, she despised its ups and downs. And these stairs, there were so damn many of them.

Her chest hurt.

Her breathing became labored.

Ten more steps.

She clutched the railing and paused. If she could only catch her breath.

The maid appeared beside her. "Are you all right?"

"Help me get up the stairs. I need ... to ... rest."

"Yes, Ma'am."

Together, they made it to the second floor. The maid helped her to the master.

"Not here." Not Phillip's bed. "The secondary bedroom."

"Of course, Ma'am."

The maid helped her into bed and stepped back.

"Don't just stand there. Remove my shoes."

"Yes, Ma'am." She undid the shoes and set them aside. She hesitated.

"Now, lift my feet so they're atop the comforter." Good God, she had to lay out every single step for this idiot of a maid.

"Shall I call for a doctor?"

Finally, a glimmer of intelligence in the girl. "No. Just let me lie here." She hesitated. "And don't tell Ruby." All she needed was some rest. Her daughter would have her drinking teas and chomping on dirty, disgusting roots all day if she knew.

CHAPTER SEVENTEEN

Tadashi watched the lawyer seated across the desk from him. Peter Wendenhall was the best, came highly recommended for cases like this. He was also highly paid. Look at that silk suit and the alligator case by his desk.

The lawyer finished looking over the papers Tadashi had brought. "And all these people will testify against the railroad?"

Maybe not all, after all, they'd been victimized into signing over their land. "I don't know that for certain," he admitted, "but the top five names on the list lost the most property. They'd be likely to stand up to Fontinello."

"But it wasn't Mr. Fontinello who approached them and beat them into submission."

No, Phillip Fontinello couldn't be caught with his fists bloodied from beating someone to a pulp. He only sent goons. "He approached them initially, asking for their cooperation." But that was the only time he'd shown his face.

"So the inference is that the beatings were ordered by Mr. Fontinello?"

"Exactly."

Peter Wendenhall sat back and sighed. "That's tough to prove. The law is obviously on the robber-baron's side regarding the sheriff and other powers-that-be, but we can try to fight Phillip in civil court with a lawsuit."

OK, so, no criminal charges, but Fontinello would still be brought to justice.

"We'd have to find the fellows who attacked these poor people," Wendenhall continued, "and get them to confess, to link this back to the railroad. The first step is locating them. That could prove problematic. They could be transients who've left town or possibly ship workers on their way to China right now for all we know."

"Yes, but somebody knows who they are." Bad guys were not known for their intelligence. They would have slipped up and bragged about what they'd done to someone, somewhere.

Wendenhall gestured. "Even if we find them, they may not confess that Fontinello is behind it."

"Offer them immunity in exchange for their testimony."

"A good idea." The lawyer nodded. "It's been known to illicit information in the past."

Tadashi stood up. "Find the men who attacked these people. Bring them in, so the farmers can identify them. Then offer the immunity and bring charges against Phillip Fontinello." He pulled out a wad of cash and set it on the desk. "I'll pay double if you can bring the charges within a month."

What good was Meifeng's inheritance if he didn't use it for a good cause? And stopping Fontinello from abusing the system was the best cause he could think of right now.

Anastasia sat at her makeup table and eyed the envelope. It was from one of her San Francisco clients, Bertrand Dodson. The man was a doll, took her out to dinner and everything. He never made her feel cheap. He even introduced her to his high society friends. His attitude was: When you had money, who cared what other people thought?

She opened the envelope. Something fluttered to the floor.

It was a check.

The zinc tincture, it was selling.

She snatched it up.

Oh, gosh, how much had it earned them?

Her shouldered dropped. Only that much? She earned more money turning tricks in one week. A girl needed a steady income for all her life.

OK, so the amount was lower than she'd hoped but it was a start. After all, the product was only in a handful of stores at this point. The important thing was that it was selling.

There was a report with it. Units sold. Pro-rated price. Handling fee. She didn't understand any of it. Bertrand would have to educate her.

Maybe he could advise her on adding more products to the line. The girls liked night cream to keep their skin soft. She'd write to Ruby and ask if she had any ideas on a formula for that.

She peered at her face in the mirror. She commanded a good price because she was pretty, but this profession could sap you dry. Or it could kill you, like it had killed Tina and that other girl. The killer was still out there. He could be one of her customers, for all she knew.

She brushed a stray strand of blonde hair out of her face.

Her wrist.

It was still bruised from that client last Saturday night.

Maybe he was the killer.

He'd been drunk and had been rough with her, holding her down with nearly all his weight as he pumped away. Try as she had, she'd been unable to get it away from his grip. Her hand had gone numb. Her wrist had throbbed afterward.

He'd thrown money at her after he was done and left without bothering to clean himself. What an oaf. Good thing Ruby had given her the herbal formula so she could buy and mix herbs for herself and assure she didn't get pregnant from *that* guy.

Hold on. Maybe that was the answer.

Forget face cream as their big money maker. Women all across the country would clamor for a tea that ensured they didn't get pregnant. She pulled out a pen and paper.

"Dear Ruby, Our first check arrived for the zinc tincture. It's not as much as I'd hoped, but this is just the beginning of our new venture. Yea. I'll deposit half into your bank account.

"How would you feel about adding more product to the line? A face cream would be nice, but I think I have a real seller – your herbal tea that keeps women from –"

The clock chimed.

Was it that time already? Anastasia sighed. She'd have to finish the letter later. She set it aside and got up from the table.

Time to put on that sheer sleep teddy that Mr. Lender liked so much. He made her face away from him and bend over while he whacked off with his hand. Why some guys didn't want to do the dirty was beyond her. As long as they paid her, she'd bend over all day. That was, until the new business took off.

Tadashi looked at the six workers seated around the table with him. "So, we're all clear on what we need to do?"

The men nodded.

"Any questions?"

They shook their heads as one.

Wonderful, then maybe this would send a message to Fontinello once and for all. Mess with the Chinese workers and you'd find your rail lines torn apart, parts of your track torn up and destroyed.

He pushed away. "Then we're done here. Thanks for coming."

This had been a good night. He'd come up with a plan to hit multiple targets at the same time. The Fresno, Ely, Carson City, Winnemucca, Redding and Sacramento lines would have rails knocked out. Whole sections, hundreds of feet of track, would be disrupted.

Not only that, the rail tracks would be carted away in the middle of the night, taken to who-knows-where and leaving nothing for the rail line to use when it went to repair the line.

Fighting fire with fire, it was only way the railroad owners would come to the bargaining table.

He stepped out into cool night air.

Funny how he had been energized in there, but now he felt tired. It had been a long day, slipping onto trains to take him to the various cities then coming back here to Sacramento. He smiled at the irony of it all. If only Phillip Fontinello knew how he hopped trains at will, riding free on the very lines he was out to disrupt.

A twig snapped.

A man stepped out of the shadows.

Not again. Didn't the beer-belly slug get the message last time?

The man stepped into the light.

It wasn't the same guy. This one was taller, leaner, and his arms bulging out from his sides.

Muscle bound, huh? I can still take you if I have to. "Look friend, I have no beef with you. You go your way and I'll go mine, all right?"

"Tadashi Moro, you're not paying attention when Phillip Fontinello tells you to lay off."

"Yeah? Well, tell Fontinello that he can come talk to the workers and work out a deal. There's no need for violence."

"Too late now." The man's fist shot out.

Tadashi ducked. His hair was brushed by the assailant's hand. Jeez, that was close. This guy knew what he was doing. He backed away.

The man's fists were up, a boxer's pose.

OK, he could handle this. Let the guy throw a punch and when he was off balance, land a decisive kick to the knee. Then, before he could recover, move in with another kick to the balls, a hard kick. Yeah, this fight would be over in no time. "You sure you want to do this?"

The man jabbed.

Tadashi ducked. Here was his chance.

Whack!

Something crashed into his back. He hit the ground. What the hell?

It was another guy. He had a baseball bat, held high over his head.

Shit.

The bat came at him again.

He rolled away.

The bat hit the street, a thunking sound.

No way could he fight off two men. He had to get away.

Tadashi jumped to his feet. He backed up.

The man with the bat came at him from the left.

The boxer came at him from the right.

His back hit the side of a building. Damn.

Look out, the bat!

The blow hit the side of his head.

He saw stars. Stars? At this hour? Where had they come from?

Another blow smashed into his arm.

A punch landed in his gut.

He folded over.

Oh, God, oh God, oh God.

Had to protect himself.

Another blow.

Another punch.

Had to get away.

He crawled.

The blows kept coming, raining down on him.

Too much. Too fast. I ...can't ...please ...make ...it ...stop.

His world went black.

Ruby pulled on her nursing smock in the hospital's back room. She'd spent the morning at Wharf Village dispensing herbal medicine and managed to grab a new book from the library. Soon, she was needed to assist in two surgeries. As long as she didn't have to work with Crimwell, the sexual deviant. She pulled out her satchel of herbs. There was still time to visit the four patients who'd been admitted yesterday and help them get better with her herbal remedies.

Three nurses were giggling on the other side of the cabinet.

"He showed it to me."

"Me, too."

"He asked me to hold it while he tried. Can you imagine? I wasn't about to touch it."

They sounded young.

Ruby peeked around the corner. "What's going on?"

One of them, a pert girl with brown hair and freckles, turned to her. "One of the patients who came out of surgery can't –" the nurse blushed "– go wee-wee."

That wasn't good. He needed to pee to help get the gas out of his system. "What room is he in?"

"Two thirteen."

She hurried to the kitchen. Mildred was there. The cook always took her suggestions for customizing meals for certain patients. "Mildred, can you spare some ice?"

"For you? Sure."

"Just put it in a glass."

Mildred handed over the glass, half full of ice. Perfect. Ruby grabbed a pitcher of water and drizzled it slowly over the ice.

The cook looked amused. "Um, I can do it faster for you."

No, no, it had to be as slow as possible. "I'm on a mission." Ruby smiled. "A mission to pee." She took the glass of water back to the locker room and found the three young nurses. "Follow me."

"We're off duty."

"This will just take a second."

They all went up to room two thirteen.

A man was in the bed, looking uncomfortable.

Yeah, she didn't need to hold her hands atop this man to know he needed relief. Ruby grabbed a potty pan and handed it to him. "You're going to be using this in just a second."

"I've been trying all day."

"So I heard."

She presented the glass of water for him to see

"I'm not thirsty."

"Just get ready to pee."

"If you say so." He sat up, set the potty pan under the sheet and adjusted his hospital gown. He looked up at her. "Now what?"

Ruby held out the glass of ice water. "Plunge your fingers in this water and hold them there."

He looked dubious. "If you say so." He dipped his fingers into the water. He flinched. "Oh, my gosh."

The sound of his stream hitting the pan filled the room.

The nurses looked incredulous. "That was all it took?"

She left them, went down the hall and nearly walked straight into someone, one of the hospital volunteers. Where had he come from?

"Ruby, you're needed in the emergency room."

Emergency? Someone needed her. "Thanks." She turned and started off. Wait a minute. She didn't work in the emergency room. No one there even knew her name. She turned to ask the volunteer. "Who sent you to find –?"

No one was there. The hall was empty. How odd.

She hurried down to the ER. A couple was there. A boy with curly blonde hair was on sitting on the mother's lap, leaning into her chest and facing the window. He was the patient here, no doubt about it.

Ruby slowed and nodded to the parents. She knelt down beside them and touched the boy's shoulder. A streak of pain shot through her. She swallowed down her reaction. That had never happened before. She'd sensed people's pain, yes, but never taken it on for herself. This poor child. He was in a real bad way. "Well, hello there, young fellow."

He turned and looked into her eyes.

Ruby caught her breath.

It was the boy her spirit guides had showed her.

Peter Wendenhall rode his gelding down the path. The farmhouse before him stood two stories and appeared old but well maintained over the years. No sag to the front porch, no missing bannisters to the railing or broken windows. No doubt about it, these were people with pride. Good. Hopefully, they were also people who stood up for themselves. Theirs was the last name on his list.

There was movement near the barn. "Hail the farm," he called out.

The figure stopped and looked his way. He was holding a pail and holding it awkwardly with both hands, as though it was too heavy for him. Oh, it was a child of twelve or thirteen. He set the pail down and shaded his eyes to better see. "Pa, company," he yelled.

Peter rode up and dismounted.

The front door swung open. A man with a shotgun appeared. "Who's there?"

He held up his hands to show he was unarmed. "My name is Peter Wendenhall, I'm a lawyer."

"For the railroad? I already gave you my best land."

"So I heard. No, I'm not from the railroad, Mr. Holmes. Quite the opposite. I'm here to see if we can't get your land back."

"Come in." The man shuffled out of the way. Good Lord, he was hobbling.

The main room was small but clean. A woman appeared, in her thirties, her hair pulled back. "Can I offer you some coffee, Mister ...?"

"Wendenhall. Peter Wendenhall. And you are?"

"Pearl."

Women were always more apt to talk about their husband's trials and tribulations. And from the way Stanley Holmes was shuffling about, his pride surely had taken a hit. He pulled out his calling card. "Well, Pearl, I understand your husband suffered an attack to persuade him to hand over his land."

She nodded and moved to her husband's side, assisting him as he dropped into a chair.

Stanley Holmes waved her help away. "I'm fine."

No, he wasn't. "I've got eyes, Mr. Holmes. You're not able to work your land. Your boy is outside trying to do a man's job when he's only, what, twelve?"

Pearl nodded and looked down. "Our eldest son. Evan."

Eldest? Even better for bargaining. "And Evan has probably given up all hope of schooling because he's had to step into his father's shoes. Am I right?"

They nodded.

"Evan should be in school."

They nodded.

Agreement always helped his bargaining chip. "You should be in a financial position to hire help."

Pearl excused herself and went back to the kitchen.

Peter turned his attention to the man of the house. It was just the two of them now. They could talk man to man. "It's got to be tough working the land, but now you're in no physical condition to do that."

Stanley cleared his throat. "Why are you here?"

"The men who did this to you, Stanley, we believe they were sent by one Phillip Fontinello."

"He came here first, all high and mighty, pushing his legal papers under my nose. But I wouldn't sign them."

"Who would? It wasn't a fair deal."

"They came at me when I was hitching up my cows to pull the plow. I never saw it coming."

"Bullies don't fight fair. And now look at you."

"They broke my leg, busted up my back."

"So, here's your chance to get even with Phillip Fontinello. We're looking for the men who did this. We're going to charge them and make them pay. But it's Fontinello who's the ultimate prize. We get the goons to fess up, yes, but we also want them to finger Fontinello as the instigator, the mastermind. Your input will go a long way in the lawsuit to show how devious this railroad bully could be."

Stanley considered it. "How long will that take?"

What an odd question. "Well, um, it could take weeks, months, a year even. But, rest assured, we'll get you justice."

Stanley flinched. "So, you're putting out the word that you're looking for these men?"

"Not yet. But we're well financed. We can place notices, big notices, in the newspapers up and down the coast and over to the mining fields of Nevada."

"So, you haven't done that yet?"

"Not yet. I can also send men into the seedy parts of town to talk to people and see what they can dig up." He nodded for emphasis. "We'll get them, I promise you." If only he was as sure as he made it sound. But he had to talk a good game to get these people on board.

Stanley paused. "I'm sorry, Mr. Wendenhall, we can't help you."

This couldn't be happening. Not again. He fought for words. "But, but, Stanley, your leg was broken. You can't walk straight. Your back was busted and aches every time you move. Fontinello would be forced to pay you recompense, enough to buy a big, new farm, two farms, maybe. How could you possibly not want justice to be served?"

"Pearl, can you come in here and show our guest out?"

So that was it. They weren't going to stand up for their rights.

Pearl appeared and escorted him out to the porch.

She was his last resort. "Look at your son over there, Pearl. Look how hard he's working. What does it say to him if your husband won't stand up to these men? They've got to be stopped. They've got to pay for what they did to Stanley."

"We appreciate you coming all the way here from San Francisco, but we can't help you."

"Mrs. Holmes, think of your family."

"I am." Pearl wrung her hands. "You don't understand, Mr. Wendenhall. The men who attacked

Stanley said that if we go to the law, they'll come back. But not to the farmhouse or the barn."

He didn't follow. "Then where will they go?"

Pearls eyes filled with tears. "To the fields, Mr. Wendenhall. They said they'd come back to catch Evan alone when he's working the fields and do the same to him. They're evil men to even *think* of attacking a child. There's no telling what they'd do to my little boy. So, you see, Mr. Wendenhall, I *am* thinking of my family."

Ruby blinked in surprise. It was a little boy, the one her spirit guides had shown her. There were the blonde curls and the dimple in his right cheek. His face was still flushed, so the fever had not abated. "How long has he had the fever?"

"Two days."

So, her guides has shown her something that had not yet occurred. Interesting. But the fact that the parents waited to get him to the hospital concerned her. They should have brought him in sooner. "I'll need you both to be silent for a little while so I can check him over. Can you turn him to face me, please?"

The mother adjusted him on her lap.

Now, the tyke was facing her straight-on. He looked up at her with big, sad eyes.

Ruby knelt down on one knee to be at his height. "Hello, young fellow. A little birdie told me you'd be coming. Your tummy hurts does it?" She let her hand hover over his abdomen. It would be better if he were stretched out, lying down so she could better pinpoint the problem, but her guides had already given her the tour. Here, she could better feel the energy emanating off the little tyke to assess things as they stood now. She looked him straight in the eye. "Chester."

The parents stared. "How did you know his name?"

It had just come to her, was all. "We need to get him admitted."

The mother clutched her arm. "It's just a fever ... isn't it?"

She got them to the check-in desk and took the three-year-old from his mother, setting him on her hip. "I'm not going to mince words. This is urgent. He has a tumor. It's in his upper intestine."

"Hold on, you don't know that. You didn't touch him." The father frowned, shaking his head. "I want a second opinion."

That was certainly fair. "One of the doctors will support what I've told you."

He peered at her, eyes narrowed. "You mean one of the 'other' doctors."

She had to be upfront. "I'm not a doctor."

"Then how do you know my Chester has a tumor?"

She didn't have time to explain. The man wouldn't believe her anyway. "There are signs. I'm taking him to the children's ward." This man was scared. He needed reassurance. "I'll have a doctor look at Chester right away."

The father stepped up to block her. "I want to be there."

Not unheard of. It was fine by her. "Then let's have your wife fill out the forms. You can come with me, Mr. Russell." She immediately regretted saying it. He'd likely question how she knew his last name. It had just popped into her head, too. "This way." She had to change the subject. "Is Chester your only child?"

He kept up with her, eyes worried. "Yes, he means the world to us."

She shifted the child in her arms. He was light as a feather. "He's lost weight over the course of the last few months, yes?"

Mr. Russell nodded. "He hasn't had an appetite for weeks."

A red flag, for sure. No healthy child refused a meal. They should have had him checked out way back then. But there was no sense to berating the parent for his lack of diligence. The situation was what it was and they were left to deal with things as they stood now.

Chester snuggled into her neck, the poor thing.

"We'll get you better," she promised him.

The killer peeked around the corner of the building and watched the girl stride down the street toward the house where she lived, where she bedded men all night long.

That slut.

Look at her, strutting around in those fine, fanciful clothes, trying to pass herself off as a decent young woman. Well, he knew what she really was.

She was a fallen woman and used her wiles to entice viral, young men like him, to trap them with her sex.

She was evil. Pure evil.

She sauntered his way, her blonde hair bouncing.

It was an illusion. She had to be taken-out, dealt with in the only way possible.

It was up to him to rid the world of women like her.

He would do it in a way that let her know he was on to her plan, the plan to bring about the downfall of men. Yes, he would do it, but when the time was right, when no one else was around, just like he'd done with those other, no good sluts.

The blonde was coming closer.

Hide!

He ducked back into the shadows.

She passed him, her heels clicking on the sidewalk and her tight little butt sashaying back and forth under her clothing.

He peered back out from his hiding place.

She was past him now, heading farther down the walkway.

Look at her, displaying herself in public like she was a decent woman. What was her name again? It was on the tip of his tongue. Oh, yeah. Anastasia.

Tadashi entered the lawyer's office building. To be contacted so soon must mean good news. "I received word that Peter Wendenhall wanted to see me. I'm Tadashi Moro."

"Yes, Mr. Moro. One moment." The clerk got up from his desk, crossed the room and stuck his head in the door behind him. There was a short conversation. The clerk returned. "Mr. Wendenhall will see you now."

Tadashi entered the lawyer's inner office. "Your note said there was news."

Wendenhall looked grim. "Not good news, I'm afraid. None of the farmers who were targeted by the railroad will testify."

Great, just great. "Where does that leave us?"

"Nowhere, I'm afraid."

Maybe they could work around this. "Do we need their testimony? Can't we proceed without them?"

"It weakens our entire case."

"We can file on each farmer's behalf. Once we find the men who threatened them, who beat them, we can just use their confessions."

"You're presuming we can find them."

"We will, I can feel it. You haven't even started looking for them yet, is all."

Wendenhall made a tent of his fingers. "You're also presuming these thugs will fess up." He sighed. "Men like that, they know how to play the system. They'll find a buddy to swear they were miles away from the scene of the crime. No, without the farmers' involvement to tell how they were harassed, and point the finger at these men, we lose the advantage and have no case." He leaned forward. "I feel for these people, Tadashi. They're good-hearted, hardworking, salt-of-the earth types."

All the more reason to stand up to Fontinello. "Maybe if I talked to them."

The lawyer shook his head. "They're scared as hell. Fontinello's men delivered a message, the beatings, then left another message – that they'd come back and hurt the kids if they brought in the law."

The kids? Tadashi clenched his fists. His blood boiled. His former boss was threatening *children?* What a low life piece of scum. Just let him kick something, right now, because he was mad as hell. "I've got to go." He jumped up, thanked the lawyer and hurried out.

He'd have to find another way to bring Fontinello to task and force him to play by the rules. He hurried down the street, took the back route and found his Chinese cohorts waiting for him. He bit his lip. "Tell the men they won't get much shuteye tonight. We have a job to do."

Ruby held her hands above the little boy's abdomen, moving them in a figure eight. She could feel the trouble spot, it was centered right ... there. The tug of the other two were fainter, but when she quieted her mind she could still detect them.

Mr. Russell hovered nearby. He'd need reassurance.

She turned to him. "The trouble's in his intestine."

He narrowed his eyes. "You sound so sure."

Of course she was sure. Her guides wouldn't have shown her the problem if they didn't think she could help. "He has one large tumor and two small ones."

The father gestured. "You barely examined him, didn't touch him at all."

"Touching him would cause him pain. I don't want to do that. Do you?"

"No, but, but," he sputtered. "Oh, good grief, I've got to get a *real* doctor in here."

Dr. Carmichael stepped in from the hall, looking at a chart. He was known for his bedside manner. "Well, well, what have we here?" He looked down on Chester. "Your tummy hurts? We'll get you better real soon."

Mrs. Russell was right behind him. "There's my boy. Mommy's here."

Dr. Carmichael herded the Russells to the corner. "Well, folks, I'm sure you're concerned about your little boy. We have a top-notch staff here and will do everything in our power to see he gets the best care. Now, when did this problem crop up?"

Ruby turned away. Let them talk to the "real" doctor, like she was a nobody. She removed the boy's shoes and pulled the sheet up.

Chester watched her intently. "How come you didn't touch my tummy?"

"I didn't have to."

"I've seen you before."

Perhaps he'd been to the hospital before. Or, more likely, at the playground when she'd go watch the children play, wondering why little Dash had been stillborn.

"You were in my room one night. We were laughing and you sang me a song."

What an imagination. "You were dreaming." She plumped his pillow.

"I gave you a daisy and you let me put it in your hair."

Felicia woke from her nap. There it was, that light-headed feeling again.

She coughed. It was a dry hacking kind of cough. Damn.

She went to get out of bed, but it took all her strength. She threw back the covers. Look at her legs, her lovely legs. They'd always been so dainty. Now they were swollen, just like her feet. She could barely shove them into her shoes these days.

"Maude," she called out. Oh hell, where was that bell?

There it was on the dresser.

She lunged for it, got it and rang it nonstop. Where was that stupid housekeeper, anyway?

"Yes Ma'am, I'm right here," Maude said, hurrying into the room.

"Help me stand up."

"You feel dizzy again, do you? Maybe I should call a doctor."

So she could be poked and prodded like she was chattel? No thank you. "Help me to the bathroom."

Maude supported her and they shuffled down the hall together.

Lord love a duck, whatever was ailing her, it sure felt like hell.

Ruby entered the operating room.

Little Chester was being slid onto the operating room table for his laparotomy. He was awake.

She went over. "How are you doing, sport?"

His eyes were big, scared. "Where's my Mommy?"

"We'll take good care of you, sweetie." She signaled the anesthetist. "Put him under." There was no need to stress the child further.

The anesthetist nodded and put the mask on Chester. "Just breathe in deep," he said. He would stay, standard procedure when a child was the patient.

Dr. Carmichael came in. He looked down at Chester and made sure he was under. "Cute little feller, huh? Well, let's get to this." He picked up a scalpel and cut into the abdomen, a lower mid-line incision from the navel down. It would allow access to the lower intestine. He slid his finger into the cut to ensure there was no adhesion.

Ruby administered the retractors to hold back the skin.

The surgeon looked at her, the scalpel wavering in his hand. "Where?"

She pointed. "There."

"You sure? I don't see any–"

"Believe me, it's there."

He cut into the intestine – the gas it emitted was notable – and whistled under his breath. "Would you look at that?"

It was larger than she recalled, but then, it had been a while since her guides had shown it to her.

He began cutting it out.

A tumor that big had to be fed by numerous blood vessels. Its feeder roots could be far reaching.

He freed the tumor from the wall of the intestine and handed it to her.

She dropped the mass in a bowl. It didn't look so big now.

He held out his hand. "Suture."

Not yet. "We have to make sure we get it all, doctor."

"Well, I suppose so." Dr. Carmichael snipped the intestine four inches farther back on each side. That would ensure that they got any leading edges.

She nodded. Much better.

They got to work attaching the two ends.

Ruby held them close while the doctor stitched around the circular opening.

She hid her amusement. Even *she* could stitch better than that.

Dr. Carmichael made the final knot and stepped back, nodding with satisfaction. "Well, that went well."

Yup, on to the next section.

"You want to close him up?" He turned to leave.

Where was he going? "We didn't get it all."

He frowned. "I certainly think we did."

"But, doctor, there are two more tumors."

"I only saw the one." He scoffed and waved away her concern. "This so-called 'ability' of yours, we all know it's just a guess."

A guess? Hadn't he just asked her to locate the exact spot to cut for the big tumor? Did he think *that* had been a guess?

He pulled off his surgical apron. "I'm done here."

But she needed him. "You can't leave."

"I can and I will." He walked out of the surgery room.

Ruby stared at little Chester, stretched out on the operating table. He was opened up. The two other tumors were there. She knew it for certain. There was the one about eighteen inches below the first. And a third one, smaller and at that turn in the intestine. "It will grow just as big if it remains," her guides had told her.

She had to make sure. Ruby held her hands above Chester's abdomen, shut her eyes and quieted her mind.

The tug was still there.

There was no way she was going to let this child suffer only to make him come back for more surgery. The tumors had to come out and they had to come out now. She opened her eyes and signaled the anesthesiologist. "Make sure he stays under."

Ruby hurried down the stone steps to the morgue. One of the recently-deceased patients had undergone the same procedure as little Chester. She needed to learn if the tumor may have had any tentacles. There wasn't time to do a thorough check when she'd been in the operating room, but a corpse? That was a different matter.

She grabbed the files, flipping through them. Larimer had been his name.

There is was: Larimer – Number 231.

The two hundreds were down this way. She located the tag and dragged the body off the shelf and onto the cart. Piece of cake. Thank goodness he wasn't too heavy.

She had him in the back room and on the autopsy table in no time.

"Let's see, Mr. Larimer, I understand you were a patient here. I hope the nurses treated you well." She pulled off the sheet and eyed his incision. It didn't look as though it had a chance to heal before he'd succumbed to his ailment. All she had to do was snip the stitches.

She grabbed the scissors and cut away.

There was a noise in the other room. A big noise.

Ruby looked up.

There were footsteps. They were coming closer.

The doorknob turned.

The door opened.

Oh, God, I'm toast.

"Ruby, what are you doing here?"

What in the world? "Mr. Jianyu?" He was the last person she expected to see in the morgue.

He stood there, holding the door open.

She stared. The mark on the door wasn't an "S" at all. She could see it better now that the light was shining directly on it. It was the intertwined snake she'd noted on his cuffs when they'd first met. No, not a snake, a caduceus, the same stylized caduceus she'd seen on some of Meifeng's library books.

Her hand flew to her chest.

It all made sense now. "Are you the honorable Bojing, the Medicine Man Most High?" Maybe she should curtsy or bow to him or something.

He entered. "Show me what you have here."

"There was a little boy we operated on today. My spirit guides –" Surely this learned man of Eastern medicine would understand such things "– showed me that he had three tumors. But the surgeon insisted there was only one. After he left, I explored further and found them. This corpse, a Mr. Larimer, his file said that he had almost the same symptoms and underwent the same laparotomy, too. So, I wanted to compare them." She was making a mess of this. She hesitated. "Your highness."

Jianyu shook his head. "I am not Bojing. He is in Shanghai."

"But you're with the Seekers of the Universe."

"You come down here often, do you?"

"Only to learn."

He lifted one eyebrow. "So, you are the ghost who keeps people away. Yes?"

"Not all people." She'd seen evidence of things moved. Someone had caused the little messes.

"You interrupted two doctors one day who were doing the same thing as you, searching for answers from men already dead."

She'd forgotten. "I thought they were just observing an autopsy, like a class." But it hadn't been a class, it had been doctors like her, opening corpses, wanting to learn more. "I haven't got time to go to med school. I want to help people now."

"You and your spirit guides, hmm?"

They hadn't let her down yet. "Your library is helping me, but hands-on work like this is necessary, too. I come here at night and use the time to investigate."

Jianyu shrugged off his jacket and rolled up his sleeves. "Let's investigate together, shall we?"

Anastasia threw her head back as she sat on the man's lap and laughed. "You're so funny, sugar." She drew her hand along his jaw and gazed into his eyes. "I like a guy with a sense of humor." What was his name again? It didn't matter. He said that he was just passing through Sacramento, so it wasn't like he'd turn into a regular customer. Too bad because, if tonight was any indication, he sure wasn't afraid to spend his money. He'd already bought everyone a round of drinks. Generous.

Beside them on the sofa, Vivian was sitting beside her next customer, playing with his shirt buttons. Her skirt was hiked up, exposing plenty of leg. The guys at the card table were stealing glances at her, hoping the skirt would expose a little more. So, she might get three takers tonight.

The others girls had also latched onto a guy of their own. Betsy had already been upstairs twice with different men. Stella had just rejoined them after servicing the mayor.

The party was a success. This was way more prosperous than merely doing three or four tricks a night. Men paid a fee to get in. They danced with the girls and played parlor games, bought drinks and got drunk, then they could pay to take a girl upstairs.

It was a win-win for everybody. Especially her.

Madams always took a cut of the action.

Her prospect – Chuck, yeah, that was his name – chugged back the last of his drink, finishing it with a satisfied, "Ahhh."

She took the shot glass from him. "We can't have you thirsty. I'll get you another." She jumped up and somebody pinched her butt. Yeah, these guys were ready for action. She smiled and swatted the hand away. "Now, you all behave."

The kitchen was cold. Maybe one of the girls had left open a window. No, they all looked closed.

Let's see, he was drinking scotch. She had a new bottle in the root cellar. She opened the door and stepped down into the darkness.

CHAPTER EIGHTEEN

There was a shaft of light from the kitchen but it only lit the top two steps. She should have brought a lantern. Oh well, it was against the wall right alongside the steps, right about ...here.

She snatched it off the shelf.

There was a breeze near her right arm.

What the heck?

Someone grabbed her other arm. "You're taking too long, sweetheart." It was her conquest.

"Why, Chuck, I'd never take long when there's a big, tall guy like you waiting for me."

He yanked her up to him. "Let's go someplace where we'll be alone," he said, nuzzling her neck.

"Sounds like fun. You want one hour or do you want two?"

Chuck pulled out a wad of bills and stuffed it down her top. "I want all night."

Music to her ears. "Right this way, sugar."

Phillip stepped off the trolley car and headed down the street. He had a full day of work ahead of him and the sooner he got to it, the better. He strode up the walkway to his office.

That was strange. The side window was ajar.

He went to put his key in the lock but the front door swung open at his touch. Shoot, someone had been there.

He hefted his umbrella with its metal eagle handle. If anyone was still on the premises, he'd rap them on the noggin with it. He stepped in.

The front office was in shambles. It looked as though a whirlwind had gone through it. Papers were on the floor, tossed here and there.

What about his own office in the back? He hurried past the mess out front. The door was ajar. "If you're in there," he called out, "I'm warning you. I've got the police with me."

There was no one. There was only the destruction they'd left behind.

His desk drawers were open.

His chair was tossed on its side.

Papers were scattered about.

Oh no, not the paperwork for the Chico line. They hadn't touched that, had they?

He dropped the umbrella and ran around the corner to the safe. The door was off its hinges. There was the smell of blasting powder. Damn them.

There were footsteps.

Jerold Fulcom peered around the corner. "What the hell?"

To put it mildly. "They got the Chico papers, Fulcom." He passed a hand over his forehead. It was Tadashi Moro who was behind this, had to be.

He'd ordered the Chinese workers to take on 18-hour shifts, made them sleep on the bare ground beside the tracks so there was no lag time getting them to the work area.

So Tadashi had retaliated.

Jerold looked lost. "What do we do?"

They had to pick up the pieces and move ahead with their vision. "We'll re-order yet another copy of the surveyor's site plans."

And put a price on Tadashi Moro's head.

Ruby pulled on her surgery apron. A man had come in who'd had a farming accident. A metal rake had splintered and pieces had lodged in his chest. This would be a delicate one. There was no telling how deep the wound went or if they'd get out all the metal slivers.

She hurried to wash her hands. Behind her, the man was wheeled in. He was awake and white-faced. Shock. She'd read about it in one of Jianyu's library books.

"Ruby, can you come here?" It was James Nueman, the hospital administrator's secretary.

"I'm about to go into surgery. It'll have to wait."

"It can't wait."

What was he talking about? A man's life was hanging in the balance. She was needed in the operating room. "Whatever this is about, it can wait."

He took her by her elbow and steered her away. "No it can't."

How dare he pull her away from her duties? She shook off his hand. "I'm due in surgery, James." Couldn't he understand that?

He shook his head. "We have a replacement for you. You need to come with me."

He was serious. She gave up. "All right, fine. Where are we going?"

James led her to the hospital administrator's office.

Mr. Judson was at his desk and gestured her to come in. "You remember Mr. Russell?"

Chester's father. She smiled. "Yes, of course. How is your son doing?" She'd meant to give him another round of herbal teas to help him regain his strength but hadn't gotten around to it. "I saw he was discharged yesterday. He's quite the young soldier."

Mr. Judson cleared his throat. "This is not a social visit, Miss Fontinello."

Why did he sound angry? Just what was this is about? "Sir?"

"Mr. Russell claims you did unnecessary surgery on his son."

"*Unauthorized* surgery," Mr. Russell added with a curt nod for emphasis.

Now she understood what was going on.

She drew herself up taller. "I did what had to be done. Chester had a total of three tumors. Dr. Carmichael only took out one and stopped there."

The administrator glared at her. "You were not authorized to do *any* surgery. You were there to assist and hand the surgeon whatever tools he needed. That's all your job entailed."

Oh, really? So all those times she'd been the one to point out and remove extra diseased flesh, all those times the surgeon's hand was too big to do the delicate work that needed to be done, those times when she'd saved the day, they didn't matter?

How about when the surgeon would just hand over the task to her because they weren't schooled in what needed to be done? Huh? Those times didn't count in her favor?

"Chester would have still been sick and he would have had to come back. I knew there were two more masses that had to be removed and I didn't think he should have to suffer through a second operation."

Mr. Russell sneered. "You didn't think? You didn't *think*? You heard the man. You weren't there to think. You were there to obey the surgeon, not make minced meat of my son."

Mr. Judson gestured that he would handle the questioning. He looked grim. "Dr. Carmichael said there was only one tumor. How did you happen to ascertain there were three?"

My guides showed me. She'd be laughed out of the city if she said that. "I felt along the length of intestine and there were two thick areas, lumps."

"Did you tell Dr. Carmichael to feel where you'd felt?"

No. "I told him there were two more masses that had to come out."

"But did you direct him to feel the lumps, as you call them, so he could use his expertise to determine whether further inspection was warranted?"

Another question to trap her in a corner. "I told him that they were farther down the intestine."

Mr. Russell turned in his chair. "You gave our son some sort of witch's brew, too."

"My teas are not witches' brews, sir. They stem directly from Eastern medicine and were tailored to your son's needs. Chinese herbal remedies have been used for centuries with great success."

So there.

"Chinese Herbs? Chinese teas?" The father scoffed. "A lot of good they did my little Chester."

"They helped your son get discharged earlier than if he hadn't had them."

He stood up and charged up to her. "You can't prove that."

He was right, she couldn't. But he should be happy that she was schooled in the discipline. "I could show you books, textbooks, with plenty of case studies on the matter but you wouldn't be able to read them."

He pointed at her face, an inch away from jabbing her. "Because I'm not some Pidgin-speaking Chink."

How uncouth. The Chinese were fine, upstanding people with a proud history.

She turned to the administrator. "I refuse to be spoken to this way. Is there anything else you need from me?"

Mr. Judson stood up and crossed his arms. "Your services here are terminated as of now, Miss Fontinello."

No, they couldn't do this. There were so many people here who needed her help.

"Gather your belongings and leave the premises. If you come back, we'll be obliged to have you arrested."

Ruby returned home.

Mother was sitting in the parlor, reading. It was probably poetry. Mother was a glutton for the stuff. She looked pale as though she hadn't seen the sun in weeks. She had a blanket across her lap as though her legs were cold. "There's a new exhibit at the museum, Mother. Shall we go take it in?"

"No, thank you."

Mother? Refuse a social event? "Are you feeling all right?" Her hair looked brittle, she skin seemed taut. Her eyes were droopy. And that paleness. She took her wrist. The pulse was weak. "How long have you been like this?"

Maude stepped in carrying a tray. "Your tea, Mrs. Fontinello. Miss Ruby, is that you?" She smiled. "Not used to seeing you around. Will you be joining her?"

Yes, if only to find out why Mother was in such a bad way. "Yes, please. Maude, have you noticed my mother having issues lately?"

Mother shot her a look. "I'm fine."

Maude hesitate. "Her balance has been off." Maude scurried away.

"All right, Mother, stick out your tongue."

It was scarlet in the middle. Menopause. Mother was forty-five, a bit early for the change of life. The tip was abnormal looking, exceedingly so. Oh, no. "How's your heart?"

Mother jerked involuntarily. "I'm fine."

"I've got my stethoscope right here. We'll see how fine you are." She pulled it out and pressed the earpiece to one ear. "Breathe normally." She pressed the diaphragm end to Mother's chest.

Weak, weak, weak. How was Mother able to stand? What could she have Mother take to get her back on the long road to health? Hawthorne. Pomegranate. Green tea. Lavender to strengthen the heart contractions. Fatty oils from fish.

Mother reached for her tea.

There was a bowl on the tray.

That cereal stuff. They were living in a spot where oranges grew in their yard, where they could see the ocean and yet Mother ate that stupid factory food? "Let me see your legs."

"What? No."

Ruby yanked the blanket off Mother's lap and pulled up the hem of her long skirt. Elephant stumps. How had Mother's legs gotten to this point? It certainly wasn't overnight. "Why didn't you tell me? How long has this been going on? What have you taken for it?"

Mother shrank in her chair and stared down at her lap.

Where was Maude? She'd be able to tell her. She hurried inside.

The housekeeper was in the dining room. "Your teacup is here on the sideboard, Miss Ruby. I saw you with your stethoscope out and didn't want to intrude."

"How long has Mother been feeling poorly?"

"More than a year. Maybe two."

That long? If she hadn't been so busy she would have seen the signs. But between the library, the poor people at Wharf Village plus her work at the hospital, she would have taken action. But Mother's heartbeat was less than half as strong as it should be. "Tell me about her diet."

Maude sighed. "She won't let the cook give her anything but grains."

"You mean cereal? Surely she has fresh vegetables and fruit that she can serve Mother."

The housekeeper sighed. "We try to suggest things, but, no."

The woman was stubborn, all right. "She's got to eat better." Ruby returned to the parlor.

Mother was spooning cereal into her mouth. No plants from the Earth. Just that processed stuff with heaps of sugar on it, sugar that had her craving more sugar. No wonder the woman's heart was giving out.

The killer thought back to that night and punched the wall. Damn it, he'd almost had her.

She'd come down the cellar stairs as though she'd been called right to his hiding place.

His fingers had actually tingled as he'd prepared to grab her. Exhilarating stuff.

Then that tall, big fellow had stepped up and snatched her away, pulling her up against him, all possessive like.

He'd been forced to shrink back into the shadows, damn.

Worse, the big fellow had stayed in her bed all night. He knew because he'd snuck up there and listened outside her bedroom door. He knew what they were doing. He could see them in his mind.

What a slut she was. She deserved to die.

His plan for that night had been foiled. So much for sneaking out of his hiding spot and slicing her throat open after he made her beg for mercy.

Laugh at him for not being able to perform? She had to pay.

So, now he had to come up with another way to catch her unaware.

Maybe that party idea of hers was the key. She'd likely hold another one. And when she did, he'd be there, ready to get her alone and make her answer for dismissing him.

"It's OK sugar, plenty of guys have the same problem," she'd said.

But on the inside she was laughing. At him. He knew it as sure as he knew she was doomed to die. Damn her.

He got out his knives and lined them up. Better prepare them. They needed to be extra sharp for what he had planned. Look at them, all shiny and clean.

He got out his rope, cordage, really. So much stronger than rope and easier to carry. Yes, this was long enough, plenty for both her wrists and her ankles.

He'd need a gag. They always screamed. This old rag would do. A dirty rag for a dirty mouth.

He'd kidnap her, take her to an isolated spot, remove the gag, then start carving into her, one slice at a time.

Anastasia the Slut had to pay.

The front door opened so hard it slammed. Ruby jumped, almost dropping the spoon as she fed Mother the castor oil in the dining room.

It was Daddy. "Where is everybody?"

"We're in here, Daddy."

He seemed to notice them for the first time. "You."

Me?

"So, *now* you're finally here where you belong, instead of traipsing off to God knows where."

He knew she'd been working at the hospital, studying at the library, helping the needy. She hadn't been traipsing anywhere. "Daddy, what's the matter? Why are you so angry?"

"Like you don't know." He threw a mesh bag on the table, full of something done up in gold wrappers.

"What's that?"

"Candies for Ross Wallace, his favorite kind from Harvey and Son's. Never shares them, not even with kids."

Harvey and Son's, the chocolatier. Maybe Daddy should have some. Cocoa beans might make him happy and would bring down his blood pressure. "What are you angry about, Daddy?"

He scoffed. "The sheriff refuses to help me. The whole company is going to go bankrupt."

So, this was work related. "Calm down."

"I can't calm down. Do you know what that turncoat did?"

She braced herself. Tadashi was not a turncoat. He was an honorable man. The workers had legitimate concerns.

"He broke into my office and turned the place upside down. We're missing documents, plans, so much stuff we're at a standstill. And it's all because of Tadashi Moro. That son of a bitch." He jabbed his finger at her. "I can't believe you laid with him."

"Daddy really!" She frowned at him. That was uncalled for, especially in front of Mother.

"I'm so glad you aren't raising that *bastard* son of his."

Her heart lurched. How could he talk about her dead child that way? An innocent infant who had been denied its first breath? It had been two years since his birth but the pain was as strong as ever.

"Damn that Tadashi Moro. He should be dead for all the grief he's brought me. Hung from the highest tree, kicking and screaming for mercy."

What a hateful thing to say. He'd brought this on himself. "If you had paid the workers a fair wage and given them proper hours, instead of treating them like slaves, you wouldn't be in this position."

He went to answer and stopped. His eyes lit up. "If the damn sheriff won't help. I know who will –the army."

He hurried back out the door and down the front steps, his boots clicking on the walk.

Ruby watched until he disappeared from view. So much had changed. Where was the man who had helped her pick flowers when she was a child? Who had pulled her up on his lap to read to her? Daddy had become so spiteful, so rabid in his vengefulness, it was as though she didn't even know him anymore.

Ruby read the letter from Anastasia with interest.

"The clothes line at the Foster's house has women's dresses hanging on it, ones that are waaaay too large for the missus in that house. Hmmm. Interesting. It makes one wonder who lives there who weighs at least two hundred pounds and is six feet tall."

The girl had a way with words. But this news would not exactly be proper for dinner conversation.

She kept reading.

"Mrs. Bremmerton let slip that she thinks 'proper ladies should have access to whatever those ladies of the night take to keep from getting in the family way.' Hey, Ruby, maybe we can sell them your herbal blend to prevent pregnancy. Women all over the world will buy it off the shelves. (By the way, our zinc tincture is selling at a decent pace, now that we've expanded to all the big cities in California. Check your bank account.)

She stopped reading. What a good idea, bottling the formula to prevent pregnancy. She'd figure out the best herbs to mix, it had to agree with everyone's constitution after all, and send it to Anastasia when she replied.

She resumed reading.

"Our customers of late have been the elite of town. Must be something in the water – the sheriff, the mayor, half of the fire department. I like those guys the best. They're gentlemen, those fire fighters, not like the miners.

"Hey, guess who slipped in late last night for a quickie? That new preacher at the First Witness Church. He had me wear his collar. Then he ate all the goodies in my candy dish. Guess he had an appetite after indulging in a little sinful behavior – ha!

Speaking of sinful behavior, I had a customer get a little weird. Wanted to tie me to the bedposts. I said flat out, 'No.' Not after what happened to my friends. He could have been the killer. I finished him up and got him out of there. Gave me the shivers."

Ruby set the letter down. She wished Anastasia would hire a bodyguard.

Ruby pulled the blanket up to Mother's neck. "Remember, lie on your right side so your heart doesn't work as hard." She smoothed the hair off her forehead.

"Yes, all right." Mother caught her hand. "Thank you."

"We'll get you better, I promise." Some promise. Mother's heart was likely damaged beyond repair.

She'd found a box of chocolates under Mother's pillow. It was from Harvey & Son's. Stashing sweets, it was the act of a child. What other little treats had Mother been hiding?

She waited until Mother went to sleep, then padded away. She got to her room, braided her hair for the night and slipped in between the sheets. Long day.

She closed her eyes and let the night tug her to sleep.

Her guides were here. They had something in their hands.

Ruby peered closer. They each held plants – foxglove, easy to identify with its tubular, purple flowers – and nightshade. A healer wouldn't use these plants. They were dangerous. "Why are you showing me these? They're both poisonous."

"Not all healing involves the body," they said. "Sometimes, wiping out evil is necessary, too."

Were they talking about Daddy? Had he become so changed in his thinking that he'd gone insane, needed to be removed from society? But instituted was a far cry from poisoning someone. She stared at the plants. Surely her guides weren't suggesting Daddy be poisoned ...were they?

She looked up.

Her guides were gone.

A boy was there. She couldn't make out his face but he was pointing.

"What? What do you want me to see?"

He was pointing at her side.

She looked down. She saw nothing out of the ordinary.

He pointed, stabbing the air with his finger, pointing to her side.

No, not her side, to her hand.

This hand? She held it up in front of her face. She had a sixth finger, right next to her pinkie.

What the heck?

He held up his own hand.

He had a sixth finger, too.

Her eyes flew open. Ruby sat up in bed.

She snatched her hand from under the blankets and held it up. No sixth finger. Just the scar she'd had all her life.

But the boy had been insistent.

She slid out of bed, lit a lamp and carried it to her mirror. She peered at the scar from her burn, not so noticeable now that she was twenty-five, but there if you looked. It was a good three inches long, all along the fleshy side of her hand. The boy had been trying to tell her something about it, using a startling sight of an appendage to get her attention, but ...what?

She peered closer. She'd seen burn victims in the hospital, had dressed their wounds, done follow-up exams. This was no burn. Maybe one part was, yes, but part of her hand was concave. This was more than a burn.

What had happened to her?

Tadashi turned over in bed and slipped his arm around Ruby, pulling her close. He nuzzled her neck. She smelled so good.

Ruby stirred and got up. She was atop a white unicorn. "Your mother wants to speak with you," she murmured. She floated away.

He looked back over his shoulder.

Meifeng was there. "Hello, son."

He sat up. "Are you all right?"

"I've come to warn you." She looked serious. "This thing that you're planning. Plan it well."

Was she joking? It was all he'd been thinking about.

"Think it through," she said. "It's one thing to attack. It's another to get away with it."

"You said before that I'd be tested."

"If you go there, many will die."

Tadashi shook his head. He scoffed. "Fontinello's men, not mine."

"Men on both sides." She beckoned him with her finger. "Come look out this window."

What window? His tent didn't have a window. He stepped closer.

Oh, maybe it did.

There was a battle taking place outside. It was from olden times in China, from the looks of people's clothing. Rockets were being shot off. Huge tufts of dirt erupted where they landed.

"This looks like it's long ago. They had rockets back then?"

"Not like today. But effective just the same."

Yeah, he could see that. What he didn't understand was why she was showing this to him. "I'm not going off to war, Mother."

"The war will come to you. At the first sign of danger, you must run."

Men didn't run from danger. "Like a coward?"

"Like a smart man."

It didn't sound so smart to him.

"Look at me." She placed a hand on his shoulder. "I won't be coming to you anymore. But I will be watching." She hugged him. "Take care of yourself. I love you."

She vanished.

Her words echoed in his brain. "I love you too, Mother."

Ruby carried the breakfast tray up to Mother's room. No cereal today, Mother. No sugar cakes. No muffins. She was getting real food this morning.

Mother was awake. She was sitting up in bed, propped against the pillows.

"Sleep well?" She set down the tray.

Mother frowned. "That's not what I usually eat."

No kidding. Ruby sat on the bed and held up her hand. "This is a scar, not a burn. What really happened to me, Mother?"

"I knew this day would come." She looked away. "The Purssington Curse."

Purssington was Mother's maiden name. "What are you talking about?"

"It affects those of our lineage. Sometimes it skips a generation. Sometimes it doesn't." She held up her own left hand. "This is where the surgeon cut off mine."

"Cut off your ...what?"

"My sixth finger."

So, the little boy in her vision was being literal. He hadn't tried to startle her with a strange image. The image had once been real. "I was born like that?" She had so many questions. How big was it? What did it look like?

Why did it have to be surgically removed? She turned her hand, trying to get a good look at it. "So why do I also have evidence of a burn as well?"

"To cauterize it."

Doctors only cauterized wounds if the bleeding wouldn't stop. "So I lost a lot of blood. I don't remember any of this. How old was I?"

"You were fresh from the womb, not even five minutes old."

One didn't subject a newborn to such a procedure. No surgeon in his right mind would agree to such a thing. And what was a surgeon doing at Mother's side if she was having a baby? Midwives were all that was needed. This wasn't making any sense. "I was born at home. Why was a surgeon even called to the house? And what surgeon would do such a thing?" To a newborn, no less?

"I did it." Mother looked down at her lap. "I did it to save you. Phillip would have declared you to be a witch and would have had nothing to do with you. I was afraid he might kill –"

"Daddy would never –"

"Oh, but he would." Mother searched her eyes. "We were only days from being married when we were out for a carriage ride and saw a dwarf. He was begging for food. Phillip sneered at him and reached into our picnic basket. He pelted the poor man with apples. 'Here's your food, you ugly troll,' he said. 'Now, go back to your cave so decent people like me don't have to look at you.'"

"Daddy said that?" No, it couldn't be.

"Your father has no tolerance for anyone with a defect. So, I passed off my scar as an accident, from a fall, I told him. But when you were born, there it was, the Purssington Curse, for all the world to see."

And what parent didn't automatically count all the fingers and toes on their newborn?

"First, you were a girl. Strike one. He wanted a boy, had already told everyone that you were going to be his spitting image. Then you were born deformed, in his eyes at least. I went crazy. I grabbed a knife and –" she took a deep breath "– whacked off your extra finger. You have to understand. I was afraid he'd strangle you, drop you off a cliff or take you out to the woods and leave you for the wolves to find."

"He would have done such a thing?"

Mother nodded. "I have no doubt."

"And the burn?"

"I must have hit a major blood vessel. You bled so much, I thought you were going to bleed out. The midwife and housekeeper ran in when they heard you screaming, grabbed the poker iron and staunched the blood flow." She put her face in her hands and cried. "I'm so sorry."

The gloves she'd had to wear, the times she'd been hushed for mentioning her hand. The effect the lack of blood at birth must have had on her brain development. It all made sense now. Ruby pulled her mother close. "Oh, Mother, I had no idea."

Mother jerked in her arms.

Poor thing, she must really be crying hard, wracked with guilt. "It's all right. I forgive you."

"Ruby, help me." Mother jerked straight up, stared into space and collapsed on the bed.

"Mother?"

No response.

She shook her. "Wake up, Mother."

Nothing.

"Mother?"

Oh, dear God, she was dead.

Tadashi woke up. Where was he? Oh, yeah, in his tent. He'd spent so much time moving from campsite to campsite, sleeping on the ground, it was a treat to be back at the camp on the mountain, high above Ruby's Sacramento home.

Ruby. God, he missed her. She must still be in San Francisco, because the windows in the big house down below were dark and all closed up.

Come home, Ruby. Come home so we can talk. So I can apologize.

There was a noise. Far away. Heavy footsteps. More than one man.

He sat up, threw his blanket aside.

He dashed outside. Shit.

Soldiers were coming up the trail, entering the meadow a hundred yards away. Way more than one man.

He had to warn the others. "Wake up. Wake up. We're under attack!"

Something whizzed past him. A bullet.

The soldiers were shooting at unarmed men.

He held up his hands in surrender. "Stop. Stop. We have no guns."

Another bullet whizzed past him.

He dropped to the ground. These guys weren't going to quit until they were all dead.

The Chinese stumbled out of their tents, rubbing the sleep from their eyes.

He had to warn them. "Xialai, xialai! Get down, get down! They're shooting at us," he yelled, gesturing at them to hit the ground.

A man, Mohan, ten feet from him took a bullet. He reacted in confusion, watching the blood flow from the hole in his belly.

"Get down." Tadashi crawled over to him on his elbows. He reached up and yanked the man to the ground. "Stay low, Mohan, and follow me. We've got to get out of here."

The bullets rained down on them, spitting up earth.

Panic hit the camp.

Men ran in all directions.

The soldiers kept marching closer.

Tadashi crawled behind a tent. Safe at last. He couldn't be seen by the soldiers here.

Mohan crawled over to him.

A bullet tore through the canvas.

No, not safe.

Meifeng's visit came back to him. Smart men ran at danger like this.

"Come on," he said. "We'll make a dash for the forest."

One, two, three –now.

He took off running, trying to stay low. A big man to his left spun in a circle then dropped. Half his face had been blown away. It was his friend Sijun, who could carry half again as much weight as any of them. Why did they have to shoot Sijun?

Another man, Erwu, had been hit. He was on the ground, bleeding from his neck.

"Erwu, come on, head to the forest," he yelled.

Erwu stared at him, eyes glazed over.

Tadashi swore. They must have hit the man's jugular.

He hurried forward, crouched down, going from tent to tent and gesturing for the other men to join him. "This way, come on."

The sound of gunfire continued.

There were yells.

There were screams.

They reached the end of the tents. He had about fifteen men with him. Fifteen out of a hundred.

It would be an open sprint from here to the woods.

"Ready, men? Let's go." He took off, running as fast as he could, not bothering to crouch down. This was his one shot at safety.

Time slowed down. It was like every second took forever.

Tadashi urged his legs to pump faster. But they were woefully slow.

Hurry, hurry. Faster, faster.

But he was hurrying. He was going as fast as he could, or he was trying to, at least.

Too slow.

Way too slow.

It was as though he was running thorough waist-high water.

A bee stung him.

Another bee stung him.

Why were there honey bees here in the meadow? They should be over by the cliff where they always were.

Tadashi looked down.

The bee stings were bleeding, no, he was bleeding.

His legs quit. He stumbled.

Someone grabbed his arm and jerked him along.

It was Tuohao. His friend who had blown Fontinello's safe open.

There were whizzing sounds going past him.

Fontinello. He was behind this. He had gotten the army to send troops here to quell their revolt.

Damn these bee stings hurt.

They hurt all the way to the center of his belly.

There was shade here. Oh, they'd reached the trees.

Tuohao was tugging at him. "We have to keep going."

What? Oh good, time was back to normal. He glanced back at the camp. Men were lying there.

There was a whoosh.

A canvas tent lit up with flames.

The soldiers were throwing kerosene on the tents.

Damn it, they weren't here to arrest people. They were here to obliterate them. Tadashi dropped to his knees. His insides hurt like hell. "I don't think I can make it, Tuohao. Just leave me and save yourself."

Ruby folded Mother's hands over her chest and closed her eyelids.

She was gone.

It had happened so quickly. There had been no time to say goodbye.

If only she hadn't been so busy with the hospital, with Wharf Village, consumed with the task of reading every book in Jianyu's library and seeking answers through autopsies, she would have been here more often and realized that Mother was ill.

The swollen legs that her skirts had hidden, she would have caught sight of them eventually.

The shortness of breath when Mother climbed the stairs to bed, that would have been another sign.

But she hadn't been here to observe those things. She hadn't seen Mother except for fleeting moments as she'd hurried out the door, off to save other people's lives.

But she hadn't been able to save her own mother.

Look at her, lying on the bed as though she were asleep. She looked so peaceful, as though nothing had happened.

She could have held her hands above Mother's body and felt what was wrong.

Then again, maybe not. Just like with Meifeng, her abilities to divine illness were no good here. She was too close to Mother for such insight.

Mother was, what, forty-five? Way too young to die of a heart attack. "Oh, Mother, why'd you have to go?"

The tears threatened. She let them come.

Fifteen minutes later, Ruby stumbled downstairs.

Maude was polishing the silver.

"She's dead." Her legs felt unsteady. She found a chair.

"The Missus?" Maude threw a hand to her chest. "Oh, no."

"She just collapsed. In her bed. At least it was quick." It was the only thing for which she could be grateful. "Go to the nearest funeral home and make arrangements for them to come get her body, will you? I want it embalmed so I can take it to Sacramento." Mother always said that she wanted to be buried there.

"Oh course."

"Daddy went out of town. Can you telegraph his Sacramento office?" It would be a hard message for him to receive, but he deserved to know. "Here, I'll give you the money." She got up and handed over some bills. "I'll go upstairs and get her favorite outfit laid out for the funeral home to take."

Maude hesitated.

Maybe she was in shock, too. "Maude? Did you hear me?"

"There's something you should know, Miss Ruby."

That Mother had stolen goodies from the cookie jar on a regular basis? Old news now.

The housekeeper looked down at her feet. She seemed afraid.

"Maude, what is it?"

"It's about your baby boy. There's something you need to know."

CHAPTER NINETEEN

Ruby strode down the street, heart pounding. Mulberry Street, Mulberry Street. Here it was.

As she searched for the address, Maude's words kept echoing in her mind.

"It's about your baby boy? There's something you need to know," she'd said. "He was born alive."

She found Dr. Welliman's office and hurried inside. Ruby ran up to the receptionist. "I need to speak with the doctor. Now."

"I'm afraid he's with a patient."

"This is urgent."

"I'm sure it is." So condescending. "Perhaps if you tell me what this is about."

Tell this rude woman, this impertinent stranger that her newborn had been stolen from her five years ago and her boss was involved? Not a chance, sister.

An inner office door opened. It was a woman carrying a child of about four and Dr. Welliman.

The doctor held the door. "If he doesn't get better in a couple days, let me know."

Ruby hurried forward and caught the door before he closed it. "Dr. Welliman, I have to speak to you in private."

The receptionist glared at her.

Dr. Welliman hesitated.

She had to get his attention. "I'd hate to have to bring my lawyer into this matter."

The doctor gestured. "Yes, well, come to my office." He ushered her to a small room.

She took the chair opposite his desk. "Five years ago, you came to my house when I was in labor."

"I'm afraid I don't recall every –"

"Fontinello. My father is the railroad tycoon." There, that ought to rattle his memory cells.

"Oh, er, yes. Your mother was very concerned about you."

"You told me that my baby was breech, that it was dead. You put me under with anesthesia and I didn't wake up for a long time." Far longer than anyone in the hospital had been put under. The tears threatened. "My baby was born very much alive, wasn't he, Dr. Welliman?"

"Well, I seem to recall –"

"Wasn't he?" She had a witness, no, two with the cook, who had seen her child alive and well. They'd held him when she'd been denied the chance to do even that. "Wasn't he?"

The doctor looked grim and he nodded. "Yes. Your mother contacted me well before your due date and insisted that you be told the child didn't make it."

And no doubt she paid plenty to make sure that's what you did. But she wasn't here to lambaste his ethics. "Where is my baby, doctor?"

Dr. Welliman gestured. "I have no idea. When I left your home, he was being cared for by the staff. They were doting on him."

Just as Maude had told her.

"But I have no knowledge what happened to him after that."

"He was healthy?"

"Oh, yes."

Thank goodness. "His color, his reflexes?"

"Above board, well, except for a couple things." He held up his left hand. "He had an extra pinkie finger, quite noticeable. It came out at about a thirty degree angle –" he demonstrated "–and nearly as long as his normal pinkie finger."

The Purssington Curse. Mother had said it could skip a generation, but it hadn't in this case. "You said there were two things."

"Yes, yes. There was a divot." He pointed to the base of his neck. "Right about here. Quite distinct. But harmless," he added quickly.

So, Dash had inherited an extra pinkie from her and Tadashi's signature throat. It was as though they'd marked him so that he could be found.

She thanked him and left. The doctor had been a dead end for locating her child. But surely someone knew something. Ruby headed out. She'd be damned if she'd give up looking for him.

Anastasia found the theatre shop.

A bell tinkled when she opened the door.

Look at all these costumes. She just had to touch them, see them off the rack. She found one in light blue and held it in front of herself before a full-length mirror. Perfect. She set it aside.

A man stepped out from the curtained off back room. "Well, hello." He motioned to her dress and made a flamboyant gesture. "I see you fit right in."

She laughed. "This old thing?" It was her gyspy-inspired dress, the ne with its flowing sleeves, always an attention getter. She'd toss it as soon as the money from Ruby's herbal formula for birth control came rolling in and she could buy that big house in San Francisco. Then she'd join the elite of society and give up being a madam. Any day now. That was the plan, at least. "I need masks."

For her next party, she was bringing in six extra girls from Virginia City, Nevada.

"What's the occasion, sweetie?"

She grabbed a feather fan and waved it in front of her face, pretending to be coy. "I'm hosting a costume party." She laughed and described the party, without mentioned the hookers of course. "I want it to be talked about for days, weeks even."

"Ooh, sister, you're a partier, my kind of person." He held up a finger. "Let me see what we have."

"I need twenty-five masks for men, twelve for women. I hope you have that many."

"We dress shows for the theater. We have oodles of masks." He disappeared into the back.

She could see it now. The men would arrive in their regular clothes, of course, but they'd be required to don masks as soon as they walked in the door. It would add an element of intrigue and fuel the sexual excitement. Of course, the booze would help fuel that, too.

She went down the list of men she would invite. They were all high society people, men who felt being with a prostitute wasn't cheating on their wives if they paid for it. Yeah, right. Should she invite that one guy? The one who got it up but never was able to finish the job, not even once?

Anastasia hesitated, then – sure, why not. Maybe the mask element would help him complete the task this time. For once.

Ruby found the building and hurried inside. Second floor. First door on the right. The sign above the door said "Pinkerton."

The man behind the desk was dark-haired, slick. He sat up and straightened his tie at the sight of her. "Steven Demming at your service. How may I help you, miss?" He was dashing and he knew it.

"I need to find a child. My son."

Steven lost the smile. "Let me guess. Your husband took him."

"I don't have a husband."

The smiled returned, brighter than ever. "I'm at your service, Miss –?"

"Fontinello. Ruby Fontinello." She took a seat. "It's a long story, so bear me out."

Fifteen minutes later, Steven Demming had two pages of notes. "You're sure the household staff doesn't know more than this?"

"I questioned them, believe me."

"No doubt, but I'd like to interview them, too." He sent her a pointed look. "I'm an expert at, shall we say, eliciting information from people."

She didn't like the way he said that. "The staff is loyal. They wouldn't hold back information from me."

"They held back information for five years from you," he pointed out.

Only because Mother held court over them. "They're good people."

He smiled at her. "Sometimes it's in the way a question is phrased."

"Fine, you can talk to them." Maybe he did know a special way to ask questions that jogged people's memories. She'd let him talk to all of San Francisco if it meant finding Dash, rescuing him from the street. Whatever it took, she'd do.

"There's one more thing," Steven Demming said.

The fee, of course. She reached in her handbag. "How much?"

"Not that."

"What then?"

"It's been five, almost six years, Miss Fontinello. Your son may *not* be living on the streets, neglected and bouncing between strangers, struggling day-to-day just to survive, as you fear."

"What are you saying? That he may be dead?" Her lip quivered. She couldn't bear such news, not after only just now learning he'd been born alive.

"No." He reached across the desk and patted her hand. "I'm saying that perhaps your mother wasn't as coldhearted as you think. There's a possibility that your son may be living a full and happy life. He may be with a family who truly loves him."

She'd never considered that.

"If we find him, are you willing to consider that ripping him out of his stable family life will be detrimental to him?"

Find him, only to lose him all over again? How could she do that when all she wanted was to rush up to her own baby, Dash. To hug him tight and cover his face with kisses? She stood up to leave. "Just find him."

Ruby found the Avery Funeral Home and opened the door. A bell tinkled above her head as she stepped inside. There was a large room with rows of seats, ready for mourners.

A man appeared. "Hello. How may I help you?"

She introduced herself and handed him a calling card. "My mother's body is to be embalmed here."

"Fontinello, yes. The makeup is being applied as we speak."

"I'd like to see her."

"Arnold is finishing up, but I'm sure he won't mind." He led her to the back.

The front door bell sounded. He excused himself.

Mother's body was in a casket. She looked as though she were asleep.

The assistant, presumably Arnold, was inspecting his work. "A little bit of rouge," he muttered and open a tin with bright red goop in it. He noticed her and nodded. "Oh, hello."

She gestured. "Please continue."

"It doesn't bother you to see –?"

"Death? I worked at the Saint Raphael Merciful Hospital. Not uncommon to see corpses there." Especially if you visited the morgue at least a dozen times to conduct unauthorized autopsies.

Arnold dipped two fingers in the goop and got a good sized gob. He hesitated and returned some of it to the tin. "Too much. Don't want her to look like a tar – I mean, a madame."

Like Anastasia was. She'd be seeing her in a couple of days. But she was here about Mother.

Arnold put on the finishing touches and stepped back to admire his work. He nodded to her. "Looks good?"

"Yes. Could I have a moment with her?"

"Of course." He wiped his hands on a towel and left.

Ruby stepped up to the casket. *Oh, Mother, look at you. We were just opening up the lines of communication when you died. There was so much I wanted to talk about, to learn.*

"I'm taking you home, Mother."

Maybe she was taking herself home, too.

Tadashi watched from the safety of the tree line as the train rushed past. There it went, the last run of the day. The next one wasn't due for eight hours.

The train chugged out of view, heading west.

He and the ten other men stepped out into the open.

He pointed. "Right here. By the time they come over the crest of the hill and see it, even if they slam on the brakes, it'll be too late."

The men nodded and picked up their shovels and pickaxes and got to work.

Tuohao hesitated. "You shouldn't be here, Tadashi."

It was his duty. He couldn't leave his men to take on all the danger. "I'm the lookout. I'll be sitting atop that rock up there." Watching in case the soldiers were tracking them and happened upon them, but they're have to be awfully good trackers to follow them through the woods.

"You should be in a bed, healing. Like the other men who got hurt."

His two wounds were fine. Wherever the bullets had lodged, they didn't seem to be causing him *too* much trouble. Some stabs of pain, yes, sometimes to the point that he had to stop and gasp for breath, but they'd always passed. He'd seek medical attention later. "Stop talking or the men will accuse you of avoiding work." Which was a joke. Everyone knew Tuohao carried his fair share of the workload.

"Where is next train coming from?"

"San Fran."

"Maybe some bigwigs will be on it and bring us publicity," Toahau said.

"Maybe Fontinello will be on it." That bastard.

Toahau smirked and headed for the site where the other men were hard at work, the clanging of their tools ringing through the air.

Tadashi made his way up to the lookout spot. He'd been joking but wouldn't it be sweet justice if the railroad tycoon *were* on it? Wishful thinking, that.

Ruby sat on the train as it surged along. She'd opted for the last one to Sacramento and had overseen Mother's casket being carried onto the freight car near the back. She'd tipped the men, then been escorted to the first class car. Everyone had treated her with solemn faces, with reverence.

The attendant, James, whom she'd known for years, had been most gracious, rushing to bring her a cup of coffee and biscuits. "We heard of your loss, Miss Ruby. If there's anything else I can do, just let me know."

But she just wanted to be alone.

Now, she watched the scenery whiz by at a dizzying speed. That's right, father had outfitted this train with the latest engine, more powerful than the older types which topped out at thirty-five miles per hour. He could probably cite its specifications, the amount of horsepower, the ratio of its gears. Men's stuff, all of it.

She was more concerned with women's stuff.

Mother was in the back, like a reminder of all that had happened. The action Mother had taken after giving birth, chopping off the extra finger – sobering. Sobering that Mother could do that to a mere infant, not even ten minutes out of the birth canal. Sobering that she'd feared Daddy's reaction so much. And the excuse that Maude said had been given to him? Laughable – that a newborn had crawled to the fireplace and grabbed a hot poker. Surely he'd questioned such a thing.

Maybe not. Father had always been so absorbed in his precious railroad line that he may have only half-paid attention After all, she'd been born a girl and his heart had been set on getting a son, a son to carry on the Fontinello name. Sorry about that, Daddy.

Then she'd learned from the doctor that her own child had been born with the so-called Purssington Curse. And Mother must have feared Daddy's disapproval again.

Here was his daughter, pregnant by a man who had betrayed the business.

Pregnant by a man who was not purely Caucasian.

Pregnant without a husband.

How would he have reacted to her baby? Her baby with the features of his nemesis? A baby whose hand was a daily reminder that he was slightly deformed?

Mother must have feared his wrath. It was the only reason there was for her whisking away little Dash.

Her heart cringed at the thought of him. Where was he? Was he in good hands? Was he happy? Would she ever see him?

If you're in Heaven looking down on me right now Mother, help me find my son.

There was a screech of brakes.

She was thrown from her seat as everything went into slow motion. What the hell?

People screamed.

Luggage flew through the air.

Everything tumbled around her.

"Hold on," the attendant yelled.

Everything went black.

CHAPTER TWENTY

Tadashi hid in the brushes and held his breath. Here it came, right on time, the mighty Fontinello machine. Well, this machine was about to be derailed.

It crested the hill, spewing black smoke from its stack. Look at that thing. It was huge, massive. He could feel the rumbling vibration coursing through the ground.

He was close enough that he could see the conductor. Look at him, probably doing things by rote, thinking this was just another day of work. When would he realize the tracks had been removed? That the entire train was about to coming crashing down?

The train rushed down the hill, picking up speed.

The conductor's face appeared in the window briefly. His mouth dropped open. Yeah, he saw it.

There was the screech of the brakes. Sparks flew.

The train engine seemed to fly for a couple of seconds, free of the Earth. Then it nosedived and plowed into the ground, spewing up dirt and rocks.

What tremendous force. What a massive crater.

The other cars careened into the mess, the sound of twisted steel and screams filling the air, and piled up in a haphazard way.

The movement stopped.

The screams changed to moans. Too many screams, too many moans.

The dust settled.

He counted quickly. One, two, three, four, five passenger cars. Five, that many? No, no, no. There was only supposed to be one. That's what the plans from the safe had indicated.

Fontinello must have changed things.

People began crawling out of the train. They were bloodied, their clothes torn.

Tadashi winced. He hadn't meant for so many people to get hurt.

A woman was climbing out of the front passenger car's window. It was the premiere car, just for the elite of society. Her clothes said, "money." Who was she? A mayor's wife? A senator's daughter?

She got free and jumped down. Her hands and arms were bloodied. She held her head as she stumbled away.

Lordie, it was Ruby. She was hurt and needed help.

Tadashi jumped up. His stomach sent him a stabbing pain. Not now. Ruby needed him.

He hurried forward, clutching his side. "Ruby, Ruby, wait up."

She didn't seem to hear him. She kept walking.

He stumbled over the uneven ground and reached the crash site. It was chaos, smelled of dust and smoke. People spotted him and reached out to him. "Help. Help me." Others hurried up to him, limped toward him, their arms outstretched.

He ignored them, tried to see past them. "Ruby, wait. Don't go." He lost sight of her. "Ruby?" Where was she? Damn, he should have stayed at his vantage point until she sat down. He scrambled around, searching. Where was she?

There was water on his fingers. He looked down.

No, it was blood. He'd deal with it later.

There she was, on the tracks. She was stumbling along, bent on getting to her destination. What did she think she was doing? Walking to Sacramento?

He caught up to her, limping as he held his stomach. They were a good hundred feet from the crash. "Ruby, stop."

She faltered and paused. She turned around, looking confused as he got closer. "Tadashi?"

He threw his arms around her and held her tight. God, this felt so right. "I'm here. I'll take care of you. Everything's going to be all right." Her head. She'd hit her head. "Maybe you should sit down."

"No time." She pointed down the track, frowning. "I'm ... going ... home." Ruby listed to one side.

"I know, sweetie. Let's sit down for a minute first, OK?"

Tuohao appeared beside him. "I'll take her." He picked up Ruby as though she weighed nothing.

Tadashi looked around. "How far is the pushcart?" It had been a stroke of genius that they'd thought to steal it from the train yard.

"Not far." Tuohao set off down the tracks with Ruby.

An hour later, they were at the new campsite. The other men gave them water and propped them up near one another then left them as they huddled together to make further plans.

Ruby's eyes looked clearer. She had a bruise on the side of her forehead and a little bit of blood where her clothes were torn. Other than that, he didn't see any red flags.

Tadashi took her hand. "I've missed you."

Ruby looked down. "You sent me away, said you never wanted to see me again, remember?"

"I shouldn't have. I know that now." He sat up and turned to face her. "Oh, Ruby, I was wrong. I was so wrong. Meifeng came to me in a dream. She told me that she's happy. I was upset over nothing, believing in some stupid superstition. Can you ever forgive me?"

She looked up and gave him a little smile. "I never held it against you."

Really? He took her in his arms even though it hurt. "I love you, Ruby. I've always loved you." God, it felt so good to hold her again. He kissed her, a long, passionate kiss. He'd missed that, too. He drew a hand down her face. Even bruised up and smudged with dirt, she was beautiful.

"Meifeng comes to you?"

Not like your guides come to you. "She warned me about the soldiers."

"That Daddy sent, I heard. Did she come and fell through Meifeng hence?"

Fell through Meifeng hence? What? What had she just said? And why was her face wavering like waves of heat? "Where is the heat coming from?"

Ruby was suddenly right in his face. She was screaming.

But she sounded so far away.

She was being swallowed up by darkness.

No, Ruby, come back.

Tadashi opened his eyes. When had it gotten to be night?

Ruby's face appeared above him. She looked concerned. "How are you feeling?"

Not good. Her face was still wavering. "My stomach, it really hurts."

"You took two bullets. That was four days ago," she said. She pressed a wet cloth to his forehead. "You've been delirious since you saved me." There was concern in her eyes. "You should have seen a doctor."

"I'd rather see you." He went to laugh at his joke but, damn, it hurt like heck. "Ugh."

Ruby looked grim. "An infection has set in, Tadashi."

The way she said it, this had to be bad. "Am I going to die?"

"I don't know. You have a raging fever, I can tell you that."

No better hands to be in than hers. "So, go get some herbs and cure me."

"Not that easy. The herbs you need are not nearby. By the time I'd could get them, they'd be worthless to you. And we can't take you to a doctor or anywhere at this point or you'll be arrested."

And that would be a death sentence for sure. He tried to breathe fully but it hurt too much. Better stick to shallow breathing. "You once told me that the body is great at healing itself."

She squeezed her eyes shut and turned away.

But not when it came to bullets, huh? He found her hand and took it in his. Such a soft hand. "Stay with me. Talk to me."

Ruby turned back to him and wiped away her tears. "I have to tell you something, Tadashi."

This sounded serious. His heart clutched. She'd found someone else? No, not that. Not when he'd just been reunited with her.

"We have a son."

His ears must be playing tricks on him, or this fever was affecting him. "I could swear you just said –"

"I did."

He had a son? Honestly? But ... when had she been pregnant? "How could that be?"

"When Meifeng was sick, I spent so much time and energy on her, I neglected my own herbal intake."

"And we had a child? A boy?"

She nodded. "Dash."

Dash. What a great name. He squeezed her hand. "Does he look like me?"

Ruby hiccupped and nodded. "The spitting image of you."

"I can't wait to see him."

She smoothed his hair off his face. "You will."

She was wavering again.

The light was dimming.

"I can't see you, Ruby. Are you there?"

"I'm here." She sounded so far away. "I'll always be here."

The darkness took over everything. The pain stopped.

He was free.

Ruby made it to the top of the trail. It sure was harder, now that she hadn't been hiking it on a daily basis.

She stopped and stared. Look at this place.

The mountain top camp, it was gone, just ...gone.

The tents had been burned to the ground. The grass was now soot.

She stepped closer. Was there anything resembling the community she'd once known and loved? How different it looked now.

No, only evidence of the fire pits remained.

She stepped carefully. Where was it?

Ah, here. This was where Tadashi's tent had been, where they'd spent time in each other's arms, where they'd made love.

Now, nothing. There was nothing.

Like her life now, without Tadashi to share in it ever again.

Her chin quivered. The tears came.

They should have been together forever. He was the love of her life. She'd planned it all out. They'd get back together. They'd locate Dash and begin their lives anew as a family, never to quarrel or be separated again.

Some plan. It hadn't taken into account real life.

He'd been taken from her and she'd never know his touch again. And worse, Tadashi would never get to meet his son.

Her only solace was that Tadashi would always have a place in her heart.

She knew who was at fault. One person and only one person.

Yes, it had been the soldiers' bullets that had caused his death, but it was Daddy's insistence, throwing his influence around, that had sent soldiers after Tadashi in the first place.

Damn him. He'd even destroyed her memories of this place.

She walked across to Meifeng's cabin. Only the foundation was left. The site was a smoldering mess. If her mentor were here to see it, she'd be heartbroken.

A bookcase had fallen over. She stepped in and wrestled it up, flipping it backwards.

The books were toppled in a pile, charred, every one. All these wonderful books, gone, useless.

Some under the pile showed promise. She kicked aside the burnt tomes, tossed the partially burnt ones.

Deep underneath, there was one book that had been almost untouched – Healing From Nature.

She pulled it out of the rubble and cradled it to her. Meifeng had heralded it as one that covered so much of what she'd need. At one point, she'd considered it her bible, the bible of all things medicinal.

Ruby opened it, flipping its pages. This book. It had started it all. She'd read it by candlelight, by kerosene lamp, by the firelight, staying up late to absorb every word. It all seemed so long ago.

A piece of paper fell out. That was odd. She'd been the last person to read the book and she'd never left any notes in the books.

She picked it up.

It was Meifeng's handwriting, "Ruby, always remember: All that man needs for health and healing has been provided by nature. The challenge is for the healer to find it."

It was the perfect summation. She must have written it before the cancer struck her down.

Anastasia opened the door. It was Ruby. When had she come to town? "Well, look who's up and about. Come in, sugar, come in."

Ruby gave her a hug. "How are you, my friend?"

"Did you look at your bank account? The zinc tincture is doing nicely, sure, but the herbal tea to keep ladies from getting pregnant? Off the charts." She swore every woman in the world was ordering it. The factory was having trouble keeping up. She ushered Ruby to the kitchen. "Tea?"

"No thanks."

"Seriously, if orders keep coming in like they have been, I'll be out of this 'madam' business in no time." She gave it another six months, had marked her calendar and was counting down the days like a kid at Christmas. But her friend wasn't here about finances. She'd been in a terrible accident and had buried her lover. "I heard what happened, Ruby. Hell, the whole town heard."

"At least I was there when Tadashi died."

She patted her hand. Poor Ruby. "You can take comfort in that." No one wanted to die alone. "How is it, living under the same roof with your dad?"

Ruby shook her head. "It's a mess. I don't talk to him. He doesn't talk to me. Half the time, it's so quiet at night that I'm not even sure he's there."

No, he was over here getting his jollies. But she'd never tell Ruby that. "Maybe that's best."

"I brought you some herbs. They were in my luggage which just got delivered." Ruby set them on the table, lining up the pouches.

That reminded her. "Lillian has a hacking cough. Will any of these help her?"

"Is she upstairs? I can better tell what she needs if I can check her out."

That 'holding out the hands' thing. "Top of the stairs, first door to the right."

Ruby got up and left.

Maybe she should make the tea for all the girls to drink. She set the kettle on the stove.

Ruby's footsteps came down the stairs ten minutes later.

A carnival dancer, feathers jutting out in every direction, poked her head around the corner.

What? "You scared me, sugar."

Ruby laughed and pulled off the mask. "You have dozens of these things."

"For the next party, tomorrow night." She told Ruby about the concept.

Her friend smiled. "So, they pay admission, they pay for the booze and they pay for the girl."

Girls, she'd come to realize. Something about the party atmosphere made all the men super heroes who wanted to do it more than once. Fine by her.

"You're quite the entrepreneur, Anastasia. Too bad Lillian won't be part of your party."

"That bad?"

"It's deep in her lungs, going to take more than just a quick tea. I'll have to brew it up at home and bring it over."

"Tonight?"

"It a three-step process. Takes time."

"Whenever it's ready, just bring it by. Anytime."

Ruby smiled. "Well, not *any*time." She held up the mask. Not during the party, she meant.

"Things won't die down until the wee hours of the morning."

"It should be ready, oh, about ten p.m. I can leave it on the doorstep."

Perfect. "The back door, here off the kitchen. I'll watch for it." She hugged her friend goodbye. She couldn't wait to move to San Fran and be a proper lady like Ruby Fontinello.

The killer sat at his desk and turned the invitation over in his hand.

A costume party, masks to be provided.

What an idiot she was. Did she honestly think having other people there would keep her safe? Then again, the mask aspect played right into his hands. This night could prove interesting, most interesting indeed.

He stepped over the mirror and adjusted his jacket.

He had the cordage.

He had the knives.

He smiled at his reflection. And soon, he'd have the opportunity to use them.

He left the building, heading to the trolley. The drivers knew him. He got aboard the usual one south, as though he was going home.

Had to make sure the driver saw him in case anything went wrong and he needed an alibi. Hi, Joe. Good to see you. How are the kids? There, that was done. The rest of his commute would be quiet.

Instead of transferring to the West-bound one, he set off on foot, zigzagging north and east. To anyone watching, he was merely out for a stroll.

Sure, a stroll to a fun night of slicing and dicing.

He reached Anastasia's house of debauchery. So much sin going on in there. It wouldn't be long before he put a stop to it.

Ruby poured the brew into canning jars and screwed the lids on them. Eight jars. Lillian would need to drink this constantly, a cup every two hours, for it to be effective. It was ten p.m., so if she got it to her now, the poor girl could start right away. Lillian needed rest. Anastasia's house was going to be far too noisy to get anything close to that. Perhaps she should invite her here to the house. She could have the bedroom at the far end of the hall. Daddy would never know she was here. And if he did hear Lillian coughing, she'd tell him it was a friend who was ill.

She wrapped the jars in kitchen towels, to keep them from clanking into one another and slid the jars in a carry sack. It was heavy on her shoulder. Too heavy when you were still bruised from a train wreck.

She set off for Anastasia's. Good thing the trolley was still running this late, she could never carry these jars all that way.

The trolley let her off three blocks from Anastasia's. This wouldn't be too bad.

She got closer.

All the lights were on. There was music and laughter coming from the house.

That's right. The party. She'd forgotten.

Anastasia wanted her to leave this on the back porch. But she needed to include instructions. Ruby felt in her pocket. No paper. No pencil. She had nothing with which to write a note. *Good thinking, Ruby.* Oh well, she'd have to knock and hope someone heard her.

She went around to the back of the house.

A man was in the kitchen. He wore a mask decorated with feathers and rhinestones. Anastasia had gone all out to make this a fun night for her guests. He pulled something from his pocket, unwrapped it and popped it in his mouth.

She knocked.

He turned, startled, and dropped the gold foil wrapper on the floor. He peered out, trying to see past his reflection. He cracked the door. "Yes?"

She set down the pouch. "I have medicine for one of the girls."

He nodded. "Shall I tell Anastasia to come get it?"

Well, she certainly didn't want to come inside and interrupt the party. That would be awkward. "Yes, please."

He went off to find her.

She should unpack the pouch and put the brew on the table. She pushed open the door and set about removing the jars. She should leave a note with instructions for taking it. Here was paper and a pencil.

She jotted down the doses and how often to take them. Oh, better add that she shouldn't have milk or cheese and to cut back on coffee until she was better.

Anastasia entered the room. She was dressed like Josephine of France. She curtsied. "Welcome to my palace."

Cute. "How is Lillian feeling?"

"Down for the count I'm afraid."

Sleeping, that was good. She pointed. "There are the instructions. She should start drinking this as soon as she wakes up."

"I'll take it up to her right now."

Excellent. She'd better get going. She stepped out into the night air and headed back to the trolley line. One should be coming along pretty soon.

Stop. You forgot.

She'd meant to suggest that Lillian come to her house to stay. But she'd been too busy writing out the instructions and it had slipped her mind. She turned on her heel and hurried back.

There was someone in the kitchen. Oh, good.

She knocked. No one answered.

She knocked again, harder.

No one answered.

That was odd, she could have sworn she'd seen a figure as she was coming up to the door. A peek in the window would tell her. But ... no one.

Anastasia came in the kitchen. Oh good.

The cellar door crashed open.

A man jumped out.

He grabbed Anastasia from behind.

He threw her to the floor.

Oh, God, he was choking her. It was the murderer.

"No!" Ruby ran to the door and yanked it open.

She ran inside.

Had to stop him.

She beat on his back with her fists. "Get off her."

He laughed.

Poor Anastasia was gasping for air.

Ruby grabbed the nearest thing, a heavy ceramic pitcher.

She smashed it over his head.

The man slumped to the floor. Cordage and a case fell out of his pocket.

Ruby grabbed the case and opened it. Knives dumped onto the floor. He was the murderer and he'd just tried to kill her friend.

Anastasia gasped, pulling in a raspy breath. Her hands flew to her throat.

"Are you all right, Anastasia?"

She nodded.

The man stirred.

Just who was this attacker? She caught the edge of the mask and ripped it off his face. "You!"

CHAPTER TWENTY-ONE

Ruby glanced at the mask in her hand, then to the knives and cordage.

This was the murderer, and he had attacked Anastasia.

Worse, she knew him.

It was Ross Wallace, the city councilman. He was the man who'd killed Anastasia's friends.

He sat up and shook off the shards of pottery. Ross Wallace jumped to his feet.

Oh, no, he wasn't getting away. She grabbed one of the knives. "You're not going anywhere." She nudged Anastasia. "Go in the other room. Send someone for the sheriff."

Wallace sneered. "And tell him what?"

Anastasia paused, unsure what to do.

Ruby narrowed her eyes. Ross was going to pull something here, she could feel it. "And tell him that you just tried to murder my friend."

He scoffed. "She slipped and fell. I was merely trying to help her."

Help her? "You had your hands around her throat. You were choking her."

He chuckled. "You had a bad vantage point, couldn't see what was really going on."

"Look at her throat." The girl's skin was mottled red, clearly marked where his fingers had been. How was he going to explain that away, huh?

Ross lifted his chin in defiance. "These tarts, they like it when a customer plays rough. She's had marks on her neck before, haven't you, sweetheart?" He reached out to pinch Anastasia on the chin.

Ruby brought up the knife.

He stopped, backed up and lost the smile. "What are you going to do, huh? Accuse a city official with an impeccable reputation? Who would believe you? Either of you?" He pointed at Anastasia. "You're nothing but a tart and *you* –" he scoffed "– *you* were branded as a fake in the newspaper. Besides, my brother-in-law is the state prosecutor." He snapped his lapels. "I bet you didn't know that, did you? Try to bring charges against me and you'll find yourself in so much shit you'll never dig your way out." He crossed to the back door, let himself out and strode away into the night.

Anastasia turned to her, hand still holding her neck. "What can we do?"

What *could* they do? He was a slippery one. "He's a psychopath. He'll attack you again."

"I have to live in fear?"

Her guides' words came back to her.

"Not all healing involves the body," they'd said. "Sometimes, wiping out evil is necessary, too."

No, Anastasia didn't need to live in fear. She'd make sure of it.

Ruby took her seat in the San Francisco Pinkerton office. Steven Demming nodded and managed to smile at her. It didn't reach higher than his mouth.

She knew that smile. It was the kind that meant: Bad News. "So, what did you find out?" she asked. Or, rather, didn't find out?

He opened a file and glanced at it. "We interviewed your staff, twice, I might add, and interviewed the neighbors to see what they recalled from that day," Steven Demming said. "We went to the orphanages and checked their records thoroughly. The hospitals, too. We even went to the camp where migrant workers and their families are in the seedy part of town."

Wharf Village, he meant. She hadn't thought of that. Dash could have been sleeping in some family's shack, just a few yards away and she would have never known.

"As you might imagine, the language barrier was a tad hard to overcome with so many ethnicities there, but we all agreed we covered it as well as possible."

"I'm sure." *Stop describing what you did and just get to the results. Did you find Dash or didn't you?*

"We spoke with private doctors. As you may know, some are specializing in treating only children these days."

"Yes, I've heard." *Get on with it.*

He spread his hands apart. "Bottom line? We could not find your son."

It was like being slugged in the gut. "So, he's probably dead."

"We don't know that."

"But you couldn't find a trace of him."

"If it's any consolation, there is a Chinese faction here in town. They look after one another. Now, it's possible your son was taken in by one of those families."

"Did you approach them?"

He shook his head. "It's not like they're listed in any kind of directory, Miss Fontinello. You happen upon these people, sure, but it's happenstance at best. Sometimes, they live in the woods."

Like Meifeng and Daddy's workers.

Demming closed the file. "We put the word out. Nothing came back." He sighed. "I'm sorry."

So, Dash was most likely dead. She'd gotten her hopes up and that hole in her heart had been opened up anew. Now, she needed to heal once again.

Ruby peeled off the rubber gloves. Scary stuff. But she'd managed to handle it without splashing any before adding it to the single candy and watching it harden. She couldn't risk adding it to all of them in the box. That would leave a trail. No, the killer liked his candy. He would get around to this one special piece in time. Maybe he'd reach for it next week. Maybe next month. He didn't share, Daddy had told her, and so there was virtually no chance of anyone else eating it.

Now, what to do with the leftovers? She couldn't very well poor it down the drain. Who knew where it would end up? Better to bury it.

She went outside and found a spade in the gardener's shed.

A half hour later, she'd hiked up the trail and turned off of it far enough to ensure no one would stumble across this stuff.

Yes, this spot would do.

She started digging.

Her guides' words came back to her as she worked. "Not all healing involves the body," they'd told her. "Sometimes, wiping out evil is necessary, too."

Well. Ross Wallace was evil in the flesh. He would continue killing girls and even if he were caught, would likely get away with it.

But she wasn't about to let him get away with the murders and his attempt to kill Anastasia. His brother-in-law, the state prosecutor, couldn't save him from this punishment.

She wiped the sweat off her brow.

The hole was deep enough. She buried the entire saucepan and began shoving the dirt back into the hole.

Eventually, the Earth would take it back and render it harmless. The Earth always took care of things.

Jianyu spotted her as she got off the train in San Francisco. She was such a lovely creature, smarter and more driven than many men he'd met. She would stand out where she was headed. He gestured to his carriage driver. "Get her bags."

She came closer and stepped up into his carriage. "You got my telegram."

And her letter a couple days before that, detailing her plans.

She took the seat opposite him. "Thank you for your help."

"My pleasure."

The carriage driver set her bag inside.

Only one bag? She was certainly traveling light for such a journey. A book, well-used, peeked out of its outside pocket. That title, "Healing From Nature", how apropos, although Ruby was well past its fundamental teachings. But he wasn't here to comment on her choice of reading material. "Welcome back to San Francisco. Do you need to stop by your father's house to retrieve anything?"

The horse started up and they clattered along the street.

"No, I have what little I need."

"You have gone over the greeting, memorized it?"

"Only a million times: Witness this traveler who wishes only –"

"Very well." He cut her off. He didn't need to hear the rest.   Ruby had proven herself a quick learner. "Everything's been arranged. The ship leaves this afternoon." He handed her the ticket for passage and her traveling papers. "Your name is now Roberta Fontaine."

She gave him a small smile. "Roberta, huh?"

It had seemed wise to choose a name close enough that she'd adjust to it easily. "Are you sure you don't want to stay?" She'd miss America, he'd bet his bottom dollar on it.

Ruby shook her head. "There's nothing here for me," she said.

"This came about rather suddenly. Shall I get word to your father of where you've gone?"

"I have no father."

"I see." Phillip Fontinello was very much alive ... to everyone but his own flesh and blood. Whatever had transpired between them, it was no business of his. But he knew this: The man was a fool. "Let me take you out to lunch then. We can converse in Chinese so no one can eavesdrop." They'd also have to stop by the bank to address her business so she'd have access to funds. Nice of her to afford the Seekers of the Universe a generous cut, but then, she'd be living a far different life soon, where money had little value.

She looked out the carriage window. "Goodbye, San Fran," she murmured.

That reminded him. "I have something for you."

Ruby shook her head. "Really, I don't need anything."

"You'll need this, especially where you're going." He pulled out a box, opened it and held it out to her.

It was a stylized caduceus pin, the pin for the xunshao hwanyu.

Her eyes teared up as she accepted it. "I am honored, Jianyu. Thank you."

"Not many achieve this. But you have."

Ross Wallace sat down at his desk. Four o'clock. What a day. And he was famished.

Wait. He smiled. *Nothing like a little pick me up to make things better.*

He opened his desk drawer and found the brand new box from Harvey & Son's. It had been left for him by some errand boy. The note was cryptic: Thanks for agreeing to our little deal.

It could have come from a number of people, he had so many "deals" going on, but all he cared about right now was popping one of those goodies in his mouth.

One? Heck, three or four were in order after a day like this.

He undid the gold wrapper and savored the taste as he let his tongue glide over it. Yum, delicious.

Two minutes later, it was all gone.

He reached for another. So good.

Ten minutes later, he'd finished half a dozen. He giggled. At this rate, he'd finish the whole box.

He popped another in his mouth, the gold foil wrappers piling up on the floor. The maid would clean them up. That was what she was paid to do. An important man like him couldn't be bothered.

He swallowed. Something was catching.

He tried to clear his throat.

It didn't help.

He tried clearing his throat again.

Nothing.

That was odd, it was like something was caught in his throat, but he could tell nothing was there.

Maybe he'd better finish this last candy quickly. He chewed it down and swallowed the final bit of it.

Ross Wallace coughed.

There *was* something in his throat. He could feel it. What the devil?

He pressed one hand to the base of his neck and stretched out the collar of his shirt.

It was suddenly hard to get a full breath, like his throat was no wider than a straw.

Oh no. This was not good, not good at all.

He pushed away from his desk, bent over and tried to draw in air.

His throat, it was closing up.

It was closing up fast.

He couldn't breathe.

He clutched at his neck, clawing like a cat.

No, no, this couldn't be happening.

The office started going dark.

He fell to the floor.

The room got darker.

The last thing he saw was the pile of gold wrappers.

Ruby hiked the last of the Shanghai trail, pausing to catch her breath.

She stood at the rusted iron gate. What a journey. It had taken her two months to get to this isolated place. Now, the moment was finally here.

There was a cord hanging to the side.

She reached over and pulled it.

A gong sounded.

A minute went by. She peered through the gate and into the garden. No one. Maybe they hadn't heard it.

She reached over and –

A Buddist monk in a mustard-colored robe was shuffling down the path.

He came up to her and nodded. He tilted his head ever so slightly, the questions showing in his eyes – "Who are you? What do you want?"

She took a deep breath. Now or never.

Ruby bowed in a formal manner and addressed him in Chinese, using the exact words that Jianyu had instructed. "Witness this traveler who wishes only to serve. I am here to learn from the Medicine Man Most High in all the land." She recited the rest of the passage verbatim, followed by another bow.

The monk's eyes narrowed. "Only the best get to train under him."

Meifeng's words came back to her. *Don't think you can just show up and be accepted. He tests people and only once. You must be prepared.* Well, she was prepared. "Then test me."

He hesitated.

It was because she was a woman, she could just feel it. Well, she hadn't come this far to be turned away by some old gatekeeper. She could do this *her* way. She crossed her arms and drew herself up taller. "Or have Bojing test me himself."

He spotted the pin on her collar – the symbol of the Seekers of the Universe – and stared at it. "You can cure illnesses?"

"Only the Earth can." Meifeng's written words returned to her and she spoke them now. "All that man needs for health and healing has been provided by nature. The challenge is for the healer to find it."

He nodded and opened the gate. "Join us."

He was letting her in! "You're taking me to be tested by Bojing?"

"No."

What? "No?"

"I am Bojing." He gave her a small smile. "You passed." He gestured her in. "Join us."

She went to step past him but her fingers were instantly pulled to a spot near his chest. She let them hover there. "You have a mass. We have to get you started on a treatment."

CHAPTER TWENTY-TWO

TWENTY YEARS LATER

Ruby heard the gong. Someone was at the gate.

She gathered her mustard-colored robe around her and got up from tending the old woman stretched out on the mat.

The woman reached out. "Healer, don't go."

"I'll just be a moment." She gestured to an assistant to stay with the patient.

Ruby started down the path.

The gong only sounded when someone needed care.

Who would it be this time? A mother with a feverish child? An old man with a goiter? A pregnant teenager, heavy with child and scared as she came to term?

She rounded the corner of the garden.

There was a young man at the gate, in his mid-twenties.

Her heart sped up.

That face.

He looked familiar, almost like –

"Tadashi?" She almost tripped but caught herself, unable to take her eyes off him.

No, it couldn't be. He'd died in her arms all those years ago.

Maybe her mind was playing tricks on her.

Maybe this was a ghost.

He was twenty-ish – not Tadashi, but Dash.

"My son," she whispered.

She stumbled closer, staring. Oh, God, he was the spitting image of Tadashi, only even more Americanized. Of course. Because if this truly *was* Dash, he had half her blood.

He gave her a polite little wave as she got closer.

His left hand – it had an extra pinkie finger.

The Purssington Curse.

It was nearly as long as his natural pinkie. It stuck out at a thirty degree angle, just as the delivery doctor had told her.

Did she dare lift her eyes to his throat? She had to. She had to know.

There was a divot at the base of it.

Her heart leapt. It was him. "Dash."

She'd found him.

Or he'd found her.

It didn't matter.

He was here. Her baby boy was here.

Look at him, all grown up. So tall, so handsome. So like Tadashi.

She threw a hand to her mouth as she stumbled closer.

Her voice was a whisper. "How did you find me?"

He nodded formally and bowed. "I have come from America, many miles by sea," he said in perfect Chinese. He hesitated and bowed to her. "Witness this traveler who wishes only to serve. I am here to learn from the Medicine Man Most High in all the land."

Wait. What?

He'd been studying medicine?

Just like her?

She barely heard the rest of the words he recited.

Look at that, he wore the same pin as hers, the one that was only granted by the Seekers of the Universe.

He'd come here to learn from the Medicine Man Most High? "You are too late," she told him. "Bojing died six years ago."

Despite all her efforts. At least she'd extended his life.

The young man straightened up, looked puzzled, and shook his head. "It is not Bojing I seek," he said. "I have come to find another, a woman whose healing powers they say come from the Earth itself as though it granted her access to its many secrets, a woman they call simply, 'The Healer.' I have waited long to meet her."

Ruby opened the gate. "Come in. You've passed the test."

She pulled him to her and hugged him as the tears poured out. "I have waited long to meet you, too."

The End